TARNISHED QUEEN

ZHUKOVA BRATVA
BOOK 2

NICOLE FOX

Copyright © 2022 by Nicole Fox

All rights reserved.

No part of this book may be reproduced in any form or by any electronic or mechanical means, including information storage and retrieval systems, without written permission from the author, except for the use of brief quotations in a book review.

❦ Created with Vellum

MAILING LIST

Sign up to my mailing list!
New subscribers receive a FREE steamy bad boy romance novel.

Click the link below to join.
https://sendfox.com/nicolefox

ALSO BY NICOLE FOX

Stepanov Bratva

Satin Sinner

Satin Princess

Makarova Bratva

Shattered Altar

Shattered Cradle

Solovev Bratva

Ravaged Crown

Ravaged Throne

Vorobev Bratva

Velvet Devil

Velvet Angel

Romanoff Bratva

Immaculate Deception

Immaculate Corruption

Kovalyov Bratva

Gilded Cage

Gilded Tears

Jaded Soul

Jaded Devil

Ripped Veil

Ripped Lace

Mazzeo Mafia Duet

Liar's Lullaby (Book 1)

Sinner's Lullaby (Book 2)

Bratva Crime Syndicate

Can be read in any order!

Lies He Told Me

Scars He Gave Me

Sins He Taught Me

Belluci Mafia Trilogy

Corrupted Angel (Book 1)

Corrupted Queen (Book 2)

Corrupted Empire (Book 3)

De Maggio Mafia Duet

Devil in a Suit (Book 1)

Devil at the Altar (Book 2)

Kornilov Bratva Duet

Married to the Don (Book 1)

Til Death Do Us Part (Book 2)

Heirs to the Bratva Empire

Can be read in any order!

Kostya

Maksim

Andrei

Princes of Ravenlake Academy (Bully Romance)

Can be read as standalones!

Cruel Prep

Cruel Academy

Cruel Elite

Tsezar Bratva

Nightfall (Book 1)

Daybreak (Book 2)

Russian Crime Brotherhood

Can be read in any order!

Owned by the Mob Boss

Unprotected with the Mob Boss

Knocked Up by the Mob Boss

Sold to the Mob Boss

Stolen by the Mob Boss

Trapped with the Mob Boss

Volkov Bratva

Broken Vows (Book 1)

Broken Hope (Book 2)

Broken Sins *(standalone)*

Other Standalones

Vin: A Mafia Romance

Box Sets

Bratva Mob Bosses (Russian Crime Brotherhood Books 1-6)

Tsezar Bratva (Tsezar Bratva Duet Books 1-2)

Heirs to the Bratva Empire

The Mafia Dons Collection

The Don's Corruption

TARNISHED QUEEN
ZHUKOVA BRATVA BOOK 2

Once he finds out what I've done, he'll never let me leave.

I lied. I ran. I hid.

But Nikolai Zhukova found me anyway.

And now that I'm his again, he's making sure I never repeat my mistakes.

He's putting his ring on my finger and marching me down the aisle—whether I like it or not.

Tarnished Queen is Book 2 of the Zhukova Bratva duet. Nikolai and Belle's story begins in Book 1, Tarnished Tyrant.

1

NIKOLAI

Some pain takes a while to be felt.

I tackle the Battiato soldier to the ground just as he pulls the trigger. Heat explodes along my right side. Right now, it's a burning sensation more than anything. But the real pain will come later, once the adrenaline and rage wears off. Once I truly realize what's happened.

I grab the barrel of the gun, burning my hand in the process, and twist it to the side. With my other hand, I clock the bastard in the jaw. His head snaps to the side while his body flails.

It's a reminder of how much can change in an instant. Seconds ago, he was on the right side of his gun, feeling supremely overconfident. Now, his feet scrabble across the dry dirt for purchase while we brawl over his gun.

Not that I need the reminder. My best friend rolled up to the scene on the back of his motorcycle and now, he's deathly still in the grass behind me. I'm trying not to think about it.

That's another pain that will come soon enough.

"There are more men coming," the soldier gasps. "You'll never make it out alive."

I twist the gun and jam it under his chin. "Neither will you."

I pull the trigger. The shot rings in my ears. The man slumps, dead. But he wasn't lying—I hear the thunder of more men approaching.

I turn to see them ripping around the corner. As soon as a head pops up, I pull the trigger. His skull disappears in a cloud of blood.

I spin around just as another man comes from behind. This one has the Greek flag tattooed on his neck. I aim for that and fire, but he veers at the last second and the shot catches him in the shoulder instead. He drops down behind the hood, groaning.

"Fuck," I mutter.

I'm still waiting for the soldier to stand up and advance, but instead, I see his gun rise over the hood. He squeezes off half a dozen shots blindly. Bullets ricochet off the light pole behind me and the concrete. Then, *click*—he's empty.

Now is the time to move. *Now, motherfucker, now.*

I force myself to my feet, even though every cell of me is screaming in pain, and race around the car.

My side is burning now. A bonfire in my ribs. I haven't taken the time to see how badly I'm bleeding, but it can't be good.

I step over Arslan's sprawled arm and corner the Greek cowering on the pavement. He's trying and failing to reload the weapon. I kick the gun out of his hand.

I could say something quippy. *Nice try* or *Any last words?* or *This is what you get when you fuck with the Bratva.*

But I'm too damn tired for that.

And far too much still hangs in the balance.

He blinks and opens his mouth to speak. Before he can say anything, I shove the gun in his mouth and pull the trigger.

"Fucking waste of a bullet." I give the dead man a swift kick in the ribs just as yet another Greek shows up.

I turn and slide down the side of the car, my knees to my chest. Arslan is in the grass next to me. I don't need to check his pulse to know he's gone. His chest isn't moving. Even the gurgling from earlier has faded into silence.

"You weren't supposed to die on me," I growl through thick, unspent emotion. "If you weren't already dead, I'd kill you for this."

The joke feels hollow, but Arslan would have liked it.

"You always said you'd die before me. I guess you were right. But not by much." I can hear footsteps on the asphalt, scuffling closer. "Being your friend was the closest I ever came to making vows. So maybe it makes sense that we go out together."

I can still hear his voice in my head. *Save the sappy shit for a Hallmark card,* he'd say.

And he'd be right. But as hard as it is to even consider saying goodbye to Arslan, the thought of saying goodbye to Belle is ten times harder.

Death comes for us all. I've seen enough of it firsthand to know that when your time is up, it's up.

But Belle is pregnant with my child. The future of my family depends on what happens in the next few seconds. On whether I can survive this attack. On whether I can haul ass out of here and save Belle from Xena or not.

"Fuck." I punch the dirt, letting the stinging in my knuckles bring me back. "I can't fucking die here, can I?"

Go get your woman, Arslan would say if he could speak. *Leave me here for the worms. They're better company than you anyway. Better-looking, too.*

The footsteps from the road are getting closer. I'm out of bullets, bleeding dry, and my vision is starting to go blurry.

But giving up isn't an option.

There is only one way to go: onward.

I lift myself into a crouch. In the distance, I hear sirens. Someone must've noticed the gunshots and called the police. They won't save me, though. Just another inconvenience. They'll only get in my way.

I hear a rock skitter across the ground as the Greek man closes in on me. I take a deep breath, count to three, and then launch myself towards the front of the car.

"Shit!" the blond man curses as he lunges back.

My movements feel clumsy and feeble. But I throw myself at him again.

"Nikolai, wait!" he hisses, his voice low. "I'm here to help."

I'd laugh if I had the energy. But I have to conserve my strength for killing as many of these bastards as I can. I lunge forward as the man pulls a gun from his waistband and fires.

I wait for the searing heat and the pain and the darkness that follows.

But to my surprise, there's nothing. Then I turn and see a Battiato soldier dying on the ground behind me. When I turn back, the blond man waves me towards him.

"Follow me. I'll get you out."

I don't trust him. I don't trust anyone right now.

But he is killing my enemies, and the more I bleed out, the less able I am to do that on my own. So I make a snap decision: I'll follow him until he's no longer useful. Then I'll kill him.

I turn back one last time to Arslan. This is a shitty goodbye. Nothing at all like what he deserves. I press my hand to my heart for half a second, resting on the eight-pointed star tattoo on my chest. Arslan has the same ink.

Then I leave my best friend behind forever.

The blond man waves me on again. We move quickly down the block. As quickly as I can, at least.

"No one else is here yet, but backup is coming," he informs me over his shoulder. "I heard on the scanner that the cops are coming, too. Can you run?"

"Of course I can."

He eyes me skeptically. I must look even worse than I feel. But he nods once and then takes off at a sprint. I follow down the block and around the corner.

Halfway down the next street, he skids to a stop next to a white pickup truck.

"Get in."

I move around to the passenger side and climb into the truck. The man gets in the driver's side and reaches for the ignition. As he does, I rip his gun out of his hold and press it to his temple.

He curses under his breath. "You don't want to do that, Nikolai."

"You don't know a damn thing about what I want."

"I know one thing," he warns. "If you pull that trigger, Belle is as good as dead."

2

NIKOLAI

The moment Belle's name slips out of his mouth, I shift my finger to the trigger. "Do you want to die? If so, say her name again. I'll put this bullet in your brain without a fucking moment of hesitation."

"It's not a threat," he says quickly. I can practically hear his heart pounding in his chest. "Not *my* threat, anyway. It's just a fact. Xena will kill her. And your unborn baby, too."

I shift back. "How do you know about the baby?"

If this man knows, then Xena must know, too. That's not good. The bitch is crazy. Belle is in even more trouble than I realized.

"Xena had you followed. She saw you go to the doctor's office this morning. She paid to find out which doctor you saw. She didn't get hard confirmation, but she assumed. And I guess you just confirmed it."

"You won't be able to pass the information along to her if you're dead," I remind him.

He shakes his head. "I don't want to pass anything along to her. Why would I be here helping you if I was working with her?"

"How the fuck should I know?"

"Well, I don't want that. And if you kill me, I won't be able to take you to where Xena is holding Belle."

The sirens are growing louder. We're around the corner from the scene, but not as far as I'd like to be. I need to decide quickly: kill this man or let him drive.

"Why would you turn on your boss?"

"She isn't my boss."

I arch a brow. "Lack of loyalty?"

"No. The exact opposite."

I snort. "You want me to believe that you're turning on your new don because you're *too* loyal? Spare me the bullshit."

"It's because I am loyal to the previous boss," he says. "To my father."

I look at the blond man's face again. He's young, his face thin and unlined. But suddenly, I see the resemblance.

"Giorgos is your father?"

He nods. "He was."

I didn't even know Giorgos had a son. Then again, we weren't exactly on friendly terms. Our arrangement was business-only. Still, it's possible this man is lying to me.

"You're Giorgos's flesh and blood, and yet you're not leading the mafia? Your aunt is?"

He grits his teeth. "Don't remind me."

The sirens are almost on top of us now. In a second, this neighborhood will be crawling with police and ambulances. If we don't get out now, we won't get out at all.

So I make the impossible choice and put my life in the hands of a stranger.

I lower the gun. "Drive."

He starts the truck and flips a U-turn in the middle of the road. As we're driving back down the street, I turn and see the first police car pass the intersection, headed towards the scene.

"What's your name?"

"Christo Simatou. Rightful heir to the Simatou mafia."

"If that's true, why aren't you leading it?"

He glances over at me. "Why is 'your woman' with Xena instead of you?"

"Watch your fucking tongue," I snarl.

"Sorry," he says. "But I'm just making a point. You know Xena. She knows how to get what she wants. And she wanted the mafia. She always wanted it. It's why she killed my father."

"She is the one who had him killed?" I ask in surprise.

"'Had him killed?' As if. She did it herself," he hisses. "If I didn't want to rip her spine out with my bare hands, I'd almost admire that she isn't afraid to get her hands dirty. He trusted her, and she cut his throat."

"Fuck." That's brutal even for Xena. The least she could have done was surprise Giorgos from behind. Give him a don's execution. But no, he had to watch his own sister gut him like a pig.

"It's not even the first time she's murdered her own family. It's old hat for her at this point."

I snap my gaze to Christo as I infer what he's saying. "Xena killed her parents," I mutter. "It wasn't Giorgos. Fuck me."

He nods. "Everyone thought my dad killed my grandparents, and neither of them cleared up the rumor. My dad thought it made him look stronger, and Xena knew it made her look like less of a threat. It worked well for both of them… until it stopped working."

"Was she calling the shots the entire time?"

Thinking back, I can see it. Xena sat in meetings with Giorgos. She spoke up without being asked. She made demands without consulting her brother. I assumed Giorgos was a pushover, but I never assumed he was the false front of Xena's operation.

But that was my own failure of imagination.

"Yes. Whether my father accepted it or not, she wore the crown," Christo says. "Your engagement is where things started falling apart. I think it might be the first time in her life that Xena didn't get what she wanted. I've never seen her so unhinged. She ran into that club you and Arslan were in by herself, armed with nothing but a pistol."

"She shot up the club?" I curse under my breath. "If I'd caught her that night, none of this would be happening."

"No, it would still be happening. My father would have declared war on you. His men wouldn't have stood for anything less."

"Yeah, but Belle would be safe."

As soon as the words are out of my mouth, I realize that she is all that matters. Getting Belle out of Xena's hands and back in mine is the only thing I care about.

Christo hits a bump in the road, and I hiss in pain.

"You need to get that looked at," he warns.

I press my hand to the wound. There's a squelch of wet, sticky fabric and another shot of agony ripping through me. "No time. It's a graze. I'm fine."

"Yeah, a graze of an internal organ maybe," Christo snorts. "You can't fight like this."

"I got your gun away from you, didn't I?"

He glances over at the gun still in my hand and sighs. "Yeah, but I'm not Xena. And I wasn't trying to kill you."

"Is that her goal now? I thought she wanted to marry me."

"So she could kill you," he says. "Marriage or not, your death was always in the plans."

I grimace. "I can't say I'm surprised."

"My aunt is ruthless when she sets her sights on something. And right now, she has her sights set on revenge."

"Which is why I need to find Belle as soon as possible. That's where you're taking me, right?" I ask. "To Belle?"

He nods solemnly. "Xena stopped trusting me once word of my father's death got out. So I only have the plan up to twenty-four hours ago. But as far as I know, I'm taking you to Belle. Where she's supposed to be, at least."

"If she's not, I'll kill you."

Christo swallows. "Might put a damper on our budding friendship if you do that."

"Is that what you call me barely deciding not to murder you? If so, you need to raise your bar," I tell him. "Besides, I had a best friend. And your comrades killed him."

He winces. "Then let's hope Xena and Belle are where they're supposed to be."

For his sake—and mine—I hope he's right.

3

BELLE

Hands are everywhere.

My arms. My legs. I feel straps around my ankles and my midsection, holding me down. But they hardly seem necessary. I barely have the strength to open my eyes.

"Heart rate rising," a male voice says. "Blood pressure, too."

"She's waking up," a woman agrees.

The strange voices are a shot of adrenaline to my system, but I keep my eyes closed. I have no clue what is going on, and I need a second to figure it all out.

It's like I'm underwater, treading water and fighting for the surface, but I don't know which way is up. I'm not even sure how I ended up here.

"Ma'am?" the male voice says, sounding far too gentle to be a kidnapper or assassin. But then again, I thought Xena Simatou was my friend, so what the hell do I know?

Xena. Her name is like a key, unlocking the part of my brain that makes sense of all of this.

Xena picked me up from Nikolai's house.

Xena tricked me into going with her.

Xena was going to kill me.

"Her heart rate is climbing again," the female voice says. "Ma'am? Can you hear me?"

I feel a warm hand close over mine, and I squeeze back without thinking. Mostly because I need a hand to hold right now. I need something firm to keep me grounded.

"Hello?" he says again. "Can you hear me? You were in an accident. You're okay."

Accident. A car accident.

More bits and pieces come tumbling to the forefront. I remember unbuckling my seatbelt and lunging across the car at Xena. She screamed and we fought, and then…

My eyes flicker open. The lights from the ceiling blind me.

"There she is." I look over and see the male shape next to me. Slowly, he comes into focus. A middle-aged Black man with a thick, graying beard. "We're taking good care of you. Try not to worry."

"Just scrapes and bruises as far as we can tell." I turn and see Elise sitting next to me.

Then I blink and realize it's not Elise at all. This woman's hair is too short and too red, her nails too dainty, her face too angular.

What I wouldn't give to have my sister next to me, though. To know where she is, that she's safe.

I hope she found Nikolai. My trust is shaken in almost everything, but I know Nikolai. He'll take care of her. He'll protect her.

The man pats my hand again. "But we have you in this brace until we can get X-rays. It's a precaution."

"My baby." My mouth feels like someone shoved cotton in it. I lick my lips and try again. "My baby… I'm pregnant. Is my baby—"

"We won't know until we get you to the hospital," the woman says. "But that is good to know. For the X-rays."

When I shake my head, it feels like my brain is sloshing against my skull. "Did I—Where did you find me? Did I fly out of the car? I'm unconscious. Or, I was unconscious. Does that mean—"

I can hear a beeping noise becoming more insistent, and the man gently pats my wrist. "Take deep breaths and try to stay calm. We think you hit your head on the dashboard, which is why you were unconscious. Right now, there are no visible bruises to your abdomen. But you do have minor scrapes from the windshield shattering. In terms of your pregnancy, that is the best news you could hope for."

Hope sparks inside of me, but I know better than to cling to it. Hope is a dangerous thing.

"Where's Xena?"

"The friend you were in the car with?" the woman asks.

"Some fucking 'friend,'" I scoff weakly.

The man doesn't seem to hear me and pats my hand again. "She is in another ambulance. She might even wind up at another hospital, just depends where they route her. You can ask when you arrive and they'll keep you updated on where she ends up."

I just hope she ends up in a grave.

I've never been a violent person, or even a particularly angry one. Given all the shit I've been through in my life, I think that's quite the accomplishment.

But Xena Simatou has earned my wrath.

If I ever see her again, I'll kill her myself.

~

"Do you see that heartbeat?" The ultrasound tech points to the fuzzy screen on the portable machine. "Your baby is perfectly fine."

The glowing little flicker is the literal light at the end of a seriously gloomy tunnel.

"Thank you," I breathe, squeezing the rails of the hospital bed until my knuckles turn white. "Thank you so much."

The woman smiles. "I didn't do anything. But I'm glad I could give you good news."

"It's been too long since I've had some," I admit. "This is… this is everything. Thank you."

She nods and starts wheeling the machine towards the door. "A doctor will be in to talk with you soon. Good luck with everything, hon. Take care of yourself."

"I'm trying." My voice cracks, and I fight back the tears until the door is closed.

As soon as I'm alone, relief overwhelms me. It's a wave, all-consuming, blotting out everything else. The only thing I can do is stifle my sobs and wait until it has run its course. Until all the pent-up emotion in me has drained out.

My baby is still alive.

Elise is safe.

I'm uninjured.

The only question mark left is Nikolai. The last thing that matters is finding out where he is.

I don't know much about the kind of tactical games he and the Greeks are playing, but if Xena was kidnapping me, it would make sense for her to have had a distraction ready. Another part of the plan running in the background to keep Nikolai busy.

Which would explain why he hasn't called me yet.

He hasn't called because he's busy, I tell myself. *Because he's wrapped up in fighting or organizing his men. It's not because he's dead.*

I say that firmly one more time for good measure. *It's* not *because he's dead.*

But the barest thought of something happening to Nikolai tightens like a steel cage around my chest, making me forget the few seconds of relief I just felt.

I need to know if he's okay. I'm reaching for my phone on the nightstand just as the door opens.

"You're up and moving, I see." A man walks into the room. He has on navy blue scrubs and a surgical mask around his face. All I can see are his deep-set eyes and thick eyebrows.

"I feel mostly okay," I tell him. "A little sore, I think."

Stiffness is already setting in along my neck and shoulders. But considering I could be dead on the side of the road, I'm grateful it isn't worse.

"Soreness is to be expected after the kind of accident you had. What caused your accident, do you know?" His voice is muffled from the mask, making it difficult to hear him. None of the other nurses have had masks on, so I want to ask why he's wearing one, but I also don't want to be rude.

"The driver lost control," I lie.

I'm not about to tell this man or anyone else that I lunged at Xena and tried to steer us off the road. I don't think I did anything wrong; Xena was threatening my life, after all. But I don't know how this kind of thing works. Nikolai seems to want to handle Bratva business himself without the police getting involved. Me telling this nurse about Xena could bring a shitstorm down on him and us. It's best to keep my mouth closed.

"I'm sorry to hear that. Did you know the driver?"

I nod, too afraid to say anything else and give myself away.

"Has anyone told you whether she is alright?" he asks.

I shake my head. "Not yet. I asked the EMTs, but they said they didn't know where she was being taken."

"She's here," he says matter-of-factly. "In this hospital. Just down the hall."

I do my best to keep my expression flat and neutral, but the machine next to my bed starts chirping out an alarm as my heart rate climbs. And as the beeping becomes more frantic, my breathing hitches. That steel band around my chest tightens cruelly, and I have to wheeze breath in and out of my narrowing windpipe.

"Are you okay?" the nurse asks, moving towards the bed. "Are you… are you frightened?"

I press a hand to my heart, trying to manually calm myself down. But that must be answer enough because the nurse leans down next to my bed, his voice in my ear.

"I'll move you to another wing of the hospital."

"Can you do that?" I rasp.

He nods. "I can do whatever you need. I want you to feel safe with us."

Just then, the door opens again. A woman with dark, wavy hair twisted back into a large bun steps into the room and then stutters to a stop when she sees the male nurse next to my bed. Her brows knit together. "I'm… I'm sorry. Are you—" She checks the paper in her hands and then looks back to the man. "This room is on my rotation. Are you from the last shift?"

"I was assigned to this room," the man says breezily. He walks towards the woman and waves her towards the door. "Let's go sort this out."

The woman looks at me and then the man again, trying to put the pieces together. As she does, an uneasy feeling settles in my gut. When she follows the male nurse out of the room, I fumble for my phone and dial Nikolai.

"Please pick up," I whisper. "Please, please, please pick up."

The phone rings and rings. But with each unanswered tone, the garden of hope I've been tending in my chest withers and dies.

Just as panicked tears are burning against my eyes, the line clicks open. I hear breathing.

"Nikolai!" I gasp right away. "Thank God. It's you. I was so—" My voice wavers, and I clear it quickly and carry on, the words falling out of me too fast. "I'm so glad you picked up. I don't know what you know or what Xena said, but things are so complicated... I was in an accident. I'm okay. The baby is okay. But something is wrong. Xena is here in the hospital, I think. My nurse is weird. He is being really nice, but it's almost too nice. God, I sound crazy complaining about a nurse who is too nice. But something feels wrong, and I need you here. I really need you here."

The words come out in such a jumble that I'm not sure if I've made any sense or if Nikolai can even understand me. Or if he even wants to understand me.

And as I sit in the hospital room, my phone clutched to my ear, listening to Nikolai's measured breathing on the other end of the line, I have a feeling he's not feeling especially sympathetic to my plight.

"Nikolai," I sob, blinking back tears. "Please. I never... I never meant to hurt you or—"

The line goes dead.

I can't actually believe it. Even when the call ends and my home screen reappears—a picture of Elise and me with complimentary green face masks from the hotel in Iceland—I keep expecting to hear Nikolai's warm assurances through the phone. I expect him to tell me he's coming to get me, that he'll take care of me.

But there's nothing.

I'm completely and totally alone.

And it's all my fault.

I drop the phone on the bed and hug my knees to my chest. If Nikolai is too upset to talk to me, what does that mean for Elise? She could be wandering around the city completely alone. Worse, Xena could have gotten her hands on her somehow.

The relief that overwhelmed me only minutes ago has been wrenched away violently. The door opens again, and I look up as the male nurse reenters. This time, with a wheelchair.

"Am I going somewhere?" I ask.

"A room transfer, remember?"

I start to shake my head, but he busies himself rolling my blanket down to the end of the bed and making my heart monitor and IV pole mobile.

"Shouldn't I talk to a doctor first? I'm waiting to see my doctor. After the ultrasound. I thought—"

"Your room number has been updated in the system," he explains. "A doctor will meet us there."

He grabs for my hand and then wrenches me awkwardly out of bed. I wince, my shoulder twinging, and he mumbles an apology.

It all feels wrong, but I don't know what to do or who to trust. I can't even trust myself.

I thought Xena was my friend, and she was using me the entire time. I thought Nikolai would never turn his back on me, but he wouldn't even talk to me. Now, my mind has been literally and emotionally rattled. I'm probably just seeing trouble where there isn't any.

So I drop carefully down into the wheelchair and let myself be wheeled out of the room.

The hospital is a flurry of movement and bright lights. No one seems to notice me being wheeled down the hallway. Until the nurse knocks my IV against a passing gurney.

"Poles go on the outside," the passing nurse reminds him, her voice low. "We don't want to rip out an IV."

My nurse shifts the poles to his right side, closer to the wall, and mumbles another half-hearted apology.

Then, a few seconds later, my entire wheelchair jerks to a stop so suddenly I nearly fall forward.

"These damn brakes," he hisses behind me. He bends down to release the brake, struggling with it for a few seconds before he stands up, adjusts his mask, and keeps moving.

With every passing second, the wrongness of this situation grows. By the time we reach the elevator at the end of the hall, my instincts are screaming at me.

"Where are you moving me to?" I ask.

"The second floor."

"What's on the second floor?"

The question is simple enough. One any nurse in a hospital would know. And yet, the man hesitates. "Oh. Um… Cardiotherapy?"

"Do you mean Cardiology?"

He chuckles awkwardly. "Yeah. That's what I meant. Sorry, I've been on for sixteen hours. My brain is fried."

I smile and nod, but my eyes are darting up and down the hallway, trying to gauge how quickly I could rip the IV out of my arm, jump out of my seat, and sprint down the hallway away from this man. If I do that and it turns out the nurse is a completely normal hospital employee, can I explain away my behavior as a concussion side effect? Or will I end up in a padded room with my arms strapped behind my back?

Indecision has me drumming my fingers on the arms of the wheelchair and rocking back and forth nervously.

"These elevators are so goddamn slow," he growls, leaning around me to jab the button again a few more times.

As he stretches towards the button, the hem of his dark scrubs lifts…

And I see a gun holstered at his hip.

He looks down and sees me looking. Just like that, the friendly eyes go cold and blank. "Don't be stupid, Belle," he hisses. "If you fight me, more people will get hurt."

"More?" I croak.

"Your real nurse is lying unconscious in a janitor's closet. She's lucky she went down easy or I would have had to kill her."

I squeeze my eyes closed for a second, cursing my own instincts.

I did the wrong thing. *Again.*

I put myself in danger. *Again.*

And now, Nikolai isn't here to save me.

Again.

4

NIKOLAI

When Christo finally parks his truck down by the docks, I'm no longer bleeding, but I'm still woozy. The world has taken on a gauzy softness, like my eyes can't find the strength to focus properly.

I'm no doctor, but that seems like a bad sign.

"There," Christo says, pointing to the abandoned factory one block ahead. "We own this whole quarter and that building is smack dab in the middle of the rest of the Simatou-owned buildings. It's where hostages go. So no one will hear them scream."

I grit my teeth and try to settle my stampeding heart.

Christo must notice the tension radiating through me because he clears his throat. "But the fact Xena hasn't called you is a good sign. She likes a spectacle. If she was going to torture Belle, she'd make you listen in. Or she'd record it or something."

"In which case I wouldn't know she was dead until after the fact," I grind out.

He winces. "Oh, yeah. Right. But I bet she'll call you and—"

I hold up a hand to silence him. "Enough. It won't matter. Belle isn't going to die."

On the long drive over, I wanted to call her on the off-chance she'd answer. But it is too risky. If Belle is with Xena, then Xena might see my name pop up on her phone. The jealous bitch wouldn't like that and anything that upsets Xena could make things worse for Belle. Plus, like Christo said, Xena might use the opportunity to torture Belle while I'm on the line for the sheer fucking thrill of it.

No, a surprise attack will work best. Even if it means I have to go in completely blind with no clue who is inside.

"Permission to arm myself?" Christo asks carefully.

His hands are tight around the steering wheel where I can see them, but his eyes glance at the glove compartment.

"If we're going in there," he explains, "I'd like a gun. No offense, but you look like shit. I don't want to count on your reflexes."

"I'm better at my worst than you will ever be," I growl. "Count on that."

"I believe you," he says earnestly. "But come on, Nikolai. Two guns is better than one."

I consider it for a minute and then nod. "Fine. But you lead the way."

He reaches into the glove compartment and pulls out a pistol. "So you can keep a gun aimed at my back."

"So if someone shoots, they hit you first."

"How thoughtful," he mutters. "I'll keep that in mind."

We climb out and move down the street towards the abandoned warehouse, Christo a few paces ahead of me. The afternoon is wearing thin, the sky darkening into early evening, and the sidewalks are empty.

"Do you have a plan?" I ask.

"As long as you have a gun on my back, my plan is to do whatever you tell me to do."

I almost smile. It sounds like something Arslan might say. "Find Belle. Help me get her away from Xena."

He ducks beneath a grimy window, and I follow suit. Bending over sends a hot flash of anguish up my side and across my ribs, but I grit my teeth through it. Once I have Belle back, I'll worry about myself. Until then, pain is merely another sensation.

"I don't know what's waiting for us in there," Christo says as he pauses outside of a metal front door. Rust is peppered across the surface, chewing away at the corners. "But last I knew, this is where Xena was going to bring her."

"Do you know the layout?"

He shrugs. "Not as well as I'd like. I haven't been here in years. But it should be a shallow entrance area that runs the length of this wall and then a second door that leads into the warehouse floor. My dad had the equipment cleared out years ago. There are some hanging walkways along the ceiling that are used for lookout positions, but otherwise, the room is empty."

"Then you focus on taking out any snipers above, and I'll focus on Xena and Belle."

With a plan, the knot of unease that's been growing inside of me releases slightly. I know how to do this: formulate a plan and execute it. Execute *her*.

But standing back and worrying? That is not in my skill set.

Christo nods. "Good. Then let's go."

He pushes open the door slowly and carefully, but the hinges still squeal with disuse. The first room is dark and empty. It smells musty, and I can't imagine Xena Simatou choosing to be anywhere near this place. She may be a cold-blooded murderer, but she also refuses to drink water unless it is handed to her in a glass bottle.

I bite back another smile, thinking about Arslan filling a glass bottle with hose water before one of our meetings with the Simatou delegation.

Then I think of him slumped against the hubcap of a car as the lights left his eyes.

That hurts worse than the bullet wound.

"Clear," Christo whispers over his shoulder.

"Yeah, I have fucking eyes," I fire back.

He ignores me and moves forward. The second door opens much more quietly, like someone sprayed the hinges recently. Christo slips through it. I follow him a second later.

He peels off to the right, gun trained upwards, as I move into the middle of the room. But there's no need for the formation. The place is empty.

I cross the distance between us in two strides and press the gun to his spine. "Where the fuck are they, Christo?" I snarl.

"Shit," he mumbles under his breath. "Nikolai, I don't know. I swear. This was my best guess."

"Your promises don't mean a damn thing to me."

"Something must have gone wrong," he protests. I snatch the gun out of his right hand, and he doesn't fight me on it. "Maybe Xena knew I would cross her. Maybe she changed the plan. Or maybe something went wrong on their way here."

"No wonder Xena is in charge instead of you," I growl. "You don't have a fucking clue what you're doing. You were in her ranks until two days ago and you don't know where they are? You don't have any way to figure out what is going on? You should have maintained a mole on the inside."

His head sags between his shoulders. "I didn't want to risk it. You've worked with her and my dad for a long time, but… but you don't know what she's really like. If anyone knew what I was planning to do, they would have told her. I'd be dead right now."

"She's a crazy bitch, not a god."

"Maybe not to you. But to them," he insists, "she's as good as such. Those men are scared shitless of her. They'll kill for her. They'd kill me. Which is why I'm not going to be safe until Xena is dead. I'm on your team, Nikolai, I swear it."

I jam the gun against one of his vertebrae. He groans, but does his best to stay standing tall. "I don't give a single fuck about your safety. I want Belle. That's all."

Christo blows out a long breath. He opens his mouth like he's going to say something, but then he pinches his lips together. "I want to help you. But I can't do that if you kill me."

I'm still weighing the option when my phone rings.

I have Christo's gun in my left hand and mine in my right, so it takes me a second to maneuver his gun into my pocket so I can reach for my phone. When I pull it out, Belle's name is on the screen.

I want to be relieved, but I know better. I answer the call and press it to my ear, waiting silently.

Maybe Xena is calling to see if I'm dead. Maybe she wants to know I'm on the line so she can torture Belle for me to hear. I don't plan to say a word until I know exactly what is going on.

"Who is it?" Christo whispers.

I narrow my eyes at him, and he shrinks back.

"Nikolai." My name is little more than a breathless sound… but the voice is Belle's. I know it. I'd know it anywhere.

She's alive.

A breath huffs out of me. Belle must be able to recognize the sound.

"Thank God. It's you. I was so—" She sounds exhausted in a way I've never heard before. There's a tension to her words that I can't decipher.

Is Xena standing over her shoulder, forcing her to call me? This could be a trap. I won't fall into it.

But I want to soothe her fears. I want her to know I'd burn the fucking world down just to pluck her from the debris and wipe the ash from her face.

"I'm so glad you picked up. I don't know what you know or what Xena said, but things are so complicated… I was in an accident. I'm okay. The baby is okay… " she says, rushing through the explanation. "But something is wrong. Xena is here in the hospital, I think."

"Is it Belle?" Christo hisses. "Who is it?"

I ignore him, focusing on the only thing that matters. Belle is in the hospital. It doesn't sound like she's okay if she's in the hospital.

She's talking so fast that I miss some of it. But her tone is unmistakable. She's scared.

"… But something feels wrong, and I need you here," she rasps, her voice almost a sob. "I really need you here."

I'm holding onto the phone so tight that I'm surprised it's still in one piece. I need her to know I'm coming.

I open my mouth to say something, anything, but Christo lunges forward.

"She's lying to you," he hisses.

My gun was aimed at his chest before he even took a step, and he looks nervously at it now. But it doesn't silence him.

"Nikolai, I have to tell you something: Belle is working with Xena," he confesses somberly. "She has been for weeks."

I'm quiet. My pulse pounds where I was shot, every throb a fresh bout of agony.

I consider shooting him for lying about Belle, for trying to drive a wedge between us. But then I remember the night Belle and Elise ran away…

At the time, I thought it was a coincidence they were nearly captured by Giorgos' men. I assumed the Greeks were surveilling my house. But maybe I didn't save Belle's life.

Maybe I interrupted her plan to escape.

"I didn't want to tell you, because…" Christo swallows. "Well, because I thought you might kill me for it. But it's true. I know it is."

Fuck.

"Nikolai." Belle is crying now. I hear the emotion thick in her voice. A bullshit act. "Please. I never… I never meant to hurt you or—"

I hang up the phone.

Christo starts talking immediately. "I'm sorry, Nikolai. I wanted to tell you, but I thought we'd find her and stop the plan and it wouldn't matter. But since they weren't here, I had no choice but to tell you before you could—"

I hold up a hand and he falls silent instantly. Then I hand him his gun. "Come on."

His eyes are wide. He grabs the gun like it might be a trick. Then he slides it quickly into the back of his pants. "What's the plan now?"

A moment ago, I had a plan. I was going to get my woman away from the psychopath I was engaged to, take her home, and keep her with me forever. I was going to make sure no one ever laid a hand on her again.

But now, that plan is shot to hell.

And Belle herself is the one responsible.

"Belle is at the hospital. She said she needs me there."

Christo huffs. "But she's lying to you. She's working with—"

I hold up my gun and arch a brow. "She said she needs me there… so that's where I'm going."

It takes the man a second, but he gets it. He looks solemn. "Oh."

5

BELLE

I want to scream, but I have no idea how many people this awful man could kill. If I scream, how many nurses and doctors will run to my aid? How many of them would get gunned down in their rush? I'm picturing bodies stacked like Lincoln Logs, red blood staining green scrubs and running in sticky rivulets down the cracks where tile floor meets baseboard. A horrific massacre.

Even if I survived, I'd never be able to forgive myself.

"Don't be stupid," the man repeats, his voice a low threat in my ear. "Come with me. Make this easy for both of us."

The elevator still hasn't moved off of floor one, and I'm hoping it never will. Because once I'm out of this hospital, I'm lost. Right now, there's a chance Nikolai could hunt me down. Arslan can probably track ambulances, knowing him. Maybe he even knows where I'm at right now. If I stay here, they could find me.

But out there? Xena could take me anywhere. I'll be lost in the ether. And dead, more likely than not.

Then a realization occurs. "Is Xena really right down the hall?"

The man makes a low, laughing sound in the back of his throat.

Of course she isn't. He was just saying that so I'd be willing to leave the room with him. So my fear of Xena might override my common sense.

"So stupid," I whisper. "I'm so stupid."

The elevator dings. I look up as the floor number shifts from one to two and then three. My captor's escape hatch inches closer while I sit here completely helpless to do a damn thing about it.

"Yeah, but you're being smart right now," he croons like he's consoling a wild animal. "Saving lives by staying quiet. Just a few more minutes, and you can scream as loud as you want."

Is he trying to comfort me? Because it is absolutely not working.

The elevator creeps closer. It feels like watching a guillotine lower against my neck. Like having a physical countdown to my own demise.

Four.

Five.

DING.

When the doors open, the man starts to push me into the elevator, but there are people inside. We're forced to back up and wait for it to clear out.

An orderly with a laundry cart is off to the right and an elderly woman with a walker stands in the center. Two men are angled towards each other in the back, phones in their hands, both wearing surgical masks. A mom and her teenaged daughter are nearest the buttons.

"... I don't even know, Charlene," the girl is arguing. "She's your friend."

Her mom groans. "And Laney's mom."

"Laney isn't my friend, either. We just have a few classes together."

The mom gives me an exasperated look in search of sympathy, but I can't muster anything beyond a grimace. Even still, I'm afraid she might see something in my face to cause alarm. If she alerts anyone to what's going on, I don't know what the man will do to her. To all of them.

So I fix my eyes on my bare feet in the wheelchair's stirrups to be safe.

One by one, the elevator empties out. As soon as it's clear, the man pushes me through the doors.

My front wheels have just barely cleared the threshold when I'm suddenly shoved forward. I have to kick out a leg to avoid smashing against the opposite wall.

When I turn around, I see the two men from the elevator standing on either side of my kidnapper.

They look calm, cool, unruffled.

But the man who just threatened my life is bleeding from the mouth in a way that doesn't look too sustainable.

"Is he—What did—Oh my God," I gasp.

Then I look up…

Into Nikolai's face.

I'd recognize those eyes anywhere. They're burning bright, looking nowhere but at me. His blond, masked companion shuffles onboard with the dead nurse held up in his grip. Nikolai peels off the surgical mask and nods towards the buttons as he steps back into the elevator.

"Basement level, please," he requests coolly.

I'm still in shock, my brain struggling to keep up with the events as they're unfolding. But I can follow a simple command. I press the basement level button and wait for the doors to close. As soon as they do, I turn to face him.

"You came," I gasp. "I didn't know if you would. You came, and—Oh my God, he was going to kidnap me."

Nikolai holds a finger to his mouth and glances up at the corner of the box. "Not here. Cameras."

I press my lips together to hold in the flurry of thoughts bubbling out of me. I use the rest of the quiet ride to silently study the blond man with Nikolai. He's young and handsome, but I can't get a good look because he refuses to even glance in my direction. He hasn't spoken so much as a word.

The elevator doors open up into a cement parking garage. The moment we're out of the doors, Nikolai and the blond man dump the fake nurse on the ground behind a dumpster in a bloody tangle of limbs.

"Come on." Nikolai holds out his hand, and I wrap my fingers through his. Grateful that these strong, capable hands will never hurt me.

Feeling the warmth of his skin against mine is like coming home. I glue myself to his side as he leads me through the parking garage towards a sedan in the far corner. When I press my palm to his ribs, I feel him flinch. But it's a quick movement, just the tiniest flicker of it before he's opening the back door for me and helping me inside.

The blond man moves around to the front of the car to drive. When Nikolai slides in behind me, I turn and wrap myself around him.

"You're real." I nuzzle my face into his neck and breathe him in. He smells like soot and sweat and blood. "I want to know where you've been and what you've been doing and who this other man is, but first—"

I grab his face and bring his soft lips to mine. Nikolai is tense. Every muscle in his body is held tightly, but as I stroke my tongue over his bottom lip and ease his mouth open, he softens.

A large hand moves over my back and around my waist. He grabs a fistful of my hair and arches my head back, giving him better access to ravish my mouth.

He's everywhere, biting and tasting me, pressing greedy, frantic kisses to my lips until I'm panting for breath and out of my mind with need.

"I didn't know if I'd get to do this again," I whisper. "I didn't know if I'd ever touch you again. If I'd ever *feel* you."

Nikolai pulls back, his irises a hard silver in the dim light filtering through the tinted windows. "Are you hurt?"

I shake my head. "I'm fine. Really. It's a miracle I wasn't thrown from the car, actually."

"A miracle?" He lifts his brow, his face twisted in an expression I don't understand. Is he teasing me?

I nod. "I don't know how it happened. It just did. A miracle."

I lower my mouth to his neck, kissing along the column of his throat, pressing my lips to his pulse. When the familiar deep rumble of pleasure moves through him, I press a hand to his chest to catch the vibrations.

Then I let that hand slide lower, trailing over the hard muscle of his chest and the flat plane of his stomach. But when I drive my fingers under the hem of his shirt, I feel the rough edge of a bandage.

Nikolai doesn't move as I pull back and yank his shirt up in growing horror. The bandage is wide, covering most of his side. I can see blood oozing through the wrappings.

"Wh… what happened?" I breathe, not even sure if I want to know. I'm not sure I can handle finding out how close to death he may have been. How close he may still be.

"You don't know?"

"How would I know?" I ask, confused. "I didn't even know where you were."

He pulls his shirt back down. Suddenly, it feels like an uncrossable barrier between us.

This isn't what I thought our reunion would be. I imagined heated touches over slick skin. Murmured cries of gratitude and pleasure that we were together again.

I want that. Doesn't he?

"Are you okay?" I ask.

He nods. "I'm fine."

He's never been so unresponsive to me or so blunt. Even when things between us were beyond complicated, *this* never was. Our bodies always knew what to do.

But it feels like Nikolai has forgotten.

"I can't wait," I whine, circling my hands around his neck. "I need you. I need you to help me forget."

I sound desperate to my own ears, but it's accurate. I am desperate. For this. For a moment of normalcy after hours of uncertainty and terror. For Nikolai to make me feel deliriously good and for me to do the same for him.

His body is still tight and tense beneath me, and I'm not sure he's going to give in. For the first time, Nikolai might set me aside.

And in that brief window, panic rises up. Has he realized he made a mistake? It would have been easier to marry Xena and leave me behind. Less complicated. Maybe he realizes I'm not worth all of the drama.

But before I can gather up the scraps of my dignity, Nikolai's large hands grip my waist. He pulls me into his lap and drags my aching center over him with a primal growl.

I moan, already lost to the sensation. "I want you inside of me," I whimper.

Nikolai shakes his head. "Not now. Finish yourself like this."

I should feel disappointed. Grinding myself against him like we're teenagers in a backseat shouldn't feel this good. But it does.

Everything with Nikolai feels good. Better than anything else.

"What about you?" I moan, shifting down so I can stroke the entire length of him from root to tip and back again. "Is this good for you?"

"This is about you."

The words are sweet, but his voice is still detached. I want to investigate more, but I can't focus on anything except the ache between my legs.

I grab Nikolai's hands and place them over my chest. The warmth of his fingers palming me drives me faster.

"How did you end up in Xena's car?" Nikolai asks.

My head is fuzzy with pleasure, and his words feel out of place with what I'm feeling now. It's the real world encroaching on this moment that I just want to last.

His hand shifts to my collarbone, his thumb drawing a line over the fragile bone. "What caused the accident?"

I squeeze my eyes closed as I squeeze my thighs around his hips. "I'm close," I pant. It's my way of begging him to let this go. To let me have this.

His thumb shifts into the hollow of my throat, and I tip my head back, surrendering to his touch. I roll my hips and shiver from the delicious friction. Nikolai growls, a deep, sexy sound. Then he curls his fingers around my neck.

I moan, leaning into his hand. The strength in him paired with the gentle way he's touching me is almost enough to send me over the edge. I've never let someone touch my throat before, but I trust Nikolai. I like his hands on me. On every part of me.

His grip tightens, and I swallow with slight difficulty as the blood rushes in my ears.

"Like that," I whisper, still bucking against him. "I'm going to… I'm going to…"

Before I can climax, all at once, my air is gone. Nikolai's hand clamps around my throat so tightly I can't breathe. I jolt, trying to move out of his hold, but the movement sends another bolt of pleasure through my body. This combination of panic and pleasure is a new high I've never experienced.

I come like that, with Nikolai's hand squeezing the air out of me, his cock hard between my legs. My eyes feel like they're bulging as it tears through me mercilessly. When it starts to recede, I tug at his hold on my neck, telling him to let go.

But Nikolai doesn't budge.

Instead, he leans forward until his breath is hot on my skin.

"Tell me the truth before I choke it out of you: how long have you been working with Xena?"

6

BELLE

Blackness creeps into the edges of my vision. I'm seeing stars, and I'm not sure if it's from the pulsing orgasm still ripping through me or the lack of oxygen. Probably both.

I claw at Nikolai's hand, too panicked to focus on his words. Too desperate for air to consider how bad it is that he knows.

He knows.

"How long have you been lying to me?" he hisses.

I open my mouth, but nothing comes out. No exhale, no inhale. The black edges of my vision are stretching towards the center, tendrils of darkness blotting out the image of his face, clenched and angry in front of me.

There's more black than color now. I can't breathe. I certainly can't speak. All this way we've come and it's going to end like this—the way I thought it would end from the start. He'll kill me right when I finally started believing that that was the last thing he'd ever do.

Blacker, and blacker, and blacker—

Then, all at once, he lets me go.

I collapse against him and suck in air. My head is splitting in two as blood surges back in place.

Weakly, I try to move off of his lap, but Nikolai holds my legs firmly in place. "No. You don't get to run away again."

"I'm not. I just…" I can't feel his erection between my legs and think clearly at the same time.

"How long have you been working with her?" he growls.

His cold detachment makes sense now. *This is about you.*

"How did you find out?" I touch my throat with tentative fingers. The heat of his grip is still imprinted there. "Did Xena tell you?"

"So it's true?"

"Yes, but—but it's not what you think. She wanted me to be a double agent. To give her information. But I didn't—"

"Don't you dare fucking lie to me."

The hospital gown is gaped open in the back and rucked up along my thighs. The last quakes of my orgasm are still moving through me, and now, Nikolai is staring at me like he can see straight into my brain.

But then, if he could see into my mind, he'd know the entire truth. Based on the black fury on his face now, I can tell he doesn't.

"She was going to help me get out of the country," I explain to him. "That's why I listened to her. She told me she could get me and Elise out."

"Away from me."

"No," I breathe. "Well, yes. At the time, it's what I wanted, but—"

"You lied to me, Belle." He breathes heavily. "You were in my house, working with my enemy to escape and hurt me in the process."

"Because you kidnapped me!"

His gray eyes flare. "Because you were falling apart without me."

He isn't wrong. It's only been a few days, but the sad, hollow version of me that floated between home and Tony's bar like a ghost doesn't even feel real.

"But you can't see how I made the decision I did?" I ask. "You flew me across the country while I was unconscious. When we first met, you kidnapped Elise to control me. I knew the only way I'd ever get away from you was with help, so when Xena offered to get me out, I accepted. I didn't see another way out."

He barks out a humorless laugh. "I guess I missed how badly you wanted to get away from me during all the fucking we did. If your orgasms were faked, then you're in the wrong line of work. You should be an actress, not an accountant."

I shake my head. "Don't act like everything between us was fake."

"It was."

"You lied, too!" I blurt.

"I made you choose," he snarls. "I forced your hand. But I never, not once, betrayed you. I was honest about how I felt. About what I wanted."

Me. He wanted me.

"I didn't lie, either," I protest, my voice wobbly and weak. The exhaustion of the day is catching up with me and all I want to do is close my eyes. "When we had sex… that's when I was most honest with you. And with myself. It felt good to be with you, but I don't live just for myself. You understand that, too."

"Don't tell me what I understand."

"Your loyalty is to the Bratva," I continue, "and mine is to Elise. I had to do what was best for her."

His jaw clenches and shifts. Nikolai understands loyalty. He lives by it. He'll have to understand this.

"My loyalty is to the Bratva, you're right," he says. "And today, my men died because of your lies. Because I was searching for you even though you left willingly."

The words steal the breath from me as if his hand was wrapped around my throat again. "Nikolai, I'm—wait, what?"

His eyes meet mine unflinchingly. "Arslan is dead."

"No." My heart cracks open. I didn't know Arslan well, but I know Nikolai, and Arslan was his best friend. The most important person in the world to him. "I'm so sorry. Nikolai, I didn't mean for—"

"I watched him bleed out. Then I left him slumped on the side of the road, so I could look for *you*." He spits the words like venom.

His fingers shake against my legs for a second before he picks me up and shoves me off of his lap. I flop into the seat next to him.

"I'm sorry," I whisper hollowly.

Nikolai stares straight ahead into a space in the middle distance that only he can see. I can't find the words to convey to him how fucked-up all of this or how much responsibility I take for all of it. I don't think there are any words for it.

I was stupid, and I made the wrong choice. Now, his friend is dead.

We drive in silence. The tension tightens between us until it's fit to snap.

Finally, I can't take it anymore. "Why did you come to the hospital?" I ask.

The slightest raise of his eyebrow is the only sign he can hear me.

"I called you, and you didn't say anything," I continue. "But then you showed up to save me. Why did you bother?"

Because I love you, Belle, is what I'm praying he will say. *Because I'm angry, but that doesn't change how I feel about you.*

Say it, I beg silently. *For the love of God, please say it.*

I want to reclaim the joy we had this morning, sitting together and staring at our baby's sonogram. I want that optimism back.

"Because of loyalty," he says at last.

I frown. "Loyalty?"

"You said my priority is the Bratva, and that's true. Which is why I have to protect every member of my Bratva."

I blink in confusion. "But… I'm not in the Bratva."

"No, you're not." He jabs a finger towards my stomach. "But that baby you're carrying is mine. And while you'll never be a part of my Bratva, my child will be. Whether you like it or not."

Aside from my stifled sobs, the rest of the drive is silent.

∼

I don't want to get out of the car once it's parked in front of Nikolai's house, but he drags me out after him.

As soon as my bare feet are on the driveway, I realize anew how exposed I am. Physically exposed in this raggedy gown. Emotionally exposed with this broken, bleeding heart.

I move towards the house with the plan to head directly to my room and change, but Nikolai grips my wrist tightly and jerks me back.

"Ow," I complain, shaking out my wrist. "Why did you—"

"You need to leave," Nikolai says.

But I realize he isn't looking at me. He's looking past me at the blond man who was with us at the hospital.

"Who are you?" I ask, following his gaze.

The man ignores me just like he did as we were leaving the hospital, instead looking at Nikolai. "Are you sure? I can stay. I can try to explain to your men about—"

"No. It doesn't matter what you say. My men won't like that you're here," Nikolai says. "Tensions are too high."

The blond man sighs and nods. "I guess give me a call when your men don't want to kill every Greek in sight."

Nikolai snorts, and I hate that this man can make him smile even a little when all he has for me are furious scowls. "Then I guess I'll never talk to you again."

The man nods grimly and disappears around the bend in the drive.

"Who was that?" I ask.

But before the question is even out of my mouth, Nikolai is shoving me towards the front doors. "Stop asking questions."

"Then start explaining what's happening, and I won't have to!"

Nikolai closes the front door behind him and, in a whirl, spins on me. I back up instinctively, pressing my spine to the wood wainscotting. It digs into my bones, but Nikolai hovers over me. "Are you really complaining about me not explaining myself to you? After everything you've done, you should count yourself lucky you're alive."

I inhale sharply, and Nikolai smirks. His mouth is a cruel slash. "There it is. Did I get through to you at last? Fuck knows your skull is thick."

Nikolai grabs my arm and leads me down the hallway to the right. It's in the opposite direction of my room. I want to ask where we're going, but I know he won't answer.

He hates me. He well and truly hates me.

And even as my heart breaks, the only thing I can think to ask is, "What about Elise?"

We're near the end of the hall. I imagine a hidden passageway opening up into a dungeon that lurks below the house. It would be just like Nikolai Zhukova to have a secret torture chamber below his house. He'll throw me down there and get rid of the key. He joked about it once—and who's to say it wasn't really a joke at all?

"What about her?"

"Did she find you like I told her to?" My lip trembles, and I do my best to keep it firm. "When she escaped from Xena's car, I told her to find you. I said... I said you'd take care of her."

"Looks like you lied to her, too, then."

Panic flares up in me, a sudden geyser of fear. I rip my arm out of his grip and back away. "I have to find her. She's out there by herself, and I have to find her."

"No, you need to start cooperating."

"I'll cooperate! I will. I'll cooperate and be your prisoner for as long as you want... if you find Elise."

Nikolai barks out a laugh. "You are not in a position to be making deals, Belle. You're already my prisoner."

"Please," I rasp. "Elise is everything to me. She's all I have."

Nikolai turns away and unlocks a normal-looking door behind me. The room behind is so dark I can't make out what it is, but I have a feeling it's not going to be as nice as my last room in his house.

He points. "Walk in."

He's right: I'm not in a position to make deals. But maybe if I cooperate—if I show him how easy life with me as a prisoner could be—maybe he'll agree to help.

I step into the dark and turn to face him. The hallway light creates a halo around his dark hair. He looks like an angel of death glaring down at me.

"So?" I ask desperately. "Will you find her?"

"You betrayed me, Belle. You lied, and now, my best friend is dead."

I choke back a sob. "I know. I'm sorry."

"'Sorry' doesn't mean shit to me," he says. "You know what will make me feel better? Revenge."

"What does that mean?"

"It means I want an eye for an eye. The most important person in my world is gone… and now, you'll know just what that feels like."

A scream rips out of my throat, but Nikolai is too fast. He slams the door shut as I hurl myself against it, pounding my fists on the wood until my knuckles bleed.

7

BELLE

I don't know if I've been locked in this room for hours or days. The window has been boarded over with a huge piece of plywood with screws as thick as my thumb, so there's no light and no clock in sight. The only way I've been able to mark the passage of time is with the ebb and flow of my hunger.

I was given a cup of ice chips in the hospital, but I haven't eaten a proper meal since Nikolai and I went to lunch after the doctor's appointment. My stomach growls and grumbles, begging for food, and I'm so desperate for someone to talk to that I talk back.

"I know," I tell it. "But he won't let me starve, right? He cares about the baby."

The truth stings.

Nikolai cares about the baby. Not me.

He's loyal to his Bratva. Not me.

Since I met him, Nikolai Zhukova has become one of the most important people in my life. Somewhere along the line, I convinced myself that feeling was mutual.

But it can't be. Not if one mistake is enough for him to toss me aside forever.

"Maybe it won't be forever," I whisper, swirling my finger in the plush carpet. I've been leaning against the side of the bed, staring at the door for… I don't even know how long. Without a television, a book, or even a sketchpad to distract me, I've taken to drawing simple designs in the carpet.

"But will he forgive me before I lose it and start draining my own blood for paint?"

I meant it as a joke, but it feels a bit too plausible to be funny. I have to get out of here.

I told Nikolai I'd cooperate with him if he took care of Elise, but he isn't going to take care of her. He's going to let her wander around the city by herself or die in a gutter or, maybe the worst of all, end up back with our mom just to spite me.

So I can't sit here and wait for him to come around and decide he forgives me.

I need a plan.

I push myself to my feet, grabbing the bed for stability as the blood rushes back to my head. Then I search the room for a weapon. Something sharp or heavy that I can use to fight my way out of this room.

Unsurprisingly, there's nothing. Every drawer and closet is empty. Unless I want to rip a sconce off the wall and wield it like a battering ram, I'm shit out of luck.

At the exact moment that I have that realization, I hear footsteps in the hallway.

I feel like a helpless rabbit, ears perked towards the noise, ready to flee at the first sign of trouble. Except there's nowhere to flee. Even if my instincts are screaming at me to take flight, fight is my only option.

A key slides into the door. I position myself in front of it, legs spread and partially bent, hands up to... I don't know, even. Defend myself? To fight him off?

Fighting Nikolai with my bare hands would be like trying to wrestle the wind out of a tornado, but I'm short on time and options and common sense.

The second the door opens, I take a deep breath and then sprint forward with my arms outstretched.

I expect my palms to meet the warm flesh of his body.

Instead, I hit metal.

It's a metal tray, to be precise. And as I collide with it, all the food resting on it squishes onto Nikolai's broad chest with a wet *slop* noise.

He doesn't even so much as stumble. He just looks down at me in disgust.

"Fucking hell, Belle."

"Food?" I'm so surprised by the humane gesture that I forget about trying to escape the room just long enough for Nikolai to close the door behind him and set the tray down.

Half of the contents are smeared across his shirt, but there's still a dinner roll and a cluster of grapes that escaped mostly unscathed. Like a starving animal, I lunge for the bread and then back away out of his reach once more.

"It was dinner, before you tried to... escape?" He says it like he genuinely isn't sure of my intentions. "Was that your attempt to escape?"

"I didn't have a lot of time to come up with something else, asshole."

"You've been in here for three hours and that's the best you could come up with?"

I blink in surprise. "It's only been three hours?"

Nikolai drops the tray on the bedside table and then assesses the sloppy mess on the front of his shirt. He flicks a smear of mashed potatoes onto the floor before he grabs the hem and, in one fluid motion, pulls the clothing off over his head.

The last few hours have been a nonstop nightmare. A top-to-bottom disaster that saw me delirious with relief, beyond reason with lust, and smashing down into rock bottom.

But Nikolai Zhukova shirtless is an experience that transcends circumstances.

I catch my breath at the sight of his broad chest and tapered waist. The V-cut above his hip makes my mouth water. I want to taste it. And not just because there's still a bit of mashed potato clinging to his skin.

I squeeze my eyes closed and shake my head.

I can't feel this way about him. I shouldn't. The sight of his naked body should not be enough to turn me inside out.

But, stupid or not, it is. The chemistry buzzing between us isn't bound by logic or reason. It's animal and wild. I *want* him.

And then an idea strikes.

I sidle closer and swipe a finger across his chest. Nikolai arches a dark brow.

"So you brought food," I murmur when our eyes meet. "Is that all you wanted to give me?"

"What else would I give you?"

I shrug, the shoulder of my hospital gown slipping down my arm. "Clothes, maybe?"

The material drops further. I do nothing to stop it. I don't want to. Especially when Nikolai is tracking the downward path of the gown with molten gray eyes.

It's nice to know that, as unaffected as he may appear, he isn't completely immune to me.

"Or," I suggest, "maybe I deserve a punishment."

His eyes peruse me from head to toe and back again before he takes a few measured steps forward. When he stops in front of me, I can't resist reaching out and pressing a hand to his chest. His skin is hot as a brand, but I don't mind the pain. I want him everywhere.

"Do you like punishment?"

His voice right now is melted chocolate and velvet. It's so different than the cold detachment from the car.

I frown. "No one likes punishment."

He reaches out and strokes a finger down my neck. "Then why did you come with my hand wrapped around your throat?"

I don't answer. He forces me back until my legs are against the mattress. He draws a line from my throat to the bundle of nerves between my legs, and when he slides his finger inside me, he growls, "You're so wet that I'm starting to think this won't be a punishment at all."

"You're smart," I mumble. "I'm sure you can figure out a way to torture me."

His pupils expand, eating away the gray. Dark thoughts I would kill to know swirl through his mind.

Then he pushes me back on the bed. "Spread your legs."

I lean back and inch my thighs apart, goosebumps blooming across my skin. Nikolai makes a disapproving groan and shoves my thighs apart wider.

"Stay like that. Don't move."

He smooths a calloused hand up my thigh, and I manage to hold still. But the second his finger dips into my warmth, I jolt.

His finger works a maddening circle up and down my slit and then up to my clit. It becomes a rhythm I can't escape and, no matter how many times he repeats it, can't anticipate. Electricity shoots through me again and again. A pressure I can't release building until my muscles are quivering with the force of holding still.

And the only part of him touching me is a single finger. What could he do with more?

"Please," I gasp, desperate for more of him.

He's giving me just enough to keep me teetering on the edge, but not enough to push me over the side.

"You're driving me crazy," I complain, arching into his touch. "I need more."

"You asked for a punishment. Punishment is what you're getting." Then he takes his finger away entirely, and I'm afraid he's going to leave me like this. "Now, be a good girl and roll over."

I flip onto my stomach. Nikolai grabs my ankles and pulls me to the edge of the bed. His warm legs step between mine, and then I feel him poised at my opening. He slides himself up and down until I go cross-eyed with need.

I shimmy my hips back, desperate to take him in.

"Nuh-uh," Nikolai warns, pressing a heavy hand to my lower back and pinning me to the bed. "Not until I say."

He teases me for what feels like forever before he finally, mercifully, nudges against my opening and slides inside. But just as the first wave of relief moves through me, he stops. One agonizing inch into me, Nikolai pulls out. Then he puts that inch in again.

It's like dying out in a desert and being given a single drop of water. I take it gladly, but I need so much more.

"Nikolai," I groan. "Please."

He ignores me, pressing his palm harder into my spine as he torments me with the tip of him until I'm practically sobbing into the mattress.

My thighs are quaking, and I can feel cramps working up the backs of my legs as my body strains towards the climax I just can't reach on my own. Not without Nikolai's help.

"I need you," I cry, looking back over my shoulder. But seeing Nikolai doesn't ease my torment. His jaw is clenched, turning his already chiseled face into a work of art. Sweat dots his upper lip and dampens the curls over his forehead. It's a reminder that this man is real. Flesh and blood, no matter how improbable that seems at times.

And I betrayed him.

I agreed to work with his enemies against him. Even if I was a shitty spy who never gave away crucial information, I turned my back on him.

Which seems impossible now. I can't take my eyes off of him.

He looks down at me, and in this moment, I'd give him absolutely anything.

"I'm sorry." My words are breathless. "I'm... I'm so sorry. For everything."

Nikolai's dark brow quirks. Then, without looking away, he thrusts all the way home.

"Is this what you wanted?" Nikolai asks in a groan as I let out a frantic scream into the mattress.

I nod desperately and moan again. "Yes. This is what I—"

"No more talking. Show me."

I extend my arms in front of me, rising up onto spread knees, and descend down his length. He fills me as if our bodies were made for this. Like we were created from the same mold, two pieces meant to connect in just this way.

I can't even remember why I started this. What my goal was in seducing Nikolai. Being filled to the brim with him, it's laughable that I'd ever think I could take him inside of me without losing my mind. As if I could engage in this and do anything aside from fall apart in every delirious moment.

I swirl down his length and press back into him. I grind our bodies together. I clench my inner muscles around him until he hisses out quiet Russian curses and bites down on my shoulder.

But when he wraps his hand around my waist and passes his finger over my clit, the last of my control is gone.

"Touch me," I beg. "Fuck me."

Nikolai takes over. He circles me with one hand and uses the other to still me so he can pound into my body. It only takes two thrusts for me to crumble. A current of warmth like I've never felt before floods my system as my body clamps down around him.

"I can feel you coming," Nikolai growls. "Such a good little *kiska*."

Nikolai follows a second later. I can feel him coming, too. Heat blooming inside of me.

He drives home into me once more and then drapes himself over my back. His cheek is heavy on my shoulder blade and the rush of air as he lets out a bone-deep sigh ghosts across my skin.

For a second, everything between us feels normal. I can imagine turning around and seeing his full lips spread in a sex-dazed smile. My body anticipates the soothing touch of his hands on me as we disengage and right ourselves.

But there is none of that.

Nikolai draws out of me all at once, leaving a hollow ache in my center. He moves to the dinner tray he brought for me and takes a long draw from the water bottle.

I'm shivering, suddenly cold without his body heat. When I sit on the edge of the bed, I almost reach for the comforter to draw around me. But then I look to the floor and notice the bulge in the pocket of Nikolai's discarded jeans.

A gun.

He's still standing by the nightstand a few feet away. I take a second to consider the geometry of the situation. The odds of me grabbing the gun and rounding on him before he catches me. A second is all I have, maybe less. Because he's capping the water bottle and if I don't act now—

Naked and with shaky legs, I lunge down to the floor and yank the gun out of his pants pocket. I lift the weapon towards Nikolai. I can't bring myself to aim it directly at his heart, so I opt for slightly wide of his left shoulder.

"Let me out of here," I whisper.

His expression is maddeningly neutral, but I see the slight rise of his brows. A flicker of surprise that is there and then gone again in an instant.

"So much for being sorry," he remarks.

I swallow past all my nerves. It doesn't help that I'm still naked. It's hard to look dominant without a stitch of clothing. Hard for me, at least. Nikolai does it effortlessly.

"I meant it. I really did. But... Elise is out there alone. I have to get out of here and go to her. I have to. I'm sorry."

He considers me for a second, his quicksilver eyes taking in my naked body as much as the gun in my hands.

Then he shrugs. "Fine."

"Fine?" I can't hide the shock from my face. "You're going to let me go?"

He nods. "You aren't worth the trouble."

I ignore the stab of pain his words cause and focus on my escape. "I need clothes."

"They're outside the door." My eyes narrow, and Nikolai sighs. "I was bringing you food and an outfit change. If you'd have let me make it through the damn door, I would have given them to you."

Without turning my back on him, I back up to the door and then reach blindly around the frame until I find the plastic bag of clothes. Then I clumsily dress with one hand.

I'm worried Nikolai will use my distraction against me and lunge for the gun while I'm pulling on the jeans, but he doesn't budge. He almost looks… bored.

My jeans are still unbuttoned and my shirt is bunched up around my waist, but I back out of the door and into the hallway. Nikolai is still standing by the bed.

More than ever before, this moment feels like a goodbye. But I can't bring myself to say it. My throat is so tight that I can barely bring myself to say anything.

Just before I turn and run to the hallway, I manage to squeak out two words.

"I'm sorry."

Then I run.

8

BELLE

By the time I make it to the police station—thanks to the reluctant help of several New Yorkers who point me in the right direction—I feel like I'm stumbling through a nightmare. The kind of dream where you try to run, but can't pick up your feet. Or try to dial a number on your phone, but keep hitting the wrong buttons.

The orgasm Nikolai worked into me still has me feeling jittery, and I'm delirious with exhaustion and hunger. The world exists beyond a haze I can't seem to clear.

Which is why the deep voice that sounds from the sidewalk behind me sends me jumping into the bushes.

"Ma'am? Do you need any help?"

I push myself out of the branches of the azalea bush and offer up my best semblance of a normal smile. "Hi. Yes, I'm here to—"

Then I look up at the man and my hope drains away.

"Officer Sweeney." He's shaved his beard short since I saw him last, but I can tell by the downward twist of his mouth that I look exactly the same as the last time he saw me. "It's so good to see you again."

"What was your name again?" he asks. "Isabel? Bethany?"

"Belle," I mumble. "Belle Dowan. I met you outside of—"

"Zhukova Incorporated. I recall." He slides his hands into his jeans. I'm not sure if I've caught him arriving for his shift or leaving, but he isn't in uniform. Aside from a shiny badge hanging from his belt loop, he's not even recognizable as an officer. "What brings you to the precinct tonight?"

I open my mouth to tell him, but then I remember that night at the Zhukova offices. When I confessed to being nothing more than a crazy ex-girlfriend. When I lied and told him I was desperately in love with Nikolai and trying to win him back, which is why I lied about my sister being kidnapped.

And now, I'm here with a very similar tale.

"Is this about your sister?" Officer Sweeney asks. "Who has her now? Wait, wait, don't tell me—"

My empty stomach twists, morning sickness merging with horror into a new level of nausea. I feel like I could hurl straight into the bushes.

"Nikolai wasn't my ex-husband," I say, sounding meek even to my own ears. "And that night… That night you went with me to his office was a misunderstanding. Mr. Zhukova manipulated me into lying—but this isn't about him, anyway. It's about my sister."

Sweeney drags a hand over his chin. I can tell he's used to having a longer beard by the way his fingers hang in the air awkwardly after reaching the end of his stubble. "Ma'am, I think you need to get on home. It's been a busy day and I can assure you that no one in there has the energy to handle… whatever this is."

"I can't go home. Don't you think that's where I'd be if I could? He brought me here against my will. Drugged me and flew me here, and now, the Greeks have my sister."

"Mr. Zhukova drugged you and brought you *here*?" he asks, pointing to the sidewalk beneath our feet.

I groan. "No. To New York City. I live in Oklahoma. I shouldn't even be here. But he brought me here, and now, my sister is gone and I need to find her before she's hurt."

Officer Sweeney blinks in a kind of daze. "How long has your sister been missing? Since I saw you last?"

"No, that was almost two months ago," I snap. "She's been missing since earlier this afternoon."

"Okay. When did you last see her?"

"I don't know where we were. I wasn't driving. Xena Simatou was." His eyes widen at the mention of Xena's name, and I hope I'm onto something now. I barrel on ahead. "She stopped the car, and I told Elise to get out. She did, and now, I don't know where she—"

"Xena Simatou?"

I nod. "Yes. I already said that. She was driving, and I—"

He holds up a hand to stop me. "You told your sister to get out of a moving vehicle?"

"No! It was stopped. Xena let her get out, but now, I can't find her and—"

"You told your sister to get out of the car?" he asks slowly. "The car that Xena Simatou was driving? And now you're upset because she isn't with you?"

It's obvious he doesn't believe me. It's just as obvious that he recognizes Xena's name. The full implications of her name.

I grit my teeth. "Yes, but—"

"It sounds to me like you might be the person responsible for her disappearance, then, Miss Dowan. You might want to take more of a grassroots approach before you involve the law."

"You are the law! If you think I've done something illegal, aren't you supposed to want me to turn myself in?"

He rolls his eyes. "After the day I've had, you'd be surprised what I'm willing to let slide. Especially when the person in front of me is here to cause trouble. Now, Miss Dowan, may I suggest you—"

"May I suggest you go home and figure out how to be a real cop?" I hiss over him. "In the meantime, I'll go inside and talk to a real detective who wants to help people."

I turn to storm inside, but Officer Sweeney slices off my path. "No one in there will help you. You watched too much news today and got bored. You don't have a case."

Too much news? What is he talking about?

I throw my arms wide. "Look around. Do you see my sister? Neither do I. There's my case."

"I'm sure you see lots of things that aren't there."

I bristle. "Are you calling me crazy?"

I realize as I ask the question that I'm standing in front of this man in jeans that are hanging off my hips, no makeup to speak of, and the rat's nest on my head is the textbook definition of "sex hair." I look deranged, to put it kindly.

"I'm not calling you anything," he says. "I'm just saying you aren't worth the trouble tonight. The people in there are mourning."

I hear the echo of Nikolai's words, and the pain I fought down back at the house comes rising up all at once now. Without thinking, I lunge forward and grab Officer Sweeney's arm.

"You have to listen to me! I'm telling you the truth and my sister is—"

"What the hell?" Sweeney swipes my arm away and holds out a thick palm to keep me back. He looks like a lion tamer. Which I guess makes me the lion. "Keep your hands off of me, ma'am. Or I'll have no choice but to arrest you for assaulting an officer."

"I didn't assault you. I'm trying to make you listen," I argue. "I just need you to do something to help me."

He nods slowly, and for a second, I think I've finally broken through to him. "You sure as hell need some kind of help. Maybe an involuntary psychiatric evaluation would be the best option for you."

I stumble away from him. "No. You can't. I was just locked up. I won't do it again."

He advances slowly, menacingly. "You're clearly a danger to yourself and others, Miss Dowan."

He is reaching for the phone on his hip, probably calling for backup, when I feel another hand land on my shoulder.

Instinctively, I jerk away and throw my elbow back. I catch whoever it is in their very firm stomach, and then look up—

To see Nikolai standing next to me.

His eyes are narrowed in silent displeasure, but then his face morphs into a charming smile.

"Officer Sweeney. Pleasure to see you again."

Sweeney's hand is frozen on his phone. He looks from me to Nikolai and back again. "Mr. Zhukova. What is going on here?"

"Another domestic issue," Nikolai says easily. "Nothing to worry yourself about."

"Well, I'm afraid I am worried. Your girl here seems to be a danger to herself and others. She's all worked up thinking she's part of our biggest case. I think it would be best if I—"

"I know what's best for her," Nikolai snaps. "Not you."

He sounds so confident that even I believe him. I mean, clearly I can't be put in charge of my own decisions. I just nearly got myself thrown in a psych ward for the night.

Sweeney sighs. "I let the two of you hash out your problems before, but at some point, I'll have to intervene. She can't keep coming here and raising alarms. If she does, we'll have no choice but to—"

"To do what?" Nikolai steps around me, towering over the officer. Even though Sweeney is an inch taller and has at least a fifty pound advantage, Nikolai is all chiseled muscle and dominance. "I think enough first responders have been hurt today, don't you think?"

Sweeney looks pale. He holds up two hands. "If you think you can handle her, then I'll leave her to you."

"I'm not a fucking pet," I protest weakly. "Neither of you gets to decide what happens to me."

But even as I say the words, I know they aren't true. I'm exhausted. This day has been the longest of my life, and wherever Nikolai decides to take me next, I'll go without a fight.

Nikolai ignores me and stares straight down at Officer Sweeney. "She isn't your concern. You're going to walk away and pretend none of this ever happened."

There's a moment where no one moves. I don't even breathe, waiting to see what's going to happen.

Then Officer Sweeney takes a breath, turns towards the road, and walks away without another word.

Just like that, he's gone.

And Nikolai and I are alone.

I spin to face him with a one-word question on my lips. "Why?"

"Why? Because you were going to get yourself thrown in jail." Nikolai drags a hand down his face. "Honestly, Belle, I've never met someone so incapable in my entire fucking life."

I ignore his barb and shake my head. "Why did you let me leave? I thought you were... well, I don't know what I thought you were doing. But you were following me."

"And you had no idea." He purses his lips in disappointment. "You never even glanced behind you."

Hot shame floods my cheeks. I was being stupid. The fact that he let me leave was surprising. I should have seen it for what it was: a trap.

"I always planned to let you go," he explains. "To be frank, I thought you'd try to escape much earlier. That's why I left you alone in the room for so long."

"There was no way to escape! You had plywood over the windows."

"Which you could have easily pulled off with your bare hands," Nikolai says. "Most of the screws were sheared off. There was also a metal coat hanger in the closet you could have used to pick the lock."

I searched the room from top to bottom and missed everything. Nikolai *wanted* me to escape, and I still couldn't manage it. "I was... scared."

"Not too scared to throw yourself at me."

My shame is molten now. I feel like I'm disintegrating into the pavement. "I was... distracting you."

He snorts. "I left the door unlocked behind me and the gun visible in my pocket. I purposefully turned away from you twice so you could grab it. I even pulled my shirt over my head, covering my face to give you an opportunity. Instead, you stood there and gawked like a lovestruck schoolgirl."

Looking back, it did take him a long time to remove his shirt. But I was so busy admiring the contours of his body that I hardly noticed. Even now, the memory of his physique has me feeling feverish.

I shake my head. "Why would you want me to escape? Why bother locking me up at all if you were rigging the room for me to get free?"

"Because I assumed you'd lead me to Xena," he says. "I wanted you to get out and take me to where the Greeks are hiding. But after a few hours of you laying around like a sad sack, I gave up and decided to go in myself. Turns out it was all a huge waste of time."

"Do you mean locking me up was a waste of time, or…?" The question is out of my mouth before I can stop it. I know instantly how desperate it sounds, but I can't take it back. That would make it worse.

Nikolai smirks darkly. "A good fuck is never a waste of time. If nothing else, you're still useful for that."

"You're disgusting," I hiss. "You're a cruel, nasty asshole."

He shrugs casually. "I guess your pussy didn't get the memo. Because it still fucking loves me."

It's not the only one, I think with misery.

But the thought is too pathetic to dwell on. I brush it aside and try to keep moving forward. At this point, it's the only thing I can do.

"Well, I didn't take you to Xena because I don't know where she is. If you'd stopped to listen to me, I would have explained that."

"Like I should trust you?" Nikolai grabs my arm and starts hauling me down the sidewalk. I don't even try to pull away. I know it's hopeless.

"You should trust me. I'm the reason she was in the hospital."

"You mean you're the reason *you* were in the hospital," he says.

I frown. "The EMTs on scene told me that Xena was loaded into another ambulance and—"

"And proceeded to slaughter the EMTs and leave the ambulance abandoned on the side of the road."

I gasp. "No."

"Yes," Nikolai bears down. "She slaughtered innocent people who were there to help her, and then fled. That's the kind of person you were working for."

"I wasn't working for her! I was working for... for myself," I fumble. "It didn't have anything to do with her."

He snorts. "Great. So you'd have worked for anyone who offered you a one-way ticket out of the country? Good to know your loyalty is only worth a couple hundred bucks."

I groan. "That is not fair. You didn't give me many options."

Nikolai lets go of my arm and spins around. We're too close, my chin nearly against his chest. He throws his arms out wide.

"Tonight, I gave you a world of options. You were free and you could have gone anywhere, done anything. You could have searched women's shelters for Elise. You could have had missing posters hung up over half of downtown by now. And instead, you came traipsing right to the fucking cops. Which is almost worse than if you'd gone straight to Xena."

I frown. "Would you rather I betrayed you again?"

"Rather than being dumb enough to accidentally rat me and my entire Bratva out to the morons in blue? Yeah," he says. "Because at least I know how to handle traitors."

The implication there is hard to miss. If I had gone to Xena, Nikolai would have killed me.

"But this..." He gestures to me and sighs. I feel like I'm wilting in place, getting smaller and weaker and sadder with every passing second. "I'll have to find a way to deal with you now."

"You could let me go," I say softly. "I'll promise not to go to the police or tell anyone—"

Nikolai laughs, stopping my words in their tracks. Then he grabs my arm. "Get in the car, Belle. I have better places to be."

9

NIKOLAI

Fifteen minutes after I get Belle back to the house—and locked in a room that isn't designed to be easily escaped this time around—I get a call from one of my lieutenants, Yuri.

"I found Elise," he reports. "She's at Urban Family Center. Just checked into a communal room an hour ago."

"Did she look okay? Any injuries? Was she with anyone?"

"Alone and unharmed as far as I could tell," Yuri replies. "I kept my distance, though. Like you asked."

All of my available men had the same mission: find Elise. I may have told Belle I'd let Elise die on the streets, but even I was surprised how easily she believed me. Then again, I don't think she could have fucked me the way she did if she really, truly thought I'd abandon her baby sister to die.

"Good work. Call the rest of the team off. All of you pivot to searching for Xena."

"Do you want me to pick Elise up?" he asks. "I'm already here."

"No. Send Ars—"

I wince and the words die on my lips. Sending Arslan is no longer an option. This fucking ache in my chest every time I think of that miserable bastard's name will not go away.

"I'll handle it," I finish gruffly. "She knows me."

I hang up the phone before Yuri says anything else.

The place is a dump.

Junked, rusted-out cars line the curbs on both sides of the street. Trash gathers in the gutters and blows across the pavement, the urban equivalent of tumbleweeds. Plywood boards cover shattered windows and seal off buildings that have been abandoned longer than Elise has been alive.

A couple teenagers are standing under a streetlight halfway down the block, passing a glowing joint back and forth between them. They close ranks as I walk past.

When I stop in front of the center's wooden double doors, a woman is sitting on the steps. It's impossible to tell how old she is. She could be thirty or a hundred or anywhere in between. Her chapped lips crack and bleed as she smiles. It's unsettling.

"If you're here to find your woman, good fuckin' luck," she slurs.

"I'm looking for my… daughter," I say carefully. It's a better label than "the sister of the woman I impregnated and am now holding hostage." More succinct, at least.

"Doesn't matter," she says. "Half the women in there are hiding from some man who looks just like you. Strong, violent, angry… They won't let you through the front doors without calling the cops."

"I'm not angry." Not at Elise, anyway.

"No dicks allowed." The woman cackles, her voice more cough than anything else. Then she snaps her attention to me, her eyebrow quirked up. "But I allow dicks. Plenty of them. All I need is a place to sleep tonight. Tempted?"

"Not even remotely." I step around her and open the door.

"Wait!" she cries. "The center is full. I'm desperate."

The woman looks pitiful. Near tears and reeking of filth. But I'm here for Elise and no one else.

"Try the next poor bastard who stumbles past."

The door slams closed behind me. I'm in a dimly-lit entryway. The tile floor is cracked and scuffed, and an older woman behind a warping wooden desk looks up as I enter. Her eyes narrow immediately.

"Women and children only," she barks.

"I'm not here to stay," I snap back. "I'm looking for my daughter."

The woman immediately starts shaking her head. "If your daughter is here, then she is safe for tonight. She'll leave in the morning and you can attempt to find her then. But as a rule, we do not reveal the identity or location of anyone who comes to stay with us."

"As a rule, I get whatever the fuck I want," I growl. "Her name is Elise…"

All at once I realize I don't know Elise's last name. She and Belle have different fathers, so it may be Dowan, but it may not. It doesn't matter anyway. The woman staring at me has zero interest in hearing anything I have to say unless it's "goodbye."

"Once she leaves in the morning, you can connect with her if that is something she is interested in." The woman talks like she's reading from a script. "We do not attempt reunification unless there is a police report filed. If you've filed a report, then the police can come and collect your daughter. We will not hand her over to you."

There are glass doors behind the woman covered with foil and cardboard. Through some of the cracks, I can see a larger space beyond. Based on the rumble of chatter, there are a lot of people in there.

"Do not attempt to open the doors," the woman warns, reading my thoughts. "We have a security guard just inside the doors who will do his job if necessary."

I can feel my gun on my hip like a brand. My fingers itch to grab it.

But there are women and children beyond this door. People who, as the elegant woman on the steps made clear, are scared and running.

I'm still debating my next steps when the doors behind me slam open. I spin just as the woman from the steps drags herself inside. She bobs and sways with every step.

"For God's sake," the woman behind the desk groans. "There's no space for you tonight, Camille. I already told you."

"But this man is looking for his daughter!" Camille is shouting now. Her voice echoes off the ceiling. I can hear the voices on the other side of the glass quiet at the uproar. "He's a good dad."

The woman behind the desk looks exhausted beyond words. "Both of you have to leave or I'm calling the police."

Suddenly, Camille rushes forward and flings the doors to the main room open. There are gasps and stifled screams.

A security guard steps in from the side and pushes Camille back. "You can't be in here," he bellows.

Camille starts screaming and fighting with him. I utilize the distraction to step into the doorway. The woman at the desk is yelling orders at me, but I'm not listening to her. I'm looking for one familiar face.

And I find it.

Elise is in the far corner of the room. She's standing perfectly still, her wide eyes pinned on me. I half-expect her to roll over and play opossum.

But then, in a move even I wasn't expecting, she spins around and sprints out of the back door.

"Fuck," I growl. "Elise, wait!"

I step forward, but the security guard has his gun out now. It doesn't matter anyway. If I follow Elise through the room, she'll maintain her lead. I need to move in the opposite direction and cut her off.

As I head back for the front door, I hear Camille talking to the woman at the front desk. "I guess a space just cleared up, am I right?"

The woman is slick, I'll give her that.

Outside on the sidewalk, I take a hard right. An alley that runs through the center of the block. It's my fastest path to the street behind the building. I turn into the alley and bear down, solely focused on the light at the other end—

When something slams into my shins.

The pain is blinding, but as I fall forward, I manage to tuck into a roll over my right shoulder. I pop up on my feet, facing the way I just came, though my shinbones are screaming at me.

The man across the alley snarls at me. He has the Battiato crest tattooed on his neck. It stands out against his pale skin, which is growing paler by the second. He clearly didn't expect me to recover as quickly as I did.

"What the—"

I cross the distance between us in two strides and throw a punch before he can even raise his arms. His nose gets pulverized beneath my fist and he falls back against the brick wall. I follow, landing two more savage hits to his unguarded middle while he helplessly shields his face with his arms.

Then he roars, drops his shoulder, and drives me back to the center of the alley. I curse under my breath. Every second I spend here with this fool is another second Elise puts between us.

"I don't have time for this shit," I grit out. I reach for my gun, but the soldier is swiping at my arms and trying to pin them to my side.

Fine. We'll do this the old-fashioned way. I drive my knee up into his face. More shit breaks. He groans and flops back. It's enough time for me to grab my gun and stick it in his face.

I'm tempted to blow his brains out right away. But I have some questions first.

"What are you doing here?"

His eyes cross as he stares at the gun. "Takin' a night walk," he spits.

I whip him across the face with the butt of my gun. "Try again, wiseass."

His nose is bleeding freely, blood flowing down his chin. His jaw works as he considers his options. Finally, he shakes his head. "I was here for the girl."

"Xena wants Elise?" I guess.

At that, his lips smash together into a flat line.

"Don't want to talk? Fine. I don't really want to listen, anyway."

He lifts his chin in defiance, but before the smug look can even settle into place, I pull the trigger. I'm already moving down the alley by the time I hear his body hit the ground.

I stop when I reach the other mouth of the alley, but the street beyond is empty. Whichever way Elise went, she's long gone now.

I reach for my phone and, on instinct, dial Arslan's number. It rings twice before I realize what I'm doing.

I freeze, my phone in my hand, and fight the urge to smash it against the wall. After a few deep breaths, I hang up and call Yuri instead.

"Change of plans," I tell him. "Elise slipped away. Track her again."

Without a single wisecrack about me letting a teenager escape my grasp, Yuri agrees. "Of course, sir."

Arslan taught these men nothing, I think. Or maybe he taught them everything. Because if anyone else tried to talk to me the way he used to do, I'd have killed them.

"I ran into a Battiato soldier. He's dead in the alley next to the building. Clean him up and find Elise before Xena does."

I've come to expect complaints about menial tasks like cleaning up murder scenes, but Yuri doesn't flinch.

"On it, boss. I'll take care of it."

I hang up and head to my car. Blind obedience has never felt hollower.

10

NIKOLAI

Belle's room is dark when I push the door open.

I didn't expect her to still be awake. I'm not even sure why I'm here. But when I got back to the house, sitting alone in my room sounded like fucking misery incarnate.

"Nikolai?" Her voice is raspy with sleep, but my heart still pangs at the familiar sound of it. "Is everything okay?"

"I'm not here to torture you again, if that's what you're asking."

The weight of those words sits between us heavily. Calling what I did to Belle earlier a "punishment" is a serious stretch. The only thing torturous about it is that I didn't wrestle the gun out of her hands and "torture" her again.

She sits up, drawing the blankets around her. "I mean, is everything okay with you? It's late."

"I'm fine. I just like to decompress after I kill someone."

Admittedly, I'm trying to scare her. I may have slipped into her room late at night, but that doesn't mean we're on anything resembling good terms.

"Who?" she asks softly.

I consider lying to her, but the truth slips out so easily. "A Battiato soldier. He attacked me."

"Are you okay?" Belle shifts to the edge of the mattress and slides out of bed. She's in a night shirt that falls just to the tops of her thighs. Even in the dark, I can see the curve of her hips. The gentle slope of her legs.

"I already said I'm fine."

When her hand skirts down my arm and clutches my wrist, I don't pull away. "If you were fine," she says, "you wouldn't be here."

"If I was fine, I wouldn't be don. No one who is 'fine' survives in my world," I tell her. "We're all fucked-up. It comes with the territory."

Her fingers slide against mine. In the dark, it's easier to give into the appeal of her. To the warmth of her body, the silky smoothness of her skin. She pulls me towards the bed, and I follow.

"Then tell me what in particular has you fucked up today."

She pats the mattress. I kick off my shoes and lie down next to her.

"Arslan was the only person in my Bratva who knew me before I was me," I whisper. "When I was a scrappy little kid with nothing and nobody."

Belle laughs softly. "It's hard to imagine you before the power and the money."

"And the harem of women at my beck and call?"

"It's very easy *not* to imagine that, thank you very much."

I sigh and run my fingers through my hair. "Having a harem of women was always more Arslan's thing, anyway. His childhood sucked, too. So settling down wasn't on his priority list."

"So there's no one—like, no immediate family to inform or anything?" Her voice is almost a whisper.

"No. I'm the closest thing he had."

I feel Belle shift slightly, drawing closer. But she doesn't touch me. "Like brothers."

"We were brothers. Arslan was my only family. Even my grandfather was... Well, I was a cog in his business machinations more than anything else."

"I'm sorry."

I fold my hands over my stomach and stare up at the ceiling. "Don't be. It's the way things are."

"But it's not the way things have to be. You don't have to do things that way." After a beat, Belle reaches out and lays her hand on my arm. Her fingers are cold, and she sighs at the contact. "You're burning up."

I say nothing. Silence descends, heavy and charged around us. Belle circles her fingers over my skin, shifting closer until I can feel her breasts pressing against my arm. Until the warmth from her thighs is radiating against the back of my hand.

"Tell me a story about the two of you," she prompts. "About you and Arslan. When you were kids."

Talking about Arslan at all feels like cracking open my chest and exposing my underbelly to the wolves. But it's painfully obvious that she just wants to know him better. And through that, to know me better.

Right now, in the dark, I want to give her both.

"When we were sixteen, we robbed a liquor store together."

Belle gasps. "Not that kind of story!"

"Those are the only kind we have," I laugh. "It's better than it sounds."

She makes an unconvinced noise in the back of her throat. It's a rumbling sound that is dangerously close to the way she groans when I'm inside of her. I feel my cock twitch.

"Arslan got invited to this girl's party, but we could only go if we could supply the alcohol."

"You robbed a liquor store to get a girl's attention? Really?"

"Well, the girl only saw Arslan, not me," I explain. "And at the time, he was sporting some teenage acne and an overbite. He had to earn his keep."

Belle laughs. "Oh my goodness. I wish I could see pictures of both of you at that age."

"Keep wishing."

"You embarrassed?"

"Me?" I scoff. "Absolutely not. But Arslan burned most of the evidence. There's nothing left."

"Except stories," she murmurs.

"Except stories." I hate the bitter taste of the words in my mouth. I take a deep breath to rinse it away. "Arslan was insistent we get the alcohol for this party. He thought we could get a fake ID or talk our way into it. I had a better idea."

"To steal it," she guesses.

I nod. "So, the night before the party, Arslan and I deck out in all-black and creep down this embankment to a liquor store right along the highway. The roar from the cars was the perfect cover for any noise we might make and it gave us a quick getaway. I parked the car along the shoulder just above us."

Belle's grip on my arm tightens. "Oh no. You got caught, didn't you? Or your car got stolen. Did someone crash into your getaway car in the middle of the heist?"

I bite back a smile. "Arslan busted out the back window with a hammer and then we crawled inside. We were able to carry the loot up the embankment bit by bit over the next, I don't know… fifteen minutes, probably?"

"Fifteen? That's too long!"

"It was," I laugh. "Because by the fifth time we crawled through the window, we could hear police moving around in the main room."

"Oh, shit."

"That's what we said. The cops clearly knew we were in the back room and they were headed our way."

"What did you do?" Belle shakes my arm with nervous fingers.

"We decided to make a run for it. Arslan pushed me through the window and told me he was coming out after me."

When I close my eyes, I can still feel him grabbing my ankles and catapulting me out the back window into the grass.

"*'Run, Niko. I'm right behind you!'* he said. But he wasn't. When I made it to the top of the embankment, I could hear Arslan yelling on the other side of the building."

Belle's fingers are digging into my skin. "They caught him?"

"No, not right away." I shake my head. "He took off running through the front door to draw their attention away from me so I could escape. He let them catch him. He got arrested and booked into jail for the night."

"He sacrificed himself for you?"

For a second, I see Arslan pale and bleeding on the ground at my feet. He rode into a shootout on a motorcycle with nothing but his pistol.

"Yeah," I whisper. "He did." Then I clear my throat. "I paid bail, took the alcohol to the party, and they finally cut him loose halfway through the party. I made sure to tell the girl what happened when Arslan arrived, and she made sure to repay him in full."

Belle sits up and looks down at me warily, eyebrow arched. "She had sex with him, didn't she?"

I grin. "Took his virginity. And it only cost him one night in jail."

"I suppose people have done a lot worse for sex," she sighs.

"Especially Arslan."

We both laugh. It feels good. For the first time since I walked away from my best friend's body growing cold on the ground, I feel lighter.

Belle's fingers stroke down my arm. When she whispers, I feel the warmth of her breath on my neck. "I'm sorry for your loss, Nikolai."

She's everywhere. Touching my arm, her heat sinking into my skin, her words rattling around in my brain. All of it has energy buzzing through my veins. My dick strains against my pants.

She must sense it, because without another word, Belle straddles me. I slide my hands up her thighs and beneath the material of her nightgown. My thumbs hook around the inside of her legs, and when I brush over the delicate material of her lace panties, Belle winces in desire.

"Are you already wet for me, *kiska?*" I ask, stroking her again.

She bites her lip and nods. "I was wet the moment I woke up and saw you standing in my room." Her hands drag over my abs and higher.

"There are too many layers between us." As I speak, I hook my fingers in the waistband of her panties and yank. The material comes apart with a loud rip. Even in the dim light, I see Belle's gaze turn molten.

She drags my shirt over my head and tosses it aside. As soon as I'm bare-chested, she bends down and works her mouth down my neck and over my collarbone. She tastes me inch by inch, licking and sucking her way down my body. When she finally undoes the button on my jeans, I'm painfully hard. It takes no encouragement at all for my cock to spring free.

Belle settles between my legs and wraps a hand around my base. As she leans forward, mouth puckered in a perfect 'O,' she glances up at me.

It's the single most seductive thing I've seen in my entire life.

The only thing that tops it is when she actually sucks me into her warm mouth. "Fuck," I groan, fisting a handful of hair at the back of her head.

She sucks and swirls, working her tongue along my underside and then teasing my tip. Her hands stroke and tease the whole time.

After a few minutes, I drag her away by her hair before I explode in her mouth way before I'm ready to finish. Her lips pops off of me, still puckered in that devastating 'O.'

"Was it not good?" she worries.

"We're always good together."

I pull the night shirt over her head and press her back onto the mattress. There's more I want to say.

Sex has never felt like this with anyone.

Since the moment you dropped down in the seat next to me on that plane, I haven't been able to think about another woman.

You're a part of me now.

But I don't say any of it.

I slide my hand down her stomach to cup the warmth between her legs. She's damp, aching for me to claim her. When I slide a finger inside, she bucks into my touch with a soft moan.

"That sound," I growl, adding a second finger just so I can wring it from her again. "It's pitiful."

"It is. I'm desperate for you. Now and all the time."

She kisses me hungrily. I bite her lower lip just as a way to pin her down and keep her in one place. With every passing second, it feels like we're in a car with no brakes.

Fuck knows I have more than enough tension to release, but this shouldn't be anything more than that. Just sex. Just fucking.

Except as I pulse two and then three fingers into Belle's aching core, and she bucks so hard she is coming off the mattress, I know damn well that that's a bunch of shit.

This isn't just "more."

It's everything.

And when she throws her head back and cries out, "I'm coming. God, Nikolai... I'm coming," I know it beyond the shadow of a doubt.

"You are so fucking beautiful."

Our movements are frantic and needy as she reaches for my length and presses me to her opening. I sheath myself all the way inside of her like it's the last time I'll ever get to do it.

"Don't leave," Belle whispers against my neck.

With slow, shallow motions, she grinds herself against me. I grab her hands and press them into the mattress above her head. Then I start to glide in and out of her wetness.

I want this to last. This universe we've created, just the two of us, wringing pleasure from each other… I want to stay here as long as I can.

But when she starts writhing up to meet me and makes that *sound* again, that sexy fucking sound, I can't hold back.

I drive into Belle as hard as I can, stay there, and empty my soul inside of her.

Belle presses a long kiss to my neck when I'm finally empty. She murmurs against my skin, "I've never felt… It's never been like this with anyone, Nikolai. And that means something, doesn't it? The way we are together. It's… it's perfect."

Her words are running away with her. Just a few minutes ago, I would have nodded along, delighting myself in the tight way her body gripped me.

But now, in the cold aftershock of my orgasm, I see this all for what it is.

A mistake.

I roll away from her and grab my jeans.

"Nikolai?" Her voice is soft and weak. "You can stay, you know. If you want."

I shake my head. "I have to go."

She pulls the blanket over herself, trying to cover her body even though I just explored every inch of it. "Are you mad at me?"

When I walked through her door, I was. Underneath it all, I was still angry.

But now, I see the truth.

I'm the problem.

Because I can't bear to let her go. I prioritized Belle when I should have prioritized my Bratva. The only reason Arslan is dead is because he was splitting his loyalties between the Bratva and her. Because he was following my lead and trying to do both.

I'm the reason my best friend is dead.

I can't blame Belle for that. I can only blame myself.

"No, I'm not mad at you."

She looks uncertain. "You said earlier you didn't know what you were going to do with me... Have you figured it out?"

I pull on my shirt and back towards the door. "Yeah, I think I have."

On my way out, I hear Belle ask what I mean. But I close the door and keep moving.

She'll find out soon enough.

11

BELLE

I dream of him. All night, every second, I dream of him.

I toss and turn in bed, and Nikolai is there with me. I can still feel him inside and out. The heat of his hands over my skin, the rush of his breath against my neck.

Then the dreams shift into nightmares. I feel him pulling away. He leaves in a hurry, rushing away from me, darting just out of reach.

When the door to my bedroom opens, I bolt upright in bed. I'm still dazed. Sleep clings to me like a fine glitter I can't shake. But still, I know enough to hope.

"Nikolai?" I blink against the darkness. Even when I see the small, thin figure in front of me that can't possibly be him, I'm convinced it's Nikolai. "You came back. I didn't know if—"

"Belle."

The moment I hear my name—the moment I hear my sister's shaky, tentative voice drenched in fear—I jump out of bed.

I'm across the room with my arms around her before I can even process what is happening.

"Are you real?" I gasp, tugging at the ends of her strawberry blonde hair and squeezing her to my chest until I can feel her heart beating against my rib cage. "Are you really here?"

Elise laughs softly. "Yeah. And I'm glad you are, too. I wasn't sure you'd be here."

"You fought like you were sure she wasn't." Nikolai's voice draws my eyes. He's leaning against the doorframe observing us. "You almost took out my eye with that brick."

"Brick?" I hold Elise at arm's length, studying her for any injuries.

"I threw a brick at him," she explains. "He was chasing me."

"Because you were running," Nikolai argues.

"It's a chicken-and-egg kind of situation," she says with a shrug.

She doesn't look hurt. Her hair is stringy and she smells like sweat and smoke. But she's in one piece. And she's here. *Thank God.*

Tears blur my vision. I try and fail to blink them away. "I can't believe you're here. I wanted to find you. It was all I wanted."

"Don't cry, B." Elise swipes at my cheeks tenderly. For a minute, it's hard to remember which of us is the older sibling.

"You were supposed to find Nikolai," I scold. "When I told you to get out of the car, I told you to find him. Why didn't you?"

Elise lowers her chin. "I didn't know if I could trust him. Everything was happening so fast."

I'm not sure what to say to that. I want to believe Nikolai is trustworthy. He found Elise for me, after all. But he also told me he'd let her die as revenge for Arslan's death.

Even as he made the threat, I didn't really believe it. I couldn't. Nikolai is a cold, calculating Bratva don to his core, but he isn't cruel. Not unnecessarily, anyway. And letting a child suffer because of my mistake would be heartlessly, needlessly cruel.

The fact that he chased her down and brought her back to me proves me right. I take a small amount of pride in knowing him so well. In seeing at least one thread of gold running through his black, shriveled-up heart.

I wrap my arms around Elise again, dragging her against me in a bone-crushing hug. "Well, you're here now. That's all that matters."

"It's not *all* that matters. I want to know what happened to you. And what happened with—" Her words drop off suddenly and her eyes widen.

"With Xena?" I ask pointedly, giving her a small smile so she knows it's okay. "The story is out. Everyone knows what happened."

Nikolai knows what happened, is what I mean.

"Yeah," she rasps. "With that."

"Xena lied to me," I tell her. "She tricked me, and I was… I was so stupid. I'm sorry I put you in that situation." More tears clog my throat, but for Elise's sake, I try to swallow them down. "I've put you in so much danger the last couple months."

"It's not your fault. You didn't know any of this would happen."

"I don't even know if that's true," I murmur. "I should have gotten us out of here the second we arrived in New York. When we saw that skeezy hotel room. No, before then—when Roger called and said he was in fucking Aruba."

Sure, leaving then would mean not knowing Nikolai and not being pregnant. I can't really bring myself to wish that was true. But for Elise's sake, I should have left.

Elise snorts. "Fuck Roger."

"Hey! Language," I warn.

"You said it first."

"I'm older. It's allowed." I smooth her hair back from her face. There's a smudge of dirt on her forehead, so I lick my thumb and wipe it off. "I'm supposed to take care of you. I'm supposed to make the tough decisions to keep you safe."

"I'm old enough to take care of myself. I mean, look at me—I did okay today, didn't I?"

"I don't even know what happened after you left the car," I say, realizing it all at once. "Where did you go?"

"Well, first, I went to a diner and drank some terrible coffee while I tried to come up with a plan. And then this woman at the counter tried to call the police for me because she could tell something was wrong, but I talked her off of that ledge. Then she told me about a shelter I could go to. It was getting late in the afternoon and I didn't have another plan, so I went there. That's when Nikolai found me the first time."

My eyes bug out. "The first time? Earlier today?"

She nods. "Just after dark. He showed up at the shelter and I didn't know what he wanted, so I ran."

When Nikolai came into my room earlier, he'd just come from looking for Elise.

I just like to decompress after I kill someone, he said. *A Battiato soldier. He attacked me.*

He'd killed someone while trying to find Elise.

The realization that Xena had people looking for Elise makes my blood run cold. And the fact that I was tearing at Nikolai, giving myself over to lust and pleasure while Elise was in danger… nauseating. Shame burns through me like a fever.

"After that, I was floating around from a park to a bus stop to a public restroom. I was trying to blend in and not get too comfortable in case Nikolai showed up again. But I fell asleep on a bench, and he found me."

My heart squeezes and my words come out strangled. "You were sleeping on a bench?"

"Yeah. And I woke up to Nikolai shaking me. As soon as I opened my eyes, I threw a punch. Or, I tried. He dodged it and then I grabbed the brick I'd been carrying for protection and hurled it at him. But his head is surprisingly thick."

I snort. "You can say that again."

In the doorway, Nikolai chuckles.

"He told me that you were safe and back at the house," Elise continues, "but I saw Xena's car on the news. It was totaled so bad, Belle. And then there were those dead EMTs. I didn't know—I thought maybe… I thought he was lying and you were dead."

As soon as the words are out of her mouth, I notice the tears shining in her eyes. Her chin wobbles for just a second. Just long enough for me to see the pain shimmering through her usually calm, stoic facade.

"Oh, honey," I whisper, pulling her in for a hug. "I'm okay. I made Xena crash the car so I could escape."

She lifts her chin proudly. "I'm just glad we're together again."

I smooth my thumb over her cheek. "And we always will be. From now on, my only priority is taking care of you and keeping you safe."

"How are you going to do that?"

I take a deep breath. "First things first, I need to get us both out of this city. We need to start over somewhere safe."

"Can we do that?" Elise asks softly.

Before I can answer, I hear Nikolai clear his voice from the doorway. When I look up, his expression is unreadable.

"You need to go take a shower and get to sleep, Elise. You've had a busy day," he says.

Elise opens her mouth to argue, but I squeeze her hand. "He's right. We'll talk more in the morning. Go rest."

I expect her to fight with me, but instead, she nods. I can see the exhaustion written in her face and in the slope of her shoulders. It's the only time in my life I've seen Elise too tired to have an attitude.

She gives me one final hug and then slips out of my room and into the hallway.

The moment she's gone, Nikolai closes the door and moves towards me.

"Thank you," I say, reaching for him. "Thank you for finding her and bringing her to me. I can't—I don't know how I'll ever repay you."

Just before I can touch him, he steps back. "I have an idea where you could start."

"What are you talking about?"

"You want to repay me," he repeats. "And I have an idea."

The warmth from our interaction only a few hours ago is gone. His posture is stiff and he's looking down at me like I'm a problem he's trying to solve. A shiver moves down my spine as I gaze up at him.

"Well, I don't... That's just an expression. I think you and I are even, Nikolai. We've each caused each other plenty of trouble, don't you think?"

He arches a brow. "Someone has changed their tune. Now that your sister's back, I guess you aren't so desperate."

"Or maybe being locked in this room has given me plenty of time to think about all the shit you've put me through," I snap.

"Oh, and I really heard you complaining about your circumstances when I was balls deep inside of you." He stalks towards me, his voice a low, rumbly growl. "Or maybe that was all an act, too? Maybe you were whoring yourself out to try and get what you want."

I flex my hand. The desire to smack him across the face is strong, and I barely resist. "Unlike you, I'm not very good at twisting love into a tool I can wield. When I sleep with someone, it's because I have genuine feelings for them."

I tried it earlier, using sex to manipulate him. But the moment we were touching, everything else faded away. I can't not mean it. I don't know how.

"What about when you lie to someone? What does that mean to you?"

I grind my teeth together until my head hurts. Nikolai tips his head to the side, waiting for my answer.

"Well?" he prods. "You let me fuck you on my desk after you tried to escape with the help of Xena the first time—what should I make of that? Do you only lie to people you have feelings for?"

"I didn't lie to you because I didn't have feelings for you," I say. "I told you before, it was because Elise has to be my priority. I had to protect her, no matter what I felt for you."

If I expect my words to break through Nikolai's tough exterior, I'm sorely disappointed. He just stares back at me with flat gray eyes. "Well, you did manage to escape, and your sister ended up sleeping on a public park bench. Seems like your priorities might be out of order."

The image of Elise sleeping out in the open, vulnerable to anyone walking by, is too much to consider. I squeeze my eyes closed to shove away the thought of what could have happened to her if anyone aside from Nikolai had found her.

The shift in the air when he steps towards me sends goosebumps down my arms, but I keep my eyes closed. When he speaks, his words brush across the shell of my ear. "Maybe you should stop coming up with plans, *kiska*. They always end with someone getting hurt."

Elise.

Arslan.

Myself.

He isn't wrong, but I open my eyes and push him away anyway. "Or maybe you're the common denominator. All of this shit started happening when you came into my life. I was fine before then."

"Is that right?"

He's goading me, talking to me like a toddler. I can feel that he's just letting me blow off steam until I get tired. Nothing I'm saying is getting through to him.

"Yeah, it is," I snap. "You and I, we're toxic. This thing between us is—well, you said it yourself. That there's something special between us."

He shakes his head. "I never said that."

"Earlier tonight, in bed," I say, jogging his memory. "You said it should just be sex between us, but it's not. It's never been that. There's something more. And whatever it is, it's dangerous. Volatile. We aren't good for each other, Nikolai."

I hear myself talking, but I don't believe it. Before I met Nikolai, I was sleepwalking through my life. I hated my job and was scared of my boss. Elise and I barely talked. Since she'd come to live with me, we hadn't had a single serious conversation about our past or our relationship. Now, I feel closer to her than ever before.

Nikolai woke me up. He taught me what life is supposed to feel like: thrilling and full and scary, yeah, but better for it. I'm not sure how I'll go back to the way it was before him.

But for Elise's sake, I'll figure it out.

"I guess we'll find out, won't we?" he says.

I frown. "No. That's what I'm saying. I can't stay here. I have to… We have to get out of here. Me and Elise. She isn't safe here, and you know that. It's why you went looking for her tonight. We are leaving."

"Not if I have anything to say about it," he snarls. "And as it turns out, I have something to say about everything."

"What does that mean?"

At that, his mouth tips up into a devastating smirk. "You and I are getting married."

For a few seconds, his words don't even sink in. I stare up at him, speechless and motionless, at a complete loss as to what to say.

Then it hits me.

"We can't get married."

"Of course we can," he says easily. "How else am I going to make you understand that you belong to me?"

My face twists in shock and rage. "I don't belong to you."

Before the words are even out of my mouth, Nikolai grips my chin hard in his calloused fingers. "Of course you do. Even if you don't realize it, you are mine. It's why you crave me. It's why you're *desperate* for me, beautiful Belle. It's why I put my child in you," he says. "And why, even now, you want my hand to drift lower and stroke across your aching pussy."

I slap his hand away from my exposed belly. "Don't pretend to know what I'm thinking."

"I'm not pretending." He grins at me. "Your face is flushed and your nipples are hard through your nightgown. You might as well be screaming it from the rooftops."

"That doesn't mean anything." I cross my arms over my chest, which only makes him laugh.

"Of course it doesn't." He rolls his eyes. "The fact that you were miserable when we were apart for the last six weeks doesn't mean anything. The fact that you throw yourself at me every chance you get doesn't mean anything. The fact that you're thrilled to be carrying my child doesn't mean anything. Live in denial if you want, but it won't change reality."

"And what is reality?" I ask.

In the span of a breath, Nikolai crosses the last bit of distance and takes my mouth with his. His huge hand curls around my neck and his thumb smooths along my jawline. We fit together without even trying.

When he pulls away, I chase his mouth instinctively. My chest is heaving, my body wanting him more than I want breath.

Nikolai presses his forehead to mine and smiles. "The reality is that you are fucking *mine*."

I shove him away and move past him. The room feels too small. There's not enough air.

Plus, my pulse is thundering between my legs, and I'm not sure what I'll do if I'm left alone with him.

I step into the hallway. Nikolai doesn't try to stop me. He just calls out, "You can't run from me, Belle Dowan. I will always find you."

12

BELLE

My nightgown barely covers the tops of my thighs, and I know my nipples are clearly visible through the material, but I can't turn around and go back to my room. Not when Nikolai is in there.

And like he said, I can't run. First, because of the aforementioned nightgown situation. But also because Elise is here now. She's exhausted and scared. I can't wake her up and charge out into the night again. Not without a solid plan.

For better or worse, I have to stay here.

"Fuck," I groan. "I'm already saying my vows."

I hesitate outside of Nikolai's office and then the library doors. I haven't explored much of the house, but I can't go in either room. No matter how comforting it would be to curl up in a leather chair with a book so I can lose myself in a world that doesn't exist.

I know the only thing I'd be thinking about is how Nikolai pressed me against the shelves. The way his strong body felt between my thighs. That is the last thing I need to be dwelling on.

Especially because I'm already thinking about it. A lot.

I groan again, stamping my foot like a kid throwing a temper tantrum. Why can he unravel me with one kiss like that? It's not fair. It's not fucking fair.

Sure, I said a lot of things in the heat of the moment. But that doesn't mean I didn't mean them. Because I did. I really did.

Sex with Nikolai is so different than it's ever been with anyone else. Hell, even standing next to Nikolai is different. Even now, I can feel him in the house. I could probably guess how far apart we are down to the inch right now. My body is tuned to his, whether I like it or not.

And when he's exploring me and finding new places inside of me to stroke and tease, it feels like the part of me that has spent my life searching for a home goes quiet. Because what is home if not feeling safe and content in the arms of the person you—

"No."

I shake my head, refusing to let my thoughts go there.

In an attempt to escape the pull of him, I walk to the opposite end of the house and into the kitchen. But as soon as I walk through the door, I realize I'm not alone.

"Whoa!" I yelp and partially hide my half-naked body behind the door. "Sorry, I didn't know—"

Then I make eye contact with the blond man from the hospital. The one who drove Nikolai and me back to the house.

"You," I say, eyes narrowed.

He's leaning against a barstool, his back straight. I don't see anything in front of him. No phone, no book. Was he just sitting in the dark and staring at a wall?

He turns to me and his blank expression pulls down into a scowl. "Belle."

Whoever he is, he doesn't like me. I'd say the feeling is very mutual.

"You know my name, but I don't know yours. Who are you?"

The man stands up from where he was sitting at the island, but doesn't make any move to respond.

"You're Greek, right? I remember you saying something about that earlier."

When he left the house earlier, he mentioned Nikolai letting him know when the Bratva didn't hate the Greeks anymore. I was still too stunned to comprehend the conversation then. Are Nikolai and this guy friends? That doesn't compute.

He still doesn't respond. His expression is icy.

"Does Nikolai know you're here?" I press. "Because he just rescued my sister from being kidnapped by your friends. I can't imagine why he'd have you sitting in his kitchen right now."

The man is a statue. It's like he can't hear a word I'm saying.

The longer we stare at each other, the more unease starts to settle beneath my skin. Maybe I was right and Nikolai doesn't know he's here. Maybe this man is a traitor. He helped Nikolai earlier, only to turn on him now. He could have broken into the house to kill Nikolai in a surprise attack.

Or maybe he's here for Elise.

My heart starts to pound against my chest. I have the urge to back out of the room and sprint back to Nikolai.

But no. Running to him for protection will be yet another thing he uses against me to show that I belong to him. That I'm too pathetic and weak to make it on my own. He'll tell me that I need him. That I belong to him.

So, before I can talk myself out of it, I snatch a butcher's knife out of the wooden block on the counter and whirl around to face the blond man in front of me.

"Get out of this house right now," I hiss.

Finally, he reacts. A flicker of surprise moves over his features. Probably because he's being threatened by a petite woman in an even more petite nightgown who has nothing except a badly wielded kitchen knife to defend herself with.

"I'm aware I look ridiculous, but that won't stop me from killing you," I assure him.

The man doesn't move. But he lets out a long sigh. It's clear that, to him, I'm an annoyance more than anything else.

I'm thrilled to show him otherwise.

"Fine," I shrug. "You were warned."

I lunge across the room, knife first, and charge the invading Greek.

13

NIKOLAI

I don't hear the scuffle until I'm a few doors down from the kitchen.

I stopped in my office and the library on the way, wondering if Belle was subconsciously aching for a round two in either of our previous haunts. But when I found both places were empty, I moved towards the opposite wing of the house.

And as soon as I hear what sounds like a fight, I remember who I left sitting in the kitchen.

I break into a dead sprint.

Based on the sounds of pans clattering around and grunts, I expect to find Yuri wrestling Christo to the ground or vice versa. Letting Christo into the house was a risk when tensions among my men are still so high. But when I turn the final corner into the kitchen, my vision goes red.

Belle is jockeying around the island in her nightgown. One shoulder is torn at the seam, hanging around her bicep, and the hem is lifted so high on her legs I can see the lace of her underwear from the back.

I can also see that she's holding a knife.

Christo is standing opposite her, a pocketknife in his hand aimed right at Belle.

"You fucking bastard!" I roar, storming into the kitchen. I don't stop at the knife block to grab a weapon. I don't reach for my gun. I don't need any of that shit.

Instead, I corner Christo against the fridge and lunge at his neck with both hands. I want to feel the life drain from his body for daring to touch my woman.

"Nikolai, wait!" he cries out, shielding his neck with both arms.

I pluck the knife out of his hand and turn it on him. I take advantage of the gap between his forearm and bicep and slide the blade in close towards his neck.

"I never should have trusted you. All of this was to get close to her, wasn't it?" I growl. "Xena probably sent you to lead me out of that shootout. This was the plan from the very beginning. Ingratiate yourself so you can kill my fiancée? Not going to fucking happen."

Christo gasps. "Fiancée?" He takes his eyes off of me just long enough to shoot a deadly gaze in Belle's direction. "She is the one you can't trust. Look at what she's wearing, Nikolai. She has 'trap' written all over her."

"Hey!" Belle says behind me. "This is the only nightgown in my drawer."

Damn right. I chose her nightwear myself when she first moved into my house.

"Has she confessed to working with Xena yet?" he asks. "Because I wasn't lying about that. They were plotting together. And she's probably just here as a spy. Don't tell her anything."

"I'll tell anyone anything I damn well please."

"Right. Of course." Christo winces when the knife inches closer to his jugular. "She came at me first, man. I wasn't going to hurt her. Not without your permission. No matter how much I wanted to."

He Hurt Belle. That's all I'm able to process. It's the only thing that makes it through the filter of my rage, broken down into the most basic language possible. *See Spot Run. Christo Hurt Belle.*

"I'll fucking kill you."

"Wait!" This time, it's Belle's voice in my ear. She's standing behind me, her hand on my back. "Nikolai. Don't kill him."

I throw out an arm to keep her back. "Get back, Belle. Stay out of the way."

God, this woman. She has the worst survival instincts of anyone I've ever met. It's a miracle she's lived this long.

"You took my only weapon," Christo says. "The knife is all I had. Check me if you want."

He watches me nervously for a few seconds, and when I don't move, Christo slowly lowers his arms. He holds his palms out, arms spread wide. I pat him down and don't feel anything else on him except a bundle of keys in his pocket. When I'm certain he's unarmed, I force myself to back away, keeping Belle behind me.

"What the fuck was that about?" I bark. "Start talking."

"I attacked him," Belle explains.

I keep my eyes on Christo. "*You* attacked *him?*"

"Don't say it like it's so crazy," she retorts. "I can take care of myself, you know."

"First I've heard of it."

Amusement flickers over Christo's face for just a second. "I was waiting here at the counter for you when Belle walked in."

"I thought he broke in," she says. "I thought he was here to kidnap Elise. Or me. Or… kill you."

Her last words are spoken unwillingly. They come out in a whisper, but the truth is there, hiding just between the lines.

"So you decided to offer yourself up to him on a silver platter?" I spit. "Good thinking."

Belle frowns. "I was holding my own."

"Because I wasn't trying to hurt you," Christo says, looking around me to talk to her. "If I had been, you'd be dead." I snap my attention back to Christo, eyes narrowed. He holds his hands up higher. "But again, that wasn't my goal. I wouldn't do anything to her without your permission, Nikolai."

That being said, based on the look on his face when he looks at Belle, Christo would love my permission.

"Don't look at me like that," Belle snaps at him. "I'm not working for Xena, okay?"

"Why should I believe that?" he scoffs.

"Because the only reason I was attacking you is because I thought *you* were working for Xena."

Christo studies her, his expression unchanging. "You already lied once. How is anyone supposed to trust you?"

"Xena is your don. How is anyone supposed to trust you?" she fires back.

When he speaks, his voice shakes with pent up rage. "She is not my don. I never swore loyalty to her. She killed my father."

Belle gasps behind me. "Giorgos is your… your father?"

"He was. And the moment Xena killed him, I decided to move against her. I won't pledge myself to someone who killed my family."

"Me neither," Belle says adamantly. "The moment I realized Xena wanted to kill Nikolai, I wrecked the car and got away from her. I don't know where she is or what her plan is, and I'm definitely not gathering information on her behalf. I want her dead."

"Something we can agree on."

I glance between them quickly. "So whatever the hell this fight was… it's over now?"

Belle nods. "If he can agree I'm not a traitor, I can agree he's not."

"I can agree," Christo says, somewhat unwillingly.

"Great," I say. Then in one swift move, I press the knife to Christo's throat again. Belle gasps, but Christo just stares at me, eyes wide. "And if you ever lay your hands on my fiancée again, I will gut you before you get the chance to take another breath."

Christo swallows. "Understood."

I turn the knife around and hand it back to him, handle out. Christo takes it from me gently and slides it back into his pocket. Immediately, the tension in the room eases.

"You two weren't engaged the last time I was here," he remarks.

"It's… new."

"Some might even say 'unofficial,'" Belle mutters.

I step back and lean against the counter next to her. My hip brushes hers, and I have the urge to shield her body with mine. But Christo, for what it's worth, is keeping his eyes very far north of Belle's equator.

Christo looks between us, brow furrowed. "So, is this—Are you doing this because of Xena?"

Belle shifts next to me. "What do you mean?" I ask flatly.

"You called off your engagement to her, and she was furious. Getting engaged now—to Belle, especially—it will send Xena over the edge," he says. "It will draw her out."

Christo isn't wrong. Even if that wasn't my plan from the start.

The truth is, I'm marrying Belle because she's a distraction to me. She is an enigma, floating just beyond easy categorization. Marrying her helps place her in an easily definable role with easily definable expectations.

It tells my men that Belle is mine. There will be no more dividing of attentions and protections. They'll protect her as they protect me. And I'll be able to keep Belle and my child under closer watch.

But Christo's line of thought is intriguing in its own right.

I tilt my head to the side. "Not a bad plan."

"Does that mean I can share the happy news?" he drawls.

"Be my guest. We won't be sending out Save the Dates, as I'm sure you can understand."

"Then I'll spread the word to the people who ought to hear it." Christo lowers his head in a small bow and backs towards the door. "Anything else you need from me tonight?"

I shake my head and wave him on. "You've done enough. Thank you, Christo. Elise needed your help."

He nods again and slips out into the night.

The moment he's gone, Belle turns to me. "*He* found Elise?"

"He spotted her at a bus station and followed her to the park."

"And you trusted him?" There's a hint of jealousy in her voice.

"I had Yuri do some recon before I showed up. But yes, I do. He has never done anything to betray me."

It's a pointed jab. One Belle clearly picks up on.

"Maybe you should marry him, then."

I grip her chin and twist her face back to mine. "And you should work harder to conceal your emotions. I can read you like a book."

"If you could read me like a book, you would have known I was working for Xena."

For the second time in just a few minutes, my vision turns red. I pivot around Belle, boxing her in against the edge of the countertop. She presses a hand to my chest, as if she has the strength to hold me off.

Our bodies are molded together. Her legs are warm between mine, shifting nervously as she tries to get her feet under her. But she doesn't need to. I'm pinning her in place with my hips.

"If I can't read you, then why do I know your precious little feelings are hurt?" I hiss.

Her lower lip pouts out for only a fraction of a second before she shakes her head. "I don't know what you're talking about."

"Oh no? Was it my imagination, then, that you didn't like hearing that our upcoming nuptials might have another purpose? You seemed put out by the idea it was all a show for Xena."

"It doesn't matter why you want to marry me because it's not going to happen."

I lean forward and brush my lips over her temple. "Is that right? You don't care if I'm only marrying you to make another woman jealous?"

There's a beat before Belle looks up at me. "Are you?"

"I thought it didn't matter."

She growls and slams her hands against my chest. I don't budge, and she crosses her arms in a temper tantrum. "It doesn't, because the wedding isn't happening. I won't agree to it."

"That would be a problem only if your opinion made any difference in my plans."

"You can't force me to marry you!" The words are forceful, but I can see the uncertainty in her eyes. It's a statement as much as a question.

"When are you going to learn, *kotyonok*? I can do whatever I want."

"Maybe with the blindly obedient automatons who work for you, but not with me."

I tug on the tear in her nightgown, ripping the seam free so her left shoulder is bared. "Wrong. *Especially* with you. You can't resist me, Belle. You're desperate for me. And now, you're carrying my baby. So we will get married, whether you're happy about it or not."

"No, we won't!"

"And," I continue, ignoring her, "if you don't want to cooperate, then you can ask some of my men what happens to people who disobey the orders of the don."

She arches a brow. "You just nearly killed Christo for pointing a knife at me. Am I really supposed to believe you'd hurt me?"

I grab a strand of her auburn hair and twirl it around my finger. "I've never been good at sharing. If anyone is going to punish my woman, it's going to be me."

A flush moves across her cheeks. I know she's thinking about the last time I punished her. With her barely-clothed body pressed against mine, I'm thinking about it, too.

Belle is staring up at me with heated eyes, anger and desire mingling in her gaze. I'm about to break the tension between us when I hear footsteps in the hallway.

I look up just in time to catch a figure moving away from the kitchen door.

"Stop right there!" I push away from Belle and jump towards the door.

But when I step into the hallway, I see Elise running down the hall towards the other side of the house. She doesn't stop to look back.

"What is it?" Belle asks. "What's wrong?"

I turn to her, hands on my hips. "Are you planning to tell your sister about what's going on here?"

"With you and me?"

"All of it."

She shakes her head. "Elise has been through enough. I don't want to overwhelm her with all of this while she's still recovering from what happened with Xena."

"Well, I'm afraid that ship has sailed." I tip my head towards the hallway. "Elise must take after you, because she was eavesdropping in the hallway. And considering how fast she ran away, I'm guessing she overheard everything."

Belle's face pales. "Everything?"

"The pregnancy, the marriage, me being a Bratva don." I nod. "Everything."

"Shit. *Shit.*" Belle races past me and down the hallway, running after Elise.

"Ask her to be a flower girl," I call after her. "That will probably cheer her up."

Belle is still running after her sister, but she takes the time to throw up a middle finger over her shoulder.

14

BELLE

"Elise, wait!"

I'm running on too much chaos and far too little sleep to be actually, physically running right now. Plus, Elise is fast and this house has way too many hallways. I'm getting dizzy. I have to stop and catch my breath before I straight-up keel over.

By the time I'm good again, there's no trace of my sister. I'm left checking the mansion room by room for her. I can only hope I don't walk in on anymore former Greek soldiers Nikolai has stashed away somewhere. I don't think I can muster the energy for another knife fight tonight.

I poke my head in room after room, whispering for my sister. I panic that maybe she ran away again. Sleeping on a public bench might not seem so bad after the horror show she witnessed in the kitchen.

But as I'm working my way back to the wing of the house where our rooms are, I realize exactly where Elise is. Where she always goes when she's upset.

The place I taught her to go.

I move through her empty bedroom and stop outside the closet. I lean against the frame and rap my knuckles softly on the wood door.

"Can I come in?"

I hear sniffling. "No."

"I thought the closet was our space?" I say with a choked laugh.

There's a beat before she opens the door and then crawls back to the nest of blankets she created next to the shoe rack. I crouch down and sit next to her, my back against the wall.

For a few minutes, we just sit together. As kids, the closet is where we went when shit was going down between our mom and her boyfriend of the month or whenever her dealer showed up. Usually, it was safest to stay quiet. For a little kid, Elise got really good at it.

When she got older, I kept paper and pencils in a shoe box and we played Tic-Tac-Toe. On good days, we'd stash snacks and water bottles in the closet in case we had to spend a long time hiding out. On bad days, we had each other.

It was never fun, but it was our space. No one could hurt us in the closet.

"Do you want to talk about anything?" I finally ask, breaking the quiet.

"I don't even know what to say."

"Well, what did you hear? We can start there."

Elise looks over at me. There are dark circles pressed under her eyes. I'm not sure I've ever seen her with those before. It breaks my heart just a little bit more.

"Nikolai is some kind of… Bratva boss?" She shakes her head. "I don't even know what that means. After he—When he killed those men who were trying to get us to go in their car, he told me he had enemies. He said he was protecting us. Was that all a lie? Is Nikolai actually the bad guy? Are we being held here against—"

Now that she's talking, the words are pouring out of her. I have to reach over and grip her shoulder to keep her calm.

"It wasn't a lie," I tell her. "The men Nikolai killed were going to hurt us. He saved our lives."

I leave out the part where I was intending to willingly get in the car with those men that night. Nikolai saved me and my sister when I didn't even realize we needed it.

"So what is a Bratva boss?" she asks.

I chew my lower lip. "Elise…"

"Come on, Belle. Tell me the truth."

"You're right." I nod. "You deserve the truth. I just… I want to protect you, E. I never meant for us to get tangled up in this."

"Tangled up in *what?*" she presses.

Deep down, I know Elise has seen more messed-up things than most fourteen-year-olds should ever have to see. Still, I feel like I'm stealing her innocence away. What's left of it, at least.

"A crime… syndicate, for lack of a better word. It's like the Russian mafia. Essentially. I think."

"Nikolai is in the mob?"

"Well, don't say that to him," I warn her. "But yeah, basically. He's the… the leader. The one in charge."

Elise presses her fingers to her forehead and gazes into the middle distance. I can practically see her reliving the last couple months, seeing everything with new eyes.

"So… he isn't the CEO of a company?"

"No. I mean, well, yes. He is. It's just not his only job. It's kind of a cover for what the Bratva is really doing."

She releases a breath and shakes her head. "This is all so weird."

"Tell me about it."

There's another few seconds of silence before Elise gasps and turns to me. She clutches my arm tightly. "You're pregnant!"

"You already knew that."

"I know," she says. "But... *you're pregnant.* Nikolai is a criminal, and you're having his baby. And aren't those crime synag—"

"Syndicates."

"Yeah, aren't those really into family lines and heirs and stuff?"

I shrug. "We haven't really talked about it much."

There hasn't been time. But more honestly, I haven't wanted to talk about it. Nikolai made it clear the day he was locking me up that my child would be part of his Bratva. I still don't know if he was saying that just to scare me or not.

"You need to talk about this kind of stuff," Elise reprimands. "The two of you are getting married."

I curse under my breath. "You really heard everything, didn't you?"

"You guys were being loud, and I wasn't asleep yet."

I drag a hand down my face and turn to her. Her pale red hair is still damp from her shower, the ends curling against her nightshirt. Without her blush and eyeliner on, Elise looks even younger than she is. She looks like she did when I first moved out and had to leave her behind.

The urge to wrap my arms around her is strong, and I can't resist. I pull her against my chest, ignoring the way she grumbles in complaint.

When I let go, she settles back into her pile of blankets and pulls one up around her shoulders. "Do you have to marry him?"

"What?" I heard her, but I don't know how to answer. I'm not sure of the answer myself.

"Is it because you're pregnant?" she continues. "Is that why he's making you marry him?"

"Nikolai isn't making me do anything."

Elise frowns, unconvinced. "He said you didn't have a choice. And you were arguing with him."

"That was just... arguing." I shrug. "I'm annoyed with him, so I was pressing his buttons."

"Then you must always be annoyed with him."

I laugh bitterly. "You could say that."

She gives me a small smile and then it slowly slips away. "You can tell me the truth, B. If he's forcing you to marry him, then maybe we could run away again. Maybe we could actually get out of here and start over."

The sight of Elise wrapped in a fuzzy blanket is juxtaposed with the reality that she was going to sleep on a public park bench tonight. And if we run away again, that's the most I can promise her.

I don't have a plan. I don't have an escape route. I don't have options.

I can't put Elise through that. Nikolai can offer her the security she's never had. Can I really rip her away from it?

"He isn't forcing me to marry him," I tell her, laying my hand over hers and squeezing. "I'm marrying Nikolai because... because I love him."

I expect the words to taste nasty on my tongue. Lying to Elise always leaves a bad taste in my mouth, but I try to reserve it for when it's absolutely necessary. For when the truth would cause her unnecessary pain.

This is one of those times.

She stares at me. Her green eyes are way too observant for her own good. "No, you don't."

"Elise," I breathe, "of course I do. I mean, we hopped on a jet and went to Iceland with him with zero warning. Would I do that for anyone else?"

"You told me that was for work."

"I lied," I say. "I didn't want to scare you. But I went because I wanted to spend time with Nikolai. I didn't realize how much I already liked him at the time. But I should have. I was just scared to admit it because he was—"

"A Bratva boss."

I wince and chuckle at the same time. "Yeah. Basically. It was scary. I probably shouldn't have gone. I should have taken you back home and carried on with our normal lives, but I couldn't bring myself to walk away from him. I didn't want to."

The words tumble out of me easily, and even now, I want to believe I've become an amazing liar overnight. I'd rather believe anything but the truth.

Which is that I'm not lying at all.

Elise has her nose wrinkled up as she thinks through everything I'm saying. "Did you know the truth about him when we went to Iceland?"

"More or less, yeah," I admit. "It still felt far away, though. I didn't know about his enemies or Xena or any of that. It was just… Nikolai. And he seemed larger than life. Untouchable. He had a private jet and the ability to whisk us both away to what felt like another world. After everything we've been through, I wanted that for us. A fairytale. Does that sound stupid?"

She shakes her head softly in the gloom. "We've never had anything like that before," she murmurs.

"Exactly. It felt like a dream come true. And it was."

"Until Xena showed up at that party."

"Yeah. Until then," I say. "God, that was the worst."

"That's when I knew how much you liked him," Elise tells me. "When the two of you were dancing, all dressed up and smiling at each other… that's when I knew something more was going on. And then we left so quickly and we went home and you got sick. It all fell apart."

I lean my head back against the wall and sigh. "I shouldn't have fallen apart like that. But I was heartbroken. I was falling for him, and I found out he'd kept an entire fiancée a secret and, at the time, he was still going to marry her. I just… I couldn't deal."

"Makes sense. That's harsh."

"Yeah, but it's no excuse. I'm supposed to be a strong foundation for you. That's the reason I brought you to live with me. I wanted to be better than Mom."

"You are!" Elise grabs my arm and draws it close to her, pressing her cheek to my bicep. "Belle, you are one thousand percent better than Mom."

"But at least Mom never got involved with any serious criminals. They were all small-time drug dealers and generic assholes. She has me beat there."

"Mom also never gave a shit about me. You've got her beat there."

I stroke her hair away from her face. "That's not true. Mom did care. She does. She loved you."

"Don't lie to me, Belle," she snaps suddenly. "You know that's not true."

I wish she was wrong. I wish I could assure her with my whole chest that our mother loves and cares about us.

But I really don't know if that's the case.

And at this point, I don't care anymore.

"The fact that you're lying to me about it is proof that you care more than Mom ever did," she says. "And that's why I'd rather be in this shitstorm with you than living with her."

"Hey. Language," I scold her playfully.

She rolls her eyes, but I'm starting to see the affection behind the gesture. The comfortability. She trusts me, whether I've earned it or not.

"I'm just saying," she continues. "I know I don't have a lot of options. It's not like I have people beating down the door to come and take care of me. But still… even if I did, I'd choose you, B. And if you love Nikolai, then I can make that work. But only if he's nice to you."

My chin wobbles as I do my best to hold back the flood of tears threatening to pour out. But I'm only human, and it was a losing battle from the start. Silent tears slip down my cheeks and Elise snorts again.

"You're such a cupcake."

"Not all of us can be as tough as you."

She shrugs. "We're both tough. We didn't get a choice. Mom was a mess. We both lost our dads. It was either get tough or give up."

There it is—the bitter tang of that old deception. But this one is mild from constant exposure. I've grown used to it. Because this way is better than the sick feeling I'd have watching Elise struggle with the truth. Watching her realize again and again that her dad is out there, living freely, and has chosen to have nothing to do with her. I'd rather her think he didn't have a choice than know he chose himself over her. One selfish parent is better than two.

It's better for her to believe he's dead.

"Yeah, I guess so," I say. "But we have each other."

She wrinkles her nose but can't fight her smile. "Ew. Corny."

"Doesn't mean it's not true." I pull her in for another hug and press a kiss to her damp head. She smells like strawberries. "You're stuck with me."

~

When I get back to my room, Nikolai is lounging on my bed.

His legs are stretched out in front of him, crossed at the ankles. His shirt is rucked up slightly, revealing a slim stripe of tan skin across his abdomen. He is sex incarnate. Sin wrapped in well-fitted jeans and a bad boy persona.

If I wasn't so pissed at him, I'd jump his bones.

"You," I hiss. I'm too tired to make it sound really vicious the way I'd like to.

He looks over at me, one eyebrow arched lazily. For the first time, I notice the shallow glass in his grip. The amber liquid in it sloshes as he turns to me. "Did you two ladies cry it out and make friends again?"

My face does feel puffy. Anytime I cry, my eyes turn red and my skin goes blotchy for hours afterward. I swipe at my eyes. "These are happy tears, you asshole. Because, despite the damage you caused, I managed to fix things with my sister."

Nikolai sits up, as unbothered as ever. "Great. So you'll be good to go to the seamstress with me tomorrow."

Of all the things I expected him to say, that wasn't one of them. It takes me a few seconds to even process what he said. "You want to go to a… a seamstress?"

"'Want' is a strong word. But you're going to wear a wedding dress to our wedding, so there isn't much choice."

I blink at him. "Are you serious right now?"

"Does it seem like a joke?" he asks. "Because it wouldn't be very funny."

Nikolai is relaxed in a way I've never seen before. The alcohol seems to have taken the sharp edge off of his anger. It should make me feel better, but instead, I'm nervous.

I prefer the devil I know over the devil I don't.

"You actually think I'm going through with this wedding? After you gave me that piss-poor excuse for a proposal and then traumatized my sister by dumping all of our baggage on her without warning?"

He snorts. "She's fine."

"Don't tell me she's fine when you don't even know her."

His glazed eyes narrow. "I know you, Belle Dowan. And if your sister wasn't fine, you'd still be in there talking to her."

Okay, I have to give him that one. He's right.

But that doesn't change anything. If anything, it makes everything worse.

"Maybe she is fine," I admit. "But I'm not."

"Do we need couples counseling before we're even a couple?" he asks in a mocking voice.

"You say that as if we aren't two of the most screwed-up people on the planet. Considering you're trying to force me into this marriage, yeah, I'd say we are in need of some counseling at the very least."

"Well," he muses, "by the time we do the dress, the catering, the ice sculptures, the fire-eaters, and the honeymoon, I'm afraid we won't have time for therapy."

He's teasing me. Toying with me. Refusing to rise to my level of anger.

And it's driving me crazy.

Which must be the reason I cross the room in a fury and slap his drink out of his hand. "I'm being serious, Nikolai! Stop being an asshole and talk to—"

Suddenly, Nikolai lunges to his feet, grabs my wrist, and spins me around. He presses me into the mattress and hovers over me, his knee wedged between my legs. It all happens in the span of time between one blink and the next.

"You lost the chance to collaborate with me," he snarls softly in my face, his breath rich with whiskey. "I took care of you and your sister at every turn, and you betrayed me. You chose to work with my enemy. You chose to willingly run into the arms of someone who wanted both of us dead."

"But I didn't know—"

"Exactly," he interrupts. "You didn't know, Belle. You don't know anything. You don't know what my world is like, you don't know what I'm capable of, and you damn sure don't know what kind of dangers are waiting for you out there. You don't know a fucking thing."

With every word out of his mouth, my anger drains out of me. He's angry, but beneath it is a thread of sincerity I've never heard from him before. A choked tension I've rarely seen.

I'm not sure what to make of it.

"When you have the freedom to choose for yourself, you choose wrong, time and time again. You go off and nearly get yourself—" He blows out a frustrated breath. "So you don't get a choice in this. We are getting married."

"And it doesn't bother you that it's against my will?" I grit out.

"Between giving you free will and keeping you alive, I choose keeping you alive."

Even though Nikolai is hovering over me, there's a purposeful distance between our bodies. He could pin me to the bed with his hips, drive his knee against my aching sex, and make me delirious with lust. But he seems to be making a concerted effort not to touch me any more than necessary.

I can't decide if it's for his benefit or for mine.

"Okay, so you want to keep me alive—today. But what about when that changes? Am I just supposed to trust that my safety will stay your priority?"

His gray eyes stroke over my face. I feel it like a physical touch. "I told you even before Iceland that I would take care of you and Elise. I've done that," he says. "I vow to you right now that I'll continue to do that so long as I'm alive. No one can stop me. Not even you."

I stare up at him, speechless. Nikolai stares back. He looks into my eyes, and I know he's serious. I know this is as solemn a vow as he's ever taken. I know he means every word.

And the power of that keeps me pinned to the mattress even when Nikolai stands up and walks to the door.

I hear the door open. I wait for it to swing closed, but it doesn't come. Instead, I hear his voice.

"You don't need to be afraid of me, Belle."

But that is where he's wrong. My heart is thundering in my chest, my hands shaking with nerves and desire. My entire body is short-circuiting because of him. Despite everything that has happened and everything he has done, Nikolai has an inescapable hold on my body, my mind, my soul.

I should be very, very afraid.

I am.

Then the door closes, and I'm alone.

15

NIKOLAI

Elise is in the kitchen when I walk down the next morning. "You're up early." I eye the mug in front of her and lean forward for a look inside. "Coffee? Does your sister approve of that?"

"I'm fourteen, not four."

I hold up my hands. "Suit yourself." I pour myself a mug and settle into the seat across from her. "Well?"

"Well what?" she asks.

"You're up at dawn and in my kitchen. You clearly have something to say."

"No, I don't."

"If you wanted to talk to me, you could've come to my office anytime. No need to lose sleep over it."

She glances down at her folded hands, a hint of the nerves she's trying hard to hide. "My sister is right: you are a know-it-all."

I chuckle and yawn. "Guilty."

"But she's a know-it-all, too. You are perfect for each other. You both think you always know what's best for everyone else."

"Only one of us is right," I say.

"I just want you to be nicer to her," Elise blurts. "If you're going to get married, you have to be nice."

I mull it over, taking a sip of my steaming coffee. Then I meet her gaze.

"I'll take care of her," I say finally. "And you."

She frowns. "How is that different from being nice?"

"Because 'nice' doesn't work with your sister. If I was nice to her, she'd still be working for the boss who tried to assault her. Twice."

"I knew it," Elise hisses, shaking her head. "I told her Roger was a scumbag, but she wouldn't listen. When she quit, I knew something happened, but she wouldn't tell me."

"Great. She'll be thrilled I filled you in."

"No, it's good," Elise says. "I need to know this stuff."

"No, you don't. That's my point. It's your sister's job to take care of you, so she's doing the best she can. And sometimes, that means she keeps you in the dark and makes decisions for both of you. That's what I have to do for her."

"I'm not a child," she grumbles.

"It's not about being a child. It's about having the right amount of information to make a good decision," I tell her. "You don't know everything about the world yet. Nor should you. Because you are still a child, like it or not. And your sister doesn't know everything about my world yet."

"The Bratva world?"

I nod. "It's a violent place. That's why I'm forced to make decisions on her behalf."

"But not marriage, right?" she asks. "You aren't forcing her into that?"

I frown. "What did your sister tell you?"

Elise chews on her lower lip for a second, and in that brief second, she looks so much like Belle. "She said she loves you."

I keep my expression neutral, even as my chest roils with pent-up emotion. "I see."

"But just because she thinks she loves you doesn't mean she's right," she snaps. "I watched my mom 'fall in love' with plenty of assholes in my life. Love doesn't mean happiness, even if it is real. It doesn't mean everything will work out in the end. It doesn't mean shit."

I lean back in my chair and study her. "People like us… we don't have any reason to believe anything works out. Not after the way we were raised. It's why we fight so hard to protect the people in our lives. It's why you're working so hard to make sure your sister is safe with me."

"And is she?"

"She is," I promise her. "And so are you. I'll do what needs to be done to take care of both of you. No matter how much you both bitch and moan along the way."

Elise rolls her eyes. "Pretend to be a hard ass all you want, Nikolai. You and my sister are more alike than you think."

"What does that mean?"

"You're a cupcake, too."

"Excuse me?"

"You heard me," she fires back, completely unfazed. She stands up and slides her still-full mug to the center of the island. "Also, coffee is disgusting. I don't know why anyone drinks it."

Then Elise marches out of the kitchen, head held high.

I can't help but smile.

~

Belle looks incredible in her wedding dress.

But I'm not the only one struggling to keep my hands off of her.

My usual seamstress, Beatrice, had to take off for a family emergency. She had her son fill in for her. Matteo is in his early-twenties—closer to Belle's age than I am—and he seems to be appreciating the way she fills out the lacy white gown. Especially the sheer panel that runs from hip to knee, which he's caressing over and over again like it's going out of fucking style.

"My mom taught me everything she knows. Don't worry; I know how to handle beautiful things," he murmurs, glancing up at Belle as he says it. "I'm very skilled with my hands. Have you considered modeling, *bella?*"

Belle laughs prettily. "Yeah, right. I can't even walk in heels without rolling my ankles. I'd fall right off the catwalk."

I'm second-guessing my choice of design now. I should have bought her a wedding parka. This low-necked lace gown with sheer panels and slits could be for the bedroom after the ceremony. One extra set of eyes on her is already enough to make my blood boil.

She belongs to *me*.

"I'm just saying," he continues, "you'd be a natural. You'd be paid to look beautiful and lie on a bed or a yacht all day. Not a bad gig, right?" He winks at her. "I don't even have a girlfriend to shop for, and I bet I'd be tempted to buy anything you were selling."

"For fuck's sake," I growl, kicking my chair back as I stand up.

Matteo snaps his attention to me like he forgot I was here. Belle turns to face me at the same time. "Don't, Nikolai. It's fine."

"It's many things," I snarl, "but it's not 'fine.'" I turn to him. "You're adjusting her wedding dress, you dumb fuck. Do I need to bend her over your sewing machine for you to understand who she belongs to?"

"Hey!" Belle steps off the platform and walks over to me. "I don't think that will be necessary. None of this is necessary, actually."

"I'd say it's very necessary. I'm paying him to do a job, and he's thinking about my wife in lingerie."

"Fiancée," Matteo corrects, because apparently, he's even more of a moron than I gave him credit for.

A low, dangerous growl rumbles through my chest. "You are severely underestimating how close I am to shoving those push pins down your throat."

"I'm not interested in him," Belle says softly. "He's just doing his job."

He's fidgeting over Belle's shoulder. I glare at him. "Pick up your phone and call your mother," I tell him. Let her know you hit on Nikolai Zhukova's fiancée. See what she has to say."

He frowns in confusion. "You want me to call my mom?"

"I want her to explain to you how badly you just fucked up," I say. "And I want you to appreciate how generous I'm being in giving you a second chance."

Matteo shrugs and shuffles into the small office off the main workspace. I hear him whispering rapid-fire Italian. It doesn't take long to have the intended effect. When he comes back out, he practically bows in front of me, and when he speaks, his tone is stiff and formal.

"I am terribly sorry to cause any trouble or discomfort, Mr. Zhukova." When he turns to Belle, he doesn't even meet her eyes. "And Mrs.—"

"Ms. Dowan," Belle corrects.

He nods and continues. "Ms. Dowan, I'm sorry about my behavior. Forgive me."

"Forgiveness. Interesting concept," I muse. The knife on my hip feels like it's glowing red-hot. Men have died for less than this *mudak* has done today. I'm not afraid to spill his blood all over Belle's pretty little gown just to teach him a lesson. He may not have seen it before, but judging by the pale gauntness in his cheeks now, he gets it: I'm not the man to fuck with.

"Sir—sir," he whimpers. "Please don't—"

"Let's let Belle decide, shall we?" I interrupt.

We both turn to her in unison. Belle is standing at my side, looking like the queen that she is. For a moment, I wonder if she's going to do the unthinkable and cut me loose on this asshole.

Then she nods imperiously, just once, and says, "You're forgiven. But don't let it happen again, Matteo."

I bite back a grin. Who would have guessed? Belle Dowan has a taste for power after all.

∽

When we get in the car, Belle is gnawing her lip uncomfortably. "You didn't have to do that back there. That guy was just being a flirt," she says softly.

"He was being an asshole."

"I'm used to it."

I hate the resignation in her voice. I hate that she doesn't still see how much power she could have. That she is still living life like some little girl locked in a dark closet, hiding from her monsters, when the whole damn world is right there at her fingertips for the taking.

"He was making you uncomfortable. You shouldn't have to be used to that."

"Is that why you did it? Or was it because he was making you jealous?"

My hands tighten on the steering wheel. "I don't like to share."

"Oh, right," she scoffs. "Because I'm yours."

"One day soon, you're going to say that and mean it." My cock jumps at the thought. At the way the words will taste when I kiss them off her lips. "You're going to scream those words like a prayer, begging for me to own every single inch of you."

Belle releases a shaky breath. Her thighs squeeze together, and I want to pull to the side of the road and drag her into my lap. I want to take her right here, right now. I want to drive her to the edge of ecstasy until she's begging for me to give her what she wants, what she needs.

I glance in the rearview mirror, trying to gauge how many witnesses our little spectacle would have. We're only two blocks down from the house now, so it's a residential area. No one else on the sidewalks, and there's only one car on the road behind us.

A dark blue four-door sedan with a toll tag stuck to the windshield.

Immediately, I slam on the brakes.

Belle screams and wraps an arm around her stomach. Around our baby. "What the hell are you doing, Nikolai?"

"Stay in the car," I growl, reaching into the center console and grabbing my gun. "We're being followed."

16

BELLE

He's gone before I can ask any questions. I turn in fear and watch him stalk down the road towards a dark blue car behind us. I can't make out exactly who is in the driver's seat, but it's clearly a man.

"No," I whisper to no one. My legs are shaking with nerves and adrenaline. "Get back in the car, Nikolai. Let's go. Don't do this."

If we're being followed, it has to be because of Xena. It's the Greeks or the Battiatos. I look around to see if there is any other movement on the street. Maybe this is a setup. Maybe it's an ambush, and Nikolai is walking to his death.

We're so close to home. I can see the roof of Nikolai's mansion peeking over the treeline. Should I crawl into the driver's seat and go get help? But he told me to stay here.

I'm arguing with myself and staring, riveted, through the back window as Nikolai gets closer and closer to the car behind us.

He's nearly to the driver's door, his gun at the ready. As he approaches, the dark blue car lurches forward, trying to navigate between our car and Nikolai's body.

I scream just as Nikolai raises his gun, aiming at the front window. The car jerks to a stop.

"Oh my God!" I cry. My heart is pounding in my chest. I was sure I was about to watch Nikolai get run down in front of me.

But then Nikolai opens the door and wrenches the driver out of the car with one hand, his other still wrapped around his gun. His mouth is moving, but I can't hear anything.

All I can think is, *He's not dead. He's alive. We're okay.*

Nikolai starts dragging the man down the sidewalk and through the front gates of his property. The guy is a head shorter than Nikolai, though a good bit rounder. He has a stocky build and a balding head. But none of that means he isn't a threat.

Without thinking, I climb out of the car.

"I told you to stay put," he barks over his shoulder.

It's clear the man isn't putting up a fight. He moves through the gates willingly and allows Nikolai to lead him into the security shed off to the right of the driveway.

"Get out of here, Belle," Nikolai orders over his shoulder.

I shake my head. "I'm staying."

"I won't hurt her," the man promises. "Or anyone."

Nikolai kicks the man in the back of the knees and shoves him into the corner.

"I don't want any trouble," the man whimpers.

"Then you chose the wrong fucking guy to follow." Nikolai steps forward and presses the gun under the man's chin. "Who are you working for?"

The man is trembling. His eyes are squeezed closed and sweat beads up on his forehead. "I'm an independent contractor."

"A mercenary?"

The man's forehead creases. "A mercen—? No. No, I'm a detective. A private investigator."

"Who hired you?" I ask.

Nikolai tenses at the sound of my voice, but he lets the question stand.

"I'm contractually obligated not to say." He looks genuinely sorry to refuse me. "It's part of the gig. I'm not supposed to reveal my clients."

"And your brains aren't supposed to be on the outside of your skull," Nikolai chimes in. "I'll let you choose which obligation seems more important at the moment."

The investigator moans, dropping his head onto his knees. "Fuck."

I move up behind him, whispering in his ear. "Nikolai, this guy doesn't look like a soldier. He's terrified. Maybe… maybe this is something else."

Nikolai regrips the gun and jabs it harder under the soft part of the man's chin. "We'll never know unless he starts talking. Because I'm going to pull the trigger in five, four, three—"

"Howard Schaffner!" The man screams the name, his eyes still tightly closed.

Nikolai arches a brow and then shakes his head dismissively. "Never heard of him. Three, two—"

"Wait!" I grab the back of Nikolai's shirt. "Say that name again."

The man opens his eyes and looks at me. His forehead is dotted with sweat and he is deathly pale. "Howard Schaffner. That's who hired me. I have his name and a single phone number. That's it. So if this is some weird thing he is tangled up in, I don't know anything about it, okay? Let me go and I won't say a word. I'll walk out of here and forget your faces. Just don't kill me."

Nikolai is still holding the man, but he looks back at me. "You know what he's talking about?"

"Let him go."

Nikolai's eyes roam over my face for a long few seconds, searching for answers. Then he drops the man in a sweaty heap on the floor and steps back.

I swallow hard. "How do you know Howard Schaffner?" I ask.

Even though the gun is hanging by Nikolai's side, the man keeps his hands up where we can see them. "I don't know him. I've never even met the man; I've only talked to him on the phone. He found my number on some site somewhere and he hired me to work for him. Paid me good money for it, too."

I clench my jaw. Apparently, he's come into money since the last time I've seen him. Good for Howard fucking Schaffner.

"What did he ask you to do?"

"To follow you," the guy answers, tipping his head to indicate me. "And your sister. Belle and Elise Dowan were the names given to me."

My stomach drops at the sound of my sister's name in this stranger's mouth. Nikolai stiffens, his body shifting even further in front of me so I'm looking at the man just past Nikolai's bicep. I feel the urge to sink against Nikolai's skin, to feel the warmth of him against me.

Instead, I stand tall and pull my shoulders back. "How long have you been following us?"

"A few weeks. I started in Oklahoma City. I was able to track the private jet you got on to New York City. But I lost track of you all until I saw your name in a news story about a car accident. I tracked you here, and I've been keeping a watch ever since to catch sight of Elise. She is the main target."

Target. It's a nasty, violent word. I can't stop myself from stepping forward. The only thing that keeps me back is Nikolai's arm curled around my waist.

"My sister is nobody's goddamn target! You leave her alone."

The guy nods. "Believe me: after this, I don't want the fucking money. No one has ever pointed a gun at me."

"I'll do a lot worse than point it at you if you threaten my fiancée," Nikolai growls.

The man raises his hands higher over his head. "No one wants to threaten any of you! Howard just wants to talk. That's what he told me. He said he was family."

"Who the fuck is Howard?" Nikolai asks me. "Do you know him?"

I nod. "Yeah. Sort of. I mean… I did. I haven't seen him in years. Not since I was ten or eleven, probably. It's been forever. This might not even be him. It could be a trap."

"Who is he?" Nikolai presses.

I bite my lip. Lies have a way of coming back around. Of revealing themselves, whether we want them to or not.

"Elise is going to hate me," I whisper softly. "She'll never forgive me for lying to her."

Nikolai keeps an eye on the man, but he turns towards me. His hand tightens on my hip. The reassuring strength of him is the only thing keeping me standing. "Who is he?"

"Howard Schaffner is her dad's name." I shake my head. "But I told her he was dead. I've told her that her entire life. She'll hate me, Nikolai. She'll absolutely hate me."

Tears are burning the backs of my eyes. It doesn't help when Nikolai pulls me tenderly against his side. Then he turns to the man still cowering on the floor.

"No one is going to shoot you," he assures him. "So long as you give me Howard Schaffner's contact information. I think it's time for a little family reunion."

17

BELLE

"I hate lying to her," I whimper.

"Too late for that," Nikolai says. "You wouldn't have had to lie today if you'd told her the truth from the beginning."

He swats my hand away from my mouth. I've bitten my nails down practically to the quick, but I still can't stop picking at them. It's a horrible habit, one I thought I'd broken.

Until today, when I told Elise to stay in her room for a few hours so I could figure out what the hell I'm going to do.

"Are we in danger or something?" she'd asked.

"No. It's just a really important meeting. One of Nikolai's biggest partners."

"We don't want any distractions," Nikolai added. "Stay here. We'll come get you when we're done."

Elise looked concerned as we left, but she didn't question me. She trusts me, despite everything. And I'm using that trust to keep her in the dark.

I'm becoming more and more certain that I'm a bad person.

I drop my face into my hands. "I was trying to protect her. He left us. Left her. I didn't want her to feel abandoned."

"She *was* abandoned."

I whirl to Nikolai, eyes narrowed. "But she didn't need to feel it! She was a little kid. And our mother was already a mess. I didn't want her to think every adult in the world was a selfish, heartless monster."

"But every adult is a selfish, heartless—"

"You are not helpful," I mumble.

"I'm not trying to be helpful; I'm being honest. You should learn the difference."

I stand up and pace in front of the couch. "If you're trying to teach me a lesson, I'm not really in the mood."

Nikolai reclines back in his chair. "When it comes to teaching you lessons, I've learned mine. I won't waste my breath."

I round on him. All of the tension from the morning is starting to condense in my chest. A tight ball of anxiety I need to either ease up or erupt, because the pressure of it is killing me.

"Could you take this seriously, please?" I snap. "I know this isn't about your Bratva or the Greeks. It may not be life and death like you're used to, but it's about my life and my sister's life. It's important to me."

"Which is why you're freaking out."

"I'm not freaking out!" I shriek, completely undermining my point. "But I'm about to meet a man who might blow up my relationship with my sister, and you're just—"

"Distracting you until he arrives."

I frown, staring at Nikolai as a smirk turns the corner of his mouth upward. "You're… you're trying to distract me."

"And considering you've finally stopped destroying your fingernails, I'd say I'm succeeding at it."

I cross my arms, failing to feel even a fraction as annoyed as I want to. "Your confidence is endlessly frustrating, you know."

Nikolai stands up and crosses the distance between us. His broad shoulders block the doorway and the rest of the world. He is the only thing that exists right now.

"I'm here with you, Belle," he breathes. "You don't have anything to worry about."

A small part of my brain wants to argue with him. *What will I do when Elise finds out I lied to her? What if Howard wants her back? What if she hates me forever?*

But a larger part of my brain—the part that Nikolai has forever and fully invaded—just nods along, certain he's right. How can things go wrong when he's here with me? They can't. They won't.

He has me.

"You're ready," he pronounces.

Then he pivots to stand next to me—just as Howard Schaffner walks through the door.

The man has the same strawberry blond hair as Elise, though his temples have turned white since I saw him last. He's grown a beard, too. It's full white. But I can still make out the same high cheekbones Elise has. The same deep green eyes looking at me with a fair amount of trepidation.

"Howard?" Nikolai asks in a harsh tone that cracks the moment open wide. I practically shake myself out of a trance. Based on the way Howard seems to wobble on his feet as his eyes shift from me to Nikolai, I think he felt it, too.

"Howard Schaffner." He extends his hand, but Nikolai doesn't reach for it. After a second, he curls his fingers against his palm and shoves his hands back in his pockets.

"Hand where we can see them," Nikolai barks.

He yanks them right back out. "Right. Yeah. I'm not armed or anything. You don't have to worry about me."

"Sending a private investigator to tail us doesn't exactly scream 'just minding my own business.'" There's more venom in my voice than I intended, but I can't help it. Too many emotions to name are coming to life just under my surface, and I don't have the energy or the strength to keep them all at bay. Nikolai might be able to bury every feeling, but I can't. I never have.

Howard ducks his head. "I know. I'm sorry. I got the best my money could buy. Which isn't anywhere close to the best. But Chris found you. I guess I'll have to leave him a five-star review now. If you leave reviews for P.I.'s, that is. I guess I don't really know the protocol."

Even as an eleven-year-old, I knew it was strange that someone like Howard would be with my mom. He was… normal. Most of her boyfriends treated me like a roach crawling across the floor. They curled their upper lips when I dared walk out of my room and they never wanted me to go anywhere with them.

"Can't the brat stay home?" they'd hiss in my mom's ear. "This place isn't really for kids."

I never found out what "place" they were talking about because my mom always decided they were right. "You can stay here, Belle," she'd say, patting my head like she was giving me a prize. "You're a big girl."

But Howard always included me. He'd choose the restaurant with the play place so I could crawl through a maze of plastic tubes while they ate. And when Mom wouldn't let me tag along, he always made sure to bring me back something to eat.

When Mom got pregnant with Elise, I wished Howard could be my dad, too.

Then he left.

"How do I even know you are who you say you are?" I demand.

"Do I look that different?" he asks. When my expression doesn't change, he grimaces. "I guess I like to think I haven't changed much."

Aside from the newly-white hair and the extra padding around his middle, he does look more or less the same. But I desperately want him to be a fake. Right now, I'd rather he be a trick from Xena than the real deal.

Nikolai grimaces. "She is saying she doesn't know you. Identify yourself."

"Right. Yeah. Okay." Howard flexes his hands nervously, thinking. Then he pats his pants pocket. "Wallet. I have my wallet. Can I get that out?"

Nikolai nods and Howard pulls out his wallet. He flashes his driver's license to me. It's an Oklahoma ID with an overexposed photo of a man who is clearly Howard. His full name is printed next to it. *Howard Ethan Schaffner.*

Still, I shake my head. Not because I don't believe him, but because I don't want to. "Tell me something about my sister."

"Elise?" He runs a hand through his hair, his back bent. Then an idea hits him. He glances up at me. "Is she allergic to cinnamon? That one runs in my family."

I flinch. When she eats a cinnamon roll, her lips swell slightly. She wolfed down two and a half cinnamon rolls before her last school picture. "Easier than lip fillers," she'd joked.

"And does she sneeze when she looks at the sun?" he adds. "If so, she got that from me, too. It's a genetic thing."

I clench my fists at my side. "Don't make guesses. Tell me something you *know*."

I've got him. Because he doesn't know Elise. He barely knew her when he left. She doesn't remember him, either. He doesn't know a damn thing.

Howard frowns, his brows pinching together in concentration. Then his face smooths and he smiles right at me. "You used to draw little houses."

The air seems to suck out of the room.

I can't breathe. Can't move. I just stare at him.

"You drew them with pencils and, when you ran out of pencils, you used your mom's makeup. She hated that." He chuckles at the memory. "I bought you a pack of crayons once, and boy, that really ticked her off. She said you were going to draw all over the walls, but I told her you were too old for that."

She's eleven, Melinda. I think she can control herself. I remember him saying those exact words. I felt so big in that moment. So seen. I can still picture the way Howard rolled his eyes at my mom and then gave me a conspiratorial wink.

But now, the memory twists my stomach.

"Something else," I snap.

Howard sighs. "Belle. Come on. It's me. You have to remember me."

"I don't have to do anything. I'm not the one who left and abandoned my daughter. I don't need to earn back anyone's trust. I know who I am," I say, jamming a finger in my chest. "I'm Elise's big sister. I'm the only person who has ever taken care of her. Now, who the fuck are you?"

Nikolai shifts towards me. "Do you recognize him or not?"

Still staring at Howard, I shake my head. "Give him a DNA test."

"He isn't worth the trouble. If you know him, we figure out what he wants. If we don't, I kill him."

Howard inhales sharply. "She knows me! You know she knows me."

Nikolai snaps his attention to Howard. "You don't know what I know. I'd keep your mouth shut if I were you, stranger."

Howard presses his lips together tightly, but I can feel him looking at me. His gaze is saying more than words ever could. He's pleading with me to recognize him, to admit the truth: I know Howard and he is who he says he is.

"Well?" Nikolai presses.

I stare at Howard, and the seconds seem to stretch and transform.

"Why now?" I ask through gritted teeth. "You missed out on Elise's entire life. Why come back for her now?"

"Your mom asked for my help."

"You're here because of my *mom?*" I spit. "All this time and you come and do this for Melinda, not for Elise? You fucking—"

"I'm not here to help Melinda."

"You just said—"

"I'm here because she told me Elise ran away," Howard explains. "She wanted my help, but I told her I'd look into it on my own. I've been thinking about Elise for… for a long time. I wondered what happened to her. So I decided to find out."

"How fucking noble of you, 'deciding to find out what happened' to your own *daughter.*" I cross my arms over my chest. "You can't see her."

"What?" he breathes. "Belle, you can't—"

"Actually, I can," I interrupt. "Because I'm the person who has been looking out for her. I'm the person who got her away from our useless mother. You're just the asshole who left her there."

"It… it wasn't like that."

"Then look me in my eyes and tell me that when you left you believed my mom would be a good mother to us." Howard tries to look away, but I snap my fingers and direct his gaze back to mine. "Look at me! Look me in my eyes and tell me you thought Elise was being well-cared for all these years."

He works his jaw back and forth, his teeth grinding. Then he looks away.

"That's what I fucking thought," I snarl, sounding harsher than I ever knew I could.

Nikolai's shoulder brushes mine. "We done here?"

"Yeah," I spit. "We're done here."

He starts moving towards Howard, ushering him towards the door. Howard seems to accept his fate. He doesn't yell or make a scene. But just before he walks through the door, he pulls a card out of his wallet and sets it on the table next to the door.

"My card," he says over his shoulder. "If you change your mind."

Then Nikolai shoves him out of the room.

I don't want to touch the card. It might as well be radioactive. But I also know it would be worse if I let it stay there and Elise found it later. Grudgingly, I stomp across the room and shove it into the back pocket of my jeans.

Just as I walk across the room again and drop down onto the sofa, Nikolai returns. He closes the door behind him.

"Considering that man is still breathing, I take it you recognized him."

"Yeah. I recognized him." I drop my face into my hands and massage circles into my pounding temples.

"Any reason in particular you decided to fuck with him?"

I snap my head up. "Since when are you against fucking with people? That's your favorite hobby."

"Exactly. It's *my* favorite hobby," he says. "Not yours."

"Maybe I'm changing. It happens. People change all the time."

"Not at their core." Nikolai touches my chin to make me look into his eyes. "And at your core, you, Belle Dowan, are a much better person than I am."

I feel hot under his gaze. I shift nervously and then spin around, unable to endure the itch growing beneath my skin. "Well, that's a low bar to clear."

Nikolai just smirks at me.

"What?" I demand. "What are you looking at me like that for?"

He shrugs. "Nothing. I'm just waiting for you to tell me what's really wrong."

"You saw what's wrong. Do I really need to break it down for you?"

His eyebrow arches, his expression smug.

"Stop it," I growl. "Stop looking at me like that. I… I hate it. I hate him. I hate you." I feel like a petulant child, but I can't seem to stop.

Nikolai just laughs, which is as infuriating as anything else he's ever done. "Go on then. You're on a roll. What else do you hate?"

More answers leap right to my tongue. "I hate that bald, sweaty private investigator who tracked us down. I hate my mom for calling Howard. I hate Howard for helping her."

Nikolai's eyes are twin black holes, swallowing up everything I'm giving him and demanding more, more, more.

"Don't stop," he rasps. "Let it all out."

I close my eyes. "I hate that a part of me—growing larger by the second, for the record—feels bad for turning Howard away. And I hate that I feel guilty for lying to Elise and taking away her opportunity to meet her father. And, most of all…" My throat clogs with emotion. I have to take a few deep breaths before I can continue. "Most of all, I hate that I'm not Elise's mom. I hate that everyone else seems to have a larger claim on her than I do, even though I love her more than all of them. I hate that she might get taken away from me. I hate how much I hate that. I hate how much it scares me."

With that, I run out of steam. I slump back against the couch and swipe the tears from my cheeks. "Elise would call me a cupcake if she heard any of that." I raise my eyes to meet Nikolai's. "You know what's craziest of all? Part of me is actually jealous. Can you believe that?"

"Jealous of what?"

"Of Elise. That Howard came back for her." I shake my head. "I'm jealous that her dad is alive and cares—or at least is pretending to care—while mine is dead and he's never coming back. He can't come back and be here for me the way Howard can with Elise. I mean… isn't that ridiculous?"

Nikolai shrugs. "Fuck if I know. Jealousy isn't something I have much experience with."

"Except where handsy tailors are concerned."

Nikolai's eyes flash. "That's different."

"I'm too emotionally exhausted to even begin to unpack that sentiment," I mutter.

"What's there to unpack?" Nikolai asks. "You live in my house, I take care of you, we're getting married. You're mine, *kiska*."

"And it's that simple for you?"

He nods. "It's that simple."

I sigh. "I wish things could be that simple for me."

"They can be."

Nikolai is watching me with cool gray eyes. I'm well aware that this is what passes as tender for him. He's being gentle with me even though he doesn't have to, even though he could be angry with me instead for bringing this mess into his life when he already has so much else to deal with.

I want to rest my head against his shoulder and close my eyes, but I force myself to sit upright and look at him.

"How?" I choke out. "I don't see how it's possible."

All at once, Nikolai closes the gap between us. He grips my chin and peers into my eyes, into my soul. "All you have to do is realize that you and you alone make your destiny in this world, Belle. You can't depend on anyone else to do it for you."

I blink up at him for a few taut seconds.

Then, before I can ask any questions, Nikolai lets go of my chin and stands up. "I have work to do. I'll be in my office."

Once he's gone, I collapse back and let the sofa swallow me up. I want to melt between the cushions and disappear.

"Figure out how to make my own destiny," I mutter to the empty room. "Gee, is that all?"

Then I press a throw pillow against my face and scream.

18

BELLE

I lie in bed and stare at the ceiling for what feels like hours, although it might be just minutes. Time doesn't seem to mean anything as the night stretches on, my brain whirring and buzzing and frothing with the events of the day and the past and the fears of what the future might hold.

When I can't take the silence anymore, I slip across the hall and peek into Elise's room. I'm not sure why because I hope she's asleep. The truth about her dad has been knocking around in my head for hours with nowhere to go, and at some point, it'll have to come out. But the middle of the night probably isn't the best time to unhash a lifetime of parental trauma.

Inside, the light is off and Elise is asleep. I wait there for a few minutes, listening to the soft, reassuring sound of her breathing. When we shared a room as kids, I would count Elise's breaths in and out until I fell asleep myself. I'm tempted to crawl into bed next to her and let the rhythm of it lull me to sleep. But I don't want to wake her up or worry her.

I close her door and wander down the hallway.

I'm not consciously aware of where I'm headed until I stop outside Nikolai's office. Light spills out of the crack beneath the door, like I knew it would. I knock softly.

"You should be sleeping," Nikolai says by way of a greeting.

I push the door open a crack. "How did you know it was me?"

"The same way you knew I'd be in my office this late."

He closes the sleek laptop in front of him and leans back in his chair. He's wearing a dark blue fitted t-shirt and gray athletic sweatpants. When he crosses his arms over his chest, his biceps bulge.

"Were you at the gym?" He doesn't look sweaty, but it would be so like Nikolai to be the kind of demigod capable of working out without breaking a sweat.

"I was about to be."

I glance at the clock on the wall and gasp. "Holy shit. It's two AM."

"Which is why I said you should be in bed."

"What about you? You're leaving to go to the gym at this hour? Do you even sleep?" I fire back. "Wait, no. Don't tell me. You probably plug into a charging port somewhere, don't you?"

Nikolai actually chuckles at that. His mouth looks best when it's pulled back in a smile. Especially when I'm the cause of said smile. "I meant to get down there a couple hours ago, but I got caught up with…" He waves his hand towards his computer. "Things."

"You haven't been into the office much since I've been here."

He nods and drags a hand through his thick hair. "Yeah, well, I've been busy. That doesn't stop the emails from coming in, though. Bridget is handling as much of it as she can, but I'm putting too much on her."

He sounds oddly sympathetic. I feel the green envy monster inside of me stir to life. "It's her job to handle it. She's a big girl."

Nikolai arches a dark brow. "Maybe you should join me in the gym. Sounds like you have some jealousy to burn off."

I hate that he has this infuriating way of seeing straight to the heart of me. I hate even more that it's one-way glass. I'm an open book when he's the one looking, but when I look back at him, all I see is stone.

"I'm not jealous. I'm just saying, I'm sure Bridget is there for more than just ornamentation. Right?"

Nikolai just smirks.

I roll my eyes. "You know what? Forget it. Surround yourself with tall, thin, gorgeous women who are allergic to the top buttons of their shirts. See if I care."

"Belle." He says my name so softly that I can't help but look at him. "I haven't been at the office much recently, have I?"

"No."

"Do people usually put their ornaments where they can't see them?"

I frown. "I guess not."

"So if anyone is an ornament, it's you."

I blush and frown at the same time. "Gee, thanks."

He shrugs. "Take your pick. Either you're my eye candy or Bridget is."

He rightly takes my silence as a concession and smiles. My heart flips at the sight. I shift on my feet and change the subject. "So when will you be going back into the office?"

"That depends on you."

"On me?"

He nods. "On what you decide to do. About Howard."

"I already decided what to do about him. He's not coming near Elise. He doesn't even know her, for God's sake. He abandoned her. Why should I let him come back now?"

"Because he's her father," he says. As if it's that simple. As if anything is ever that simple.

"Allegedly," I snort. "With my mother, who the hell actually knows? Elise could belong to some random dealer or a guy at the bar."

"Which is why Howard left here today and went straight to a company that could provide a paternity test."

I freeze. "What?"

"You said you wanted a DNA test."

"And you refused!" I snap.

"And I'd refuse again," he says with zero remorse. "But Howard decided to take things into his own hands. You said you wanted a test, so he said he'd get one."

"I didn't hear him say that. When did he say that?"

"Yesterday, when I escorted him out."

"Why didn't you tell me?"

"What do you think I'm doing now?"

I know he's done nothing wrong, but I need someone to be angry at. And since Howard isn't here, Nikolai is the easiest option.

"You could have told me earlier."

"And you would have taken it so well if I'd done that," he drawls sarcastically.

"So you decided to lie to me instead?"

"I decided to keep information from you that I thought would upset you. The same way you told Elise her dad was dead rather than a deadbeat. We all make choices, don't we, *kiska?*"

I stare at him for a few seconds, trying to muster up a glare. But I can't. Because he's right.

"Fine. You win."

He smiles. "Surprise, surprise."

I fold my arms over my chest. "So do you expect me to call Howard and set up another meeting with him or something? I'm sure that's why he left his business card."

"I don't expect you to do anything," he says. "This is your decision, not mine."

My eyes widen. "Wow. Has Mr. Control Freak ever said those words before?"

"Start making choices with your head instead of your heart, and you'll hear them a lot more often," he growls. Then he tucks his hands behind his head. "He left an address where he'll be for lunch tomorrow. He'll have the results by then. If you want to talk to him, all you have to do is show up."

"Did he want me to bring Elise?"

Nikolai shakes his head. "I don't think he has any expectations where Elise is concerned. You made your feelings about him pretty clear."

"Why does it sound like you're defending him?"

"Because you're looking for a reason to be pissed with me."

I cross my arms over my chest. "Usually, you're more than happy to supply me with a reason. This is a first."

"I can lock you in your bedroom tonight if you want. For old times' sake."

"How generous. I'll think about it," I snark back. "I'm really just annoyed because you're the guy who is all about loyalty, but you don't seem to care that Howard abandoned his kid. Doesn't that go against all of your core Bratvian tenets?"

"Bratvian what?" he asks, biting back a laugh.

"You know what I mean! You're supposed to care that this guy abandoned Elise."

He shrugs. "Why? He isn't my father. He didn't abandon me."

"Because Elise is worth sticking around for," I grit out. "Because I love her."

"I don't make it a habit to feel things on behalf of other people. This is between Howard and Elise. It has nothing to do with me."

"Yet you have no problem at all inserting yourself into my business."

"Because you have a lot to do with me," he says. "You're pregnant with my child, for one."

I snap my fingers. "See? You're already an involved parent and our child hasn't even been born. How do you not hate Howard?"

"I don't think it's fair to go around comparing men to me. The rest of them really don't stand a chance."

It's my turn to bite back a laugh. "Humble as ever."

"The point stands. I am the leader of a Bratva. I have hundreds of men under control and enough money for several lifetimes. It's not exactly fair to compare the kind of father I'll be to the average Joe. Maybe Howard is doing his best."

"If this is his best, it's not good enough!"

"At least he gives a shit," Nikolai snaps. "At least he wants to make things right."

"Why does he deserve a second chance? Why should I give him the chance to have a relationship with her after he fucked it up the first time?"

"You're right."

My jaw nearly drops. "Pardon?"

"You're right," he repeats grimly. "Howard doesn't deserve it. But doesn't Elise?"

I clamp my lips together and look away, but Nikolai slides his chair to the side, staying in my line of vision.

"You said yesterday you were jealous of Elise because her father came back for her. Maybe you're trying to keep them apart because yours never came back for you."

"Oh, so you're an armchair therapist now?" I seethe, even as I feel the hot sting of incoming tears. "My dad died, for the record. He didn't abandon me."

"Tell that to nine-year-old Belle," he says. "I'm sure she didn't understand the difference. All she knew was that her dad was gone overnight. And considering you're now an adult who is jealous of her teenage sister, I don't think you ever quite let go of that bitterness." He pauses, then adds, "I understand what you feel, Belle."

"I thought you didn't make a habit of feeling other people's emotions."

"I don't. I feel my own. My parents are dead and never coming back. So yes—like it or not, I know how you feel."

The wind in my angry sails dissipates. I sag. "What happened to them?"

"Cancer took my mother," he says. "She went quickly since we couldn't afford the treatments. And that ate my dad up inside. He couldn't handle the shame. He killed himself not long after. I was a little younger than Elise."

"Oh, Christ, Nikolai." My throat clogs, thinking about him as a little boy, navigating that kind of loss. It makes me want to cross the room and wrap him in a hug. "I'm so sorry. That must have been—"

"It was shitty, but so is life. It either makes you or it breaks you. I let it make me."

I settle into the leather chair across from his desk and pull my knees up to my chin. The buzzing in my head has dulled. All my anxieties quieting for the first time in hours. The world sounds so simple and clear-cut when he describes it. *Do this or that. Choose A or choose B.* When I look out at it, though, all I see is an ever-shifting haze of things that always stay just out of reach.

"Does that mean you wouldn't change anything if you could?" I ask.

He frowns, but it's not angry. Just… brooding, I guess. "I don't have time for regrets or 'what if?' I like who I am now and that's all that matters."

I shake my head in quiet disbelief. "It must be amazing to exist in the world that way. To let life wash over you, taking what you need and leaving what you don't."

"You should try it," he suggests.

I snort. "Try it? I can't even imagine it. I've spent my entire life wondering where Elise and I would be if my mom had put us first. Where we'd be if our parents gave a single shit."

"Howard gives a shit, Belle."

"Maybe half a shit," I mumble, resting my head on the arm of the chair. Nikolai's office is surprisingly warm, and the overhead light is off, so the room is lit by the gentle glow of his desk lamp. It's soothing.

"You don't have to decide anything about Howard now. But I'll text Yuri and have him scope out the restaurant where he'd like to meet. He can make sure everything is above-board and that you'll be protected if you choose to go."

"I thought you said this doesn't concern you?"

"How many times do I have to say it?" he snaps. "*You* concern me, Belle. And if you're going to be there, I intend to make sure it's safe."

I know better, but it's nice to pretend he cares what happens to me. I want to stay in this fantasy for a minute. So I close my eyes and let myself lull into a doze.

"You should get to bed," Nikolai murmurs.

His voice surprises me, making me jump. But I don't open my eyes.

I know I should get to sleep. I need more rest because of the baby, anyway. But I'm not ready to give this up. Just a few more minutes.

When I do finally open my eyes, I'm surprised to find I'm not in Nikolai's office anymore. The room is dark, and I recognize the furniture in my bedroom. He must have carried me to bed when I fell asleep.

The comforter is wrapped around my shoulders and soft against my cheek. I nuzzle deeper into the blankets, smiling at the thought of Nikolai tucking me into bed.

It's nice. It's simple.

If only anything else was like that.

19

BELLE

"Come with me."

Nikolai doesn't look up from his phone, though he does arch an intrigued eyebrow. "It's a little early for that kind of dirty talk, don't you think?"

I groan. "I didn't mean—To the lunch with Howard, I'm talking about. I want you to come with me."

"You're going to go?"

"Yeah. You were right," I admit grudgingly. "Howard might be a shitty dad, but Elise deserves the opportunity to know him. So I need to meet with him and vet this whole thing."

At that, Nikolai finally looks up from his phone. He's freshly showered, his hair wet and curling across his forehead. The morning light slanting through the windows makes it look like it's carved from dark marble. "I'm right?"

"Don't look surprised. You're always right, remember?"

"I know that. But you usually need reminding."

I roll my eyes. "Are you coming or not?"

"Not presently," he says, spreading his legs and leaning back slightly. "But if you're interested in changing that, then by all means—"

"To the restaurant with me," I growl. "Do you want to accompany me to the restaurant to meet Howard?"

"Of course I'm going with you."

I blink in surprise. "Really?"

He sighs. "Someone has to make sure you don't get yourself killed."

"It's lunch. I think I can survive a lunch."

⁓

But two hours later when I walk into the diner to meet Howard, I'm suddenly not so sure that's true.

Because Howard didn't come alone. He's sitting next to a walking, talking nuclear bomb. And there will be no survivors.

I inhale sharply and stumble back. Nikolai lets me fall against his strong chest. He curls an arm around me and whispers in my ear. "What is it?"

My answer is a single, horrified word.

"Mom."

Nikolai's breath is warm against the back of my neck. "Do you want to leave?"

Yes. One hundred times yes. I want to turn around and sprint out of this diner without looking back. But that's what she wants, too. For me to run. For me to look like the guilty party. She doesn't expect me to face her. And maybe I wouldn't—if this was just about me.

But Elise is all that matters.

I shake my head. "No. No more running. I want to stay."

Nikolai's arm brushes mine, and I reach down and squeeze his hand. I need the extra courage. Then I cross the diner and stand in front of the table, my expression icy.

"Howard," I say with a nod. Then I turn to the woman next to him. "Mom."

I took Elise from her house in the middle of the night, so it's been years since I've looked my mom in the eyes. It could be centuries, though, and that still wouldn't be long enough.

She smiles lazily. Even when she isn't drunk, she has a permanent dopey expression on her face. Like her muscles never fully sober up. But her eyes… those are sharp. Cunning.

"'*Mom*,'" she mimics with a sneer. "After everything you've done to me, that's how you greet me?"

Somehow, she still has the capacity to surprise me with her awfulness. I scoff. "Everything *I've* done to *you*? Are you—"

"I'm sorry, Belle," Howard interrupts. "I didn't know she was coming to town. I didn't ask her to be here for this, but she wouldn't leave."

"Oh, screw you," Mom coughs, scowling at Howard. "The only reason you're here is because I asked you to come."

Howard looks at me imploringly. "That's not true. I came because I wanted to find Elise. This has nothing to do with Belle."

I redouble my grip on Nikolai's hand. "This isn't what we agreed to, Howard. You were supposed to be here alone."

"I would have called and explained, but I didn't have your number. And I didn't just want to not show up," he says. "I didn't want you to think I was flaky."

"Yeah, that would've been bad," I grit out. "Instead, I just think you're a traitor."

My mom tips her head back and cackles maniacally, though it's clear she doesn't think any of this is funny. "Always so damn dramatic. This isn't a war, Belle. There are no traitors."

"Whatever you want to call it, you and I aren't on the same side. We never were."

"Giving you life means nothing, then?" she snaps.

"You gave birth to me, but you didn't give me a life. You weren't a mother to me."

She shakes her head. "I didn't realize it was a crime to be poor. Sorry I couldn't spend all my time baking pies and… and gardening or some shit like that."

"No, you were too busy searching for your next fix and being passed out drunk by noon. Your schedule was all full."

Her eyes narrow. "I lost my husband, you know. I was mourning."

"And I lost my dad!" I can feel other people in the diner watching us now, but I can't bring myself to care. All of this baggage with my mom has been tucked out of sight for too long. It's time to air it out. "I lost the only parent who even halfway cared about me, but you were too focused on yourself to see that I was mourning, too."

"Kids always bounce back. You were fine."

"Because I had to be!" I scream. "Because I was always the adult in our house. Even when I was a little kid."

She purses her lips. I notice a slew of new wrinkles around her mouth. Time and drugs are leeching the life from her. "You've always been impossible to talk to. So hysterical. So much like your father. Elise was my girl, but you poisoned her against me, too."

"You did that yourself. I wasn't even there."

I should have been there, though. I was so young when I left, but I should have taken Elise with me. I should have figured it out and gotten us both out of that house sooner.

"That's why she liked you. Because you weren't around. Absence makes the heart grow fonder," she says. "After you ran off, she forgot how miserable you could be."

At one time, my mom had the ability to hurt me. I cared what she thought.

Now, I just want her gone.

"You're not getting her back."

Her eyes narrow. "I'm her mother. You can't keep her from me."

"Then call the police," I tell her flatly. "File a missing person report or list her as a runaway. Get the authorities involved."

Her jaw tightens. "Why should I? The person responsible is right in front of me."

"I think the question you should actually be asking is, 'Why shouldn't I?' And lucky me, I know the answer. It's because you're afraid the cops will care more about the nasty, shady stuff you're up to than finding Elise."

All the ease has left my mother. She is tense now, pulled taut and ready to spring at me. "I'm not 'up to' anything."

"Is that right?" I arch an eyebrow. "Open your purse. Let me see what's inside."

Her hand closes around her bag in a possessive claw. That's all the answer I needed.

Howard sighs. "Girls, come on. Can't we be civil?"

I have a sudden, jarring flashback to when he and my mom were dating. When I wanted to leave the house with them, but my mom wanted me to stay. *"Girls,"* he'd said, as if my mom and I were on the same level. As if she was as immature as I was, and he was above it all. *"Let's not do this."*

It hurt then, too. I hoped Howard would be on my side, but at the end of the day, he'd rather stay out of it. It was me against the world, like always.

"You shouldn't even be here," I seethe at him. "The moment she showed up, you should have left. You know where Nikolai lives. Leave a fucking note. But don't ambush me with her."

"'Her'?" my mom hisses. "That's the kind of respect I get? Like it or not, I'm your mother. You can't cut me out."

"Wrong." I face her, my expression hard as steel. "You aren't my mother. You're just the bitch I lived with for sixteen years."

I don't even see her move—I just feel the crack. Her palm hot against my cheek.

Then the room explodes.

Other diners gasp in shock. Howard yelps. But it's all drowned out when Nikolai steps forward.

He moves around me easily and wraps his hand around my mom's throat. As soon as that happens, the entire restaurant goes blaringly silent.

"Touch my fiancée again, and I'll kill you." His voice is measured and calm, which makes it even more terrifying. Because it's clear this is no idle threat. He means it.

A waitress moves over reluctantly, her eyes wide. "Sir! I'm sorry, but… you all need to leave."

My mom's face is turning red, but it's mostly with embarrassment. He isn't holding her tightly enough to cut off air. Just enough to make his point. He lets go one finger at a time, peeling back slowly. Then he retreats back to my side.

"Are you okay, Belle?" he murmurs.

My cheek burns, but it's actually a nice feeling. It means she's desperate. Bothered enough that she can't just ignore me. She can't just shut me away in a closet and forget I exist.

Right now, finally, my mom has to look me in the face and hear what I'm saying.

And she fucking loathes it.

"I'm okay." I give him a small smile. "I just need another minute to talk to her."

"You need to leave," the waitress says again. "I'm sorry. But my manager wants you out. He's going to call the cops."

"My fiancée said she wants another minute," Nikolai snaps.

The woman jumps, but I hold up a finger. "I'll leave as soon as I'm done. Nikolai, could you take Howard outside?"

Nikolai leans in and presses a kiss to my cheek. The same cheek my mother just slapped. I know it's just his way of claiming his property, but the gesture sinks into my skin and shoots warmth straight through my chest.

"Howard," Nikolai barks, "let's step outside."

Howard seems relieved to be free of this disaster. He gets up quickly and follows Nikolai outside, leaving me alone with my mother.

She's sitting down again, looking up at me with a smug smile. "Howard is Elise's father. In case you wanted to know the results of the paternity test. Sorry to disappoint you. I'm sure you would have loved it if it came back negative. Just one more reason to hate me."

"I don't need another reason," I tell her. "I have plenty."

Her smile slips slightly. I want to wipe it all the way off. So I keep going.

"You're not taking Elise home with you. I know that's why you came here, but it isn't going to happen. She belongs with me. With someone who will actually take care of her."

"I took care of her for fourteen years."

"You didn't kill her," I correct. "There's a huge difference. But now, she is well taken care of. She can be a kid. She can have a family."

She snorts. "A family with you and that woman-beater out there? How sweet."

"You want to know a secret, Mom?" I blurt suddenly. "I'm pregnant."

Her eyes widen. Then she looks me over quickly, trying to see how far along I am.

"Nikolai and I were broken up when I found out, but Elise called him and told him. Him, not you. Because she trusts him, not you. Because she wanted us to be together again. Not with you." There's no reason I can't fudge the truth a little bit here. I don't plan to ever see this cunt again after today, anyway. "And Nikolai loves us. *All* of us. Me, Elise, our baby. We are going to be a family, and you can't be part of it."

Her jaw twitches with built-up tension. "You'd really keep me away from my daughter and grandchild because of your feelings towards me?"

"I'm not doing any of this because I hate you," I tell her. "You might not believe that, but it's true. If the only problem was that I hated you, I'd grin and bear your presence. I'd endure. But the problem is that you're toxic. You ruin everything you touch. You are a parasite, latching on and sucking everyone else dry. And I won't let you do it anymore. Not to me and sure as hell not to the people I love."

I see the panic in her eyes. The realization that I mean what I'm saying.

"You can let me see Elise just once," she whispers. Her voice cracks with the desperation that's been there all along. "I came all this way. I spent money to come and see her."

I laugh out loud, right in her face. "Not a fucking chance."

She lifts her chin, looking at me down the length of her nose. Her lips pucker in distaste. "Look at you, Miss High and Mighty. Judging me like your boyfriend didn't just try to choke me in public. Ask around. I have a restaurant full of witnesses."

"Nikolai is my fiancé, not my boyfriend. And the difference between him and whatever loser you're shacking up with these days is that Nikolai cares about me." The words slice through the fragile coating around my heart. I wish every word I was saying was true. I hope I look more confident than I feel. "Unlike you, Nikolai cares about his child. He'll do anything to take care of his kid. You've only ever cared about yourself."

She crosses her arms and leans back in her chair. "Don't come crawling back to me when he dumps your ass and you have nowhere to go. He'll disappoint you."

"No, Mom, he won't. That's your job."

I don't wait for her response. I don't need one.

I turn and face the exit. Then, for the last time, I leave my mother behind.

20

NIKOLAI

I watch Belle talk to her mom through the diner's front window.

If that *pizda* so much as breathes wrong, I'll kill her. I wasn't kidding with that threat. The woman is lucky I didn't snap her windpipe for slapping Belle. Even the thought of it makes my fists clench again.

"Melinda is all talk," Howard says from behind me. "She won't hit her again."

"For her sake, I hope not." I feel Howard watching me, but I refuse to take my eyes off of Belle.

"You really care about her, don't you?" he asks a moment later.

I don't answer. I don't owe him anything.

Not that the answer isn't blindingly obvious. Even after her betrayal and my oath to myself not to let her become a distraction, my mind is once again filled with Belle.

Not with Xena, wherever the fuck she is. Not with Arslan. Not with my empire.

Just with Belle.

"You better," Howard continues. "Belle has been through… well, you can probably tell that she didn't have it easy growing up. Not with Melinda as a mom. She deserves someone who will take care of her."

"Spoken by the coward who brought that bitch here. The same coward who abandoned his own daughter."

He lets out a soul-deep sigh. "I know I don't have much room to talk. Or maybe the ways I've fucked up are exactly why I have the room to talk. I know what the other side of those kinds of mistakes looks like. Belle deserves better."

"Better than you? You might want to set a higher bar."

Howard actually chuckles. "You're probably right."

Belle turns around at that moment. She strides through the diner of gawkers and onlookers with her head held high. I don't even bother looking back at Melinda. She doesn't deserve the attention.

I open the door as Belle approaches, and she gives me a tight smile. "Can we go?" she asks.

"If you're ready."

She nods. "I'm ready."

She starts to turn right, but then Howard steps forward to intercept her. "I am sorry about Melinda being here, Belle. I genuinely didn't know she was coming."

"It's fine."

"No, it's not," he says. "If I'd known, I would have warned you. I'm sorry."

Belle shrugs. "It's not like Elise was with me. That would have been worse."

With that, she brushes past him. I fall in step, take her hand in mine, and together, we walk away from the flaming ruins of her past.

"I wasn't sure you were going to show," Yuri comments when I walk into my office.

He's sitting in the leather chair across from my desk. The same one Belle fell asleep in last night.

She was talking to me, being honest, being vulnerable… then her voice stopped. When I looked up, she was asleep with her cheek resting on the arm of the chair. Her auburn hair fell around her shoulders and her hands were tucked under her chin. She looked perfectly at peace. I was content to watch her breathe for a long time.

When I finally picked her up and carried her back to bed, I paused outside my own bedroom door. For a second, I considered putting her in my bed. I thought about waking up to the sight of her wrapped in my sheets.

But then I thought better of it.

Belle is taking up enough of my brain space as it is. I don't need her invading my unconscious hours as well.

"I always show," I growl back at my new right-hand man.

"That's my point. You usually aren't late, either."

"And my seconds aren't usually so mouthy."

He lowers his head, sufficiently cowed for a moment. But then he smirks. "Arslan probably just rolled over in his grave hearing you say that."

"Arslan is the reason I said 'usually.' You are stepping into his role for now. But you aren't him."

He bows his head fully this time. He was trying to connect with me, but that was his mistake.

"I like you, Yuri," I say, folding my hands on my desk. "You've always been loyal to the Bratva and dedicated to your work. You follow orders and ask the important kind of questions. The kinds that save lives and firm up plans. You're a vital asset."

"But…?" he asks, seeing where I'm headed.

I nod. "But I'm not interested in a new friend. I need you to serve me well and do your job. I need you to trust what I tell you and not push back when it's unhelpful. Can you do that?"

"I can do that, Don Zhukova," he says.

"Great." I knock three times on the surface of my desk and call to the door, "You can come in."

Yuri frowns, confused. But then the door behind him opens. He spins around just as Christo comes into the room.

I knew the first meeting would be tense, but I'm still surprised by the speed with which Yuri jumps out of his chair and turns to face Christo. He reaches for his gun before he remembers he doesn't have it.

"And that is why you were required to leave your weapons at the security shack," I say. "Stand down, Yuri."

Yuri retreats back half a step, but keeps his body ready. Christo isn't convinced the danger has passed. His shoulders are high and tense. He watches Yuri with wide eyes as he skirts around the edge of the room towards my desk.

"What the hell is that Greek motherfucker doing here?" Yuri growls.

"I invited him."

He turns on me almost as quickly as he turned on Christo. "What is this, Nikolai? Is this your way of telling me you're in bed with the Greeks? Because I don't want a part of it. Kill me if you have to, but I'll never turn on the Bratva."

"Christo would have to be a lot prettier before I'd be tempted to crawl into his bed," I drawl. "No offense."

Christo shrugs. "Some offense."

Yuri lets out an incoherent growl.

"Calm the fuck down and then sit the fuck down," I tell him. He hesitates and I snap my fingers. "Now."

Reluctantly, he sits back down. But rather than slouching back in the chair like he was when I entered, he's perched on the very edge with his spine ramrod straight. Christo is standing in the corner like a ghost, practically blending into the wallpaper.

"Christo isn't working for the Greeks. He's working for me."

"He's a fucking liar," Yuri hisses.

At that, Christo stiffens. His face flushes with rage. In a second, I'm going to have a brawl on my hands.

"If either of you touch one another, I'll kill you both," I say. "How about that? Will a death threat cool some tempers?"

"I'm fine," Christo grits out.

"And I'll be fine once he's gone." Yuri shakes his head and then spits in Christo's direction. "I lost brothers because of your people."

"You would have lost your don, too," I sigh, "if it hadn't been for him."

Yuri finally gives me his full attention again, eyes rapt.

Satisfied that I have his focus, I continue. "Arslan was dead next to me. I was cornered with no way out. Christo gave me a gun and helped me fight my way free. Without him, I'd be dead."

Yuri mulls that over for a second. "He has a motive, then. What does he gain by keeping you alive?"

"My aunt's head on a fucking spike," Christo answers grimly. "Xena killed my father. I want her to pay. Nikolai is the only man who can make that happen."

"But he won't be able to if he's dead," Yuri says. He turns to me. "And you will be, Don, if the men find out you're working with the Greeks."

"I'm not working with the Greeks. I'm working with one Greek. And he's left the family business."

He shakes his head. "It doesn't matter, Nikolai. Everyone is already on edge with Belle being back in the house. And with the rumors that the two of you are getting married."

I clench my jaw. "They aren't rumors. Why does it matter who I marry?"

"Is it a rumor that she was working with the Greeks, too? Because the men think she partnered with Xena. That's why it matters."

Christo stiffens. I can tell he wants to answer. He still hasn't fully forgiven Belle for her betrayal. These two could probably bond over their mutual distrust of her.

"That isn't a rumor, either. But Belle doesn't understand this world. She didn't realize what she was doing."

"Do you think the men will care about that?" Yuri spits. "I'm not trying to question you, sir, but—"

"But you are," Christo interrupts.

Yuri throws a glare in his direction before looking back to me. "The men are on edge, Don Zhukova. We've lost brothers and friends. Now is not the time to look sympathetic to the Greeks."

"No one is sympathetic to the Simatous. Least of all me," I growl. "I watched my best friend die in the dirt because of Xena and her men. Fuck them all."

"Yeah, fuck them all… Except Christo and Belle," he adds quietly.

I stand up, my hand on my gun. "You're getting dangerously close to pissing me off, Yuri."

"You'd shoot an unarmed man?" he asks.

"I won't need to. I'll strangle you. It'll be more personal that way."

His nostrils flare, but he eventually holds up his hands in a silent surrender. "I told you I trust you, sir, and I meant that. Even now, I trust your judgment. But everyone else might not feel the same way I do."

"What are you saying?" I ask, my voice laced with warning.

"I'm saying that the Bratva is on edge. And if they thought you were grieving Arslan's death, maybe they could be convinced you weren't thinking rationally."

"Who would convince them of that?" I snap. "You're the next in command after me. Those men answer to you. A fish rots from the head. If they're disloyal, what does that say about you?"

Yuri goes still. "You can't make me personally responsible for how they feel."

"I can do anything I fucking want, Yuri."

"What do you want me to do?" he asks, desperation creeping in.

"Whatever you see fit," I tell him. "But if you'd like to live, then I suggest you find lots of nice things to say about your don. Convince the men I'm of sound mind and that Belle isn't a threat."

When he nods, his skull shakes like a bobblehead.

I wave my hand. "Good. You're dismissed. Get to it."

Yuri leaves without another word. His eyes are unfocused. He doesn't even glance at Christo as he walks out of my office and into the hallway.

As soon as he's gone, Christo lets out a low whistle. "Attacks coming on all sides, it seems."

"So it seems," I growl. "You're not winning me any popularity contests."

"I'm not winning any myself, either. Xena is sending men after me."

I look him over and notice the dark circles under his eyes. "Is that why you look like shit?"

"It's hard to sleep when trained assassins are coming after you." He walks around my desk and drops into the chair Yuri just vacated. "I'm guessing you'll know all about that feeling soon."

"Do you have confirmation Xena is planning something?"

He shakes his head. "I wasn't talking about Xena."

"Yuri?" I ask, intuiting his meaning. "Yuri won't come for me."

"No. But if he's right, your men might. You could have a mutiny on your hands. Especially if you keep Belle around."

The way he says her name so flippantly has my hackles rising. I sit a little taller, and Christo notices. The man notices everything.

He holds his hands up in surrender. "She's a target on both sides. Your men want her because they think she's a traitor, and Xena wants her because you want her." He snorts. "Hell, the Battiatos, too, for that matter, though they're mostly just Xena's puppets at this stage. Point is, anyone gunning for you will be gunning for her, too."

"You think I should cut her loose?" It's not an actual suggestion, but I am curious what he thinks.

"Only if you want her to end up dead," he sighs. "It's too late for that now. She's tangled up in this mess with you. Fiancée or not, you put a target on her back. And a target in her womb to boot. The Zhukova heir will come with a hefty bounty."

I nod slowly. "I know."

"So what are you going to do?" Christo asks.

"Keeping her close is dangerous. Setting her free is dangerous." I shrug. "It seems like the only option is to get her out of here. Hide her somewhere."

"I doubt she'll like that."

I snort. "What else is new?"

21

BELLE

"I'm glad you're back," Elise says as I come in. She's sitting cross-legged in the middle of her bed with a laptop open in front of her. "I want to run this idea by you so that you can run it by Nikolai."

She seems excited. I hate that I'm about to take it all away.

But surely that horrible moment can wait at least one minute longer.

"What idea is that?" I say after a painful swallow.

She turns the laptop to me so I can see the article she's pulled up. ***10 New York City Sights That Separate Locals From Tourists!***

"If we're going to live here, I need to explore the city. I mean, it's New York! City of Dreams, Alicia Keys style." Elise spreads her palms through the air like her words are written on a Times Square billboard. "We've been here for weeks and all I've seen is the airport, a women's shelter, and… two murders."

I grimace. "Are you okay, E? I haven't asked you that question enough."

She gives me a sad smile. "Yeah, I'm okay. And even if I'm not, Nikolai has the money to send me to some top-notch therapy. I'll sort through it all. Especially when I have one of the coolest cities in the world to distract me."

My sister sounds upbeat—more than she ever did when we were living in Oklahoma—but I can't shake the feeling that she's doing this on my behalf. Now that she's glimpsed what an utter hot mess I am, I get the sense she's trying to pick up the slack. Paste on a happy face.

The way I always tried to do for my mom.

Even when she didn't deserve it.

I sit on the edge of the bed and touch her knee. "You know, if you're not okay you can tell me, right? Whatever you're thinking or feeling, I can handle it."

"That goes both ways. I'm here if you need me."

"No, Elise. I mean… thank you. That's sweet. But I'm the one who is supposed to take care of you, not the other way around."

She dips her chin. "You're not my mom, Belle."

I can't count the number of times she's said that to me since she came to live with me. But this time, the words are tender. She isn't yelling them at me to get me to shut up and leave her alone. She's trying to take some of my burden.

It breaks my heart.

"No, I'm not," I admit. "But I'm the closest thing you've got right now."

"You're all I've got. The only family I need." She pokes my stomach. "Until little baby comes along. Then I'll be a super fun aunt."

She unknowingly segued perfectly into what I'm here to talk to her about, but I hesitate. Am I ready for this? Is she?

I want to say no, I'm not ready and I will never be ready. But as bad as this conversation is going to be, it will be so much worse if Elise hears this news from anyone but me.

I repeat this to myself again and again and take a deep breath. "Actually, that's what I came here to talk to you about."

Elise's expression shifts to horror. "Oh my God. Belle. Is the baby all right? Are you okay? Did something happen?"

"Oh my—no!" I shake my head. "No, nothing like that. We're both fine."

She exhales sharply and grabs my wrist. "Holy shit. Don't scare me like that. I thought something bad happened."

"Well, it's not anything bad, per se. It's just… news. New news." I wrinkle my nose. I should have practiced this speech more. It's coming out all garbled. "I have some news about our family. Your family."

She stares at me, her forehead creased in confusion. I don't blame her. I'm not making any sense.

"I'm sorry," I exhale. "It's hard to talk about this."

"Talk about what?" she says. "You're killing me."

I pull both my legs onto the bed and press my palms to my knees. "Okay. Do you remember when Nikolai and I asked you to stay in your room yesterday?"

"Yeah. For a big meeting, right?"

"Right," I nod. "Except it wasn't with one of Nikolai's clients. And it wasn't Bratva-related. It was about… you."

She stiffens. "What does that mean?"

"Someone came to see me… about you," I say. "They have been looking for you. They tracked us from Oklahoma to here."

"What does that mean, 'they tracked us'? Am I in danger?"

"No, honey. Nothing like that. You're safe." Her face is pale. I reach out and smooth her hair back. Drawing this out is worse, but I don't know what's going to happen once the words are out of my mouth. "Really, this could actually be a good thing."

She shakes her head. "No, it can't. If it was a good thing, you would have already said it."

Welp, she isn't wrong about that.

"It could be a good thing for you," I clarify. "But it might not be a good thing for me. Because… I lied to you."

I'm not sure if Elise even realizes she's doing it, but she shifts away from me. It's a tiny movement, just a fraction of a degree's change in her spine. But she pulls away from me and just like that, the pit in my stomach yawns open.

"I did it to protect you," I tell her. "I know that's no excuse. I should have told you the truth, but I guess I never thought it would matter. I never expected him to come back and—"

"Never expected who to come back?"

"That's what I'm getting to. I just thought that—"

"Never expected *who* to come back, Belle?" she repeats in a low, dangerous monotone.

I suck my cheeks in, trying to find the courage to say what I need to say. But I quickly realize I'll never find the courage. There's no point at which I'll be ready to do this. The only option is to run into it screaming and fearful, braced for disaster.

"Your dad."

Emotions flicker across her face like a jittery old movie, the screen flashing from one photo to the next while she stays perfectly silent. My blood is thundering through my veins, roaring in my ears as I wait for her to settle on an emotion, to say something. To say anything.

It's all there. Confusion, worry, shock…

Then, finally, anger.

Elise looks up at me, her green eyes glimmering. "You told me he died."

"I know," I admit. "He left when you were so small. I didn't think he'd ever come back."

"You told me he died," she repeats, the words hissing between clenched teeth. "You told me my dad was dead."

"I'm so sorry, Elise. I guess Mom told him you and I were missing, and he hired a private investigator. I didn't even know she was still in contact with him."

"She never talked about him," Elise says, thinking back. "When I mentioned him once, she said he was dead to her. I thought she was saying he died, but she was… Did she know you lied to me?"

I shrug. "I don't know. I really don't. I just wanted you to have what I had."

"You wanted me to have a dead dad?!" she shrieks.

"No! No, not like that. I just—" I squeeze my eyes closed, trying to find the words. "Mom sucked. She was the worst. But at least I had the fantasy of what could have been if my dad had survived. I could imagine what life would have been like if he'd never gotten in that accident and Mom never went off the deep end. I could imagine I had one decent parent, even if he couldn't be there with me. And I wanted you to have that instead of some deadbeat dad who abandoned you."

Elise jumps off the bed and turns to me. Her face is red and I can tell she's about to cry. She keeps swiping her arm across her nose. "You keep talking about what *you* wanted for me. But what about what *I* wanted?"

"I know. You're right. I should have—"

"You should have backed off!" she yells. "My entire life, you've always been so protective and overbearing. I get it, I do. Our mom was shitty, and you protected me from a lot of that. But you were so busy protecting me that we were hardly sisters, Belle."

Her words slice through me like a hot knife through butter. I feel gutted to my core. "What?"

"I love you," she says flatly, her anger melting into a stony distance. "Of course I do. But you were so busy pretending to be my mom that I never knew what it would be like to have a sister."

"We've always been sisters. We always will be."

"But we didn't fight about clothes or over who got to hold the remote. We didn't listen to music or talk about boys. You were always pretending to be my mom. Always. Even when I never asked you to."

"Well, someone had to be," I say softly.

"It wasn't until we came here and lived with Nikolai that I felt like we could be sisters. Like you backed off a bit and let me breathe."

Elise has changed so much since we've come to New York. I assumed it was the new environment and Nikolai putting us up in fancy hotel suites and mansions.

But it was because of me. Because I was too distracted to hover over her all day. Because I gave her room to be herself.

I guess I always just wanted to hold her close. I never realized I was suffocating her while doing it.

"I was just…" I shake my head. "I was trying to take care of you, Elise."

"I know you were. And you did. But we don't get to have both, I guess." A tear rolls down her cheek and she swipes it away. "Instead of going through our terrible childhoods together, you went through it alone. You shielded me from a bunch of it and lied to me and... and it made me feel like I was going through it alone, too."

My heart cracks open. "Elise, I'm so sorry. That isn't what I wanted for you. I never wanted—"

"God, Belle." She shakes her head. "Stop! It's not about what you wanted for me. It's about what I wanted!"

"You're right. I'm sorry."

Her jaw clenches. "And what I wanted was a sister I could talk to. Someone I could be honest with about what was going on at home. About our family. Maybe I would have wanted to reach out to him. Maybe I would have wanted a relationship. But you took that away from me."

"He took it away," I insist. "He's the one who left you behind. He left you with Mom. I was just trying to fix it."

"Yeah? And how did that go for you?" she demands.

I open my mouth to respond, but the words lodge in my throat.

Elise shakes her head. "Get out, Belle."

"No, Elise, please," I rasp. "We can talk. Can we figure this out?"

"You don't get to ask anything of me right now. Just leave."

Part of me would feel better if Elise was yelling. If she was screaming and raging out at me, then I could tell myself this is just like the hundreds of times before that I pissed her off and she forgave me.

But the calm, clear, icy way she asks me to leave... I'm worried she'll never ask me to come back. I want to say something, anything, to convince her to let me stay.

But before I can, Elise turns into her bathroom and slams the door closed.

22

NIKOLAI

The knock on my office door sends Christo jumping out of his chair.

I arch a brow in his direction. "Nervous?"

"The last man who was in here wanted to kill me," he says. "So, yeah. Nervous is a good word."

I wave his worry away. "Come in."

The door cracks open, and Belle peeks her face in. "Am I interrupting anything?"

"No. We were just finishing up," Christo says. His voice is tight, but he dips his head in greeting. It's not a warm welcome exactly, but it's a start. He turns back to me. "We'll talk soon. Good luck."

He closes the door behind him. Belle stares after him for a second before looking back at me. "Good luck with what?"

"Leading a Bratva, probably. It's a dangerous business."

"No more dangerous than being a big sister." Belle drops down into the chair with a groan. "I don't know why I said that. That's obviously not true; your job is way more dangerous. But I'm feeling sorry for myself. I came here to throw a pity party. You want to join?"

"My RSVP is conditional. Why are you feeling pitiful?"

She leans her head back against the leather and stares at the ceiling while I stare at the curve of her throat. At the way her collarbones cast a shadow over her skin, beautiful hollows where my lips fit perfectly. When she breathes, her chest rises and falls and it's hard to pay attention. Everything about this woman is a distraction.

"I went and talked with Elise," she says, gaze rooted upward. "Things did not go how I hoped."

"You told her about Howard?"

"Yeah. That's the point in the conversation where things started going south." She closes her eyes and whimpers. "It was a disaster."

"You knew it would be bad."

She nods. "Yeah, I did. But I still hoped she would forgive me on the spot and we'd talk it out. I hoped she would understand why I lied to her."

"She's fourteen. Grudges are what she does best."

Belle lowers her chin and narrows her eyes at me. "I know that. I didn't say it was a realistic thing to hope for."

"How mad is she?"

"Beyond mad." She blows out a breath. "Not only is she mad that I lied, but she had a lot to say about the choices I've made for, oh, I don't know… my entire life. I'm a bad sister, a bad fill-in mother, a bad everything. The overwhelming conclusion is that I'm a terrible person."

"If she thinks she hates you, tell her to go back and live with Melinda. She'll change her mind."

"I don't want to blackmail her into forgiving me." Belle sits up. "She didn't actually say I'm terrible quite that explicitly. She understands my instincts to protect her, but she thinks I handled it poorly. Essentially, I ruined her childhood and lied to her and forced my will onto her. She just said a bunch of casual, heart-shattering stuff like that."

"I lie and force my will on people all the time. Join the club."

"Is that supposed to make me feel better?"

I shrug. "Depends. Is it working?"

Her hazel eyes are wide and sad. I can practically feel them tugging me across the room, drawing me closer.

"Maybe," she says softly. She tips her head to the side. "Keep talking, please. I like listening to your voice. It's nicer than the one in my head."

"Christo and Yuri met."

"Really? I'm sure they became fast friends. Instant pals."

"It went about as well as your talk with Elise," I mutter. "I had to threaten to kill them both so they wouldn't kill each other first."

"Sounds counterintuitive."

"It worked. They agreed not to kill each other, but Yuri is uneasy. Anyone even sort of connected to the Simatous is under heavy scrutiny right now."

Belle nods, giving me a sympathetic smile for a moment… until she goes still. "Am I included in that group?"

I hesitate and sigh. "There are… rumors circulating amongst my men that you worked with Xena."

"Shit." She takes her lower lip in her mouth. "What did you tell him?"

"I told him I have it under control and there's nothing to worry about."

Her shoulders sag in obvious relief. "That's good."

"But Christo made a good point. He said you're top of the hit list of three different criminal organizations."

Her brow knits together. "Wait. Three? The Simatous, the Battiatos… what's the third one?"

I stare at her, waiting for the reality to sink in.

"*Your* men want to kill me?" she bleats in disbelief.

"They think you're distracting me. It's absurd. It's also hard to blame them. When you showed up, all the shit hit the fan. My deal with the Simatous fell through, we were attacked, and now, you and I are engaged."

Belle leans forward. "Can't you just tell them not to kill me? Like, forbid it?"

"Power doesn't work like that. I can't just order them to feel a certain way about you. I can order them not to harm you, but the only thing that will change their minds and ensure no one takes matters into their own hands is for me to show them you aren't a distraction."

"Okay… and how are you going to show them that?"

I lean back in my chair, hoping if I look relaxed that Belle will take the news better. "I have hotels and houses and apartments all around the world. There are beautiful safehouses where you and Elise will be comfortable. Places where you can—"

"Run and hide," she snaps before I can finish. "Why bother with the villas and finery? You're shoving us in a closet, Nikolai. There are plenty in this house."

"If maintaining control of my Bratva and keeping you alive means I'm 'shoving you in a closet,' then sure, that's what I'm doing," I fire back. "I'll be able to handle the threats here better if I know you are safe."

"And if I'm out of the way. Not a distraction." She sighs. "When will I be allowed to come back? At what point will I not be a 'distraction' anymore? Before or after the baby is born? Or maybe I'll just stay hidden away until the kid is one or two? Or, better yet, I'll raise our kid and then send them back to you when it's time for them to take over the Bratva. Then, having served my purpose, I'll rot in whatever foreign hidey-hole you've dropped me into while you live 'distraction-free' here."

"You're being dramatic."

"We're supposed to be getting married," she says, pushing herself to standing and facing off with me across the desk. "Is that still happening?"

"Last I checked, you didn't even want to get married."

Her jaw twinges, but she doesn't say anything.

"Or have you changed your mind?" I ask. "You were ready to throw yourself on the sword to avoid it, but now, you're suddenly ready to be Belle Zhukova?"

I meant it as a jab to draw her out, but hearing her name mingled with mine does something to me. My body heats, and I can feel that magnetic pull between us working both ways. The distance between us seems so much larger now. I need her closer.

"Have you changed *your* mind?" she fires back. "You're the one trying to send me away. I thought my mom was exaggerating when she said I made everyone miserable, but now, I'm not so sure. Elise wants nothing to do with me, and you're trying to get rid of me. Maybe I'd be better off leaving everyone alone."

I round my desk before I even realize what I'm doing. My body is drawn to hers. Before, I thought she was throwing a temper tantrum, but I can sense the desperation now. She's like a person drowning, so panicked that she's willing to take her rescuer down with her for one gulp of air.

I pull her in close and press my palm to the back of her neck. I can feel her quick breaths against my chest. "I'm not getting rid of you, *kiska*. I'm protecting you."

Her voice is meek. "Is there even a difference?"

"In terms of your response? No. You'd be a pain in the ass regardless." I feel her chuckle and I hold her tighter. "But in terms of my motivation, there's a pretty big difference."

"And what's your motivation?" Her voice is so soft I can barely hear it. Her fingers curl in the fabric of my shirt.

"I told you: to keep you safe."

She pulls back and looks up at me. "Me or the baby?'

I stare deep into her eyes so she knows I mean what I say next. "You, Belle. Always you."

Instantly, her eyes brim with tears and her chin wobbles. She's barely holding it together. Mere seconds from a breakdown.

"Are you really that surprised?" I grab her hand and bring her fingers to my mouth. One by one, I press a kiss to each of her fingertips. Belle watches me like it might be a dream.

"All I've done is make things more difficult for you, Nikolai." She's arguing against herself even as she draws closer to me. "I betrayed you and brought my family B.S. to your doorstep. And I've fought you every step of the way."

"Why is that?"

"Why what? Why did I fight?" She frowns, seriously considering the question. "I guess… I guess I didn't know how to let someone else take care of me. I've been handling everything on my own for so long."

"For too long," I interrupt. "Maybe it's time you let someone else call the shots for a while."

She leans forward and presses a kiss to my jaw. Then her lips move to my ear. "Tell me what you want, Nikolai. Tell me what to do."

She doesn't have to tell me twice.

"Unzip my pants," I command. "Wrap your hand around me."

Belle obeys, her small hand making efficient work of my pants and boxers. When she slides her fingers around me, I groan. "Stroke me."

She moves in slow, deliberate strokes. Her thumb works over my ridges and across my tip. She swirls her palm on the way back up, applying an excruciating friction that has me pumping into her hand while we're both still fully clothed.

If I'm not careful, this will end well before I'd like it to.

I pull back and gesture to her clothes. "Off. Take these all off."

Belle pulls her shirt over her head while I undo her jeans. She lifts her hips so I can slide them down her legs, pressing kisses to the warm skin of her thighs and her calves.

"You're perfect," I tell her. "Every fucking inch of you. Perfect."

Her face flushes. "I never took you for a liar."

"You don't believe me?" She shrugs and tries to drag me closer, but I pull out of reach. "We can't keep going until you believe that."

"I thought power didn't work that way," she argues. "Aren't you supposed to convince me of your way of thinking?"

I smirk. "Good point. Touch yourself."

Her eyes flare. "What?"

"Touch yourself and you'll know." I grab her hand from her thigh and slowly place it on her belly. Her fingers twitch like she wants to move them lower, but they stay still. She isn't sure yet. "Make yourself feel good. Explore how perfectly you're made. Do it until you understand."

"Nikolai, I don't know if I can—"

I cover her hand with mine and slide her fingers between her legs. Her skin is warm, and when she curls a finger against her slit, I can feel how wet she is.

She sighs, and I draw my hand back. As much as I want to stay here, touching her… I want to watch her even more.

Her movements are timid at first. Small strokes, her legs pressed tightly together. But as she finds a rhythm, her body has no choice but to respond.

Belle lets her thighs fall apart. Her head falls back and her eyes flutter closed. I watch her lips part in a sigh as she rocks her hips against her own fingers.

I give my cock a rough stroke, but I hardly need it. Watching her is more than enough.

"Tell me how it feels."

Her eyes meet mine, the pupils blown wide with desire. "Good. Better with you watching. Everything feels better when you're with me."

She moves to slide a finger between her folds, but I grab her wrist. "No. Like that. Just your finger."

Her eyes widen, but she obeys. The tension is ratcheting up and up with every passing second. Every cell of my skin is quivering, burning. One look at Belle says she feels the exact same.

Keeping myself away from her is exquisite torture. She's moaning now and rolling her hips, desperate for a firmer touch, to be filled. But she's being a good little *kiska* and restraining herself to just the one finger, like I told her.

Her chest is flushed pink, her nipples pebbled and begging for my mouth. I'm at the end of my patience. And when her eyes close and my name crosses her lips on a sigh, I can't hold back another moment.

I step forward, grab her hips, and wrap her legs around me. With one thrust, I'm inside of her.

We both pause, looking at one another as I stretch her, sliding home until I'm filling her and she's everywhere around me.

"Take me right here," she gasps. Her fingers drag through my hair. "Just like this. Please."

I drive into her and she rocks against me. Back and forth as we find our rhythm. It's as natural as breathing, and every bit as vital.

I plant a hand on her chest and push her flat on her back on the desk. Then I pluck her wrist from her side and lay it on her sex. "Don't stop touching yourself."

Her legs hook over my shoulders, and I pulse into her as she circles her clit. Within seconds, her back is arched and her breath is coming in gasping hitches.

"Nikolai," she gasps. "Can I? I need to… please."

"Come for me."

Instantly, I feel her body clamp down. The orgasm works through her and then through me. It takes me tumbling over the edge. I pump everything into her, stroking my hands down her legs as they quiver.

When it's finally receding, Belle reaches out and grabs my hand. She twines her fingers through mine, eyes still closed. "Please don't send me away, Nikolai."

I'm still inside of her, and I already want more. This whole plan was foolish from the start. How could I send her half a world away?

I can't. I won't.

I lean over and press a kiss onto her lips. "So be it. You're not going anywhere. You're staying right here with me."

23

BELLE

My body is humming. Just the memory of Nikolai's touch, the way his voice settled over me like silk as he filled me, is intoxicating. The thought sends an orgasm aftershock through me, and I want to charge back into his office and chain myself to the desk so we can go for a repeat performance or three.

But he has work to do. And so do I.

Back in my room, I grab a pad of paper and a pen and settle into an armchair to write Elise a letter.

I want to give her space to process everything. I made the decision to lie to her about Howard, and I have to own that. But I also want her to have the entire story. I want her to understand why I did what I did.

I write one draft of the letter from start to finish and then rip it out of the binder and toss it in the trash can next to the bed. Halfway through the second, I tear it out, too.

Everything I say sounds like an excuse. Like I'm trying to pass blame to Mom or Howard or anyone but myself.

Finally, after countless pieces of crumpled paper, I settle on the simple truth:

I love you more than anything in this world, Elise, but I didn't know how to express it. I'm sorry I failed and hurt you. I'll always try to do better.

It's short and to the point, but after five rereads, I can't find anything to cut or add. I rip it carefully out of the notebook and fold it into neat thirds. Then I hop out of bed and pad into the hallway.

Elise's door is open, but there's no answer when I knock. I peek around the doorframe and the room is empty, so I head towards the kitchen. Nikolai's snack cabinet has become a watering hole for the two of us. Maybe a neutral meeting place will be for the best, anyway.

But when I get to the kitchen, it's empty, as well.

"Where is she?" I mutter to myself.

I pull out my phone and check for any missed messages, but there's nothing. My finger is hovering over Elise's name in my contacts list when I hear a peal of rough laughter. I turn to the sound and notice the patio door is cracked open.

I creep towards the door, poking my head around the corner to look through the glass pane in the door. But I don't see Elise or Nikolai.

Instead, there are three large men hulking around the empty patio furniture.

Yuri is standing further back, glancing furtively towards the side of the house like he's making sure no one is watching them. The other two men are decked out in security gear. I recognize one of them from the guard shack by the gate, but not the other.

The one I recognize shakes his head. "All this shit might be funny if it wasn't our livelihood on the line. Who the fuck is gonna pay us when the don gets himself killed for this bitch?"

I freeze, my feet glued to the spot. I couldn't move right now even if I wanted to.

"He'll survive, Makar," the unknown man says. "So far, it's just everyone else he lets die for her."

"RIP Arslan." The one named Makar kisses his fingers and points to the sky.

Yuri works his jaw like he wants to respond, but isn't sure what to say. Finally, he leans forward. "You know Arslan was always throwing himself into trouble. Nikolai tried to save him and almost died in the process."

"And Arslan had plenty of trouble to throw himself into once the accountant showed up," Makar retorts. "She was probably a plant for the Greeks from the start. Send a tight little ass in as a distraction while they pull the rug out from under us."

The other man nods in agreement. "Nikolai should've fucked Bridget if he wanted someone outside the Bratva. She's hot and easy."

Jealousy flares hot and bright in my chest. Before I can really consider what I'm doing, I pull the door open and step onto the patio.

The three men turn, momentarily dumbstruck. Yuri looks horrified.

"Evening, gentlemen." I give them all a warm smile. "Taking a break?"

"Shift change, actually," Makar grumbles. "We were just leaving."

He starts to turn, but I shake my head. "Stay. Hang out. You all deserve the break."

"Don't need it," the other man grunts. "We'll work as long as the Bratva needs us to."

Makar nods. "And anyway, we usually wait for an invite from the don before we linger. It's his house, after all. Not for the riff-raff."

If the first comment was an obvious jab, the second hits me right in the chest.

This isn't your house. You don't belong here. We don't trust you.

I give up my half-baked plan to kill them with kindness and settle on blunt honesty. It's how I'm hoping to handle things with Elise, so might as well test it out here.

"Listen, I know things are tense right now with—"

"Your friends," Makar adds under his breath.

I narrow my eyes. "Xena tried to kill me. She tried to kill Nikolai. She is not my friend."

He shrugs. "That remains to be seen."

"No, it doesn't. It has been seen. I'm not working with her."

Makar backs away with his hands raised. "So you say."

I turn to Yuri in hopes of finding an ally out here. "You trust me, don't you? Nikolai wouldn't be working so closely with you if he didn't."

Yuri grimaces, and I'm sure I've said the wrong thing, though I don't know why. I apparently know even less about how a Bratva works than I thought.

"Because you have him wrapped around your finger?" Makar snarls. "He probably doesn't make a decision without checking with you first."

What he's saying is so ridiculous that I laugh, but that only cements my villainy even more in his mind.

Makar's top lip curls in disgust. "I can't wait until Nikolai figures out you're a spy, and I get to watch you die a traitor's death. Gutted like a fucking pig."

I'm so stunned by the hatred in his voice that I can't even formulate a response. I gawk dumbly as he turns around and stomps around the corner of the house, his friend following him.

Yuri shakes his head before he leaves, too. "Maybe you should keep your head down, Belle," he says on his way out. "Keep quiet."

My cheeks are burning with shame. "Maybe Nikolai is right. Maybe I should flee the country." I sigh and head back into the house.

I've almost forgotten about the letter for Elise still clenched in my hand until I step into the kitchen and see her standing in front of the fridge, a distant, dreamy smile on her face.

How can she be smiling right now? I'm her big sister. I'm supposed to want my sister to be happy. But not now. Not right after we just had the biggest fight we ever had. She's supposed to be as miserable as I am.

God, I'm a selfish bitch.

"Hey. I've been looking for you."

She jumps and spins around. Her smile dries up when she sees me. "Why?"

"Because I wanted to give you this." I hold up the letter. "There's a lot I still wanted to say."

"You already said enough, don't you think?" she snaps.

And just like that, my hopes of her cooling off since we last talked wither and die.

"Well, I guess you can read this and decide for yourself." I extend it to her, but she doesn't make any move to take it from me. "Come on, Elise. It's just a letter. You don't have to read it now if you don't want to, but I'd like you to—"

"I talked to Howard," she blurts.

"Who?" I ask on instinct even though I obviously know exactly who he is. It just seems so impossible I can't compute.

Elise chews on her lip. "My dad. We talked."

"How?" I grit out.

"On the phone. It's how you reach people these days when you want to talk."

I shake my head. "He shouldn't have reached out to you. It was—that's so inappropriate. I told him I would decide if—"

"It's not your decision," Elise interrupts. "It was mine. I should have had this choice from the time I was a little kid. None of this should have ever been your choice."

I swallow down my words. "I know. You're right. But… you don't actually know him, Elise. We don't know what his motivations are."

"The only reason I don't know him is because of *you*." The acid in her voice is undeniable.

I groan. "I know, okay? God, I know! I fucked up. You've made that clear."

"Apparently not, since I have to keep reminding you!" Her hair is twisted back in a large bun on the top of her head and it bobs around as she talks.

"I know you're mad at me, but that doesn't change the fact that Howard is essentially a stranger to us. You can't talk to him without me knowing about it."

"I'll talk to my dad if I want to. I don't need your permission."

I snort. "You've known this man for half an hour and now, you trust him more than me?"

"I trusted you before and you lied to me, so I won't make that mistake again."

"That's a popular feeling today." I drag a hand down my face. "Where did you even get his number?"

"I found his business card in your pocket." She pats her leg and I realize she's wearing my jeans.

So much for us not acting like sisters. Ever since she realized we wear the same size, half my clothes end up in her room.

"What did he say?"

Elise crosses her arms. "It's private. Father-daughter stuff."

For the second time today, the green envy monster inside of me roars. But this jealousy is different than thinking Nikolai might be attracted to Bridget. This one is primal and fierce.

Howard Schaffner will not steal my baby sister from me.

"As long as I'm taking care of you, nothing is private," I hiss. "We don't know that man, Elise. If you want to see him or speak to him, you'll talk to me about it first."

"That's not fair!"

"It doesn't need to be fair. It needs to be safe."

"Why not just lock me up then?" she yells. "If I can't be trusted to think for myself, you might as well not let me outside. Chain me up like a dog."

I roll my eyes. "Don't be dramatic. You didn't even know this man existed yesterday, so having supervised calls with him won't be the end of the world."

Elise's face flushes red. Her lips pucker as anger builds behind them. I can practically see the words gathering at the end of her tongue, ready to let loose.

Then, all at once, tears roll down her cheeks. "You're such a bitch, Belle."

And she's gone.

The moment I'm alone, everything crashes down on me at once. I stumble back against the kitchen counter, overwhelmed by the weight of it. I grip the cold granite for stability.

"She hates me," I murmur.

I'm not handling anything right. I don't know how to take care of Elise. I can't be her sister or her mom or whatever weird mix of the two I was trying to be. I don't even know what I am to her anymore. I don't know what I'm supposed to do.

And now, I'm about to be an actual mom to another human.

I press a hand to my stomach. A whimper forces its way out of my lungs.

Suddenly, it's hard to breathe. I try to inhale, but my lungs don't expand. The panic is an iron band around my chest that I can't release.

How am I going to raise a baby and take care of Elise? How am I going to prove to Nikolai's men that I'm trustworthy? How am I going to prove to Nikolai that I'm not a distraction? How, how, how—

"Belle?"

The sound of his voice forces my eyes up. Nikolai is standing in the doorway, silhouetted by the light from behind.

"I can't—I can't do this," I croak. "I'm pregnant. And Elise… And the Greeks and loyalty and… Any of this. I'm fucking everything up and—"

His arms are around me before I realize he has even crossed the room. His lips brush across my ear. "Breathe, Belle. In and out."

For some reason, my body listens to Nikolai. The tension in my chest eases enough for me to take a full breath. Then I force it out between tight lips.

"What happened?" His strong hands caress my arms, massaging feeling back into my limbs.

I shake my head. I can't get the words out. But it doesn't matter now anyway.

Nikolai is here.

That thought alone is what carries me through. It's my anchor in this storm.

Because I've never had anyone to depend on. It's always been *me* making the calls, *me* muddling through, *me* making a mess of everything. But now, there's Nikolai.

I don't know when or how, but he became the person I can trust. And right now, that's the only thing I have to cling to.

So I squeeze him tighter and decide to never let him go.

24

NIKOLAI

The elevators open to the Zhukova Incorporated lobby, and I immediately regret coming into the office today.

Bridget is looking at me, her teeth worrying at her lower lip. But I'm focused on the man sitting in the waiting area behind her.

"What the fuck are you doing here, Howard?"

He stands up, flatting the lapels of his jacket. "I needed to see you. Can we speak in your office?"

"Instead of that, how about you get out of this city before I bury you beneath it?"

Howard glances at Bridget, expecting her to show some kind of reaction. But Bridget is a consummate professional. She's seen me do a whole lot more than make threats.

He takes a deep breath and straightens to his full height. "I'm not here to be disrespectful, Nikolai, but… well, I've waited too long and come too far to leave now. I want to meet my child."

I snarl as I sweep past him down the hallway towards my office. I don't invite him to come along, but he does. It doesn't piss me off as much as it should.

I can't help but respect his dedication. Most men would have slipped away the moment I raised my voice. But the fact Howard stood his ground shows some kind of loyalty to his daughter.

I, of all people, can admire a father who cares.

"Your child isn't in my office, so I'm not sure what exactly you hope to gain from coming here."

"I hope to gain your trust."

I unlock my office door and push it open. Howard followed me down the hallway, but he hesitates at the threshold. With a sigh, I wave him in and point to the chair across from my desk.

"Showing up at my office unannounced is a bad way to do that. So far, all you've done is make my pregnant fiancée cry and tear open a rift between the women living under my roof."

His mouth turns down in a frown. "Are they fighting? I told Elise to take it easy on Belle. None of this is her fault."

"Well, congratulations, then. You've earned your first parenting badge," I tell him. "The 'My Daughter Doesn't Listen to a Damn Word I Say' patch. Because Elise is blaming Belle for everything."

He curses. "When Elise called me, I thought Belle must have given her my number."

I shake my head. "Elise stole it and called you behind her sister's back."

He pushes a hand through his red hair. "Well, fuck it all. She hates me, I'm sure."

"Elise? No. If she did, you'd know it. She's not one to hide her emotions."

"I meant Belle." Howard says her name with concern etched on his face. "I thought maybe we were getting somewhere, but if Elise is disobeying her to talk to me, that can't be good."

The man is irritatingly hard to dislike. There's something almost noble about him. His persistence, his stubbornness.

Arslan was the same way.

The thought of my best friend hurts like a knife in the gut. I set it aside and focus on the sorry bastard in front of me.

"I'm not sure Belle is capable of truly hating anyone. She tries—she tried to hate me, actually—but her heart is too soft. Still, you'll need a lot more than 'not hate' if you want to get close to her and Elise."

"Like what? I'll do anything," he says.

"You abandoned them. Belle may act like she's only concerned about Elise, but you hurt her, too. You gave Belle hope and then you snatched it away. So you'll have to figure out how to undo that."

Howard's eyes shift towards the ceiling. He's actually sitting in front of me trying to come up with a plan. I'm about to tell him to take this kumbaya brainstorming session somewhere else when he snaps his fingers. "I have an idea."

I frown. "What?"

"A drawing. Something Belle gave me a long time ago. I'll have to find it. I think I know where it is."

"Best of luck to you then."

I stare at him for a few seconds, waiting for him to note the intentional silence in the room. When he doesn't, I sigh. "Now, get the fuck out of my office, Howard."

His attention snaps to me and then he jumps up. "Right. Sorry. Yeah."

He sees himself out, waving twice before finally closing the door behind him.

⁂

When I get back to the house, it's late. My eyes are burned-out husks in their sockets from staring too long at the computer screen. It turns out billion-dollar businesses aren't easy to run, even when they're just covers for the real work that takes place in the shadows.

In the kitchen, I find the remains of the lasagna the chef must have dropped off in the sink along with two dirty plates, but no one is around.

I search through the house and find Elise's door shut with the light on. Belle's is empty. I take my phone out of my pocket to call her before a thought strikes me.

I turn around and walk straight to my room. Before I even open the door, I know she's going to be lying in my bed with a certainty I can't explain.

Belle smiles when I walk in. She is tucked underneath my comforter in a tank top, her hair falling around her shoulders in loose waves. A book rests open in her lap.

"I hope this is okay," she says. "I didn't want to be in my room alone."

I push the door closed and walk towards the bed. "So you decided to be in my room alone?"

"Yeah. I guess I feel a little less lonely in here."

I drop onto the bed and drag her body against mine with one hand looped around her middle. "And what about now? Do you feel alone now?"

She laughs against my chest. "Definitely not."

I kiss the top of her head and lean back against the pillows. "Howard came to my office today."

She stiffens and pulls away. In an instant, she's cross-legged and upright. "What did he want?"

"To talk to me."

"About what?"

"You."

She frowns. "Me? That doesn't make any sense."

"Doesn't it? You're Elise's gatekeeper. He has to go through you to get to her."

"Yeah, right," she snorts. "Elise has his number. I know she's texting with him. He doesn't need to woo me anymore."

"Well, he thought you gave Elise permission to call him. He had no idea she did it on her own."

"And why should he care?" she asks. "He got what he wants. Elise wants to talk to him. She wants to get to know him. So fuck what I want, right?"

I twirl my finger in her silky hair. It smells like my shampoo. It's a strangely intoxicating observation. "Elise might feel that way, but Howard doesn't. He cares what you think. How you feel."

She narrows her eyes at me. "Are you still defending him?"

"Are you still doubting whose side I'm on?" I tug on the strand of hair I'm holding. "I'm Team Belle. Do I need a shirt or something? Should I tattoo your name on my neck?"

A small smile lifts the corner of her mouth. "You've got enough tattoos as it is, and a shirt is a little ostentatious, I think. Your men already think I'm crazy. Labeling you might be a bad idea."

"True. So how about some artwork?" I suggest.

"You mean the drawings you have framed in your office?"

I arch an eyebrow. "You noticed?"

Her cheeks flush. "The second I walked into the room. I didn't expect a Bratva leader to be so sentimental."

"I'm not the only one."

Belle's face goes pale. "What are you talking about?"

"Howard kept one from the last time he saw you. A drawing."

"From the last time—like when I was a kid?"

I shrug. "Something like that."

Belle chews on her lower lip. Her eyes are unfocused, lost in memories. "After he left, my mom… well, she did what she does best. She convinced me that I was worthless." Her voice drops into a convincing imitation of her mother. *"Why are you crying? Howard didn't care about me, so he damn sure didn't care about you. You're another man's brat.'"*

The words make me clench my fists. If I could beat a memory to death, I would. I'd bludgeon this one and bury its body so Belle never has to relive it.

She sighs mournfully. "I wish I could blame her for all of it, but honestly, it hurt when he left. A lot. I didn't need my mom's encouragement to hate him; I figured that out all on my own. It's why I'm scared."

"Scared of what?"

"Of being a mom," she whispers. "I just worry… I worry about everything. But mostly, that I'll be like her."

"The fact you're worried you'll be like your mom is the reason why I know you'll be nothing like her."

Belle's eyes glisten with emotion. She looks down at me, and I can see all the way to the core of her. To the aching, tender part she keeps tucked away.

"Really?"

I nod. "I've told you, Belle, I'm not going to lie to make you feel better. You'll always get the truth from me. Always."

She lies down next to me, her head propped on her hand, and smiles. "Me, too."

I kiss her forehead, and she closes her eyes as if absorbing my kiss. Then, all at once, she rolls over so her back is to me. "I want to cuddle with you."

She grabs my arm and belts it around her waist. Then she presses her body back against me, tucking her soft curves into my growing hard parts, and sighs contentedly.

In a few minutes, I'll work my hand down her body and stroke her until she's begging for me. I'll take her from behind and empty everything into this moment with her.

But right now, I let her lean into me and feel safe. Because knowing that I can make this woman good and truly happy is enough.

I press my lips to her ear and whisper one word.

"Done."

25

BELLE

"That's for me?" I ask the delivery man, who's waiting impatiently for me to take the huge, flat box from him. "Are you sure?"

"Are you Belle Dowan?" he asks. "Yeah? Then it's for you. Can I leave it here?"

"Sure, Yeah. But… you're sure this is for me?"

He sighs and holds out his scanner and a pen. "Listen, I get paid to deliver the packages. All I know is that one has your name and address on it. Please sign so I can leave."

I sign my name and close the door behind the man. I'm about to call Nikolai at the office and ask what it is when I see the name listed as the sender. *Beatrice Aguilar.* It hits me all at once.

"The dress," I breathe.

With everything else going on, I honestly forgot Nikolai and I are getting married.

A couple days ago, I would have chucked the box in Nikolai's room and left it for him to deal with. He's the one who is enforcing this marriage. He's the one who wanted me to get fitted for this dress. Let him deal with it, right?

But things have changed.

I carry the box back to my room immediately, rip the lid off, and lay the dress out on my bed. I want to try it on, but I want to do it right. I change out of my black bra and panties and into a lacy white thong. The dress has a built-in bra, so there's no need for that. And even if it didn't, the bodice is all sheer panels and beautifully intricate lace. I wouldn't want to ruin the design with any visible undergarments.

I should probably ask for help with the dress, but I do my best splaying it out on the floor and stepping into it. Slowly, I slide the material up over my body.

I have to say, Matteo may have been inappropriately flirty, but the man knows what he's doing. The fit is perfect.

The hem is a little long since I'm barefoot, so I grab my white heels out of the closet and try them on to make sure the length will work okay. The last thing I need is to trip over my dress as I'm walking down the aisle.

I buckle the strappy shoes on and then walk slowly towards the full-length mirror. As I move closer and closer to my reflection, I bring my hands up as if holding a bouquet. And my chest tightens.

The dress looks beautiful, yes. And I feel great in it, sure.

But that isn't causing the burble of emotions inside of me. No, it's the fact that, in just a couple days, I'll be walking towards Nikolai just like this.

And he'll become my husband.

A smile I can't contain spreads across my face. I look *radiant*. I never knew it was possible to see "happy" until this moment. But I can see it in every single inch of me. Glowing. Shimmering.

"I want this," I whisper aloud, letting the words shiver over my skin. "I want to marry Nikolai Zhukova."

I'm still riding the high of my admission and admiring the delicate lace work of the dress when I hear footsteps moving down the hall.

Elise has been scurrying around the mansion like a mouse the last couple days, only creeping out at night for sustenance. Otherwise, she stays locked away in her room and refuses to talk to me. The heavy footfalls probably don't belong to her.

Then the door to the room next to mine opens, and I panic.

Nikolai. No one else—aside from me—would go into his room. They wouldn't dare. But he's supposed to be at work. Nikolai is scheduled to be in the office all day today. He can't be here.

"Belle?" Nikolai calls.

"Shit, shit, shit." I hurry back towards the closet, fumbling with the few buttons I managed to close on the back of the dress.

Nikolai was there when the dress was getting fitted, but it all feels different now. I don't want him to see me in it until our wedding day. I want it to be special. Call me stupid, call me old-fashioned, I don't care. So much of me is exposed to him at all times. He can see everything there is to see. So this—this one little thing, this one silly thing…

I want to keep it to myself until it's time.

"Belle?" he calls again, his voice closer. "Where are you?"

"Don't come in!" I yelp.

The dress slipped on like a dream, but now that I'm trying to take it off, it's like I'm in a straitjacket. I can barely get the damned thing down over my hips, and my heels keep getting caught in the layers of material.

I hear him just outside the door. "What are you doing?"

"Don't come in!" I yell again. "I'm trying on my dress."

I reach around and undo another button, which does the trick. The dress falls into a puddle at my feet just as my bedroom door opens.

"When did the wedding dress get—" Nikolai's voice cuts off. When I turn to face him, I instantly understand why.

His eyes are black and moving over every inch of me. Like he's trying to memorize this moment to come back to later.

There's not a whole lot to memorize, though. Without the dress, I'm standing in front of him in a lacy thong and high heels. Nothing else.

"That's not a wedding dress," he rasps. The faintest ghost of a laugh shimmers on the edge of his voice.

I cross my arms over my chest, trying and failing to give myself some coverage. "I took it off. You're not supposed to see me before the wedding."

"Too late for that. I'm seeing all of you right now."

My skin tingles under his watchful gaze. I've never been more aware of my body. "You're not supposed to see me in the dress. I didn't think you'd be home for a few more hours. I thought I was alone."

He's still in the doorway, covered from neck to ankles in a black button-down shirt and dark gray trousers. We make a compelling couple—him huge and clothed in darkness next to my pale, skinny near-nakedness.

He doesn't say anything. I step slowly out of the center of the dress so I don't trip on my heels. "Let me put the dress away, and we can—"

There's a low groan behind me. "Belle. Fuck."

I'm picking my dress up off the floor, confused about what Nikolai's problem is, until I realize… I'm bent over. In a thong. In high heels.

I know exactly what his problem is: me.

"Oh I'm—I'm sorry," I fumble, scrambling to make myself more decent. "I didn't mean—"

But Nikolai's hands are on me before I can get the words out. He grips my waist and pins me flat against the wall. "You didn't mean to drive me absolutely fucking insane?"

His lips are on my neck and my collarbones. His hands rove over my curves, palming my breasts and grabbing handfuls of my exposed ass. He's everywhere all at once, and all I can do is hold on and pray I survive the beautiful storm that's coming.

"I didn't mean to be naked. I just didn't want you to see me in the dress. I told you not to come in."

"I've never been more grateful I didn't listen." He runs his fingers along the inside of the band of my panties. "Are you going to wear these for the wedding?"

I shrug. "I was debating."

"Between?"

"These," I say, wriggling my hips against him, "or nothing."

He groans again and brings our bodies flush together. I can feel the hard length of him through his pants. "Let's test out both."

In an instant, my thong is around my ankles. Nikolai steps back to admire me. Normally, I'd be self-conscious, but the heat in his gaze burns everything else away. I step out of the panties and kick them to the side with the toe of my heels.

"With them, without them… you can't go wrong." The man actually licks his lips as he moves towards me. "You look incredible either way. But I am a fan of the shoes."

"Is that right?" At this height, I can hook my arms around his neck without even moving onto my tiptoes. I'm a fan of the shoes, too.

He hums his assent as we kiss. His tongue swirls against mine and he nips at my lower lip. "Big fan. In fact, I don't think you should ever take them off."

I laugh. "That might make it a little hard to walk."

Nikolai scoops me up and carries me towards the bed. "You won't need to walk. I plan on spending a lot of time horizontal."

"And do I get a say in any of—oh God." Somewhere around the fourth word, Nikolai drops to his knees between my legs and presses a kiss to my throbbing center. I lose all power of speech. All I can do is moan and babble incoherently.

He opens me with his tongue and sucks at me with his full lips. His hands find my ankles and hook my heels over his shoulders.

If I'm going to be treated like this, I really will wear these shoes all the time.

Nikolai dives in. He flicks and strokes and sucks until I'm rolling my hips against his mouth, wild and desperate. Then he slides two fingers inside of me.

Immediately, it tosses me over the edge. The orgasm rages through me, hitting new highs as Nikolai curls his fingers inside of me to the pulse of my pleasure.

I'm still gasping and crying out when he slides out of me and crawls over my body, kissing his way across my skin. "That was so hot."

"Hot for you?" I gasp. "Think about me. I'm pretty sure I caught on fire."

I twine my fingers through his hair and bring his mouth to mine. His lips are slick with me, but I don't mind. It feels like claiming him. That thought sends a new urge through me.

"Take your clothes off," I beg, unbuttoning his pants with clumsy fingers as he peels off his shirt.

His body is forever a distraction to me. It's impossible to see Nikolai shirtless without wanting to rub across his washboard abs like very dirty laundry and taste every inch of his golden skin.

But today, my interests are singular. I slide his boxers down and free his impressive erection.

"Down." I'm not capable of more words as I push him back onto the bed and straddle him. I slide up his strong legs until he's pressed flush against the length of me, but I don't take him in. Instead, I slide myself up and then down the underside of him, covering him with the orgasm he just gave me.

"Tease," he snarls deliciously. His fingers are white where they grip my knees.

I smile and cup my hands around the other side of him so he's wrapped in me on all sides, but still not *in* me. Again and again I stroke him this way, working his length with my pussy and my palms until he's panting.

"Belle," he growls, "you're killing me."

I'm killing me, too. The anticipation of him—the way he'll fill me—is almost too much to bear. My body is quivering with need.

"Good. It's a punishment."

I slide to the tip of him and tease him between my lips, toying with the idea of taking him inside of me before I drop back to his base. He snarls again, breathless. "For what?"

"For coming in my room when I told you not to. For seeing me in my dress before our wedding. For making me want you so badly."

His forehead creases as I stroke him again. I can practically see him gathering his thoughts through the haze of lust.

"In case you've forgotten, this is my house, *kiska*. I can go wherever I like in my house, including your room. Second, you shouldn't have even been in here," he says, his fingers digging into my skin. "You should have been in my room. That's where I went first to find you."

I try and fail to bite back a grin. "Is that what you think?"

"It's what I know," he breathes. "Third, you weren't wearing the wedding dress when I came into the room, which is why we ended up in this situation."

"And lastly?" I press. "What's your excuse for making me want you so bad?"

He smiles cruelly. "I don't have an excuse for that. I do have a solution."

Before I can ask what that solution is, Nikolai grabs my hips and drives himself into me.

I bite my lip to stop from screaming. It's only my palms planted against his chest that keep me from collapsing on top of him. When the initial shock passes, I start rolling my hips, riding the new fullness.

But Nikolai is done going slow. He palms my ass and grinds our bodies together until I've forgotten any attempt I was making at claiming control or teasing.

I want him. All of him. Now.

"Be careful what you wish for," Nikolai growls. That's when I realize I was talking out loud.

Still inside of me, he rolls us over so I'm on my back and pins my arms above my head. He slams into me again and again, each thrust driving me further up the bed until we're crashing against the headboard.

His body is glistening with sweat, and I'm clawing at his chest and the sheets, searching for something stable to cling to because the Earth's gravity no longer seems to be holding me down.

Then, just as I feel the rumblings of a second orgasm, Nikolai flips me again. He presses my palms against the headboard, tilts my hips back to him, and enters me from behind.

"This is the hottest moment of my life," I gasp.

Never one to settle, Nikolai works his hand around my hip and slides between my legs. His finger circles my clit, and I nearly jolt off the bed. I arch my neck back, and he grabs my hair with his other hand, coaxing me back even further.

"Belle," he grits out. I can hear the restraint in his voice and feel the tightening in his body.

I shake my head. "I don't want this to end."

In response, his finger circles faster. He flicks and pinches until I'm almost crying with the effort to hold back.

"Come, dammit," he growls. He shifts his hips higher, entering me at a new angle.

Just like that, I'm gone.

This orgasm isn't a wave—it's a tsunami. I'm lost in the pleasure, dizzy and breathless as I cry his name and dig my fingernails into the wooden headboard.

"Fuck," Nikolai grunts, pulsing into me, his warmth spreading so he's everywhere, inside and out, above and below.

When we're both done, he maneuvers us carefully onto the mattress so my head is pillowed on his chest. I can hear his heart pounding in his chest, and I press my ear there as the beat slows back to normal.

"I know I'm not supposed to see the dress before the wedding," he muses after a silent minute or two. "But what are the rules on fucking you within an inch of both of our lives before the wedding?"

"Generally frowned upon," I chuckle.

He kisses the top of my head. "My favorite kind of thing to do."

We lie like that for a few minutes before I let myself explore him the way I resisted before. My fingers play over his pecs and the ridges of his abs. I stroke his body lower and lower until my finger circles the curls around his shaft.

"No, Belle," he growls. "You'll actually kill me. Plus, I just came back for a quick lunch. And that was… forty-five minutes ago."

I turn my face and kiss his ribs. "You're the CEO. That has to come with perks."

"I get whatever the hell perks I want. The problem isn't that I can't do this," he says, stilling my hand just before I can wrap it around his twitching cock. "It's that once we start, I'll never be able to stop."

I give him a devilish grin. "Don't make promises you aren't prepared to keep."

I see the decision forming behind his eyes. I'm anxious for permission to touch him. Then the pile of his clothes on the floor starts to ring.

He gives me an apologetic smile, plants a quick kiss on my forehead, and slides out of bed. "Probably best for the hundreds of people I employ that we don't stay in this bed until we fuck each other to death."

"Boo," I pout. "Party pooper."

Nikolai fishes his phone out of his pants and answers it. His voice is casual, but the moment the other person starts talking, he goes rigid. "Where? Okay. I'm on my way."

"What is it?" I ask as soon as he hangs up.

"Bratva business. Emergency."

I watch as he pulls on his pants and shirt, covering up the body I was just wrapped around. "Is everything okay?"

"It will be." He shoves his phone in his pocket and then stands back. His eyes trail over the bed and over me. I'm still lying on top of the comforter, one leg curled up, my arm draped over my stomach. He lets out a ragged breath. "I want you in this exact position and in this exact outfit in my bed when I get home tonight."

A blush creeps over my skin. "Yes, sir."

"Fuck, Belle. You are—" He shakes his head. "I have to go. I'll call when I'm on my way."

Before either of us can tempt the other back into bed, he rushes out of the room.

I lounge on the covers for a few minutes, trailing my hand over my sensitive skin and luxuriating in the memory of being with him. Only when I'm positive my trembling legs won't collapse under me do I get up and tug on real clothes.

I've just pulled on jeans and a t-shirt when there's a loud, pounding knock on the front door. I have no clue who it could be until I step on the keys that must have fallen out of Nikolai's pants. I scoop them up and jog down the hallway and through the entryway.

"Did you forget your keys on purpose?" I yell at the dark shape just on the other side of the fogged glass. "You don't need to create an excuse to come back to my room. You're always welcome to fuck me wherever—"

I pull the door open and the words die on my lips. Nikolai isn't standing on the doorstep.

Instead, it's three police officers standing in a triangle formation.

"Belle Dowan?" the first asks. He's a bulky man with a deep frown.

I nod slowly and fearfully. "Yeah, that's me. I'm Belle. How can I—"

He grabs my wrist and yanks me outside. "Belle Dowan, you are being charged with the kidnapping of Elise Dowan. You have the right to remain silent. Anything you say can and will be used against you—"

"What? What are you talking—" I try to pull my arm back, but his grip is like iron. The other two officers step up to assist while the first officer continues reading my Miranda rights.

"What is going on?" I scream. "You can't—I didn't kidnap anyone! What is—"

I look back into the house and see Elise standing frozen in the middle of the entryway. The female police officer notices her, too.

"Elise Dowan?" she calls.

Elise nods dumbly, her eyes flicking from me to the officers and back again.

The officer steps into Nikolai's house and grabs Elise. "You aren't in trouble, honey. You're safe now."

She was already safe, I think. My voice won't work anymore. *Don't fucking touch her.*

But I don't want to scare Elise. I don't want her to see me fighting and flailing with the police.

So I let myself be dragged to the police car. I watch helplessly from the backseat as Elise is loaded into a separate vehicle.

Then we are both hauled away to God-knows-where.

26

NIKOLAI

Smoke pours from the parking garage of the Zinc Hotel, spiraling up into the clear blue sky. Worried guests and staff whisper and pace around the sidewalk. No one knows where to go or what to do.

"When did this happen?" I growl to no one in particular.

"I called as soon as I heard about the *fire*," Yuri says. He doesn't actually place air quotes around the word, but I hear it in his intonation. He knows as well as I do that this was no accident. "The security guard saw a few dudes with neck tattoos cruising around the lower level of the garage on their bikes a half hour before the fire. He managed to tell that to the cops before he died from his wounds. Two gunshots to the chest."

I clench my jaw. "Fucking Battiatos."

Yuri nods. "The cameras were all conveniently down, but my guess is the guard was in the wrong place at the wrong time. This seems more like a warning than anything else."

I nod in agreement. I'd say it was a distraction, except I know for a fact Belle is safe. I've tripled security measures around the house, and my guards know better than to let anyone through the gates when I'm not there.

Still, I decide to call her as soon as I have a free minute. Just to be sure.

"Has anyone talked to the firefighters?" I ask.

At that moment, Makar joins our group. "I just did. They're going to blame an emergency light in the parking garage for the fire. A stray bullet hit the outlet and it sparked. Something like that. But there's not much that can be done about the murder."

"This'll be great for business."

I can practically hear Makar's teeth grinding together. "I doubt Vadim cares about the ding this will put on the bottom line. They fucking murdered him, Nikolai. We need to retaliate."

"Retaliate against who? Where?" I ask. "I want revenge for Vadim and Arslan and every man we've lost as much as you do, but going into this blind will only cost us more men. We need to be prepared."

"Maybe we would be if—"

I'm in his face in an instant, towering over him. "If what?"

I silently dare him to finish his sentence, but he doesn't. He shakes his head and steps away, hands raised. "Nothing."

But we both know exactly what he was going to say.

If you weren't so distracted by Belle.

"Nikolai is right. We need more information," Yuri chimes in. "We could reach out to some contacts. See if anyone knows what the Simatous and Battiatos are up to."

"Already done."

"Christo is probably on it," Makar grumbles. He glances at me nervously and shrugs. "Yuri told us he's part of the Bratva now."

Yuri shakes his head. "I did not say that. I said—"

"He isn't in the Bratva. He's a contact," I interrupt. "But even if he was, it would have been my decision. And you would've sucked it up and fucking dealt with it."

"Bloodlines aren't worth shit anymore, I guess."

My fists tighten painfully. "Nothing matters more than loyalty. And that seems to be running thin these days."

Makar's beady eyes sharpen. "Christo should know. He turned his back on his family to work for you."

"And right now, he might be the only person able to tell us what the hell Xena is up to and offer some valuable information. That way, when we do actually retaliate, you don't end up among the dead."

Makar takes the implied threat just as I intended and shuts the fuck up.

Satisfied, I turn back to Yuri. "If there's any salvageable footage from the security cameras, I want it as soon as possible."

"I already had the equipment sent over to the tech guys. If there's anything, I'll send it to you straight away."

Yuri is oddly on top of things today. Probably because the last time we spoke, I threatened his life. Death threats have a way of inspiring hard work.

"If Vadim was in the wrong place at the wrong time, we need to figure out what the Battiato soldiers were doing here and what they have planned next. Then—and *only* then," I say, turning pointedly to Makar, "will we execute our plan and anyone who stands in our way. Is that clear?"

They're both nodding when my phone rings. "What is it now?" I pull it out with a grimace. "Hello?"

"Nikolai, it's Kostya… from the security—"

"I know who you are, man." I shake my head. The kid is relatively new. I added him when I beefed up security at the main house. Even though I hired him personally, he can't seem to stop introducing himself. "What is it?"

"The, uh… the police came to the house."

I thought I got the detectives looking into me as a suspect in Giorgos' murder off my back, but apparently not. I'll have to pay them another visit, it seems. "Did you tell them I wasn't home?"

"I did," he says, his voice taking on a weird, strangled quality. "But they… they weren't here to see you."

"Then what the fuck did they want?"

There's a pregnant pause as I wait for Kostya to spit it out. Finally, he sighs. "They took Belle."

My heart pounds hard against my ribs. It feels like every beat shakes my whole skeleton from head to toe. "What do you mean, 'They took Belle'?" I growl finally.

Yuri and Makar are watching me, but I barely register them. My entire being is focused on this call. Everything else is white noise.

"They came to arrest her. I saw them drive her and Elise away just a couple minutes ago."

I flash a wave at Yuri and Makar and start running towards my car. Could this be an undercover operation? Mafia members in police uniforms? It sounds a little espionage thriller-y, even for me, but it's possible. Maybe this fire and murder were yet another distraction.

"And why didn't you stop them? Your job is to protect Belle. It's the entire goddamn reason I hired you."

"I tried to delay them so I could call you first," he says. "But they had an arrest warrant. Then you weren't answering when I did call. This is the first time my message went through."

I stopped answering calls during the initial flurry of notifications about the fire at Zinc. Everyone from the general manager to the investors to the security team were calling me, and I was already on my way. I ignored them. Then I didn't have service in the parking garage.

"When did they take her?"

"Just a couple minutes after you left."

I check the time and curse under my breath. "That was almost an hour ago."

"There was nothing I could do," he says pitifully.

"You could have fucking killed them."

Kostya doesn't respond, and I don't have time for his excuses anyway. I hang up and jump into the driver's seat.

I'm going to get my woman.

~

The female officer working behind the glass is in tears by the time Officer Sweeney comes through the locked door to my left to see what's happening.

"Sir, I don't have the authority to release anyone," she whines to me for the dozenth time since I stormed in here spewing hellfire and brimstone.

But I'm not listening to her anymore. The second that Sweeney steps into the lobby, I lunge for the door. He just barely manages to close it and initiate the automatic lock before I can yank it open.

"Move," I growl as I consider ripping it off the hinges.

"Nikolai, just listen."

"No, you listen," I snap back. "Bring my fiancée out or I'll kill everyone in this room."

The receptionist whimpers again, but Sweeney just sighs and waves me towards the corner of the room. "You probably shouldn't be overheard threatening a police officer in a precinct, okay? Besides, I'm on your side here."

"Like hell you are. If you were on my side, my fiancée wouldn't be in a cell right now. Belle would be at home waiting for me."

Naked. In my bed. I want to kill Sweeney all over again for stealing the promise of that reunion away from me.

"Some hotshot new judge issued the warrant, and they sent a new cop to carry it out," he explains with a weary sigh. "Also, Belle doesn't have your last name. We didn't know who she was."

"That will change in two days. We're getting married. Which will be hard to do if she's in a jail cell."

He holds up his hands in surrender. "She's being released right now. It's all being taken care of."

"You act like making this right is going to save you. When did you mistake me for a forgiving man?"

Sweeney grimaces. "And when did you mistake me for someone who wants to poke the bear? Whether they're working for you or not, no one in this precinct wants to cause you any trouble."

"Weird, since you all keep causing me so much trouble."

"There's plenty of evidence she's guilty of the charge. I might not have been able to stop her arrest even if I had caught who she was before the warrant was served."

"Guilty of what?" I bark. "You're acting helpless, but you managed to undo the damage pretty quickly once I showed up."

"No, this wasn't me. The charges were dropped. That's why she's being released."

"What charges?" I ask again. "Belle hasn't done a damn thing wrong."

He hesitates before he answers, like he already knows the reply is going to absolutely infuriate me. "Child abduction."

"Child abd—Are you fucking insane? Who the hell would Belle have—?" Then it comes to me. Elise. *"Blyat!"*

Sweeney is watching me parse through this new information when the door opens again and Belle comes out. A tall, skinny officer has a vise-grip hold on her upper arm, hard enough to bruise. She's staring down at the floor, shame flushing across her face, so she doesn't even see me standing in front of her.

"The charges were dropped," I growl, grabbing her hand and pulling her out of the officer's grasp. "She isn't a criminal and she sure as fuck isn't yours to touch. Let her go."

Belle lets out a whimper at the sound of my voice. She instantly falls against me and buries her face in my chest. "Nikolai. You came."

Right now, I could rip this building from its foundations and tear the place in two. Seeing Belle trembling and terrified is enough to send rage pumping through my veins. It takes all of my restraint to stand next to her and keep my voice level.

"Where's her stuff?" I ask Sweeney. "We need it all. Now."

His tongue slicks over his lower teeth. Talking to him like this in front of other officers is not going to earn me any points with him, but after this fuck-up, he's the one in my debt. "I'll get it."

Belle curls against my side as Sweeney goes to retrieve the plastic bag full of her belongings.

"Are you okay?" I whisper, wrapping my arm tightly around her waist.

She nods. "Just take me home, please."

Every fiber of me wants to rip Sweeney a new asshole and not leave the premises until I've paid a visit to the chief and had the arresting officers fired, tarred, feathered, whatever the fuck.

But Belle needs to get out of here. Making sure she's taken care of will feel better than revenge.

Just barely.

Once we have her things, I level Sweeney with a glare and lead Belle out of the precinct. With every step away from the building, she seems to stand a little taller. By the time I get her buckled into the passenger seat and engage the ignition, the tight ball of tension and anxiety inside of her is unraveling. She's fidgety now, her eyes darting up and down the street.

"What is it?"

She startles at the sound of my voice and then shakes her head. "Elise. I don't know... I don't know where she is. When they arrested me, they took her, too. I thought I'd get to talk to her, but I didn't say anything. She might not even know what is—Can you get her back, too?" When she turns to me, her eyes are wide and hopeful.

Belle believes in me. Belle has faith in me.

"Did they bring her here?" I glance up at the building. If Elise is still inside, I really will rip the place from the foundations. Sweeney will be dead before the last brick crumbles to the sidewalk.

"I don't know." She unzips the plastic bag and pulls out her phone. It takes a few seconds for it to power up, but as it does, notifications start coming in rapid-fire. Her phone buzzes again and again and again.

"Elise called," she hiccups, biting back a sob. "She left messages."

She presses play on a voicemail and Elise's voice cuts through the silence in the car. "Um, hi. It's me. Mom picked me up at the station a few minutes ago. I asked to see you, but they said I couldn't."

Her voice wavers. It's clear she's trying not to cry. Belle presses a hand to her mouth, stifling her own tears.

Then Melinda's voice comes over the line. "Hurry up, Elise. Tell her I dropped the charges and you're coming with me. That was the deal."

"I will! Just give me—" Elise sighs. "I'm sorry, Belle. But we're going to the airport right now. I hope you… Well, I hope things work out. But I gotta go. Bye."

After the message ends, Belle stares at the phone like she's waiting for Elise to say something else. Finally, she shakes her head.

"After everything, Elise is back with my mom. We came so far. I… I honestly thought it was over. But now, she's back where she started. I guess it really is over. Just not how I ever expected."

"Fuck no, it's not over." I reach over and grab her hand fiercely. "Your mom made an unexpected play, but that isn't the end of the match. We can fight back."

She blinks. "What options are there? I'm not Elise's legal guardian. The warrant was right; I did kidnap her."

"The worst-case scenario is that my lawyers take a week or two to beat in the skull of every judge between here and Oklahoma until Elise is back where she belongs. This won't last long, Belle."

She chews on her lip. "I don't know. I want Elise back with me, but this is… a lot. She's been ripped back and forth across the country over and over again. Across the world, even. I don't want to put Elise through even more drama. Maybe I should just—"

"Then fuck the lawyers. I'll go handle it myself."

Her chin wobbles, and she shakes her head. "No. No, I don't want to put Elise through that. Or me, either. God, is that selfish?" she asks. "Maybe it is, but I don't have the energy for this right now. Elise doesn't even want to live with me anyway."

"That's bullshit and you know it."

"It's not," she protests. "She may like me better than our mom, but that's a low bar. And you heard the message she left. Elise didn't even ask for my help."

I have a strong suspicion the only reason Elise didn't ask for help is because she wanted to make sure Belle didn't end up in jail. She made the deal with her mom to go with her so long as Melinda dropped the charges. Otherwise, Belle's phone would be blowing up with messages from Elise asking to come back and live with us.

Deep down, I'm sure Belle knows that.

But this isn't my decision to make.

When it comes to the Bratva and my men, I call the shots. But Elise is firmly Belle's territory. I have to let her decide what's best for her and her sister.

"Whatever you do, just know that my offer stands," I tell her. "Elise is your sister. You have to decide what's best. But she can come back and live with us or we can adopt her once we're married. Whatever you want, Belle."

She turns to me, eyes wide. "You'd… you'd adopt her?"

"Of course I would. If it's what you wanted. I'll give you whatever you want."

A tear slips down her cheek. She wipes it away. "Can you… can we go home for now?"

Home. I've owned my house for years, but it's never felt like a home before. Not until I had Belle to come home to.

I nod and bring her hand to my lips to press a soft kiss there. "Yes. Let's go home."

27

BELLE

My bridal room is humming with activity. The hairdresser and makeup artist are arguing about whether my eyeshadow should match the flowers in my hair or not. The wedding planner, a high-strung woman who can't stop complaining about the quick turnaround time on this whole affair, is on the phone with the security team, begging them to try and look presentable.

"Forget the boutonnieres," she's saying. "I'll settle for black button-downs at this point. You're guest-facing, so the cotton polos have got to go."

It should be exciting, seeing my big day come together.

But all I can think about is who isn't here.

Elise should be with me. There hadn't been a good time to ask, but she was going to be my Maid of Honor.

And in another world—another life—my parents would be here, too. A loving mom, worrying over all the details and helping fix my veil in place. A proud dad trying and failing to hold back tears as he walks his baby girl down the aisle.

Instead, I'm alone with a group of strangers, about to marry a man for whom "love" is just another four-lettered word.

"Forget the matching eyeshadow," the makeup artist finally says. I think her name is Amanda. Or maybe Annie. She doesn't seem to care what my name is, so I decide not to worry about hers. She grabs my chin and turns my face from side to side. "We'll do a bit of white eyeliner and some nude shimmer on the lid."

I don't know a thing about makeup, but she must notice my expression because she wags a finger at me. "Don't give me any of that sass. You've put your face in my hands. I know what I'm doing."

"Go ahead," I mumble. "I surrender all creative control to you."

Mostly because if it was up to me, I'd use the same shine control powder I've used since high school, pat on some pink blush, and swipe on my favorite strawberry chapstick.

"And me," the hairdresser says. Her name is easy to remember because it's stitched above the pocket on her shirt that holds a comb and an extra pair of scissors: Kara. "I would have loved to see you a few weeks ago so we could have done a deep conditioning treatment and some honey blonde highlights, but this will do."

"'This will do.' High praise," I mutter sarcastically. I'm being bitchy, I know that, but I just can't shake the sourness creeping in at the edges of my mood.

Kara smiles at my reflection in the mirror. "I didn't mean it like that. You're gorgeous. But there's always room for improvement. Nothing is perfect."

"You can say that again."

If today was perfect, Elise would be sitting in the chair next to me. Unlike me, she'd love getting dolled up by two professionals. For her last school dance, I couldn't afford to get her hair done at a salon, so I watched approximately one trillion video tutorials on YouTube and did it myself. After two hours of arm cramps and arguing, we ended up with a slightly lopsided, but still pretty braided bun that made her look like a Greek goddess.

I'm tempted to pull out my phone and scroll back through the pictures I took of her in front of my apartment door, but I don't want to cry off all of the makeup artist's hard work. Because she wasn't wrong—the white eyeliner really makes my hazel eyes pop.

I'm about to tell her that when there's a knock at the door. Everyone in the room acts like a bomb went off.

"The ceremony isn't for another two hours. No one should be here," the planner groans.

"Don't come in!" Kara screams. "The bride is in her dress. No grooms allowed."

"I'm not the groom," a male voice responds. "I have a delivery."

I don't recognize the voice, but when Kara carefully opens the door, I see Makar standing in the hallway.

"Is everything alright?" I ask in alarm.

I'm imagining invading forces marching through the reception hall. Or maybe Nikolai has fled the building. It would be unlike him to retreat, but maybe the thought of marrying me was enough to send him running for the hills.

"Everything is fine. The security team is on the perimeter. No alarms raised yet."

"Did Nikolai send you to get me?" I ask.

He shakes his head. "No. He doesn't know I'm here."

Amanda and Kara are busying themselves with other tasks. So long as the person at the door isn't the groom, they don't seem to care who's here to see me.

I wish they did. Makar and I haven't spoken since the day he made known he thought I was a traitor. He isn't exactly the first familiar face I'd choose to see on my wedding day.

"Okay," I say, trying to keep the suspicion out of my voice. "So what's going on?"

In response, Makar holds out a long, thin black box with a gold ribbon. "It's a gift. From me and some of the guys."

"A gift?" I frown. "Like a wedding present? I thought the groom usually did that."

Makar shrugs. "I'm sure Nikolai will give you something. He's traditional that way."

I snort. "I don't know if that's the first word I'd choose to describe him."

"Well, he decided to marry you," Makar says.

I still, slowly looking up at him. His expression is pleasant enough, but something about what he's saying feels insulting. It's made even worse by the fact that I can't decide if I should be offended or not.

"I know he likes you," he course-corrects. "After all, he almost threw away his Bratva for you."

"I don't think that's exactly fair to—"

"I just meant that you're pregnant and he's marrying you. A tale as old as time, right?" His smile is thin and false, and I just want him to leave. Whatever this is, whatever he's doing, I want it to end. Now.

"Yeah, okay. Well, thanks for the gift."

"Open it." He tips his head to the box.

The last thing I want to do is feign fake gratitude for whatever gaudy necklace Makar and the other Bratva goons put in this box. It's probably made from the teeth of their enemies or something equally morbid like that. But I'll do anything to get him to leave. Quickly, I tear off the gold ribbon and lift the lid.

But it isn't a necklace sitting inside the box.

It's a knife.

The handle is long and thin, tipped with gold, and the blade is equally slim. But it's deadly sharp. I don't need to touch it to know that.

"In case this wedding is a sham and you need an out," Makar says, leaning in too close to whisper to me.

I search his face for a sign of whether this is a joke or a threat, but his expression is frustratingly neutral. Is it customary for the Bratva to gift the don's wife a weapon? Why does it feel so creepy and wrong?

"Do you like it?" Makar presses. "This knife is special. It's the one we took out of Nikolai's back."

That clears things up: it's an insult. At best, this is an insult. At worst, Makar is threatening me.

But by the time I put the pieces together and am ready to tell Makar he better get the fuck out of my room before I plunge this knife into his face, he is at the door.

"Congratulations on your wedding," he says with a finger-wagging wave. "*Big* day."

Then he's gone.

My heart is thundering. But that's exactly what Makar wanted, isn't it? Maybe what the entire Bratva wanted. They gave me this knife to unsettle me, to make me question what I'm doing marrying their don. As if I'm not already questioning it enough.

I want to marry Nikolai; I already decided that. But everything else is a mess. None of this is how I pictured my wedding day, and now, I'm not only marrying Nikolai, but I'm marrying into an entire criminal organization that, fun fact, absolutely hates my guts.

Suddenly, the conversation Amanda and Kara are having in the corner about their favorite retinoids and which products are best for curly hair feels too loud. The wedding planner still jabbering into her phone might as well be a jackhammer into my temple.

I squeeze my eyes closed, trying to cut through the noise, trying to lower my heart rate and calm down. But the world is pressing in on me from all sides. I just need a minute. I need quiet. I need…

"Can you all leave?" I say suddenly.

All eyes turn to me.

I clear my throat and try again. "Sorry, but I—I need to be alone for a few minutes. Is there any way you all could… get out?"

Kara shrugs. "I'm done with your hair anyway. I can come back and touch it up before the ceremony as needed."

Amanda nods. "Me, too. Don't touch your face and if you start to sweat, dab your forehead, don't smear."

"Great," I tell them. "Thanks."

The wedding planner is still talking on her cell phone as the three women leave through the side door to my suite. When the door closes, I'm alone.

I drop down onto the pink velvet sofa and count my breaths.

It's only been a few seconds since the room cleared when there's another knock on the door. My eyes snap to the closed door, but I don't move. Don't speak. Is it Makar back to make use of the knife he gave me?

There's another knock. "Belle?"

The sound of Nikolai's voice vibrates through me like a gong, shaking me out of my trance and propelling me to the door.

"Nikolai," I breathe. "What are you doing here?"

"I came to see you."

I press a palm to the door. "You're not supposed to see me in my dress."

"Crack the door open at least. I can barely hear you."

Slowly, I twist the handle and pull the door open. Nikolai's arm darts in, his hand open and searching. "Where are you?"

I twine my fingers through his. At the contact, my heart finally slows. The last few minutes melt away. "I missed you."

"That's your own fault. You're the one who wouldn't sleep in my bed last night."

"We can't wake up in the same bed on our wedding day!"

"But we can fuck the night before?" he scoffs through the door. "I think you're picking and choosing traditions here, Belle."

My face flushes at the memory of his body on mine last night. I told him I had to leave by midnight, which he took as a challenge to wring as many orgasms as possible out of me before then. When I woke up this morning, my body still felt warm and oversensitized.

But it's coming alive again now.

"And I think you're trying to break all of them," I tease back.

I hear him shift on the other side of the door. His next words are velvet whispers dripping over my skin. "Damn right. As many as I can."

My hand tightens on the knob. I have to fight the urge to yank the door open and pull him inside. After Makar's unplanned visit, I could use the distraction. This empty room isn't making things any easier.

I cleared everyone out of here, but it wasn't because I wanted to be alone. It's because I wanted to be with someone who could make me feel better. Someone who knows me.

Elise's absence feels like a tangible thing. An elephant in the corner, a fourteen-year-old-sized hole in my heart. I can't bite back a sigh.

"What is it?" Nikolai asks, instantly alert. "What's wrong?"

"Nothing."

"If you lie to me, I'll break this door down."

I have no doubt at all that he's completely serious. "Really, it's nothing. It's probably pregnancy hormones or something."

"If it's nothing, that means you can tell me."

I chew on my lower lip before I remember Amanda specifically told me to "stop picking before you ruin your lip stain." I groan. "I just wish Elise was here. And that I wasn't in this room by myself."

"You're alone in there?" he asks.

"Yeah. I sent everyone out a minute ago. I needed some space."

"To think?"

"Yeah. To think and decompress. It's been a kind of stressful day."

"It's been a stressful few months," he says. "Your life has turned upside down, Belle. We didn't know each other two months ago and now, you're pregnant and we're getting married."

I blow out a breath. "It sounds crazy when you say it like that."

"It is crazy," he laughs. "But I don't regret anything. Do you?"

"You don't have time for regrets. That's what you told me."

"It's true. But even if I did, I'd never regret you, Belle."

His voice is soft and tender, and tears press against the backs of my eyes. Amanda would hate it if I cried off all my makeup. I try to will them back, but Nikolai keeps talking and making that obnoxiously difficult.

"You've been through more in your life than most people ever experience, but you've come out of it a stronger person. Without sacrificing the hope and purity that makes you who you are."

I dab—*dab, not smear*—at a tear rolling down my cheek. "How can you know that? Like you said, you didn't know me two months ago."

"Because I've seen the way your sister looks at you," he says confidently. "I know how hard you worked to take care of her. You're always focused on helping everyone around you, which is why I'm ready to become your husband and make it my official responsibility to take care of you. You deserve it."

A beat of silence. My heart is ready to leap up my throat.

"Why wait until the wedding? You can take care of me now," I whisper.

Nikolai leans in. I can see a glimpse of his dark hair through the crack of the door. "What does that—"

Before he can finish, I yank the door open.

He's standing in front of me in his tux, all sharp lines and smooth edges. His body looks broad and strong, his jaw is clenched as he takes in my sheer lace wedding dress. His dark hair tumbles artfully over his forehead.

We only look at each other for a second, but the moment stretches and burns like wildfire. By the time I grab his arm and pull him into the bridal suite, I feel like it's been eons. I'm dying of thirst.

"Touch me," I beg, throwing my arms around his neck.

Nikolai wraps his arms around my thighs and scoops me up. We stumble back towards the couch where he sets me on the low back. He leans away, his eyes and hands trailing down my body. "You look fucking incredible."

"You're the one who picked out the dress."

"I have impeccable taste." He leans forward and kisses the exposed skin of my chest and then lower, dragging his tongue over the swell of my breast.

He has barely touched me, and I'm already panting. "Everyone is going to come check on me soon. We don't have much time."

"How am I supposed to rush this?" he whispers against my neck.

"There will be time for taking it slow later tonight," I remind him. "Once we're married."

A low growl rumbles through his chest. His hands skirt down my side and over my hips. "Once you're mine."

I hook my ankles around his calves and pull him closer. "I'm already yours in every way that matters."

He looks down at me and his gray eyes are black. It's the animal shift in him, the moment when desire takes the wheel and reason goes out the window. A shiver of anticipation moves down my spine just as Nikolai shoves the hem of my dress up and parts my legs.

"Shit," he growls.

I'm fumbling with his pants, and I hesitate. "What?"

His hand slips between my legs. I gasp when his finger strokes over my slit. "You decided against the panties."

"I didn't see much point," I breathe. The feeling of him against my nakedness confirms my decision.

He captures my mouth in a kiss. "I couldn't agree more."

Finally, I regain the motor skills required to unzip his pants. I wrap my hand around his hard length and stroke, pulling him closer. Nikolai doesn't need the encouragement. He deftly maneuvers under the layers of tulle in my dress, positions himself at my opening, and slides inside of me in one thrust.

Instantly, we're moving together. It's hurried and hot and it breaks every rule in the book—and I never want it to end.

"I'm going to take my time with you tonight. But right now… Fuck." He bites lightly on my jawline and my neck, thrusting into me at a feverish pace. "You feel so good."

God, he feels good, too. But between the soft cries of pleasure coming out of my mouth, I can't find the words. I tug at the silky hair at the back of his head and arch back, working my body against him, grinding until I see stars.

"There you go," Nikolai urges. His strong hands are wrapped around my shoulder blades, holding me up. "Take what you need, Belle."

My thighs are shaking and the sounds coming out of me are more animal than human. When Nikolai holds my weight with one arm and slides his free hand between our bodies, I'm lost.

I moan a string of curses, repeating the same things again and again.

Nikolai, I'm coming.

So good.

I'm coming.

The pleasure is warm and comfortable, and I need it bottled up for later. Micro-doses of this feeling could bring about world peace, I'm convinced. Who could be hateful when they feel like this?

I'm still mumbling to myself, lost to my own oblivion, when Nikolai pumps into me and lets out a soft grunt. Then he's coming, too.

"It will never be enough," he whispers as it rips through him.

I couldn't agree more.

When we're done, Nikolai helps me clean up. He wipes me down and tucks stray bits of hair back into place.

"No one will ever know," he whispers, bending to kiss the pulse in my neck.

I believe him. Right now, I feel like the most beautiful woman in the world.

"Still, you should get out of here," I tell him. "They'll probably come looking for you any minute."

Nikolai wrinkles his nose. "I doubt it. Everyone is pretty busy carrying out my surprise right now."

I'm trying to push him towards the door when his words register. I stop and come around him, looking up into his face. "What surprise?"

His smile is mischievous. If I had panties on, they'd be dropping. "The one that should be knocking on the door in three, two, one..."

Part of me thinks he is teasing, but sure enough, a soft, tentative knock sounds from the door.

I stare up at him, suspicious. Nikolai just laughs. "Well, go get it. I didn't distract you for nothing."

"Is that what this was?" I ask, feigning offense.

"Well, actually, my job was to talk to you through the door to kill time, but one thing led to another and..." he shrugs. "You were distracted, so I think that means I did my job."

"Nothing you're saying makes any sense."

He waves me on. "Open the door and it will."

I run my hands over my hair again to smooth it down and swipe my finger under my lips. My lip stain is probably long gone, but otherwise, I feel mostly put together. So I walk across the room and open the door.

To see Elise standing in front of me.

She smiles and opens her arms for a hug, but it takes a few seconds for my body to catch up with my brain. When it does, I lunge forward and wrap my arms around her.

"What are you doing here? How did you—When did you—" I squeeze my eyes closed and hold her tighter. "It doesn't matter. I'm so glad you're here."

"I'm here for your wedding," Elise says, extracting herself from my crushing hug and holding me at arm's length. "Nikolai and Howard got me here. As for when… well, right now. I would've been here sooner, but my flight was delayed. I think that answered all of your questions. Did I miss one?"

I swipe at my eyes, but it's no use. So much for not ruining my makeup. Between Nikolai and now this, I'm a disaster.

"I… I can't believe you're here."

Elise grabs my shoulders and turns me to face Nikolai. "Thank your baby daddy. He made it all possible."

I wrinkle my nose. "Don't say 'baby daddy.'"

"As soon as you're married, I'll start calling him your husband," she says. "Until then, that's his title."

I look at Nikolai through tears. "How did you do this?"

"It wasn't that hard," he says. "Everyone wanted Elise here except for your mom. And she was easy enough to convince."

"Thanks to Howard," Elise chimes in. "The only reason Mom called the police at all is because Howard called and reamed her out for the way she treated you at the breakfast. He said he didn't want anything else to do with her, so Mom tried to snatch me up and run."

I shake my head. "I'm so sorry, Elise. I should have come after you. But I—"

"Was busy being arrested," Elise interrupts. "It's okay, Belle. I get it. I'm not mad. Besides, I had Howard on my side. He threatened to call the police on Mom and report her for… oh, you know, everything. He said he'd fight to get her in jail so he could get full custody of me unless she let me come back and be with you. It was that easy."

"I'm sure it was." I roll my eyes. "Mom has always looked out for herself first."

Elise waves her hands like she's clearing out a bad smell. "Forget her. You're getting married!"

I grin. "I am."

And now that the tears have stopped falling quite so heavily, I can see Elise clearly. I gasp. "Oh my… You look incredible. I guess I know where the Glam Squad snuck off to."

Her strawberry blonde hair falls in large, shiny curls against her shoulders and her pale green dress compliments her creamy complexion and brings out her eyes.

She does a little half-turn and curtsy. "Nikolai set me up with your hairdresser and makeup artist. I picked out this dress. He paid, though. So, like, give him an extra smooch or something to make up for it."

"It's perfect. You're perfect," I say, reaching out and grabbing her hand. "I'm so glad you're here."

We smile at each other until Nikolai moves behind me, his hands on my waist. "And now that she is here… it's time."

My heart stutters in my chest. I turn around, feeling suddenly nervous. "It's time?"

Nikolai nods. "Are you ready?"

Panic wants to creep in, but Nikolai's presence is bright and warm as the sun, dispelling all the shadows.

I place my hand over his and nod. "Let's go get married."

28

NIKOLAI

When Belle walks through the double doors and into the ceremony, I feel like I'm seeing her for the first time.

It's not the form-fitting dress or the professional makeup. Belle is beautiful in nothing but her own skin, when her hair is mussed from sleep and her face is pillow-creased.

No, it's that the cloud that has been hanging over her head since Elise was taken has lifted. She's radiant, practically glowing from the inside out.

All at once, it hits me that I never want that glow to fade. I'll kill anyone who tries to so much as dim it.

She stops in front of me, tears shimmering in her eyes. I reach out and take her hand.

"Hi," she whispers, her chin wobbling. "You look so good."

"And you look perfect." I lead her onto the platform and stare into her eyes as the minister starts to speak.

He's going on about the importance of marriage and our union, but I don't need the lecture. Looking at Belle standing in front of me, her small hands wrapped in mine, I know I will do anything to make her happy. Anything to keep her safe.

Since the moment I met this woman on the plane, something deep and instinctual in me wanted to care for her. I wanted to ease her worries and help her stay calm. I wanted to help find her sister. I wanted to get her away from her sexual harasser of a boss. I wanted to rescue her from my enemies.

And now, I want to make her my wife and spend my entire life caring for and cherishing her.

Even if it means giving up my own life to do so.

So when it comes time for our vows, swearing to honor her "until death do us part" is the easiest promise I've ever made.

The minister tells me to kiss the bride. I pull Belle against my chest, bend her back, and cover her mouth with mine. She wraps her hand around my neck and kisses me back until I'm tempted to clear the hall and take her on this stage. Before God and everyone, this woman is my wife.

But when she gently taps my chest, I reluctantly separate myself. Her cheeks are flushed, and she squeezes my hand tightly as we turn to face the guests.

"May I present for the first time," the minister announces, "Mr. and Mrs. Nikolai Zhukova!"

The crowd cheers, clapping and whistling. I do notice a lack of enthusiasm from the middle rows where Makar and some of his closest comrades are sitting, but nothing can bring me down today.

My men think Belle is a distraction. But soon enough, they'll see the truth. They'll understand that she is my motivation. That Belle makes me a better, more formidable leader.

Belle is the perfect Bratva wife.

And once they realize that, they'll love her almost as much as I do.

We walk out of the ceremony hand-in-hand and climb into the back of a waiting limousine. "Oh my God," Belle says the moment the doors are closed. "We're married."

"We are," I agree.

She turns to me, eyes wide. "You and I are *married*, Nikolai."

"I know. I was there," I chuckle.

She shakes her head. "I can't believe it."

"Do I need to convince you?" I lean over and kiss the soft skin of her cheek and jaw. She leans her head back and I suck on her pulse point, working my way down to her collarbone.

"The reception hall is right around the corner," she gasps, breathless. "We'll be there in a minute."

"Then let's not waste a second," I growl.

Belle arches into my touch and kisses me. She throws her leg over my lap and curls her fingers in my air. But then she pulls away. "Wait. Wait."

I shake my head and grab handfuls of her back side. "No."

She laughs and pulls my hands away. "We're married, Nikolai."

"Hence the consummation."

"We're married… which means we have all the time in the world." She rubs her nose against mine. "Every night. Every morning. Every lazy Saturday afternoon. Every long lunch."

"Having sex that often is a big ask, but it's a sacrifice I'm willing to make."

Belle laughs. It's the most beautiful sound I've ever heard. I press a kiss to her chest, feeling the vibration of that laughter against my lips.

"Let's go inside and thank our guests," she says, sliding off of my lap.

"And then?"

"And then you take me home and claim every part of me."

"Fuck, *kiska*," I whisper. "You can't say stuff like that to me. Not if you want me to walk into the reception and keep things decent."

She snorts. "You're never decent."

I wrap my hand around her neck and bring her mouth to mine for one last kiss. "Exactly. Don't make it harder than it already is."

∽

I threw the entire wedding together in less than a week, but the reception is beautiful. String lights and tulle hang from a chandelier in the center of the ceiling, casting the entire room in a magical glow. The tables are decked with flickering candles and massive bouquets. A five-tiered cake in the corner stands almost as tall as I am, blooming with pink and green fondant.

But nothing can outshine Belle.

Music swells as we walk in. I immediately sweep Belle into an unofficial first dance.

"We've barely walked through the door and you're already causing trouble," she says, complaining weakly.

I hold her close, swaying with the music. "If dancing with my wife is trouble, then I plan to be in trouble a lot."

"You're a big dancer, are you?" she asks, eyebrows raised.

"That depends. Do you like it?"

Belle snuggles close to me, her body fitting against mine perfectly. "I love it."

"Then yes," I tell her. "I'm a big dancer."

We finish with a twirl and a bow, and then I escort Belle to the head table. Servers swirl around with appetizers that I barely even look at. For the first time in weeks, my Bratva is in order and my woman is safe. I'm sustained on that alone.

But when Belle notices, she grabs a forkful of chicken from my plate and holds it out to me. "You need to eat."

I snort. "You're taking care of me now?"

Her eyes flash with mischief. "You're going to need energy for everything I plan to do to you later."

Without hesitating, I take the bite and then shovel in a few more. Belle's laugh is a constant soundtrack to our dinner.

As much as I want to tear her wedding dress off with my teeth, the reception remains busy. Elise makes a very brief toast that sends Belle into sobs, and then the caterer directs us to the cake to cut it.

"If you smear this on my face, I will punish you," Belle says, arching a dark brow.

"Is that a threat or a promise?" I ask.

She laughs. "Nikolai, I'm serious. I hate the messy cake-eating crap at weddings. Don't do it."

"Only one way to find out."

I hold out a bite of cake and Belle takes it. But the way she wraps her mouth around my fork should be a crime. I groan, the low rumble shooting straight through my cock. "Do you want this reception to end right this second?" I hiss. "Because I swear to God, I'll clear every person out of here."

She giggles, swiping frosting off of her lip with her finger. It's clear she knows exactly what she's doing to me.

As the guests line up for cake, Belle and I stand next to the table and greet everyone.

"Do you actually know all of these people?" she whispers between well wishes and hugs.

"I do, but not well. A lot of them are contacts."

"Contacts? Like… Bratva contacts? Criminal contacts?" she hisses. "At our wedding?"

I shrug. "That's what weddings are for in the Bratva. You're either marrying to bind a contract or you invite everyone you know to verify you're not enemies. It's all politics."

"I don't know why I'm surprised," she says after shaking hands with the head of a small drug syndicate from New Jersey. "Hopefully, our wedding can do some good and make you some allies, at least."

"It doesn't matter to me. So long as you and I do some good tonight, I don't care."

"My God," she laughs. "You have a one-track mind today."

I reach behind her and grab her ass. "Because you still have this dress on. It's distracting."

We're still smiling at each other when the next guest in line clears their throat.

Makar is standing in front of us, a sad attempt at a smile on his face. He looks like someone just spit in his catered dinner.

"Congratulations to the bride and groom," he says. "Or is it best wishes? I never remember. I'm not good with traditions."

He tosses a look in Belle's direction that I don't understand. Her jaw tightens.

"'Keep the cake line moving' is a tradition you'll want to remember," I growl at him, nodding my head towards the table. "We have other guests to greet."

Makar and his friends file through stiffly. Belle seems to deflate with each stony glare. As soon as the line of guests has finished, I whisk her to the center of the dance floor for our official first dance. But dancing is the last thing on my mind.

"What is going on with Makar?" I ask her quietly.

She snaps her attention to me, eyes narrowed. "What are you talking about? Nothing. Nothing is going on with us. Did he—"

"Did he say something to you?"

Belle's lips press together into a thin line, and there it is; I have my answer.

"What was it?"

"Nothing," she lies. "Really. It's nothing."

"If it was nothing, your face wouldn't look like that. Tell me," I demand.

"I won't," she says. "It's not worth ruining our wedding over. And it wasn't a big deal, anyway. Just let it go."

The music starts, and I take Belle in my arms. "Whatever happened, it's probably not as bad as what I'm imagining in my head. So you might as well tell me before I tell the band to stop playing and kill him."

Belle tries to smile as we dance, but it's thin and pursed. Her forehead is wrinkled in concern. Finally, she sags. "Okay. Fine. He came to see me before the wedding."

"Before I came to see you?" I ask.

"Just before. You missed each other by seconds. He was only there for a minute or two, but he gave me a gift. A knife."

"What the f—Why would he give you a knife?"

She winces. "So it isn't some Bratva wedding tradition, then? I kind of hoped it was customary to give the bride a weapon. I wanted this to be no big deal."

I can feel my hackles rising. My eyes are on Belle, but I know exactly where Makar is standing behind me. I'm tracking him now. If the bastard tries to run, he won't get far.

"What did he say?"

"He was being weirdly pleasant. Smiling and all that. But he said that he… that he pulled the knife out of your back," she admits. "A not-so-subtle reminder that I once worked with Xena. He told me the knife was a way out in case our wedding was a sham. I don't know what he meant by that, but—"

"It's a threat," I say. "It doesn't matter what he meant; it was a threat."

Belle nods slowly. "I know. I figured as much. But Nikolai, please don't take care of this now. Let's just enjoy the wedding and—"

I bring her hands to my mouth and kiss her knuckles. "This kind of disrespect has to be dealt with immediately, *kiska*. Everyone in this room needs to know that you are mine. You are protected by me. You are cherished by me. They have to know that an attack on you is an attack on me and the Bratva as a whole."

"Please don't," she whispers. "This won't look good. They already think I'm a distraction for you. Maybe we can let it go and—"

"No. This has to be handled now." I kiss her knuckles again and then wave for the band to stop.

The music cuts out. The room goes eerily quiet. I turn to Makar's table and watch as the man's face goes white. "My sincerest apologies for the interruption, everyone. But my wife has been disrespected on our wedding day."

Muffled whispers move through the room. Makar doesn't move.

"If you are here as our guests today, it is because we wanted you here. But that invitation comes with the understanding that you support our marriage," I continue. "More than that, it's an understanding that you will respect our marriage. If you were paying attention during the ceremony, you heard that marriage is a union. It is a combining of two people into one." I face Makar, leaving no question who I'm talking to. "I am Belle. Belle is me. You'll respect us both equally."

Makar's jaw shifts like he's grinding his teeth, but he doesn't make a move to respond or defend himself.

"And if you can't do that, then you should get the fuck out now," I say. "While you still can."

The room is deadly silent. Everyone is holding their breath, waiting for the fallout.

After a few seconds, it comes.

Slowly, Makar stands up and pushes his chair in. He lifts his chin and moves towards the door, his walk all swagger and confidence. After a beat of hesitation, the two men on either side of him follow.

I keep my eyes on them as they saunter out of the room. The security at the ballroom doors escorts them through the lobby. Only once they're out of sight do I smile and turn back to the guests.

"Again, my apologies, all. Some business can't wait." Then I turn back to Belle. Her face is flushed a deep red, but she holds out her hand for me. I take it in mine and gesture to the band to carry on. They pick up right where they left off, and Belle curls into my body.

"You didn't have to do that, Nikolai. I could have made things right myself."

"You make things right with people who deserve it," I tell her. "Makar doesn't deserve your time or effort. If we weren't having such a lovely day, I'd give him what he actually deserves. As it is, I let him walk out with a pulse. Most men don't get that mercy from me."

Belle lays her head on my chest and sighs. "Let's just forget about him and enjoy the rest of the night."

I kiss the top of her head. "Already done."

The mood in the room settles and shifts as the song carries on, and for half a song, everything and everyone is in their perfect place.

But just as I'm turning Belle out for the final spin, the speakers cut out.

The band fumbles for a few more confused notes before they give up playing their instruments. I turn to look for the source of the issue, but the DJ just shrugs.

Then loud static cuts through the room, broken up only by a voice.

Belle's voice.

I turn to her. She's standing next to me, her mouth hanging open in dumbstruck confusion even as her own voice echoes around the room.

"... I'll do anything," Belle's voice is saying over the speakers with the crackly quality of an audio recording. *"But I have to get out of here and as far away from Nikolai as possible."*

29

BELLE

I never thought I'd be terrified by the sound of my own voice, but I'm trembling from head to toe.

The words are coming from everywhere. I keep searching for speakers or something, but it's like they're coming out of the walls and rising out of the floor. It's like they're speaking inside every cell of my body.

"I'll do anything. But I have to get out of here and as far away from Nikolai as possible. If you can make that happen, then that is all that matters."

More static fills the room. A few people cover their ears. Then I—the old me, the stupid me, the me that thought Nikolai was my enemy and Xena was my friend—start talking again.

"I can't thank you enough for all your help, Xena. You've been so good to me and Elise, even after everything... If I'd known Nikolai was engaged to you, I never would have started anything with him. If I'd known who he actually was, I never would have started anything with him. I wish I'd never met him."

Nikolai is turning in a slow circle, examining the room. I know he's trying to determine if we're in danger, but I want to grab his face and force him to look at me. I want him to know that I don't believe a word Past Me is saying.

"How do we turn it off?" I beg. "We have to stop this."

He just growls like a wild animal.

The security team by the doors are fanning out down the halls, doing a sweep of the hallways and the perimeter. A few more men are unplugging everything from the walls, hoping to disconnect whatever system is playing my voice.

But I have a feeling they won't find that system. Because only one person could have these recordings of me, and that person wasn't invited to the wedding.

"Xena," my voice says, *"there's nothing to report today, but I'll keep listening for anything you could use against Nikolai. Just get me out of here as soon as you can, please."*

I didn't find anything, I want to scream. *I was the world's worst spy. I was never an asset to the Greeks.*

But even if I could find my voice, none of it would matter.

Makar and his friends may have been my loudest detractors, but I know most of the men in the Bratva doubt me at least in part. Actively hearing me betray their leader isn't going to change any minds.

Finally, the recordings stop and the reception hall falls into silence.

"Thank God," I groan. "It's over."

Nikolai's arm loops around my waist. "No, it isn't. We have to get you out of here."

Oh. Right. Because where there's smoke, there's fire. And where there's a terrible knot in my stomach, there's Xena.

Before we can even move, the security team comes through the doors. Yuri hustles through the tables of guests towards Nikolai.

"Xena is here," he hisses.

I gasp, but Nikolai doesn't even flinch. "Where?"

"She and a few of her men are at the front doors," Yuri says. "They're unarmed. We've checked. Three times."

"What does she want?" I whimper.

Yuri glances at me and then at Nikolai, trying to decide whether he should answer me or not. Ultimately, he looks to Nikolai and answers my question. "She wants to see the both of you."

Nikolai nods grimly. "Let her in."

"Nikolai, no!" I tug on his arm, as if I can disappear and take him with me. Like we can fall through the floor and escape this. "Don't let her in. Let's just send her away."

"I'm not going to hide behind my men," he barks. "She wants a confrontation? So be it. We'll have one. I'm not afraid of her."

That makes… one of us. I haven't seen Xena since I crashed her car. I hoped I'd never have to face her again. But if I do have to see her again, at least Nikolai is standing by my side. I tighten my grip on him and stand tall.

The doors open again a moment later. Xena flows into the reception hall, brutish men flanking her on either side.

I glance towards the table where Elise was sitting, but her chair is empty. My heart jumps into my throat until I see her standing nearby. She is in the far corner of the room, her eyes wide. But she seems to understand that it's best if she isn't seen. She backs into the corner, hidden in shadow.

"Wow. More flowers than I would have imagined," Xena says, looking around. "I'm guessing you didn't have much say in the decorations, Nikolai?"

She's wearing a shimmering silver dress with a thigh-high slit and a plunging neckline. The color matches the cool gray of Nikolai's eyes. Knowing Xena, that's on purpose.

My attention is glued to her. Everyone else's is, too. She's transfixing. She knows how to command a room better than I ever could. Even though I know Nikolai doesn't want her, I can't stop the jealousy that rises up in me.

It's made even worse by the fact that Xena doesn't even glance in my direction. Her attention is wholly focused on Nikolai.

"He planned everything, actually," I interject. "He wanted to get married as soon as possible."

Xena glances at me and her nostrils flare. I'm poking the bear, I know. But I can't help it.

Then her face smooths. "Probably for the best. As it is, I didn't have a lot of time to plan. Rigging some speakers up in the walls was the best I could manage. Another day or two and I would have poisoned the cake or pumped carbon monoxide through the vents."

A shiver moves down my spine. Nikolai's hand presses to my back before he engages her. "Someone is feeling confident. Considering how badly your last plan failed, I'm not sure where you're finding the will to go on. But good for you."

"You're not sure where I'm finding the will?" Xena scoffs. "You backed out of our deal and disrespected me to be with another woman. A woman who, by the way, betrayed you. She was my spy for weeks. Truthfully, I don't know where *you* are finding the will to carry on. It's embarrassing. You ought to spare us all the trouble and just kill yourself."

My entire body is flaming with shame. Everyone in this room just heard the truth. They heard my conversations with Xena. They know how willingly I was participating in her plans. And without her side of the conversation, they don't realize that she was lying to me every step of the way.

Not that it would make a difference. A Bratva wife probably isn't supposed to be as easily manipulated as I was. No matter how you slice it, I'm an embarrassment.

"You had a spy in my house. In my bed, actually," Nikolai agrees, "and you still couldn't beat me. Someone ought to be ashamed of themselves, but it isn't me."

Xena offers up a smug smile. "Yeah, but I killed your best friend."

The room has a collective intake of breath. I'm surprised there is any oxygen left.

Is Xena trying to be killed on the spot? Because that's where this is headed.

Nikolai's posture goes rigid. His fingers turn to stone against my skin. It's like I can feel the warmth dripping out of him. "That's not something I'd walk around bragging about if I were you."

"But you aren't me," Xena says with a shrug. "If you were, you'd have control of two families and the respect of all of your men. Instead, you have a woman standing next to you who is more of a nuisance than an asset, and you're down a rather mouthy right-hand man."

Suddenly, Xena turns to the left and stares right at Elise. As if she knew she was there the entire time. The bitch even has the audacity to lift her hand in a cutesy wave. "I forgot you were still alive, little one. We'll see how long the baby sister lasts in this war. Seems pretty expendable to me."

The threat stokes a fire to life inside of me. I lunge forward, prepared to rip Xena limb from limb. Only Nikolai's grip around my wrist holds me back. "Don't even fucking look at my sister! Touch her and I'll kill you. Actually, look at her again and I'll kill you."

Xena's eyebrow arches and she laughs. "You're not a killer, Belle. You're also not a fighter. Or even a lover. You know what you are? *Boring.*" She shakes her head and looks back to Nikolai. "You could have had so much more. You could choose anyone to be your wife. You could have had me."

"You wanted to kill me once we were married," Nikolai drawls. "Or are you forgetting that part?"

"Yeah, well… technicalities," Xena says. She licks her lower lip. "We could have had plenty of fun before then. More than you're having with Little Miss Stick Up Her Ass, anyway. But you threw that all away for her. And now, you're both going to die for it. Shame."

"Get out, Xena," Nikolai snarls. "Bitterness doesn't look good on you."

"No, but it does inspire me." Her eyes flash as she turns to the doors. "You'll see me again, Nikolai. Soon."

She waggles her fingers once more in a mocking wave. Then she and her security swoop out of the room as fast as they arrived.

30

BELLE

It's well after midnight, and I'm still fully clothed. At the reception, I didn't assume my wedding dress would stay on longer than the car ride back to the mansion. But not only am I still in my dress, I'm not even with my groom.

"Are you sure you're okay?" Elise asks. She unwinds the final braid from my hair and pulls a brush through the tortured strands. "Today was... a lot."

The way she's taking care of me, I could believe she is the bigger sister. She's grown up so much in the past couple months. Not that she really had a choice. I've thrown a lot at her.

I turn back and smile at her. "I'm okay. Really. It's not as if I didn't know Xena was still after us."

"Yeah. But knowing it and seeing it are two different things. She was scary."

The memory of Xena's threats sparks a fire in me all over again. I grab Elise's hands with both of mine. "You have nothing to be scared of. I won't let anything happen to you."

"I know that. Nikolai has been checking the security system for the last hour."

"He wants to make sure there's no way for her to get to us," I tell her. "Either of us. He's going to protect you."

Elise nods and then her lips part in a huge yawn.

"That's it." I stand up and push her towards the door. "You need to go to sleep."

"No. I'm fine. I just—"

"You were on a plane and in a wedding and then you were threatened by the leader of a mafia. It's been a big day. You need sleep."

Elise snorts. "My life sounds so dramatic when you say it like that."

"It's dramatic no matter how you say it. And that's probably my doing. I'm sorry."

"Hey, it's not your fault." Elise pulls me into a hug. "I mean, this is happening because of you and Nikolai, but you can't help who you love."

Even if I could help it, would I? In the recordings Xena played, I said I wished I'd never met Nikolai. But is that true?

I don't even have to think about it. Definitely not.

I'd never undo him.

That feeling is only cemented when Nikolai walks through the door and looks at me. He's still in his tuxedo pants, but he ditched the jacket in the car. Now, his shirt is unbuttoned and his sleeves rolled up, revealing a slice of his tan chest and a swath of rippling forearms. He looks at Elise. "What are you still doing awake?"

"What is with you two?" she groans. "I'm not a baby, you know? I can stay up late."

Nikolai tousles Elise's hair as he passes. She wrinkles her nose and ducks away from him. "Yeah, you can. But you shouldn't. You need to get to sleep."

Elise throws a middle finger up as she backs towards the door. But just before she ducks into the hallway, she blows a kiss.

"Was that for me or you?" Nikolai asks, slowly wrapping his arms around my waist and pulling me to his body.

"Do you mean the bird or the kiss?" I ask. Then I wave the question away. "Doesn't matter. Either way, I think it was for both of us."

He chuckles and massages his hands down my arms. I sag against his chest and let him rub warmth into my limbs. "Crazy day, huh?"

"Not in the way I anticipated." He sighs. "I should have killed her when I had the chance."

"Everyone at the wedding may have been in the Bratva or sympathetic to it, but with that many witnesses, you'd probably be in jail right now. So I'm glad you didn't."

His jaw ticks. "She threatened Elise."

"I know." I take a deep breath. "I want to believe Elise is safest here with us—"

"She is safe in this house. I can watch over her."

I nod. "In this house, yes. But… I want more for her than that. I want her to feel free wherever she goes. Can she have that here?"

"Once I kill Xena, she can."

"And until then?" I ask.

He grimaces. "You're thinking we should send her away for a while."

Immediately, emotion clogs my throat and tears flood my eyes. "Since the moment Xena walked through the door, it's all I've been thinking. I didn't want Elise with our mom because she wasn't safe there. But she isn't safe here, either. She can't have the life I want for her until Xena is dead, and I don't want her here if there's a war going on."

Nikolai swipes his thumb over my cheek, pushing a tear away. "You're right. She's leaving. And you're going to go with her."

Of course he knows exactly what I'm thinking. He probably realized it before I even did.

But God, this hurts. The words lodge inside of me like shrapnel, tearing and ripping through my chest as I force them out. "That was your original idea, right? To send me away until the heat dies down? I'm just doing what you wanted."

"Sending you away is never what I wanted, Belle. Never. But it might be what is best."

I wanted Nikolai to agree with my plan, but now that he is, I want him to argue. I want him to fight for me to stay. Because we just found each other again. We can't be separated already.

Whatever is left of my makeup is streaming down my cheeks. I don't even bother dabbing at the tears. "You could come with us. It isn't safe for you here, either. Your men could handle the fight while you call the shots from offsite. It could work."

Nikolai doesn't answer, but his hold on my arms tightens. We both know it's an impossible ask. He pulls me against his broad chest and pats my back while I sob.

"I want you to come with me," I cry. "I don't want to be away from you."

"I know. But I can't leave. The Bratva is fractured enough as it is. If I leave, it will fall apart. We have to present a united front right now. I need to regain their trust."

I know he's right, but that doesn't make the truth any easier to swallow. "You'll bring us back the moment she's dead?"

"You'll be the first call I make once her pulse stops." He kisses my forehead and draws back. "It could be nice bonding time."

"Elise and I are pretty bonded."

"Not for her and you," he says. "For the two of you... and Howard."

I do a double-take. "You want to send Howard with us?"

"It would be easier to stay anonymous if everything is done under his name. The plane tickets, the bills, all of that. But I also like the idea of there being someone else there with the two of you."

"A man, you mean?" I ask, ready to hit him with a feminist rant about how I've taken care of myself my entire life without a man's help.

"No. Just someone who wants to take care of you both almost as badly as I do," he says softly.

And just like that, the tenuous hold I have on my self-control snaps.

My makeup is smudged and blotchy and my face is damp with tears, but I loop my arms around Nikolai's neck and kiss him.

He responds immediately, dragging me against his body with a groan. Already, I can feel how ready he is. His erection is obvious even through the layers of my dress. But he still stops.

"We don't have to do this, Belle. Not tonight." His forehead is pressed to mine, his eyes closed. I can tell he's speaking from an extraordinarily deep reserve of restraint that I don't possess. "It's been a crazy day. We can just go to sleep."

I reach up and gently begin unbuttoning his shirt. "Yeah, we could. But Xena would love that, don't you think?"

Nikolai freezes at the mention of her name.

"She'd love knowing that she got in our heads and ruined our night. Plus," I say, swallowing down a fresh wave of tears, "we don't have as much time as I thought we would. Turns out, we need to fit a lot of sex in before I have to leave for… I don't know how long."

"Not long, if I have anything to say about it."

"You have something to say about everything."

He nods. "Exactly. You'll be back in no time."

"Okay, well, until then…" I stretch onto my toes, my lips against his ear, "I'd like you to make me scream so loud Xena can hear. Until everyone in this city knows I'm your wife."

"Ask and you shall receive, *kiska*," Nikolai growls. Then he takes two fistfuls of my dress and tears it apart. The buttons along the back of my dress pop like firecrackers and skitter across the floor.

"That was so hot, I don't even care that my dress is ruined." I push the lace material off and stand in front of him completely naked.

He sucks in a sharp breath. "And you are… you are so fucking beautiful, *moya zhena*. My wife. My brave, perfect wife."

Before I can say anything, Nikolai's mouth is moving over mine. We kiss until my lips feel swollen and I'm not sure how to exist without this. Until I can't remember what it means to live without his breath on my skin and his hands in my hair.

And then he slides his knee between my legs, and I'm awakened to an entirely new level of feeling.

I slide my bare skin across his pants and moan. "I'm already so wet. Your pants are going to be ruined."

"Then they'll match your dress."

I'm the one getting myself off on his strong thigh, but Nikolai's breaths come fast and heavy against my neck. Like my pleasure is enough for both of us.

He leans me back onto the mattress and drags the bulge in his pants over me. Dry humping like this shouldn't be enough to send me over the edge, but I'm already on the verge of coming.

"I want you inside of me," I gasp even as I roll my hips into him. "I want to finish around you."

Nikolai kisses me quiet and circles his thumb over my clit. "You will. But not yet."

Slowly, torturously, he flicks and pinches and massages me into a borderline blackout. I'm clawing at his clothes and moaning like I've lost my mind. When the orgasm hits, it is sudden and devastating.

I shudder and shake beneath his weight, almost embarrassed by how needy I am for him. But Nikolai just lifts himself over me and kisses my jaw. "And now that that's out of the way, I can take my time with you."

I release a breathy laugh. "What does that mean?"

"It means that you were going to end this night too quickly for both of us unless I took care of you first."

"You think I'm that desperate for you?" I demand, trying to muster up some offense.

Nikolai palms my sex and curls a finger into my wetness. I nearly lunge off the bed, and he smirks. "Yeah, I think you are."

He has a point. So instead of arguing, I push him to standing and make quick work of his shirt and pants.

He thinks I'm the needy one? Then I won't rest until he's just as desperate for me as I am for him.

If that's even possible.

I wrap my hand around the base of him and then lean forward and take him into my mouth.

"Belle." His voice is a warning growl. He grabs a handful of my hair, holding me in place. "You trying to get back at me for calling you desperate?"

He's still in my mouth, pressed against my cheek when I hum in response. He curses incoherently, the word lost to a moan. I have to suck him off around a smile.

Nikolai lets me take control for a few minutes, swirling my tongue over the tip of him and then plunging back down. But as his breathing becomes irregular, he pulls me off of him and presses me back on the bed.

His eyes trace over my face and my body. Then his hands take a turn. The room is quiet, but nothing about this moment between us is awkward. I close my eyes and let him explore. Finally, he bends forward and takes my nipple in his mouth. Then the other.

His tongue follows the path of his hands until he presses a kiss directly over my heart. "Xena was wrong."

"About what?"

"Nothing could be better than this," he murmurs. "Not her. Not anyone."

His words are shockingly sweet. I don't know what to say back. But it doesn't matter, because right then, Nikolai slides his body over mine and kisses me. And kissing him is as easy as breathing, and it says everything I could possibly capture in my words.

All day, I imagined this moment would be heated, bordering on vicious. But the way we kiss and touch is more of a controlled simmer. A slow-moving heat that's all the more powerful for how it takes me by surprise.

He crawls over me slowly and twines his fingers through mine. One at a time, he shifts my hands over my head, pressing them into the mattress. When he finally pushes into me, he slides in so deep that I can lean forward and kiss his chest. I'm caged in by him, surrounded by his warmth and his strength, and it's all I could ever want.

He moves in slow, deliberate thrusts. It's like I can feel our individual nerve endings moving together, creating a delicious friction that is sending me higher with every touch.

Nikolai buries his face against my neck and growls. I curl my fingers in his dark hair. We slide together again and again. We're too focused on the single point of connection to kiss or talk. The room is filled with the sound of sliding skin and our breathing.

It's the most intimate moment of my life.

I hold my orgasm at bay as long as I can, but eventually my body clenches around him. I take a bite of his shoulder to try and swallow my cries. But then he arches up, driving his hips into me. I feel the pulse of his pleasure deep inside just as our eyes meet.

We come that way, me looking up at him while he looks down at me. We're sweaty and panting, but I have to bite my lip to keep from crying.

Because this is the best sex I've ever had…

But it feels dangerously close to saying goodbye.

31

BELLE

Two days later, the real goodbye arrives.

It's midweek and early morning, so the airport isn't as busy as it could be, but it still feels like there are too many people around. Especially since I'm crying like a baby.

"You'll be back before you know it," Nikolai says, swiping a calloused thumb over my cheek. "It won't be long. I'll take care of everything here and then you all can come back."

I nod, but I don't really believe him. Because right now, this feels like the end.

Elise is sitting against the windows with her headphones on. She took the news about going to Iceland surprisingly well. Especially once I told her Howard would be coming with us.

"I don't even know if Elise will want to come back," I mumble to Nikolai. "She wants to spend time with Howard."

"That's a good thing, Belle."

There's nothing but sincerity in his face. He believes that, so I guess I'll try to do the same.

"Speaking of," Nikolai says, inclining his head towards the doors, "he's here."

I turn around just as Howard lugs a rolling suitcase through the automatic doors. I've seen him a few times now, but it's still surprising how much he looks like Elise. Even the way he kicks at the stuck wheel of his luggage in a burst of frustration reminds me of my sister.

Elise is still lost in her phone, scrolling and paying zero attention. I'd be frustrated with her being so oblivious if it wasn't useful to me at the moment.

"Watch Elise for a sec?" I ask. "I want to talk to Howard before she sees him."

Nikolai nods and leans back against the wall. "Don't give him too much hell."

"I'm not going to give him any hell," I say with a frown.

Nikolai just gives me an amused smile. He doesn't look convinced.

Howard is scanning the lobby for us as I approach. When he sees me, his face splits into a wide grin. "I'm glad to see you, Belle."

"Were you expecting not to?"

I've been ironing out the details of our travel with him for the last two days. I was so anxious that I made sure we had everything planned out to the minute.

"Well, kind of," he admits with a shrug. "The last two days have been so crazy that I was starting to think I made up all of this. I mean, Iceland? I've barely even thought about Iceland as even, like, a general concept before, and now, I'm going to be there indefinitely."

"That was Elise's choice. She had a few options—South Korea, France, New Zealand. Italy was her second choice. But she wanted to go back to Iceland."

He strokes his chin thoughtfully. It looks like something she does, too, and I can't help but feel a frisson of heartsick familiarity ripple through me. "I probably would have gone for France. If I could eat bread, cheese, and chocolate for every meal, I would. What about you?" he asks. "Where would you have gone?"

Strangely, the thought hasn't even crossed my mind. I gave Elise full control over the destination without a second thought. "Wherever Elise wanted to go," I say. "That's why we're doing this in the first place. To keep her safe."

Howard's expression turns serious. "Right. Of course."

"That's why you're coming, too, right?" I ask. "Because you want to keep Elise safe?"

When asking him to come, I tried to bury the lede that we were leaving the country to live large somewhere else. For all he knew, Howard agreed to spending weeks on end in some kind of cement underground bunker, eating tuna out of a can. I didn't want him to agree to an all-expenses paid vacation instead of taking care of his own daughter.

"Yeah. I want to spend time with her. And you," he adds. "It's been so long. I couldn't turn down this opportunity to be together and—"

"This isn't a family reunion, Howard. I tried to make it clear over the phone, but maybe I need to clarify: Elise is in danger."

"And you are, too." It's not a question, but a statement. "Aren't you? You're both in danger."

I shrug. "Yeah. But Elise didn't ask for any of this. She's innocent."

"You were innocent once, too," Howard says softly. "When you were about her age. Actually, that reminds me: I brought something along."

Howard digs into the front pocket of his suitcase and pulls out a small journal that's held together with a leather cord. Carefully, he unwinds it and flips open the front page. Inside, pressed between two of the pages, is the drawing I made for him.

The edges of the paper look thin and fragile and the pencil marks have faded over the years, but I recognize it. It's a princess tower on steroids, all curlicued ironwork banisters and ivy flowing delicately over weathered stone.

It's clumsy and it's childish, but it's mine.

"I just wanted you to see it," he says, closing the journal and sliding it back into his bag. "I wanted you to know I wasn't lying when I said I kept it."

I tilt my head to the side, seeing him in a new light. "I didn't think you were lying, Howard," I say softly.

He gives me a tender smile. "That's good. Because I wouldn't. Wouldn't lie, I mean. You'll get the truth from me, Belle. And the truth is, I'll protect Elise with my life."

Just like that, the anxiety that has been brewing inside of me for two days dissipates. Knowing Howard is here for the right reason, that he understands how important this trip is, helps me take a deep breath for the first time in ages.

Maybe this will all be okay.

"Great. Then let's go."

As soon as Howard and I clear the corner to the alcove where Nikolai and Elise are waiting, Elise jumps up and runs over to greet him.

"You're here!" she crows with a huge grin. Then she frowns and adjusts her tone to something cooler and more teenagery. "You're here."

"Sorry you had to wait on me," he says.

"That's okay. We've been waiting here forever and a half, but only because Belle made us come hours early."

"Because usually, you are running a full hour late getting out of the house," I retort. "It's not my fault you were on time today for the first time in your whole entire life."

She shrugs. "I was excited. Sue me."

That makes Howard grin, and then they're smiling at each other, both of them the same kind of lovable, looney goons who don't know how to share their feelings. I'm happy for both of them, but I'm not feeling especially smiley today. So I peel away and sidle up next to Nikolai against the wall.

"How long do we have before the flight leaves?" I ask quietly.

"Ninety minutes," he says. "Actually, eighty-seven minutes. But who's counting?"

I lean my head against his shoulder and sigh. "I hate this, Nikolai."

"Which part?"

"A couple days ago, I would have said all of it. Except the Icelandic vacation. That is always a pro," I say. "But I would have complained about letting Elise take a trip with her absentee father. I would have complained about being forced out of the city by Xena."

"But…?" he presses.

"… But I think Howard genuinely cares about Elise. He told me he'd protect her with his life."

Nikolai nods in a very masculine kind of approval. "Strong statement."

"I really think he meant it. At least, I'm choosing to believe he did. So I trust Howard, and I'm happy to get Elise out of here. But…"

"Another but?" he teases.

"Yeah. But *you*," I finish.

Nikolai arches an eyebrow. "Is this the part where you finally admit you hate me?"

My chin wobbles as I think about exactly how much I *don't* hate Nikolai. That's the entire problem, actually. If I hated him, this would be the best day of my life. Also, the easiest. Instead, it's neither.

"I hate leaving you," I clarify.

There's a beat of silence. Then, suddenly, Nikolai comes around to the front of me and lays his hands on my arms. "You'll be safer if you leave, Belle. So will the baby. It's for the best."

We've talked about this too many times to count over the last few days, and I know this last conversation isn't going to do anything to make this easier. There just isn't anything left to be said. So instead of responding, I stretch onto my tiptoes and wrap my arms around Nikolai's neck.

I squeeze the heck out of him until Howard clears his throat, drawing my attention. "We should probably get through security, girls."

My instinct is to wrap my arms and legs around Nikolai's body and cling to him like a scared cat. But Elise is standing over Howard's shoulder, watching me. I have to be brave for her. I also have to be brave for myself.

Reluctantly, I pull away from him and grab my suitcase. When I look up, his gray eyes are watching me intensely. He's assessing me, looking for any signs of weakness. I'm sure he's finding plenty, but I lift my chin and take a deep breath.

"As soon as possible?" I ask.

"As soon as possible," he repeats. "The second it's safe for you to come back, I'll bring you home myself."

Home. I shiver at how good that sounds. I kiss him one final time and then spin away and move into the flow of people moving towards security.

It's easier this way, just ripping off the bandage. No drawn-out goodbye, no weeping. I need to look confident in this decision. I need to be certain. Plus, if I have to watch Nikolai turn and head for the exit, I'm not sure I'll be able to force myself to keep moving.

Elise steps up alongside me as we wait in line. "Are you okay, B?"

"Yeah. I'm fine."

She's quiet. When I look over, her eyebrow is arched.

"What?" I demand. "I'm fine."

"You're a liar is what you are. Pinocchio nose, pants on fire, the whole nine yards."

I groan. "I'm sad, but I'm fine."

"You're sad and you're miserable," she agrees. "That is not fine."

We kick off our shoes and place them on the conveyor belt. Howard is a bit further behind us, untying the laces of his thick-soled dad sneakers.

"I'm not miserable," I say as cheerfully as I can muster, which is "not very." "How could I be miserable when I'm going to go on a vacation with you?"

"It's okay if you're not excited, Belle. I know you're not, like, totally thrilled about Howard coming along."

I drop my phone, wallet, and keys in a plastic bin and slide it towards the scanner. "It was my idea. Or, well, partly my idea, anyway. Nikolai suggested Howard come with us and I thought it was smart. This will be a good time for you two to reconnect."

"And you?" she asks. "What about you?"

"This isn't about me, okay?" I sigh.

I walk through the body scanner as a male TSA agent stands off to the side. He doesn't attempt to stop me or tackle me for setting off any alarms, so I assume I'm good to go. I'm pulling on my shoes at the end of the line when Elise comes up behind me.

"So it's all about me?" she asks with a bit of an edge in her voice. "The only reason you're here is because of me?"

The answer is yes, obviously. But I get the feeling that response won't make Elise feel any better. So I end up staring at her for a few seconds, unsure what to say.

She shakes her head. "You don't have to do this for me, Belle. You've done enough."

"You're right. I've done way, way more than enough," I scoff. "You're fleeing the country, because of what I did, because of who I trusted, because of who I was afraid of, because of what I misunderstood. You're less safe than ever because of all the 'enough' I've done. All of this is my fault. So now, I have to—"

"No, you don't," she cuts in. "You don't have to do anything. You're getting me out of the city. Howard is coming with me. You're doing more than enough. You don't even have to come with me if you don't want to."

"You can't go alone with him."

"Why not?" Elise asks. She stares at me, waiting for a response. "Don't you trust him?"

I nod grudgingly. "Yeah."

"Do you think he'll take care of me?"

I sigh. "Yes, but—"

"But you're a control freak who can't admit that I don't need you for every single thing all the time?"

"Hey!"

"It's true. Spoken out of love, though." Elise steps forward and grabs my shoulders. "Look, B: you wouldn't have asked Howard to come if you didn't trust him, so that's not the problem. And I was going to let you come with us because I thought it was what you wanted, but clearly it's not. You want to stay with Nikolai, don't you?"

The answer is at the tip of my tongue, but I can't bring myself to say it. Guilt keeps me quiet.

"Don't you?" she asks, shaking me playfully as one corner of her mouth tilts up in a wry grin. "Just admit it, you clown."

I whimper. "Fine. Yes. I want to stay. But only because I know you'll be safe. I'm not sure Nikolai will be, so it's hard to leave him."

Even the passing thought that Nikolai might get hurt while I'm on the other side of the world and too far to do anything makes me feel nauseous.

"So don't leave him," she says. "Stay here. Be with him."

As if it's that simple. *Be with him.* There's more baggage in those three little words than in this whole airport put together.

Howard ambles up behind her, sliding his wallet back into his pocket. "What's going on, ladies?"

"Belle is deciding whether she is going to stay behind or not," Elise explains bluntly. "She doesn't want to leave Nikolai."

I cringe when she lays it out like that. "I'm not deciding anything!"

Howard nods serenely. "That makes sense. You just got married."

"And you're pregnant," Elise adds. "You'll want to be close to your baby daddy."

"Husband," I correct with a warning glare. "You said you'd stop calling him that after we got married."

"You're right. He's not just your baby daddy anymore. He's the man you love."

Elise says it so easily, but the words send a blush blooming across my cheeks. For most people, getting married is the ultimate sign of love. But things have been different for us. Nikolai is clearly fond of me. But admitting my own love? It feels a bit too much like offering my heart up to the guillotine.

Which is part of why I want to stay.

Whatever is going on between us, I don't want to let it go. It's too fragile to survive in the wild, cruel world we live in.

"I'll be okay, Belle," Elise says gently. "Really, I will. And I won't be mad if you stay."

"You won't?" I ask. Before she can answer, I shake my head. "I can't believe I'm actually considering letting you leave on your own."

Howard throws a casual arm over Elise's shoulder and pulls her in for a side hug. "She won't be alone. She'll be with me."

Elise smiles up at him. They look good together. Pretty as a picture. Anyone who saw them would think they'd been together like this since Elise was born, that they are just like any other father and daughter.

And suddenly, it hits me: *I'm happy for them.*

I'm happy for Howard and Elise. I'm glad they've found each other and that Elise has the chance to have the father I couldn't. But just as much as that, I realize that I'm happy for me, too. Howard can bear some of the weight of taking care of Elise. None of that means I love her any less, but maybe it means I can afford to pull back a bit. Maybe I can finally be a sister instead of her mom.

That realization locks my decision in place.

I pull Elise in for a bone-crushing hug. "You'll call me every day?"

"You're staying?" she asks, like she never actually believed I'd go for it.

"That depends. Are you going to call me every day?" I ask more sternly.

She laughs. "Yes. Twice a day, if I have to to keep you off my case."

I kiss the top of her head and look at her through the haze of tears in my eyes. "If anything at all goes wrong, call me immediately. Nikolai and I will be there in an instant. Do you hear me?"

"I hear you."

"Say it again."

"I hear you, sheesh."

I hug her one more time, hard, and then move on to Howard. "Are you going to take care of my baby sister?"

"With my life," he promises softly. "You can trust me, Belle. I won't let anything happen to her."

I give Howard a slightly awkward hug and then push them both off towards the gates. "Go. Go before I change my mind."

I watch until they're swallowed up by the crowd. Then I turn and walk the wrong way through security.

Nikolai probably left the moment we walked away from him, and I don't want him to have to turn around and deal with airport traffic again. Maybe I'll take a taxi back to the house. At least that will ensure he can't chuck me back through security and force me onto a plane immediately.

That's the vague plan I'm outlining in my head as I'm walking down the long hall towards the main entrance.

Then I look over and see a familiar figure standing at the viewing area.

Nikolai is standing with his back to me, watching planes taxi down the runway. I know he's lost in thought because he doesn't realize I'm walking up behind him until I'm only a few feet away. Unusual for a man like him, who's always so aware of his surroundings.

When he does finally turn to face me, his mouth is set in a stern frown. But that isn't so different from usual. It's hard to tell what he's thinking.

I give him a weak shrug. "Would you believe me if I said they kicked me off the plane?"

He stares at me silently for a few more seconds. Then he drags a hand down his face. "Fucking hell, Belle."

"I'm sorry." I surge forward and throw my arms around his middle. He's solid and reassuring and he smells like the forest after it rains, and I'm not sure how I ever managed to let him go. "I couldn't do it. I want to stay with you."

His body is tense under my touch. His voice sounds pained. "We decided leaving was for the best, Belle."

"And since when do I do what's best for myself?"

"That's the problem." He holds me at arm's length. "That's why I have to make the hard decisions. Because if it's up to you, you'll get yourself killed."

"This decision was hard for you?"

"It's not like I imagined marrying you and then sending you away."

"So don't." I grab his arms and wrap them around my waist for him. "Howard can take care of Elise. And I can stay here with you."

"Sending you away isn't what I imagined, but it's what is right." Nikolai grits his jaw and starts pushing me back down the hall. I try to fight, but it's hopeless. He's so much bigger than I am.

"I'll be on a plane back to you the moment this one lands," I snap feistily.

He growls. "Then I'll put you on the next one."

"And we'll do that forever?" I snap. "Doesn't sound like a good use of time."

"*This* isn't a good use of time."

"Says the guy who was standing by the window watching planes take off! Were you going to stay there until we left?"

The way his jaw tightens tells me I'm not far from the truth.

I press my hands flat against his chest. "Nikolai… please."

"You'll be safer there."

"But I'll be happier here," I say softly. "Doesn't that mean anything?"

He doesn't respond, his eyes focused just over my shoulder. I grab his chin and force his eyes to mine. "Tell me you don't want me here. Tell me you'd rather I be in Iceland, and I'll get on that plane and I'll leave. If you don't want me here, I'll go. But if there's even a single part of you that wants me to stay… then I'm staying."

We stare at each other for no more than a few seconds, but it feels like a lifetime. The anticipation nearly kills me dead.

Then Nikolai picks me up by the waist and hauls me against his body. I slide down his front, my arms settling over his broad shoulders as he leans his face back to look at me. "I want you here, *moya zhena*."

"You do?" I ask, failing to hide the goofy grin on my face.

He nods solemnly. "Of course I do. Every single part of me wants you to stay right here with me."

I slide a bit further down his body. When I feel a steel rod somewhere south of his belt, I get an idea of which part of him in particular is most excited for me to stay. Warmth zips through my spine, and I hug him close.

"Then it's settled. I'm staying."

He grabs my suitcase and takes my hand. "Stubborn woman," he growls darkly.

But he smiles all the way to the car.

32

NIKOLAI

I'm normally loath to reward disobedience. But Belle's palm is warm on my upper thigh, and I'm not sure how much longer I can control myself. She knows how close I am to yielding, too—she's been inching her hand higher and higher up my leg since we left the airport. The fact I haven't pulled over and taken matters into my own hands is a miracle.

"You better not be writing a check you can't cash," I murmur.

She has the audacity to look over at me, her lips parted in innocent obliviousness. "Huh?"

I rest my hand over hers, dragging it even higher.

She smiles. "Oh."

"*Oh*," I mimic. "As if you didn't know."

"I'm sorry. I'm just happy to be with you."

I arch an eyebrow. "How happy?"

Her cheeks flush, and I want to make her entire body do that. I want to undress her and watch as that blush blooms across her skin.

We pull up to the compound, fingers still entwined as that familiar, addictive tension builds in my gut. I'm so focused on Belle that I don't immediately notice the white truck parked along the curb.

Or the person slouched over in the driver's seat.

It's not until Belle grabs my arm and points in shock that I see. "Nikolai!"

I curse and pull up alongside Christo's truck. Whatever is going on here, it's not good. I want Belle as far away from this as possible. "Get in the driver's seat and go inside the gates. I'll be there in a second."

I get out of the car, and Belle climbs over the console and takes my place. A second later, she drives forward through the gates.

I approach Christo's truck with my gun in my hand.

I can't see his face, but he doesn't move when I knock on the glass. When I pull the driver's side door open, he flops to the side. The only reason he doesn't splatter on the pavement is because I catch him.

"What the fuck happened to you, man?" I demand.

Christo responds with a muted, pain-filled groan.

Grimacing, I push him across the bench seat to the passenger side and then get behind the wheel of the truck. There's blood caked on the steering wheel and more of it dried on the seat beneath me.

"Pretty early in the day to look like this," I remark. I elbow him lightly in the side, forcing another groan out of him. "How long have you been here?"

Christo groans again, but I can't tell if he can hear me or not. He's still mumbling something incoherent when I pull up to the security shack. The guard inside is ready to refuse entry until he does a double take and sees me behind the wheel.

"Don Zhukova!" he sputters. "I saw your car, and I thought—"

"That's why you should make everyone roll down their tinted windows. Even me," I tell him. "Lucky for you, that was only Belle."

"I will, sir. I'm sorry." Then he looks past me to Christo. If he's shocked to see me sitting next to a partially-conscious, bloody Greek, he doesn't show it.

"How long was this truck parked on the street?" I ask.

"It showed up ten minutes after you left for the airport. Might have been during shift change. I didn't see the driver get out. Kept an eye on it, though. I was gonna go check it out in a few minutes."

I give him a wave of thanks and he opens the gate. As soon as I park, Belle appears at the driver's side door. "Is he okay?"

I climb out and walk around the car, Belle trailing behind me. "Are you worried about Christo now?" I ask. "I thought you two weren't friends."

"That doesn't mean I don't care if he dies," she snaps. "Who did this to him? This is clearly a message, right?"

"Looks like it. But from who, I don't know exactly. Though I have my theories." I hand her the house keys. "I'll carry him. You unlock the doors."

Belle grabs the keys and jogs up the steps. By the time I get Christo to the porch, the door is open and Belle is in the foyer telling a maid to get supplies.

"Towels, a bowl of water, some bandages, and some kind of antiseptic." She waves for me to follow her. "Put him in the living room."

"I keep a doctor on call, Belle. You don't need to do this."

She pushes aside the throw pillows on the sofa and lays out a blanket for him. "We technically don't even know that it wasn't your men who did this, right?"

"If any of my men did this, I'll kill them," I growl. Outright disobedience like this would have to be dealt with swiftly. This is the kind of resentment that festers and gets kings killed.

"So I'll take care of him until you're sure. The last thing Christo needs is the Bratva doctor slipping him some poison."

"Poison isn't the Bratva way," I say, gesturing to Christo's bloody body. "We're more hands-on."

Belle grimaces. "Clearly."

I stand back and watch her work, only occasionally stepping in to lift Christo up so Belle can wrap a bandage around his middle or adjust the blankets. But mostly, I observe. I didn't love finding an unconscious man practically on my doorstep, but I do love seeing Belle take charge.

She's so confident right now. So sure of herself.

Belle may not have been born into my world, but she knows how messy life can be. She understands better than most that people have to do whatever they can to survive their circumstances. As much as I hate Belle's mother for what she did to her daughters, I offer her up a silent thanks of gratitude.

You made her like this. You didn't mean to and you don't deserve an ounce of fucking credit for it. But her strength is needed.

In the end, I decide "gratitude" is a little too strong of an emotion. "Acknowledgement" feels like plenty.

"What are you staring at?" Belle asks suddenly.

I blink and realize she's looking up at me, a small smile playing on her lips. "Your hands," I say honestly.

She looks down at where she's smoothing a bandage around Christo's forearm. "Do you have the hots for caretakers, Nikolai Zhukova?"

"Just one particular caretaker, Belle Zhukova."

Her face flushes at the sound of her new name, and fuck, do I wish Christo hadn't been waiting for us when we got back from the airport. She'd be tangled in my sheets right now.

I'm imagining the curves of her hips when Christo groans. It's the first noise he's made since I elbowed him in the truck.

I crouch down at his side. "You finally coming around?"

His eyes flutter and he coughs weakly. "Unless you two… are gonna keep… flirting," he rasps. "I'd rather… die."

I bark out a laugh. "Without us, you'd already be dead."

"He wasn't hurt quite that bad," Belle comments. She stands up and backs away from Christo, visibly more nervous now that he's conscious. "Mostly bruises and cuts. Maybe a fractured arm, I can't tell."

He squints against the light and tries to look down at himself. "My shirt is bloody."

"Oh, and a broken nose," she adds.

He lifts his hand to his face and taps the end of his nose gingerly, then winces. "Oh. Right. I remember that one. Hurt like a bitch."

"You remember what happened?" I ask.

"In vivid, painful detail," he grumbles. "I'll probably be remembering it for a few days, at least."

Belle hands him a couple pills and some water. "You should really be seen by a doctor. I'm barely proficient in applying bandages and Neosporin, so you'll want to see a professional and make sure you don't have any internal bleeding or anything."

Christo takes the pills from her with a wary expression. "Thanks."

"Yeah, of course."

The air in the room goes stale, the seconds stretching into a weird silence I have no intention of breaking. These two can get themselves out of their own awkward situations without my help.

Finally, Belle glances at me and then wipes her hands on her pants. "Well… I'll let you two talk."

I nod and wait until she's out of earshot before I sit down on the coffee table facing Christo. "She nursed you back to health."

"She wrapped me in bandages and gave me some aspirin. I could've done that for myself when I came to."

"I was going to drop your ass on the tile floor so you didn't get blood on my furniture," I tell him. "So you can at least be grateful you came to on the sofa instead in my foyer."

He repositions himself on his pillow and sighs. "I am. Shit, I am. Besides, Belle isn't the one who broke my nose and put me in this position, so she isn't top of my shit list by a mile."

"She shouldn't be on your shit list at all."

He looks at me over the rim of his glass. "Time will tell."

I roll my eyes. "Maybe one day the people I trust will trust each other and I can have a tiny sliver of peace in my life."

"I wouldn't count on any peace whatsoever until Xena is dead."

"Is that who did this to you?"

"Not herself," he clarifies. "Fuck, I wish she would have tried to fight me herself. There's nothing I'd love more than to strangle that backstabbing bitch with my own two hands. But no—as always, someone else did her dirty work. Her soldiers made sure I knew she sent her regards before I went unconscious."

"Was it a surprise attack, then?"

He shakes his head and his eyes go unfocused. The movement is too much for him and he presses two fingers to his temple for a second to steady his skull before he looks back at me. "I was trying to meet with a contact. You wanted information from inside Xena's ranks, and I thought there was one person I might be able to trust. It was a risk, but I guess I didn't realize how much of one."

"You're saying you did this for me?"

He grimaces. "I didn't have a lot of options. The family I grew up in has turned their back on me. I have no one to trust and nowhere to go. Earning your trust is my only chance to turn this mess around and not lose everything I've worked for."

"Let me tell you, it's wildly flattering to be your last choice."

"It's not—" Christo shakes his head. "It's not like that, Nikolai. I just—"

I hold up a hand to stop him. "Breathe. I get it. And I don't care. Loyalty is loyalty, and I'll take it either way."

He looks relieved. "Thanks."

"You risked your life to get me information. We'll call it even."

"I just wish I'd gotten something out of the meeting aside from a bruised kidney. My contact didn't give me shit."

"I'm honestly surprised Xena didn't try to feed you false information. Seems like a good way to set a trap for me."

A small part of me wonders if this whole thing could be a trap. But I don't see how. Christo has gotten inside of my house before and he didn't need to be unconscious to do it. Plus, I made sure Belle and I kept our chit-chat while Christo was knocked out to a minimum. You can never be too careful.

"She probably knew I'd be on the lookout for something like that," he says with a shrug. "I was going to triple-vet any information I got in case she was feeding me bullshit. I've learned the hard way not to trust

Xena. Part of the reason I left in the first place is because I knew Xena would kill me next to make sure her claim to leadership couldn't be contested."

I arch an eyebrow. "I thought you left out of loyalty to your dead father."

He shrugs. "It was both."

Christo's honesty is refreshing. Not for the first time, he reminds me of Arslan. If half of everything he says becomes a sexual innuendo, I might start to wonder if Arslan wasn't reincarnated.

"Instead of setting a trap, she sent a message," he says. "*'This war will end soon.'*"

"That's the message? I usually can't shut Xena up, and now, she decides to be brief and cryptic?"

Christo gestures to himself. "Blood is worth a thousand words, I guess."

"I guess. But it still seems strange. No offense, but why would she think I'd care that she beat you up?"

"Offense taken, actually," he mumbles.

I snort. "Don't be so sensitive. Why not attack someone closer to me?"

"She still might. You should take stock of the people in your inner circle. Make sure they're okay."

"You just saw Belle," I remind him.

"Is she it? There's no one else."

My mom is dead, my father is as good as, no siblings, Arslan is gone...

I nod grimly. "I keep my circle small."

"Usually, I'd say that's a good thing, but in this case, it might just place a bigger target on the people you do have. Have you considered sending Belle away for a while? You have safehouses, right?"

I stare at him, and he holds his hands up. "You don't have to tell me where or anything. We aren't on that level yet, and that's fine. But you should take her somewhere safe."

Christo is right—we aren't there yet. I'm not going to tell him or anyone else where I sent Elise and Howard or where I might send Belle. But if I actually thought the Greek was a mole, he'd already be dead.

"I tried to send her away. She… resisted."

He raises a skeptical eyebrow. "I get the feeling you didn't fight her very hard."

And why the fuck should I have? Belle didn't want to leave, and I didn't want to send her away. We should be on our honeymoon right now, not bandaging a bloody maybe-ally who was dumped on the porch. But I'd rather be doing this together than be apart.

"I can keep her safe," I snap.

Slowly, Christo sits up. It takes obvious, painful effort, but he doesn't stop until he's perched on the edge of the couch facing me. "That's what I thought."

I frown. "What does that mean?"

"I thought I could keep the woman I loved safe," he says, casting his gaze down to the carpet. "But I failed her."

"How?"

Christo is silent for a long time. I can practically see him dredging the story up from the deep, dark part of himself where he has kept it hidden away.

"There was a woman once. Just once. Mariana. Her father was a caterer. No one in her family had any connections to the mafia. My dad just liked her dad's cooking. That's how we met—her family catered a party we threw, and Mariana was a server."

"You dated the help? I bet your father loved that."

"Dad didn't care, actually," he says. "But Thia Xena was a bitch about it."

"She's a bitch about everything."

"You're not wrong. But this time, Xena found a whole new level. She said I was marrying below my station and muddying the bloodline, or some appalling shit like that. And she said it right in front of Mariana. To her face." He shakes his head like the memory of it still makes him angry. "But none of that mattered. I'd dated plenty of women 'below my station' before. The problem with Mariana was that I was serious about her."

"Xena is a control freak, sure. But why would she care if you liked someone?"

"Because a serious girlfriend would lead to a wife, which would lead to a family," he says, trying to lead me to the answer. When I stare back blankly at him, he shrugs. "I didn't see it at the time, either. But now, I understand: she didn't want me creating an heir."

I grimace. "Of course. Xena always sees the big picture."

"It's her gift," Christo agrees. "When I proposed, Xena lost her shit."

I nod in understanding. My ex-fiancée certainly knows how to play the long game.

"Mariana was afraid of Xena and everything to do with the mafia. She wanted to back out of the engagement a few times, but I convinced her I'd take care of her. Ironically, if I'd stayed with her, I probably would have given up my birthright. Mariana wouldn't have wanted to be the boss's wife. And I woulda done it, too, you know. I would have given everything up for her. Xena could have waited and everything would have worked in her favor. But she wasn't going to take that kind of chance."

It's easy enough to see where this story is headed. "Xena killed her?"

I expect him to nod, but instead, Christo shakes his head. "No. She didn't. I did."

I recoil in surprise. "What? But you were going to give everything up for her. You loved her."

"I was going to. And I did," he says solemnly. "I loved Mariana more than anything. It was the first time I'd ever felt that way about anyone. Maybe that's why Xena was able to convince me that I was making a mistake. She convinced me that Mariana was a plant from another family. That she was with me solely to extract information. And the more she whispered in my ear, the more I saw guilt everywhere I looked. I was so afraid of being caught out and made a fool of that I believed everything Xena told me. It was months of lies and manipulation and, by the end of it, I…"

Christo shakes his head. I urge him on. "You what?"

Finally, he looks up at me, and I glimpse the brokenness in him. His eyes glisten. "I did what she said I had to do. And I did it myself."

"Christo," I sigh. "Fuck."

"I know, I know," he whispers. "Xena demanded justice. She charged Mariana as a spy, and the night before what would have been our wedding… I killed her. I executed her. While she screamed for my mercy."

The horror of it plays across his face. I know for a fact he's seeing that moment in his mind's eye. Reliving it. Succumbing to it anew every single time he remembers what he did, the blood he spilled.

I've seen a lot of shit in my life, but a small shiver works down my spine. "When did you know your aunt lied to you?"

"I suspected it within days after I killed Mariana," he says quietly. "But I didn't know for certain until she killed my dad. I was so blind... as blind as the rest of the men following her. She has them all fooled."

But not me. Never me. I knew from the start that Xena was a crazy bitch. It's why I didn't marry her. It's why I'm not dead right now.

"It's a sad story, Christo. It is. I'm sorry for you. But that story doesn't have anything at all to do with me and Belle."

"You say that now, but you don't know what she's capable of. No one does." He turns and eases himself back down onto the sofa. "Just keep her safe, Nikolai. That's my warning. Don't lower your guard for a second."

I open my mouth to respond, but I hear footsteps in the hallway. A second later, Belle appears in the doorway.

"Sorry," she says, wincing as she steps into the room. "I didn't want to interrupt, but I just realized I may have given Christo pain medication with a sleep aid in it."

Christo lets loose a long yawn. "You may have, or you did?"

Her shoulders lift to her ears. "I did. I'm sorry."

"That makes sense why I just spilled my guts to Nikolai, then. You drugged me."

"Not on purpose! I'm sorry. This is why I'm not a doctor."

Christo waves her away and closes his eyes. "It's fine. I could use a nap anyway."

Within seconds, his breathing becomes deep and even.

"I'm so sorry, Nikolai," Belle whispers to me. "I really didn't mean to. But it's what the maid brought me. I didn't think anything of it until I got back to my room and looked at the bottle. I hope I didn't mess anything up for you."

"No. We were done talking."

Belle looks from me to Christo, a million questions burning in her eyes. One slips out. "What did he spill his guts about?"

I look down at Christo. He looks dead asleep, but I know better than to take a risk. Besides, I'm not sure I want to tell Belle his story, anyway. There's no need to scare her.

Things ended in blood for him. My story will not go the same way.

I won't fucking let it.

I smile up at her. "Nothing important," I say. "Nothing important at all."

33

BELLE

"You're just now getting ready for dinner?" Elise asks. Her face is blurry and pixelated on the screen of the computer, but I can tell she's stunned. "Miss Hangry Pants is waiting until almost 10 PM to eat? Next thing you know, a pig is gonna fly into my window."

"Excuse you, but Miss Hangry Pants is pregnant, need I remind you? And also, it's not even five o'clock here yet."

Her face falls. "Oh, right. Time change. I forgot about that."

Turns out half a world apart is a really long way.

"I miss you, E."

She perks up, but her face twists in disgust. "We've only been here for, like, an hour. I saw you literally this morning. You and Nikolai have probably been going at it too much for you to miss me."

"Ew, Elise! Don't talk about that. Ever."

"What?" she asks innocently. "Sisters talk about this kind of stuff. Besides, I shared a suite with you when we were all in Iceland. I saw things."

The endless amount of compromising positions Elise could have caught us in flashes through my mind. I'm too horrified by the sheer magnitude of trauma I may have inflicted on my sister to speak.

"I mean, I came out one day and saw rumpled bedding on the sofa," she says finally. "Your bra was hanging on a kitchen barstool. And I may be the one with red hair, but you're the one with reactive skin. Nikolai just had to glance at you and you'd blush from head to toe. It was so obvious."

Relief courses through me. So long as she didn't see me naked, I can move through life guilt-free. "Well, still. I don't want to talk about… *that* with you."

"You're pregnant, Belle. Cat is out of the bag. I know how the X's and O's of that whole shebang work."

"There's no cat in any bag," I argue. "There is simply human decency and privacy. I'm not going to pretend I'm a nun, but I do not want to talk about that with my little sister or anyone, please and thank you."

"Okay. No sex talk," she says. "No discussing the sweaty, steamy lovemaking you and your husband have partaken in since I left."

I bury my face in my hands. "Moving on."

"Yes. We won't talk about the filthy, raunchy—"

"I said we're moving on!" I practically shout. "How are you and Howard getting along?"

"Good," Elise says, just as another voice chimes in from the back, "Fantabulous!"

I frown. "Was that Howard?"

"Yeah. He's in the kitchen making grilled cheeses."

I lean close to the screen like I'm whispering in Elise's ear. "And you said all that sex stuff in front of him? Elise, he's your dad!"

"What? I'm not the one doing it," she shrugs. Then she grins. "There you go again. You're blushing so hard. You could see that blush from space."

I narrow my eyes. "I will hang up on you. That's the benefit of you being so far away. I can turn you off whenever I want."

"Yeah, but you don't want to," she says confidently.

I want to slam the computer shut just to prove her wrong, but I can't. She's right—I'd sit here and talk to her forever if I could. If teleportation existed, I'd be there to brush her hair and paint her toenails and lie next to her watching trash TV until the wee hours of the morning.

"Don't worry, I'm not listening," Howard calls from the background. "I have earbuds in. I'm listening to a podcast. Elise put me onto it on the flight."

Elise grins. I can't remember the last time I saw her so genuinely and openly happy. "Yeah, by the way, tell Nikolai thanks for paying for the Wi-Fi on the flight. I don't know if he knows he did that, but he did. Anyway, it's a true crime podcast. We both like true crime, isn't that cool?"

"That's great." I really do mean it. Howard and I may have our own stuff to work through eventually, but when it comes to his relationship with Elise, I'm at peace. I want this for her. She deserves to know her dad and have at least one parent who isn't an active hot mess. And clearly, she's happy. What more could I want?

What more could I want? The question rings through me like a gong, reverberating way further than I expected.

I could want a normal life, for starters. One where a crazy woman isn't tracking down my family and trying to kill them.

I could want a husband who doesn't find unconscious, bloody men in his front yard.

I could want a small, cute house with no security shack out front.

I could want my sister sitting next to me on the bed while I get ready for my date instead of languishing in a hotel room in another country.

I don't have those things… but I do have Nikolai. Doesn't that outweigh the rest?

"How are you and Nicky Boy doing?" Elise asks, her voice cutting through my thoughts. "And you can keep all of the naked details to yourself."

I roll my eyes. "We are doing fine."

All we've done so far is bandage Christo. Nikolai said we'd go get dinner, then took off to get some work done. I haven't seen him in hours.

"Then why don't you look like it?"

I smooth my face back to neutral. "What?"

"You're worried. What's wrong?"

I consider lying, but what's the point? Some of the early cracks in this marriage are obvious. "Well, let's see… my baby sister just had to flee the country. I'd say that's 'something wrong.'"

"As a precaution."

"But still. It's not exactly ideal," I protest. "And things are just… kind of overwhelming at the moment. Honestly, part of me worries we rushed into this."

"Into marriage?"

I nod. "Kind of. It's a small part, but this is crazy, right?"

"Of course it's crazy," she laughs. "It's nuts. Like, bonkers to the extreme."

"Gee, thanks, E. You make me feel so much better."

"I'm not trying to make you feel better. I'm being honest."

I wonder if she has any idea how much like Nikolai she sounds. The two of them are more alike than they know. They both put up walls to keep people at arm's length. But under it all, they care more deeply than most people could ever fathom.

"So you think I'm nuts then?" I ask.

"Nope," she declares. "Sane people do crazy things all the time. What matters is why you chose to do it. So let's hear it: why did you decide to marry Nikolai?"

"Because I love him." The words slip out easily. I don't even have to think about them; I know without a doubt they're true.

And all of the doubts that were just shouting at me go quiet, just like that.

"Wow," I breathe, impressed. "You're smart, Elise. Very wise."

She shrugs. "I know. I'm just glad you finally figured it out."

"Sorry it took me so long, Oh Wise One."

She waves me away. "The Wise One forgives you. Where is your husband, anyway?"

"He had work to do, but he should be back soon." I glance at the clock in the corner of my screen and wince. "That's actually why I need to hang up and get ready. He's taking me out to dinner."

"Ooh. Like a date?"

"Can we even call it that? We're married now."

"Sure you can," she says. "Married people go on dates all the time. You have to keep things fresh."

"We got married two days ago. I'd say things are pretty fresh."

Elise ignores me and tucks her legs underneath her. "Show me what you're planning to wear."

I look down at myself and then hold my arms out. "Um… This."

I have on my favorite pair of ripped jeans with a scoop neck tank tucked in. It's casual, but fashionable. Paired with some delicate gold necklaces and a pair of leather flats, I'll look positively posh.

But Elise wrinkles her nose. "You're going to dinner, not brunch. Put on a dress."

"Since when did you become the fashion expert?" I want to remind her that a couple months ago, she didn't even own a pair of shoes that weren't held together with duct tape. When we came to live with Nikolai, he didn't just upgrade my wardrobe—he also made sure Elise could buy whatever she wanted. Apparently, it's turned her into a critic.

"I'm not. But I follow people who are," she says. "And unless you know you're going somewhere casual, you want to be prepared for anything. That calls for a little black dress."

"Isn't that a little cliché?"

"It's timeless," she retorts. "There's a difference. Put on a little black dress with a pair of flats, some basic jewelry, and pull your hair back with that bronze clip you have. That way, you'll look casual, but if the place you go is really fancy, you can take your hair down easily."

I want to be a cynic for no other reason than that I don't want to get fashion advice from my barely-teenaged sister, but the girl knows what she is talking about. It's a good plan.

"I can tell you want to thank me," she adds, "but you are just far too overwhelmed and/or hideously ashamed of how washed-up you are. Either way, you're welcome."

I snort. "You're ridiculous."

"But you love me." She blows me a kiss just as I hear Howard's voice in the background calling, "Sandwiches are ready!"

"Ope, my food is ready." She waves her fingers under her chin. "I'll call you tomorrow, okay?"

"First thing in the morning," I remind her.

"That'll be the middle of the night for you, goober."

"So?" I shrug.

She rolls her eyes. "You're ridiculous, B."

"I love you."

She tries and fails to suppress a smile. "I love you, too."

As soon as I close my laptop, I fish through my closet for everything Elise said I should wear. And when I pull on the outfit, there is no denying that my sister has an eye for fashion.

I look great.

The black dress cuts way up on my thighs, but the high neck balances everything out so I don't look too flashy. With my hair up, I could be going to a concert or a bar. But as soon as the hair comes down, I'm ready for a formal sit-down restaurant.

I snap a quick picture and send it to Elise. A millisecond later, she responds.

Elise: Yep. You're welcome.

I smile and check my messages, but there's nothing from Nikolai. No word from him yet. As if on cue, my stomach rumbles.

My outfit isn't the only thing Elise was right about: I'm getting hangry. I consider texting Nikolai to see when he's coming back, but I don't want to seem clingy. Instead, I decide to head down to the kitchen to wait for him. And if I just so happen to look in the pantry and grab a small snack while I wait, who would ever know?

With the promise of a packaged blueberry muffin in my future, I hurry down to the kitchen. I'm so busy beelining for the pantry that it takes me a couple seconds to realize the kitchen isn't empty.

I skid to a stop in front of the island just as Nikolai's personal chef looks over her shoulder at me.

"Hi there!" she greets. "I am finishing up and then I was going to have one of the maids come get you. But I guess I don't need to do that anymore."

The woman is on the backside of fifty, but just barely. She has gray-streaked black hair pulled back in a ponytail and a green apron tied around her waist. Her name escapes me, but Nikolai said he's had her on staff for years. Typically, she cooks his meals in her own kitchen and then delivers them each morning to be reheated. But sometimes, she cooks things fresh when he requests it.

Considering she's standing over a sizzling skillet right now, he must have requested it. The smell of garlic and spices has my sputtering stomach practically leaping out of my body to get at whatever she is cooking.

"Is Nikolai here?" I ask.

She shakes her head. "No. He told me he'd be out tonight, but he wanted to make sure you were fed."

"I'm sorry… he isn't going to be eating with me?"

"No, I'm cooking for one," she explains. "Just you tonight. But between you and me, I made extras for myself. No sense cooking if I can't eat some, too, right?"

I try to smile and nod, but my mind is spinning. Did I misunderstand him when he asked me to dinner? I assumed it was a date, but maybe he was just offering to feed me.

But no, he said we'd talk over dinner. We can't talk if he isn't with me.

I watch the chef's ponytail swish as she starts plating my food, and I want to ask her if she knows where Nikolai is. If she knows when he'll be back. If he said anything to her about me. But how pathetic would that make me look? Two days into a marriage and I don't know where my husband is.

Instead, I sit down at the island and wait for my dinner.

A minute later, the chef turns around and slides my plate across the island to me. "Salmon pasta with a creamy garlic sauce. Rumor is you're pregnant, so I wanted to make sure to get those omega-3 fatty acids in."

I raise my eyebrows. "The omega-whatty whats?"

"This is why I'm the chef and you're the diner," she laughs. She holds out her hand. "I'm Francesca, by the way. I'm not sure we've actually met."

I shake her hand and then practically lunge for my fork. "We haven't met officially. But your cooking is incredible."

"Thank you. Nikolai is a great client to work for. He lets me have free rein to cook whatever I want. Some clients can be really demanding."

"Not me," I say. "So long as I'm fed, I'm happy."

"My kind of woman."

Francesca pulls a Tupperware container out of her bag and starts to fill it with pasta.

"Is that for you?" I ask.

"Yeah. I'll take it with me and eat at home."

"Or you could eat now," I offer. "It's not like I have some hot date I'm waiting on."

There's a bit too much bitterness in my tone for my liking, so I slap on a smile.

Francesca hesitates for a minute, but the woman is clearly not shy, so she quickly grins and plops down on a stool next to me. "Thanks. Food is always better fresh. I tell Nikolai that all the time. 'I'll cook in your kitchen for every meal if you want. I can make your food fresh.' I mean, he's paying me enough that I'd spoon-feed him gold-leaf caviar if he asked me to. But no, he wants me to cook from my house and store the food in his fridge. I guess his schedule is a bit unpredictable."

"A bit, yeah," I agree. Though I'm guessing Nikolai's logic has a lot more to do with the fact that bloodied men occasionally show up at his door and knife fights break out in his kitchen every now and then. The less of that Francesca sees, the better.

She shrugs. "Doesn't matter to me, though. I was hustling between four different clients when Nikolai hired me. Now, he's the only one. I'm living the dream."

"Four clients?" I shake my head. "How did you manage that?"

She laughs. "I didn't. I had no work/life balance. I worked constantly, never slept. It was ridiculous. They say if you love what you do, you never work a day in your life, but in my experience, it just means you work way more than you should and don't know how to take a break."

"Maybe I should sit you down for a talk with Nikolai." The words are out of my mouth before I can stop them. My bitterness leaking out through a crack I try quickly to patch. "Just that unpredictable schedule, you know? But he's great. Amazing. The best."

There are a few seconds of silence, and heat blooms across my cheeks. I hear Elise's voice in my head: *There she goes again, Blabbermouth Belle.* Badmouthing Nikolai to his employees is probably not something a wife should be doing. It's not a great look, to say the least.

I open my mouth to take it all back when Francesca finally responds. "You can be upset with amazing people and still think they're amazing," she says softly. "They can still be amazing, even. They are just also a person who upset you."

I huff out a weak laugh. "Am I that transparent?"

"Well, maybe I'm just used to people walking into the kitchen and being thrilled to see me because I'm making them food, but you looked downright depressed at the sight of me. I could tell you were expecting someone else."

"I thought he was taking me out to dinner tonight."

Francesca winces. "Maybe that's why Nikolai requested I make a special dessert, too. He was trying to soften the blow."

"What kind of dessert?"

"Cinnamon caramel cheesecake."

"Damn him," I hiss. "That sounds incredible."

"Well, you can thank me for that. I need to get rid of some of it before I eat the entire thing myself."

"I'll happily take it off your hands," I promise. "Especially if I'm nursing the sting of canceled plans and can't have a glass of wine."

We eat in silence for a few minutes, stopping only so I can moan incoherently about how good my pasta is. Maybe it's a carb-induced mania, or maybe the pasta has given me strength, I can't be sure. But without any preamble, I turn to Francesca and ask, "So how many women have you done this for?"

Francesca, to her credit, slowly chews her bite before she turns to me. "Excuse me?"

"This," I say, gesturing to the pasta. "How many women have you cooked for after Nikolai canceled plans? Or how many women that he's been with have you cooked for, period?"

She sets down her fork, and I am starting to feel like I crossed a serious line. "Well, I'd say that is a conversation you should probably have with Nik—"

"You're right," I interrupt, blushing so hard it's a miracle that there's any blood left elsewhere in my body. "I'm sorry. I shouldn't put you in that position. It's uncomfortable and unacceptable. Please let's just forget—"

"But," she continues, "I don't mind telling you the truth. And the truth is… none."

I blink, letting her words sink in. "None?"

"None. You are the only woman Nikolai has ever asked me to cook for, both in this specific scenario and in general. In fact, I don't know if I've ever even seen him bring a woman home before."

"That cannot possibly be true."

She shrugs. "I only know what I've seen. But I've always made his meals in one-size portions… until you came along. Then he started asking for enough for three people. I secretly thought he had a harem living with him, if you want to know the truth."

"I'd believe that long before I'd believe he was celibate."

"Okay, let's be clear. I don't think Nikolai was celibate," she says in a near-whisper. "But he never had anyone staying over for breakfast, I can tell you that."

"Good. Or, well—Fine. Whatever," I sputter. "I just mean, thanks for telling me."

She waves me away dismissively. "Yeah, yeah. I know how this kind of thing goes. It's hard to ask him this kind of thing yourself, and it's not like there are many people in Nikolai's life to ask."

"He keeps a small circle," I agree.

Francesca elbows me gently and winks. "Quality over quantity."

I smile back.

It shouldn't matter to me. I mean, we met by having sex in an airplane bathroom. It's not like we had some storybook meet-cute. And I certainly didn't think Nikolai was a virgin. But still, hearing that I might be special in some way, it eases the sting of him standing me up tonight.

Just a little.

"I'm definitely still going to need that cheesecake," I announce.

Francesca laughs and grabs both of our plates. "Coming right up."

We chat a bit more while I eat my cheesecake, but soon after, Francesca needs to get home. I thank her for the food and the conversation, walk her to the door, and then head back to my room.

Passing by Nikolai's room causes a physical ache in my chest. It's late enough that we probably would be done with dinner and headed back to the house by now. It's not hard to imagine where the evening would have taken us.

Instead, I'm plodding back to my room alone.

Outside my door, I glance down the hall at Elise's room, but the fact that it's empty, too, is too depressing to contemplate right now. So I hurry into my room and change into a pair of lounge pants and a matching tank top.

I've been single for most of my adult life. I know how to spend an evening alone in my room.

Except, tonight, Nikolai is everywhere. All I can think about is what he could be doing right now. Why did he stand me up? Why didn't he call to tell me what was going on?

And the most pressing question of all: should I call him?

"No," I say aloud, tossing my phone to the end of the bed so it's out of reach. "No, you shouldn't."

But still, the idea is tempting. I try to distract myself with a book or painting my nails, but my phone keeps winking at me from where I dropped it.

"You'll look desperate," I say again. "Don't do it."

But I'm quickly losing the battle. So the only option is to retreat. Before I can sabotage myself, I slip out of bed and get into the hallway, leaving my phone behind.

So what if Nikolai calls or texts? Who cares? I'll talk to him later. I don't care.

I move into the sitting room and plop down on the sofa, already itching to run back and check my phone. Instead, I grab the remote and power up the TV.

The news is on. I'm not surprised. It's all Nikolai seems to watch when he is rarely seated long enough to watch television.

Just as I'm about to turn the channel, I see a familiar name flash along the chyron at the bottom of the screen.

"Am I having a stroke?" I mutter, sitting up to get a closer look. But no matter how close I get, it doesn't change.

I turn the volume up just as the same familiar name comes out of the news anchor's mouth.

And now, I'm positive I'm losing my mind. "What did Nikolai do?"

34

BELLE

I can't sleep and I can't sit still. For the next ninety minutes, I pace around the house like a madwoman, repeatedly calling Nikolai and repeatedly getting nothing but his voicemail. By the time his car pulls down the driveway of the house, I'm a ticking time bomb of anxiety and confusion.

I catapult down the porch and meet him just as he's opening the driver's side door. "What did you do?" I demand.

Nikolai doesn't look fazed at the sight of me, despite the fact I'm one worry line away from donning a tin foil hat and pinning newspaper cutouts to a corkboard.

"Hi to you, too." He grabs me by the shoulders and gently moves me so he can step to the side and close his car door.

"Hi?" I snap. "That's what you have to say after standing me up for dinner and then not calling or answering your phone? *Hi*?! You could have been dead."

"You knew I wasn't dead."

"How do you know that?"

He gestures to me as if I'm proof enough. "Because clearly, you saw the news."

Yes, I saw the news. And I haven't been able to stop thinking about the news since I saw the news.

"What does that even mean?" I ask desperately. "You know I saw the news, which means you knew there was news to see. So that means… you did this?"

"Did what?"

"You know what! The news anchor said a university building—an entire freaking building!—was being named after Petyr Dowan. That's my dad's name."

Nikolai nods. "I'm aware."

"Why would they name a building after my dad?"

"Well, it's an architecture building," he says. "He liked architecture, didn't he?"

I nod.

"And you like architecture, don't you?" he continues.

I nod again.

"So there you go. An anonymous donation was made to revamp the college's school of architecture. It was named after your dad."

Nikolai makes it all sound so reasonable that I'm not sure why I was freaking out so much at the start.

"I—You—I mean… what?"

"Are you pleased?" he asks after a pause.

"I'm—Well—" In the shock, I never really stopped to think about it. But… "Yeah. Yeah, I am. It's—"

Oh Lord, there I go. Just like that, I'm crying. Weeping, actually. Blubbering like a big damn baby.

Nikolai laughs and pulls me against his chest. "I didn't want to make you cry."

"So you did this for me?" I blubber.

"Of course I did." He kisses the top of my head. "It was a wedding gift. I had it all lined up, but then they wanted to announce my name with the press release. I knew all the stories would be about me donating money instead of the name of the building. So I had to cancel dinner to negotiate. It cost me another million, but it was worth it."

"Another million?" I swipe at my eyes. "How… how much did you spend?"

"It doesn't matter."

"It matters to me."

"No, it doesn't. You don't care about money," he says.

"Well, I certainly care if you spent too much! And I'm guessing you did. They probably don't name buildings after people for a couple grand. And you're talking about a million like it's loose change." I shake my head, the news still not fully penetrating. "Why did you do this?"

Nikolai sighs. I can tell he doesn't want to rehash everything, but he's being remarkably patient with me. "I told you."

"Not really, though. If you wanted to get me a wedding gift, you could have given me jewelry. Or a knife. That's what Makar gave me."

"Don't talk to me about Makar," he growls.

I hold up a palm in apology. "But the point remains. This is a huge, massive, absurdly extravagant gift. I just don't understand—"

"Your father isn't here to see us get married or have a baby," Nikolai interrupts. "He can't be with you physically, but I'm only lucky enough to have you because you were lucky enough to have him. He helped you see a brighter future for yourself. He did for you what the Bratva did for me. He gave you drive and purpose. He helped you become who you are today. And I wanted to say thank you to him for that gift. This is my way of doing that."

My throat is clogged with emotion. I can't even form the words.

Nikolai wanted to tell my dad thank you… for *me*. He's thankful for me.

I thought seeing my dad's name on the news was surreal, and realizing that people are going to learn and study under my dad's name and go on to make the world a better, more beautiful place is overwhelming.

But realizing that Nikolai did all of this *for me*?

That is what steals my breath away.

"Are you going to cry more?" Nikolai asks warily.

Yes. Absolutely. If I try to speak, the dam will break. I'll lose it. I have to channel all of this emotion into something else.

So without another thought, I jump into Nikolai's arms and kiss him.

He catches me easily, molding me against his strong body. I hook my legs around his back and swirl my tongue into his mouth. He tastes like wine and peppermint, and I moan against his lips.

"Fuck. That sound," he growls. Within seconds, he's carrying me up the porch like this was the plan all along. Hell, maybe it was. He had to know this was one heck of a wedding gift. The kind that can only be repaid with vigorous, energetic sex.

We bang through the front door and into the entryway. What Elise said earlier about the two of us "going at it" runs through my mind, and I bite back a smile. She'll never know how right she was.

I pull my tank top over my head and throw it on the floor of the hallway.

"Much better." Nikolai's gray eyes burn across my flushing skin. I knew it was a good decision not to wear a bra.

"You think so?"

His response rumbles through his chest. "Absolutely. Never wear a shirt again."

"I'd never be able to leave the house."

"I fail to see the issue, *kotyonok*."

We reach Nikolai's room and he presses me back against the door. The breath whooshes out of me, and then he is everywhere. His hands grip my backside, his mouth is on my skin, his chest and hips move against mine in a slow, tortuous kind of friction.

He leans forward and takes my nipple into his mouth. I'm already pert and ready for him. When his tongue flicks over my puckered skin, I drag my fingers through his hair and moan.

"You're going to drive me crazy with that," he says, his lips moving across my chest.

His fingers work around the backs of my thighs, spreading my legs even further apart. I feel every inch of him through my thin lounge pants. He's huge and hard against my center, and I roll myself against him.

My movements are clumsy and feverish, but Nikolai kisses my neck and my collarbone. He dips back down to my breasts, sucking one nipple and then the other. It feels like we're discovering something new.

"No one knows what this is like," I pant crazily. "If they did, they'd never do anything else. Everyone would be doing this. All the time."

He chuckles. "We aren't even doing anything yet."

I'm about to ask what he means, but then he opens the door. For a second, I feel like I'm falling, but Nikolai's strong arms have a firm grip on me. He carries me to the bed and I instantly sit up and tug on the hem of his shirt.

"I'm naked. Now, it's your turn."

"You're not naked," he says, pinching my lounge pants. "If you were naked, we wouldn't be having this conversation. Our mouths would be otherwise occupied."

"Okay, but top for top. Take your shirt off."

Nikolai grabs the hem of his shirt with one hand and pulls it straight over his head. And my heart explodes.

He was right. We weren't doing anything before. Because now, his skin is right there for me to touch, and that changes everything.

Before he's even dropped the shirt on the floor, I lunge forward and unbutton his pants. In a sexed-up haze, I shove his pants and boxers down and wrap my hand around his erection.

"What the—Fuck." He closes his eyes and tips his head back. His Adam's apple bobs with obvious effort. "Belle, what are you doing?"

"You can't rip your shirt off like a lifeguard from a sex fantasy and expect me to be cool about it."

He chuckles, but the sound transitions to a groan as I add my other hand to his base. I work him in both directions, my hands meeting in the middle. I love the way he feels velvety against my palm, soft and hard at the same time. I get lost in the touching.

"If I'd known this was waiting for me, I would have paid so much more money," he sighs. "Fifty million doesn't begin to cover it."

I inhale sharply. "Fifty million. Holy—I've never even thought about that much money, let alone had it or seen it. You shouldn't have, Nikolai. You really, really shouldn't have done that for me."

Suddenly, Nikolai pulls my hands off of him and presses me back onto the bed. His hands shackle me to the comforter, and I never, ever want to get free.

"You're right—I didn't have to do this for you. But you're worth it, Belle."

He hooks his fingers into my waistband and pulls my pants and panties down my legs. His fingers trail fire across my skin.

"Worth fifty million?"

I don't even realize I've said the words out loud until Nikolai leans over my naked body and presses his lips to my navel.

"Worth everything," he answers. "Every fucking penny."

Kiss by kiss, he moves down my stomach and over my hip. He licks around my thigh and then, with a rough shove, slides my legs apart. I yelp in surprise, but then his breath is warm against my damp center, and I go gasping quiet. My entire body is humming with anticipation. I chew my lower lip, waiting for him to touch me, shaking with need.

When he finally spreads me with his fingers and licks across my clit, I explode.

"I'm coming," I cry out, barely believing my own words. He hardly touched me. But the pulsing pleasure at my core doesn't lie.

Nikolai sits up and watches me, awe written on his face. I'm pretty sure my entire body is fire engine red right now. I'm flushed with ecstasy and embarrassment as I buck and writhe on my back.

When I finally start to come down, I cover my face with my hands. "I can't believe that just happened."

"You came with one lick," Nikolai snorts. "One touch."

"Not one touch! There was all the kissing in the hallway. And the… the grinding." A laugh bubbles out of me. "This is embarrassing."

He kisses the inside of my thigh and shakes his head. "No, it's not. You may not know this, Belle, but being wanted by a woman is incredibly attractive."

"Then you must find lots of women attractive. Everyone with eyes wants you."

His fingers massage the still trembling muscles of my thighs. "And I want *you*."

"You do?"

"Knowing I can do that to you… that you react like that to me… it's sexy as hell."

"Really?"

He crawls over me, hooking his arms under my knees and bringing them slowly up until he's directly above me. "Really. But you know what's going to be even sexier?"

I feel the tip of him brushing against my center, teasing my opening. It makes it hard to focus on what he's saying. But I'm pretty sure nothing could be sexier than this. I might actually die from how freaking sexy Nikolai Zhukova is.

But distantly, I hear myself respond. "What's going to be sexier?"

"Making you come again," he announces.

Then, with one thrust, Nikolai fills me.

He moves into me, stretching and pressing until I think there's nowhere else for him to go. No possible way we'll fit. And then he slides deeper.

A guttural sound I've never heard before comes out of me. I dig my nails into his shoulder blades. "Please," I whisper.

I don't know what I'm asking for, but Nikolai must have an idea. Because he sits back on his heels, grips my thighs, and drives into me again and again.

I throw my arms over my head. I arch my back. I grip handfuls of the comforter in search of anything to hold onto. None of it does much good to slow the tide swallowing me whole right now.

The slap of our bodies coming together fills the room, and I'm not sure there's anything better than the sound of his heavy breathing. Nothing beats the way Nikolai falls apart.

"You take me so good," he growls.

His hand slides down my thigh and his thumb finds my center. In slow, steady circles, Nikolai takes me to the next level. I lift my hips to meet his touch and his thrust, and it's all too much in the best way possible.

I press my hand over my eyes, but he grabs my wrist and yanks my arm away. "I want to see you come."

I meet his eyes, and the dark desire I find there is what sends me over the edge. My brows pull together and my lips part in a moan as my body clamps around him. Nikolai's face creases in a mixture of pleasure and pain.

"I can feel you around me."

"Is it good?" I ask, even though I know the answer. Because there's no way he isn't feeling what I'm feeling. With every thrust, he drags out my pleasure. It feels like it could go on forever like this.

His eyes flutter closed. "So good. You feel so good, Belle."

I reach down and hook my hands around his thighs. Then I slowly grind my body against him. Nikolai goes perfectly still.

"I came. Now, it's your turn." I push against him in deliberate, intoxicating strokes. "Eye for an eye. Orgasm for an orgasm."

He looks down at where we're connected, his eyes heavily lidded, pupils blown wide. This is the closest I've ever seen him to losing control.

"Let me do this for you," I purr.

Nikolai slides his hands down my thighs. His fingers dig into the soft skin of my hips, and he pulls me more tightly against him.

With each wave of my body, friction drives me towards yet another peak. I palm my breasts, pinching my nipples between my fingers. And I hear Nikolai curse again.

"Touch yourself, *kiska*," he commands. "Don't stop."

Part of me distantly suggests that I should be embarrassed, but this man has seen everything. My highs, my lows. He's seen me crazy with rage and with lust. He's seen me crying on the floor and moaning in ecstasy.

What's crazy is that I *want* him to see it.

I want him to have all of it.

All of me.

I arch my back, and the new angle has me clenching my thighs around him. "I'm going to come again, Nikolai. I need it. I can't stop."

"Come with me," he rumbles.

And just as the first wave of warmth moves through me, I feel him release.

This orgasm is a lazy kind of heaven. A bliss that presses me into the mattress and drags me to the edge of consciousness. It's soft and delicate and perfect.

I feel Nikolai slide out of me and crawl onto the bed to lie next to me, but I don't move. He kisses the swell of my breasts and chuckles. "Are you still alive?"

"Can someone die from too many orgasms?"

He laughs. "We could find out."

"Don't tempt me. I'm alive, but just barely. I'm alive… and deliriously happy. And exhausted." I reach over and squeeze his hand. "Thank you."

"For the sex or the gift?"

I bring his hand to my mouth and kiss his rugged knuckles. "For you."

35

NIKOLAI

She falls asleep naked on the bed, her fingers twined through mine. She doesn't stir when I slip out of bed and pull on my clothes.

It feels like a crime to walk away from Belle right now. My wife is gorgeous, her skin practically glowing in the dark room. She looks like a painting. I want to capture this moment and hang it on my wall. If I could, she'd sell for millions. Billions.

But I'd never give her up. She's mine.

That thought alone pushes me out of the room. Who the fuck am I?

I've never let a woman fall asleep in my bed. *Until Belle.*

I've never let a woman live in my house. *Until Belle.*

I've never let anything come before my goals and the Bratva. *Until Belle.*

She is breaking all of my rules, and I don't care in the slightest. She's worth it.

Fifty million dollars, fifty billion. I'd give it all.

I'm so lost in thought that I don't even realize where I'm going until I walk through the patio doors and cut across the lawn. The night is still warm. The moon is out, casting pale shadows across the lawn, and bugs hum and buzz from the trees. I want to wake Belle up and bring her outside. Right now, freshly fucked and still buzzing with an orgasm, I feel like a wild animal. Like a king. The world seems to be bowing to me, so now is not the time to mourn. I want to fuck Belle in the grass and fall asleep under the stars.

So maybe it's actually the best time to mourn.

"God, you're a fucking sap," I mutter to myself in a voice that sounds like Arslan's.

Tucked in a small alcove off of the main garden is an elaborate stone bench and tall hedges. A well-manicured, shaded place where I can sit and visit my mother.

I drop down onto the bench and pat the placard on the backrest. "Hey, Mom."

Her name is smooth under my fingers, worn by years of sun and rain. Her headstone at the cemetery was in much worse shape, which was part of the reason I had her moved to the grounds. Here, I can make sure she's well taken care of.

"You'd like her," I say aloud. I always feel stupid talking to my mother, but there's something calming about it, too. I just pick up like we've been talking all along. Like we never stopped. It's all I have. "Her name is Belle. She's a lot like you. Tender-hearted, loyal, headstrong. She'll make a great mom to my children."

Children. It's the first time I've said it out loud. The first time I've admitted how serious this thing with Belle is. I mean, sure, we're married. But I see a life with this woman. I see her by my side for a long, long time.

It's another first. I've never imagined a future with any woman I've ever dated.

Until Belle.

"I'm not exactly an expert on the subject of love, but I think I might—"

Footsteps crunching across the gravel pathway have me biting off my words. I jump up and face the entrance to the alcove just as a security guard—Aleksei, I think—appears from the shadows.

"Sorry, Don Zhukova," he says, lowering his head. "I didn't mean to interrupt."

"So why did you?" I growl. "What's wrong?"

I just left Belle a minute ago, but the worry that she could be in danger is instant. The fear that I could lose her rises up in me unbidden and uncontrollable.

"Nothing is wrong. You have a visitor."

I relax, forcing out a breath between my teeth. "Who is it?"

There's a small hesitation before he responds. "Your father."

Arslan always referred to my father as "The Lion." I preferred the distance that threw up between us. Seeing him as his code word and nothing more was easier than recognizing who he actually was to me. Who he *is* to me.

Just another reason to miss my right-hand man.

"What the fuck is he doing here?"

Aleksei shrugs. "He said he wants to talk to you. He won't say about what. I asked, believe me."

I should turn him away. I don't owe him anything. I said everything I wanted to say when I stopped by the treatment center where he was living a few weeks ago.

But that doesn't mean he doesn't have something to say to me.

My dad wasn't built for the Bratva world, but he still has the connections. Maybe someone knows something about Xena or the Battiatos. Maybe he's come to bring me something useful. Something that could help me protect Belle and bring her sister home sooner.

"Fine. Show him in."

I follow the guard across the lawn to the patio, and then I wait there as he goes to let my father in. When Ioakim's slumped shadow moves around the corner of the house, regrets instantly rise up in me.

How could someone so weak have given life to me? He can't even hold up his own weight, let alone carry a family or a Bratva. It's pitiful.

And he seems to know it. As he approaches, he keeps his head down. Only his eyes rise up to me, the whites glowing in the moonlight.

"Nikky—" He pauses and shakes his head before correcting himself. "Nikolai. It's good to see you again."

"Wish I could say the same. You look like shit."

He holds up his right arm. There's a cast on his wrist. "I had a bit of a relapse."

"And the treatment center broke your arm over it?"

He chuckles humorlessly. "I actually broke my wrist. Accident. Fell cleaning gutters, if you can even believe it. And then there were painkillers… It wasn't anything serious, but I started losing control. I'm clean again, but it was hell there for a week or so."

That is precisely my definition of hell: being controlled by something beyond myself. Addiction has a firm grip on my father, even now.

"Is that why you're here? You looking for money for your next fix or something?"

He finally looks me full in the face, his creased eyes wide. "No. Nothing like that. Like I said, I'm clean again."

"Then why are you here?" I snap. "The sooner we get this over with, the better. I have a beautiful woman lying naked in my bed. I don't want to waste another second with you."

I don't need to brag to him. I don't care what he thinks. But I want him to know my life is bigger than him. That I have more than he could ever or will ever have. And I did it all without his help.

"Your wife?" he asks. "I saw the news in the paper. There was a picture. She's pretty."

"Thanks for your approval. I was dying for it."

He nods. "The two of you looked great together. I cut out the picture and put it in my top drawer."

"Am I supposed to be touched?" If anything, the image he paints is sad. Imagining him clinging to news of me from the outside, stashing away newspaper clippings like a rat hoarding treasure.

"No. Well, I mean, if you want to be," he says with a small laugh. "I'm just saying that… I'm here because I wanted to congratulate you, I guess. You're building a family for yourself. I'm proud of you."

Some people wait their whole lives to hear those words from their father.

I could not care less.

"I don't need your congratulations. I don't need anything from you."

He nods. "I know. You're a self-made man. Independent. You're better off than I ever was."

"That's a low bar."

He smiles again. I want to punch the expression off his face.

"That therapy the center forced on you must be working if you can stand here and smile while I remind you what a piece of shit you are."

"You don't need to remind me," he says solemnly. "I know. I've never forgotten. Not for a single day."

"I'm sure there are lots of days you've forgotten. Most of the ones you spent in the gutter."

He shakes his head. "The days like that are the days when I remembered most. I wasn't as strong as you. I needed something to take the edge off of the pain."

I don't remind him that I was twelve years old when all this went down. When the Battiatos stole what was rightfully ours. When cancer took what was rightfully ours, too. He already knows. It didn't change anything then and it won't change anything now.

"And you don't need to take the edge off anymore?"

"No, I don't. Don't get me wrong: I do want it," he says. "I still want it often. But I don't need it the way I did right after… right after I lost your mom."

It's been decades, but the words come out stilted. I can see the grief in his eyes. The deep pain that, until a couple months ago, I never fully understood.

Until Belle.

"You really loved her."

He takes a deep breath. "I really did. It was the best and worst thing I ever did."

I frown. "What does that mean?"

"Your mom was my world. My life. I would have given up anything for her, would have done anything. But then she got sick, and I couldn't do a damn thing." He swallows, dragging his teeth over his bottom lip. "I hated myself for that. I hated myself more than anything for not being able to get her the treatment she needed. And when I looked at how much you missed her, when I realized what a hole she had left behind, I knew I'd never be able to fill it. I knew I wasn't enough."

"So you didn't even try." It's not a question or an accusation. It's just a fact.

He shrugs weakly. "I thought you were better without me. I didn't think I was worthy. Because, without your mom, I didn't feel worthy. She was my everything. And sometimes, I think I would have been better off if I'd loved someone else a little less… does that make sense?"

Yes. The voice in the back of my head is nodding along. *You care about Belle like that. It's too much. It will ruin you both.*

"None of it matters," I grit out. "I managed fine without you. If you're still tortured over how badly you fucked up, you can let it go. I'm great."

"Are you… Is that your way of saying you forgive me?"

He's gone perfectly still. I can feel him holding his breath. He's been waiting for this, working towards this for months, years. I don't give a shit about any of that. But at some point, not forgiving him takes more effort than just letting all of this shit go.

I shrug. "I don't care enough to forgive you. Which means I don't care enough to hold a grudge."

"I'll take it," he says eagerly. "That's part of why I came here. I wanted to ask for forgiveness. I wanted to—"

"I thought you came to congratulate me on my wedding."

"That, too. Both. I saw you moving on with your life, and I just didn't want you to carry your resentments towards me forward. Hate is poison, son. I can't undo any of my choices, but I can try to make sure you don't repeat my mistakes."

"I'd never turn my back on my child," I snap. "I'll never repeat your mistakes."

"God, I hope not," my father murmurs. "Because I want more for you than that, Nikky. I've always wanted more for you."

"And I have it. Now, it's time for you to find more," I say, realizing how genuinely I mean every word. "Let this shit go—me, Mom, your guilt—and move on."

It's only been a minute, but he looks years younger. He holds himself a little taller, lifts his head a little higher.

He smiles. I can see tears in his eyes, but he has the self-respect to hold them back.

Finally, he nods.

"Thank you, son. I really... This is what I needed. Thank you."

He turns and shuffles away. But as he heads around the side of the house, disappearing back into the shadows, all I can wonder is whether I'm repeating his mistakes after all.

36

BELLE

I feel the familiar dip of his weight on the mattress next to me, and I can't help but wonder when his body next to mine became so familiar. When did Nikolai become this foundational part of my life?

I roll onto my side and drape an arm over his chest like I've done it a million times before. His skin smells like the night—dewy and lush. "Where were you?"

"Nowhere."

There's a strange note to his voice. Something that wasn't there when I fell asleep, but I'm drowsy and comfortable and it's late. I let it go for now.

"You weren't sleeping?"

"I'm not tired," he says. But he sounds dead exhausted. "Why aren't you asleep?"

"I was just thinking about when things switched," I murmur, my eyes still closed.

"Switched?"

I feel the subtle shifts in his breathing as he responds, the way his chest rises and falls. It's a steady thing. I squeeze him tighter.

"Yeah. Like, when things between us switched. When did we go from... whatever we were before... to this?"

"What is 'this'?"

It's embarrassing to have to define it, but Nikolai might be as new at this relationship stuff as I am. Neither of us know what we're doing. There's some strange kind of comfort in that.

"A marriage," I say, sort of ducking the question. "When did we become two people who like each other and, for the most part, get along? We talk now. We're honest with each other. It just feels... easy, doesn't it?"

I listen to the in and out of his breathing, the thudding of his heart beneath his rib cage. I'm so preoccupied that I don't immediately realize how long he's been silent.

Finally, I open my eyes and sit up. "Nikolai?"

"I have to tell you something," he says suddenly.

The bubble of bliss bursts in an instant. I turn to him, my pulse twice as fast as a second earlier. "Okay."

He doesn't feel the same way. You're coming on too strong. Three amazing orgasms and you're suddenly writing poetry and pretending you're in a fairytale. And he's going to rip it all away, watch him, brace for it, get ready because—

"I lied to you."

I try to quiet the naysayer in the back of my head, but I can't. As I watch Nikolai, his expression as unreadable as ever, every insecurity I've ever had comes rising up inside of me.

I inhale sharply and then force the air back out. If I keep breathing in and out, then I'll be okay. Actually, that's a lie—I've been through enough to know that's not true—but it's all I have right now.

"Lied about what?"

"About my family."

"Your family? You mean… they died, right?" I say, repeating what I remember. "Your mom died and your dad killed himself."

"That's what I told you. That's what I wanted to be true."

I frown. "You wanted your mom to die of cancer and your dad to kill himself? What the—what does that even mean?"

Nikolai sighs. "My mom did die of cancer. That was true. But the other part… well, if my dad had killed himself, it would have been easier than the truth."

"And what's the truth?"

But Nikolai just sighs again and passes a hand over his tired face. He looks so weary suddenly. Like he's been carrying the world on his back for so long and his legs are finally starting to tremble.

I groan. "Just tell me, Nikolai. I'm dying over here. What's wrong?"

"Nothing is wrong," he says. "But I lied about my dad killing himself. My dad didn't kill himself. He isn't even dead. He was actually here tonight."

My eyes widen. "Here? Like… *here* here? In the house? When?"

"After you fell asleep. He stopped by to see me."

"You see him? Not only is he not dead, but he drops by for visits? I don't understand why you'd lie about that. Is it because of my dad?" I ask. The words are all coming out in a torrid rush. "Did you feel bad that my dad was dead so you lied to me about yours?"

My stomach roils. I'm not with Nikolai because of his family or his past, but being with someone whose situation is just as messed up as mine has been comforting. And now, I'm finding out it was all bullshit.

"It isn't like that," he says, shaking his head. "Tonight is the first time he has dropped by. Ever. And it's only the second time I've seen him since I was a kid. He saw our wedding announcement in the paper and wanted to come offer his congratulations."

"You haven't seen him since you were a kid, but he came to congratulate you on getting married? Am I still asleep? Because none of this is making any sense at all."

"It's because I'm doing a shitty job of explaining it." For the first time, I see a shot of anxiety streak through Nikolai. He drags his hand through his hair. "He came to see me because I visited him a little while ago. I'd just found out you were pregnant and that I was going to be a dad, and I wanted to see him. That kind of opened the door, I guess."

"Okay," I breathe, setting that aside to process later. "So what's true then?"

"My mom really died, and my dad lost it. He couldn't handle that she died and he couldn't do anything to stop it. He fell into drugs and drinking. Anything to numb the pain."

"Wow. He must have really loved her," I say softly.

Nikolai's attention snaps to me. His gray eyes are narrowed. "He did. And it destroyed his life."

"Well, love didn't do that—" I start to say.

He interrupts me. "My father was beyond help. In many ways, it would have been easier if he'd died."

"He abandoned you," I guess.

Nikolai nods. "I was just a kid, and I lost both my parents in one fell swoop. He was too far gone to care much about me, but I cut him out of my life anyway. Everything else I've ever told you is true. I grew up as if he was dead. I made it without him."

The panic starts to fade as the admission settles. "So your dad is alive. Is he going to be part of your life now?"

"Not in any way that matters," he says. "I've learned everything I need to learn from him. Mostly how not to live my life."

For the first time, I can imagine Nikolai as a little kid. I can see him scared and alone, making his way through the world without anyone there to guide him.

I reach out to stroke my fingers through his hair, but he turns his head at the last second. I curl my hand into a fist and let it fall against the mattress. "You're a better man than he could ever be, Nikolai. You're loyal and dependable. You take care of people."

"I'm not worried about being like him," he snaps. "I'm nothing like him. I'm not going to abandon my children. I'm going to make the world better for them."

"Children?"

Nikolai's expression is open and vulnerable, but as soon as I voice that silly question, I watch it shutter closed.

"Child," he growls. "I only have the one. Unless you have a secret you're keeping."

"No, just the one. For now," I say gently. "But we could have more… if you wanted. We could have a family."

The idea settles over me like a warm blanket. The image of a whole brood of dark-haired, gray-eyed babies is enough to bring tears to my eyes. Though that could be the pregnancy hormones speaking.

I want it. All of it. I want a future with Nikolai, and I'm tired of tiptoeing around that fact.

"Do you want a family?" I press. "Would you want more children?"

His jaw works side to side. "I don't know what I want, Belle."

Some small part of my mind is waving a red flag, trying to warn me off. But I'm too high on this night. Nikolai dropped tens of millions of dollars on a wedding gift for me and we spent one of the most passionate hours of my life together.

Even if he can't say it, he feels it. I know he does.

"Well, I know exactly what I want," I say, charging ahead. "I want *you*, Nikolai. I want the whole happy picture with you. I—I love you."

I hold the words out to him like my own little gift. Waiting for him to take them, to do something with them. Waiting for him to do anything to let me know he feels the same way.

There's one moment where I believe he might say it back. When all my hope hangs in the balance.

Instead, Nikolai's top lip curls. "Then you're with the wrong man."

The next few seconds pass in slow motion.

I feel the smile slip from my face bit by bit as his words sink in. I shake my head. "No—what does that mean?"

"I'm never going to have a picture-perfect family, Belle. I'll never give you that."

I shake my head, trying to push away what he's saying. "You can, Nikolai. You're not your dad. Remember what you said? You'll be there for me and your kids."

"I'll never abandon my child," he corrects, his voice cold and flat. "And I'll take care of you. But—"

"But." I draw away from him, sliding off the edge of the bed and landing on shaky legs on the floor. "But… you don't want this?"

His full lips press together into a flat, silent line.

And the world around me starts to crumble.

"I thought you… I thought we wanted the same things." Tears burn the backs of my eyes, but I blink them away. "You didn't want me to go to Iceland. You wanted me to stay here with you. And the building… My dad's name is on the building. The wedding gift."

My words are becoming more and more disjointed. As my world falls apart, so does my ability to form full sentences.

Nikolai shrugs. "I don't want you to be miserable. So I let you stay. But that doesn't mean…"

His voice trails off, and oh God, how bad can it be that even Nikolai doesn't want to say the words aloud? The man has killed people with his bare hands. If he can't tell me what he's thinking, then what he's thinking must be devastating. He's trying to spare me, but there's no saving this.

I'm already lost.

"Oh my God." I press both hands to my chest to keep my heart from lurching out of my ribcage. "You're… you don't love me. Okay. Alright."

My head is bouncing like a bobblehead, but none of this is okay. I'll never be alright.

"How did I convince myself you loved me?" I ask with a wheezing kind of chuckle. "I am so, so stupid. I can't believe I… I'm sorry."

Nikolai is sitting on the bed and watching me. That makes it even worse.

He's not trying to talk me down or correct my assumption. He's sitting quietly while the reality sinks in.

He doesn't love me.

He never did.

I turned this into something it wasn't.

Embarrassment swiftly turns to rage. I set my jaw, clenching my teeth purely so I won't sob. "Well? Are you going to say something?"

"I... I never wanted to hurt you, Belle."

At that, I bark out a laugh. "Well, thanks, I guess. That doesn't help at all. But at least you didn't *mean* to rip out my heart and stomp on it. You just did it."

He drops his face and sighs. "You're a good person, Belle."

"But not good enough, apparently." I move towards the door. "Why did you let me stay here? If this is how you felt, why did you—I could be with my sister right now. I chose to be here, and you knew why."

"I didn't know you were going to do this," he snaps.

"Maybe not. But you know everything. You knew why I decided to stay. And you let me."

I lean back against the door and remember the last time I was pressed against it. When Nikolai was holding me, his hands and mouth on my body.

The memory feels tainted now.

"I knew you could be vicious, but I never thought you'd be cruel." A sob nearly bursts out of me, but I swallow it down. "Especially not to me."

He's sitting up in bed now, staring at me. I feel like some kind of freak show on display. My skin is hot enough that I'm surprised I'm not steaming, and I know every emotion must be written plainly on my face.

The love. The pain. The heartbreak.

I can't be here anymore. I can't look at him. And I sure as hell can't have him looking at me.

I spin around and yank the door open. Maybe Nikolai says something, maybe he doesn't, but either way, I don't hear it. By the time I step into the hallway, the tears I managed to hold back have sprung free. I'm sobbing and running away from him.

It doesn't matter what he says now anyway. There's nothing he can say to fix this.

The only thing I want to hear is an impossibility.

I love you, Belle. Of course I love you.

But he doesn't. He never did.

I'm just the naive fool who believed he could.

I run to the opposite end of the house before I realize there's nowhere to go where he won't find me. I can't leave in the middle of the night, and I can't just sit in the kitchen or the sitting room while I'm like this.

I need somewhere private. Somewhere quiet.

That's when it hits me: the place I've always gone to hide. The safe space I created as a little kid when I was alone in the world, unloved and terrified. Just like now.

I double back to the discreet doorway across the hallway I've never opened before. During the initial tour of the house, Nikolai said it was storage. It's exactly what I need now. I need to hunker down in a dark closet, take a few deep breaths, and figure out how to carry on from here.

"Belle!" Nikolai's voice echoes through the dark house. "Belle, wait!"

Panic creeps up my spine. I can't see him now. Not yet. I need a few minutes.

I yank open the door and step into the darkness...

But I meet no resistance where the floor should be. No ground under my foot. No rail or wall to catch myself on. I can only throw my arms forward as I tumble headfirst into the pitch black, a scream on my lips.

37

BELLE

It's dark. It's so unbelievably, blindingly dark.

"Belle. Belle, are you okay?"

The words are coming from all around me. Somewhere far away and inside my own head at the same time.

"Are you okay?" Nikolai's voice asks again.

I blink hard and open my eyes. When I do, there's only more darkness. But I feel Nikolai around me. The real Nikolai. He is damp with sweat. The room around us smells like musk and earth.

"I'm going to pick you up," he says. "Tell me if something hurts."

Everything hurts, I think. But I can't force the words out. My lips won't move, and the harder I try, the more tired I get.

My eyes drop closed and the world fades away.

Nikolai looks like a god. He's shirtless and jogging towards me, sweat glistening across his skin.

"Did you have a good run?" I ask, swallowing back the lust clogging my throat. I want to lick him clean.

He slows to a stop in front of the porch and shakes out his limbs. Muscles ripple. It takes physical effort to keep my tongue from lolling out of my mouth.

"I finished, so I guess it was fine. I prefer getting my cardio in other ways," he says, wagging dark brows at me. "But you said you were busy, so—"

A blush creeps across my chest, but I hold my chin high. "Next time you want to have sex in the middle of the afternoon, I'll tell the kids to make their own damn snacks."

"Good. It's about time they learn." He grins and swipes a hand across his forehead. "Where are the kids, anyway?"

"Aunt Elise came and picked them up. She's taking them to the children's museum and then for ice cream."

Nikolai's gray eyes lock on mine. "Are you telling me the house is empty?"

"That is exactly what I'm telling you, Mr. Zhukova." I lean back on my palms, back arched, shamelessly ogling him. "What are you going to do about it?"

He crosses the distance between us in two strides and scoops me into his arms. I yelp, but there's no need. He won't drop me. He never has.

"You're all sweaty." I swipe my fingers across his golden chest, trying to be disgusted with him. But I'm only human.

"And about to get sweatier." He leans down like he's going to kiss me, but I barely feel the brush of his lips.

"Hey!" I wrap a hand around his neck and pull him down to me. Once again, his lips move across me, but I don't feel a thing. "Why aren't you kissing me?"

I open my eyes. Nikolai is still holding me, but his face is suddenly, bizarrely blank. His gaze is flat. Lifeless. He looks down at me, slack-jawed and vacant, and asks, "Why would I kiss you?"

"Because... because you're my husband?" *I laugh, but it's a weak, nervous sound.*

He shakes his head. "No, I'm not."

"Is this a joke? This is a weird joke."

"It's not a joke."

"Then what is it?" *I demand, suddenly angry.* "We're married. You and I, we—we had a wedding. And how do you explain the kids? There are three of them."

Nikolai shakes his head again. "I don't know what you're talking about."

"Nikolai, stop! We have three kids. Their names are..." *I think hard, but no names come to me. My mind goes perfectly blank. I grunt in frustration.* "I know we have kids! What are their names?"

"We don't have kids," *he says, his voice shifting to a lower pitch with every word, into baritone, into something too low to be real. I barely recognize it now.* "We don't have anything. There is nothing between us."

"What are you even saying? This doesn't make any—"

I look up and Nikolai's face is gone. It's like he was a graphite drawing and someone smudged the image. His features shift and slide and blur until he is a cloud. Until he doesn't exist.

Until nothing exists.

I scream, but it doesn't make a sound.

∼

I try to sit up, but a strong arm around my chest forces me back into the thin mattress. I claw at it, a scream rising in my throat. But it isn't an arm; it's a strap. I'm pinned to a bed.

"You're okay, Belle."

Nikolai's voice is close and familiar, but there's no comfort there. Not after the dream I just had.

I try to turn towards him, but my neck is locked in place. "You have a neck brace on," he explains from just out of sight when I try to thrash against the restraint. "It's a precaution. You kept throwing yourself around in your sleep, so they strapped you down so you wouldn't get hurt."

"Where are you?" My voice is little more than a rasp, but Nikolai hears me. He gets up out of the armchair he was sitting in and stands next to my bed where I can see him.

He isn't shirtless or sweaty like he was in my dream, but his facial features are all exactly where they should be. I guess that's a good thing, more or less.

"What happened?"

"You hurled yourself down a flight of stairs." He looks down at the floor. His hands are shoved deep in his pockets, and I wonder if there's room in there for me to hide. Because I want to be anywhere except for right here. "You could have killed yourself."

"I thought it was a closet."

His eyes snap to mine. "What?"

"I didn't know there were stairs there." The memory of falling through empty air rushes over me. I feel nauseous.

All at once, I jerk against the strap again. It cuts into my chest, and I can only whimper.

"What the fuck are you doing?" he growls. "Stop—"

"The baby."

His lips press together. I want to pry them open. I want to make him talk.

"Nikolai," I whisper, "is the baby okay?"

"You've been through the ringer tonight. You need to relax. The doctor wants you to rest."

I reach around my side and unhook the strap from the side of the hospital bed. My body is sore as I sit up, but I feel okay. I'll be covered in bruises, but I'll survive.

Now, I want to know if my baby will.

I swing my leg over the side of the bed, but Nikolai grabs my ankle. "Belle, no."

"Don't touch me." I try to kick his hand away, but he dodges and then moves up to press my shoulders back into the mattress.

"Lie down."

Only a few hours ago, I would have grabbed his arms and pulled them around myself. I would have sunk into his touch and lost myself there.

Now, his hands on me are hollow comfort.

"I'm fine," I snap, shoving him away. "If the doctor gets mad, I'll tell them standing up was my idea."

"I don't give a fuck whose fault the doctor thinks it was."

"Then why do you care?"

We stare at each other, our last conversation ringing in the silence between us. He doesn't care. That has been well-established.

"No, I know," I blurt, talking before he can. "It's because I'm pregnant. That's why you care. Isn't it? The only reason. You just don't want anything happening to the baby."

He's silent for a long time.

Then he says the only words that could break my heart any further.

"There is no baby anymore, Belle. The baby is gone."

He says it so fast that I almost miss it. I pause, waiting for him to say something else. To somehow restate the sentence in a way that won't cut me to the bone.

"Wh… what?" I finally splutter when he offers nothing else.

He sighs and shakes his head. "They said they didn't hear anything. No heartbeat. The baby didn't make it."

I drop back onto the bed, the weight of my body too much to bear.

It's over. Everything is over.

Even when Nikolai told me that he didn't care about me, some small, pathetic part of me thought he would come around. If I gave him a child and we raised it together, he'd learn to love me. All the time we'd spend together, playing and making food and changing diapers… Deep bonds are formed in the trenches. I thought we'd go through the trenches of parenthood together. I thought that one day everything would work out.

But now, the baby is gone and we have nothing.

"I've lost everything," I whisper.

I squeeze my eyes closed. I don't want to cry anymore. Especially because I don't think Nikolai will comfort me, and crying in front of someone who couldn't care less would only make it all worse.

Suddenly, a shrill ring cuts through the room. I glance back at the machines around my bed, but they're beeping along as usual.

"It's mine." Nikolai holds up his phone for a second. Without looking at me, he backs towards the door. "I have to take this."

I nod weakly. "Okay."

The second the door closes, I collapse on the bed. I can't hold myself up another second. But I can't cry, either.

My eyes burn, my throat is clogged, but the tears won't come. The rug has been pulled out from under me in every way, and I don't know how to respond. So I press my face into the stiff, over-bleached blankets and focus on inhaling and exhaling.

When Nikolai comes back, I don't want to look as shredded to pieces as I feel. I have to be able to face reality: he doesn't love me and our baby is gone.

Physical pain lances through me at those twin thoughts. It's a snake eating its own tail, two sides of the same coin, one leading into the other, the other leading right back into the first. He doesn't love me and our baby is gone. Our baby is gone and he doesn't love me.

Slowly, I press up to sitting. Just as I get myself resituated in the bed, the blankets pulled up around my waist, the door opens.

I turn to the window. I don't want to see him. Not yet.

Footsteps pad across the floor, but I focus on the window. The blinds are halfway open. I can see slashes of the sky and the buildings surrounding the hospital. The day looks bright and warm—a far cry from the chill creeping into my chest.

I feel a presence behind me, the magnetism of a body close to mine.

Then there's a sharp pinch in my bicep.

I spin around and see the syringe in my arm first. The needle is long and thin, gleaming in the sunlight.

As I watch, a pale, delicate hand pushes the plunger down all the way.

"What—" Realization is already coming over me as I look up into the face of the last person I ever wanted to see again.

"Good to see you again, Belle," says Xena.

Her face is clean and makeupless, making the sharp lines of her cheekbones even more brutal. When she smiles, I instinctively pull back. It's like a she-wolf showing me her teeth before she rips my throat out.

I inhale to scream, but the sound stays locked in my lungs. My tongue has disconnected from the rest of me. Piece by piece, my body is going offline. My arms hang uselessly at my sides and my legs are lumps beneath the blankets.

"Don't bother trying to fight," Xena murmurs, brushing my hair away from my forehead in a weirdly tender gesture. "The medicine is already taking effect. You'll be gone in a couple seconds."

Gone? I want to ask what that means, but I can't ask anything. Even thinking is becoming difficult. My thoughts float behind a gauzy veil I can't seem to break through.

But one thought is crystal clear, even as my vision goes dark: I wish Nikolai was here.

38

NIKOLAI

"What do you mean you don't know where she is?" I growl.

A crowd of nurses and orderlies are cowering around me. They've been scurrying around like mice for the last few minutes, trying in vain to figure out where Belle might be. But no one has a satisfactory answer.

"She was here when I left," I snap. "Belle was in that bed when I walked out of her room. I talked to a hospital executive for ten fucking minutes, and now, she's gone? Where the fuck did she go?"

No one has any answers. The only reason I left Belle when I did was because I thought it was her doctor calling, but instead it was some C-suite idiot calling to kiss my ass and apologize for a clerical mistake. I was on my way back to the room to tell Belle the news.

But now, she's gone.

She's gone.

For fuck's sake, she's *gone*.

"I checked the cameras," a scrawny male nurse stutters, squeezing his way into the panicked circle. "A woman in a nurse's uniform walked into her room minutes after you left, Mr. Zhukova. She wheeled Mrs. Zhukova out a minute later."

"Which nurse was it?"

His face pinches into a grimace. "I didn't recognize her. She wasn't even wearing a badge."

And instantly, I know.

"Mr. Zhukova?" The head nurse calls after me, but I'm already pushing through the double doors at the end of the hall. "Where are you going?"

My answer is too low for anyone to hear.

"I'm going to kill her."

∽

Xena isn't stupid enough to move into her brother's old house—not while I'm still alive, anyway—but there are lights on inside nonetheless.

Considering she killed her own brother inside these walls, any sane person would think she'd sell the place or demolish it. But Xena isn't sane. And soon, she'll join her brother.

There's only a single guard in a shack near the front gate. When I approach, he isn't even watching the monitors. His eyes are trained down at his phone, and based on the moans coming from the tinny speakers, I've caught the man with his pants down.

"Security is a little laxer now that Giorgos is dead," I remark.

The man whips around at the sound of my voice, his hand wrapped around his dick. His eyes are wide and terrified. He opens his mouth to say something, but I don't have the time for banter. I shoot him between the eyes and reach over his slumped body to disconnect the perimeter cameras.

Xena may control the Simatous and the Battiatos alike, but even she can't win a war with zero soldiers. When I'm done sweeping this place, that's exactly how many she'll have left.

I storm down the walk. The front door is locked, but it's pitiful protection. One kick and the wood swings inward and careens against the wall. Hinges break.

A Simatou man is standing in the middle of the entryway, a cellphone pressed to his ear and a smile frozen on his face. He blinks in confusion, and then he's on the floor, too. Blood pools around where his head once was. I step over the mess and keep going.

Everything is white and bedazzled with gems or covered in mirrors. I see the reflection of my feet in the mirrored entryway table pressed against the wall. I also see the shadow of a man closing in from the living room behind me.

He lunges just as I turn around and catch him in the chin with an elbow. His head whips to one side, and I follow the blow with a kick to the side of his knee. He buckles, hitting the floor with a pained groan. It gives me enough time to aim and fire.

"Three down."

The sound drew some attention, so by the time I get back to the hallway, two more men are there, trying to figure out what is going on.

"Sh-she isn't here, N-Nikolai," the shorter man stammers as I approach.

"I don't know if you're talking about Xena or Belle, but it doesn't matter." I raise my gun and fire just as he dives to the side. The shot catches him in the shoulder, and he roars in pain as he hits the ground. "You will die either way."

The second man scrambles for his weapon, but I kick his right arm and his gun goes flying across the floor. It fires as it hits the tile, shattering a nearby mirror into jagged shards.

"We didn't take her!" he cries. "No one here knows where she is."

I knock him to the floor, stand over him, and press my boot into his chest. He wheezes against the crushing weight, but he's too busy staring at the barrel of my gun to be overly worried about breathing.

"I'm not here to find Belle. I know she isn't here."

The other man drags himself against the wall, his right arm hanging limply. "Then why—"

"To kill you," I sigh. "As if I need a better fucking reason."

Before either of them can argue, I pull the trigger on the man under my foot and then turn to the man slumped against the wall. He raises a hand to hold me off, as if that might help.

It doesn't.

The rest of the house is easy to clear. It's embarrassing how inadequate the security is. If I wasn't already certain Xena wouldn't bring Belle here, I'm positive by the time I comb through the final wing of the sprawling mansion.

"Anyone back here?" I call, kicking open a door to a linen closet. "I'm sure you've heard your friends die by now. So if you are back here, it's because you're a fucking coward."

No movement from within. No sirens from without, either. Maybe the neighbors know to keep their mouths shut about strange happenings inside these grounds. I peek into an empty bathroom and keep moving.

Yuri and Christo are separately searching for where Xena may have taken Belle. I called them both on the drive here. But I couldn't go home and wait. I couldn't sit in my empty house while I knew Xena had my wife.

Every time I think of the way she looked at me in my bedroom—the same way she looked at me in the hospital—I feel sick.

She looked utterly broken. Because of *me*.

And in a clumsy attempt to convince her I cared, I made it all worse.

I tighten my hand around my gun. The heat burns into my palm. I'll tear the Simatou mafia apart limb by limb before I let Belle die thinking she has lost everything.

My phone rings. At the same time, I hear movement in the room to my right. Looks like I do have one final coward on my hands. A soldier who would rather hide than come out and face me. Pathetic.

I answer my phone as I tiptoe around the corner of the doorway. "What do you have, Christo?"

"Nothing," he growls. "I've looked fucking everywhere, Nikolai. Wherever Xena has taken her, it isn't one of the usual spots. It's somewhere new."

"She doesn't want me to sneak up on her."

"Or she doesn't want to be found," Christo suggests.

I shake my head. "Xena always wants to be found. The woman needs an audience. She just wants to control the performance."

"What does that mean?"

"It means I need to send her a message."

"What kind of—"

I hang up before Christo can finish. With one swift movement, I kick the door to my right wide open. It bounces off the wall, and I hear a yelp from deeper in the room.

"Come out now and I'll let you live," I boom.

There's a long pause before the man speaks. "Bullshit. You're going to kill me like you did everyone else."

"Maybe. But would you rather die facing me or cowering behind the bed?"

The location was just a guess, but a good one. A few seconds later, the man stands up, facing me across a queen-sized bed. He's young—barely twenty, if that—with a patchy beard and red-rimmed eyes.

"All your friends are dead."

He swallows nervously. "They weren't my friends. I barely knew them."

"Are you trying to tell me you aren't one of them?"

"I am. But only for a week." His chin wobbles, but he quickly shakes his head to try and maintain his composure. "I was just recruited and initiated. I moved into this house yesterday, and now—"

"Death is here." I give him a cold smile. "But I told you if you came out, I'd spare you. I'm a man of my word."

He swallows hard. "Why would you do that?"

"Because you're going to deliver a message for me," I inform him. "You're going to tell Xena that I want to meet. You're going to find her and tell her that this war ends now. Can you do that?"

He nods. "But… why me?"

I look him up and down, from his buzzed head to his scuffed sneakers. "Because you're the only one still alive. And because I want Xena to know that the sole reason you're alive is that I spared you."

His frown deepens, but he doesn't argue. He isn't really in the position.

"Can you do that or would you rather join your friends?" I ask.

"I can do that," he says quickly. "I'll tell Xena."

We stare at each other for a few seconds before I snap, "Then what the fuck are you waiting for?"

The man gasps and then hurries by me, keeping a wide berth. I could follow him and find out who he is calling or where he's going to deliver the message, but it isn't necessary. Xena will reach out and tell me where to meet. She won't be able to help herself.

Once that happens, I'll find her.

Then I'm going to wring her neck for what she's done.

39

BELLE

A sharp pain radiates down my arm and vibrates through my bones.

"Wake up already," a distant voice whines. "This is boring."

I feel like I'm underwater. My ears are full and my vision is blurred. I can't tell which way is up.

"Come on."

There's a sharp jab against my hip. The pointed toe of a shoe, if I had to guess.

The last thing I remember is laying in the hospital bed, waiting for Nikolai… and then Xena. The syringe. Her laugh. I thought she was killing me. But I should have known better—Xena would never make it that easy. Why kill me in a hospital bed when she could toy with me in what I have to assume is some kind of sadistic torture dungeon?

"You're awake now," Xena croons in my ear. "I know it. You just can't stop pretending, can you? Can't stop lying and wasting my time."

Someone grabs me by the arm and hauls me up. I'm conscious, but barely. Not enough to open my eyes or respond. I'm just starting to realize that I'm sitting upright when there's a hard crack across my face.

Stars burst across my vision and my face burns from the heat of the slap. And one thing becomes crystal clear: I'm in a lot of trouble.

"Oh, Bellyyy?" Xena taunts in a sing-song voice. "Wake up and play."

I pry my eyes open, squinting against the dim lights above me. I have no idea how long I've been unconscious or where I am. It should be terrifying, waking up with Xena looming over me like Death's eager minion, but I can't find the energy to really care.

"There you are!" Xena grins. "Finally. I worried I gave you too much of the sedative. It would have been no fun if you'd died in your sleep. What a waste that would be, right?"

I don't know if she expects an answer from me, until she's suddenly yanking on my hair, arching my body up so she can snarl into my face.

"I said, *'Right?'*" she spits.

"Dying would be preferable to ever seeing you again." I think the words come out alright, but my mouth feels like it's full of cotton. It could be a garbled, incoherent mess for all I know.

Xena lets go of my hair. I drop to my knees on the concrete floor.

"What's the matter?" she asks, pacing in a circle around me. "Trouble in paradise?"

Paradise? I want to bark out a laugh, but I don't want to give her the satisfaction. She doesn't deserve an explanation.

"I figured you'd be begging for me to spare you and your baby." She narrows her eyes at me, her expression turning acidic as she glances at my stomach. "I bet you didn't know Nikolai put a target on your back when he put that baby in your womb."

"I actually think he put a target on my back when he put his dick in me," I snap back. "Again and again and—"

Xena rears back and strikes. I barely have a millisecond to brace before her palm cracks across my face again. The metallic tang of blood fills my mouth this time.

"You'd be a lot better off if you could keep your mouth and your legs closed," she hisses.

I would remind her that she is the one who forced me to talk, but there's no point. Xena sees the world the way she wants to see it. Logic and reason don't factor in.

She bends down and snarls in my face, "You destroyed my plan. You wrecked everything. And now, I'm going to do the same to you in the most painful, agonizing way possible. If you had any idea what I have planned for you, you'd start begging."

"Begging for what? My life?" I shrug. "You can have it."

She pulls back, arching an eyebrow. She's put on makeup since the hospital, I notice. The wings of her eyeliner flare out nearly to her temples. She looks more like a cartoon villain than an actual person.

"Are you trying to make me feel sorry for you? You steal my life—my fiancé, my baby—and now, it's not good enough for you?"

I didn't steal anything. To steal it, you have to possess it. And nothing about Nikolai has ever been mine.

Not his heart. Not his baby. Nothing.

The only thing I have left is Elise. And even she is safer without me around.

Emotion creeps up my throat, but I won't cry in front of Xena. I won't. She's like a shark in the water—if she smells blood, she won't fetch me a bandage; she'll take a bite.

I swallow it all down. "He doesn't love you," I croak aloud. "He doesn't love you at all."

Xena's eyes flare, and she slaps me again, harder than ever.

But she doesn't realize I wasn't talking to her.

40

NIKOLAI

I'm back at the warehouse Christo took me to the first time we went looking for Belle. The rusted-out shell in the center of a ring of Simatou-owned buildings.

Chasing Xena is like a game of Whack-A-Psycho. Just when you think you've beat her down, she pops up again.

But this time will be the last.

Tonight, this all comes to an end.

Her message told me to come alone, so I ease through the unlocked front door and into the long, narrow entryway by myself. Christo is parked nearby, a group of my men on standby a few blocks away. But I don't think I'll need them.

The last time Christo and I were here, I knew instantly the building was empty. The air was stale and every noise rang through the space like a hollow drum. But today, there's an electricity in the air. I feel myself being drawn forward like there's an invisible string attached to my chest.

Belle is here.

I know it.

My gun is on my hip. I rest my hand there as I step through the door into the main space. Dust swirls in front of the fluorescent lights in the ceiling and dim shafts of moonlight cut through the few windows that aren't blacked out. It's into one of these patches of light that Xena emerges.

"You came," she trills happily.

I fight an eye roll. The woman is staging this like a fucking movie. I wouldn't be surprised if she had some of her men come and stir up the dust just to make it more cinematic.

"Did you think I wouldn't?"

She lifts a lazy shoulder. "Maybe I had doubts about your true feelings for your darling bride. I wondered if she'd be worth the trouble."

"You clearly thought so," I reply. "You've tried to abduct her three times now. Maybe we should question if you're the one in love with her."

Xena laughs. "You know I only have eyes for you, Nikky."

"You only have eyes for yourself. The only reason you give a shit about me is because I don't give a shit about you."

Proving my point, Xena's smile sharpens. Her eyes brighten, and I half-expect them to shift into something predatory and inhuman. She doesn't scare me in the slightest, but she's a hunter, no doubt about that. I'd be foolish to underestimate her.

"Don't provoke me, Nikolai. I still have your wife. Or have you already forgotten?"

I've been actively working not to scan the room. I don't want Xena to think I'm panicked. But the fact I haven't seen any proof that Belle is here—or alive, even—is weighing on me.

The last conversation we had… Things between us can't end that way.

"I haven't forgotten a thing," I tell her. "I'm just not surprised. I held up my end of the bargain and showed up, but I doubted whether you'd hold up yours. Maybe no one has told you this before, but you're kind of a sneaky bitch."

Xena tips her head back and cackles. The light glints off her teeth, and for a second, they look like fangs. "Such a charmer. Shame our wedding didn't pan out. Though maybe we'll get a second chance. Nothing is guaranteed. People die all the time these days. Especially people close to you."

I gnash my teeth. "Where is she, Xena?"

Xena stares back at me for a few seconds, her brow arched. It's a wordless challenge. A quiet game of Chicken.

I bite my tongue and wait. She can't bait me the way she can everyone else in her life. I won't fall for her tricks.

Finally, Xena sighs and waves an arm over her head. "God, you're no fun."

A door at the back of the warehouse opens and two figures break through the gloom. Even in the shadows, it's not hard to figure out which one is Belle.

She's small and pale, and her head snaps in my direction the moment the door opens. She has a gag belted around her mouth, and at the sight of it, my hands ball into fists so tight I think my knuckles might burst.

The man holding her, however, keeps his gaze trained on Xena. As they move across the room, he holds onto Belle's arms. I'm distracted by his hands on her biceps, by the delightful thought of breaking his fingers one by one for even daring to touch her.

But when they step into the light next to Xena, my anger bubbles to the surface. A low growl rumbles through my chest.

"Makar."

He turns to me, and sure enough, my ex-soldier is the one manhandling my wife. He grimaces like he's tasted something bad. The feeling is more than mutual.

"A little family reunion," Xena burbles. "You two know each other, don't you?"

She knows we do. The only reason Makar is here is because Xena, for some ridiculous reason, thought I'd give a fuck that one of my men left me for her. If Makar is stupid enough to think Xena is a good leader, then I'm happy to let him go.

"Careful there, Xena. Your little stooge there broke his vow to my Bratva. I'm not sure I'd put him in charge of the captives."

"Only because you turned your back on us to make vows to her," Makar hisses, tightening his hold on Belle.

"And unlike you, I take my vows seriously," I tell him. "Which is why I'll tear your head off with my own hands if you hurt a hair on hers."

I can feel Belle's eyes boring into me, but I can't look at her right now. Xena brought her out to distract me. I won't let that happen.

"Promises, promises," Xena purrs.

She walks in a circle around Makar, her finger dragging across his shoulders. He looks over his shoulder at her, a small smile on his face. If the two of them haven't fucked already, I'll fall over dead.

"That's the problem with you, Nikolai," Xena continues. "You talk and talk, but there's no follow-through."

"When are you going to get over the fact that we didn't get married?" I fire back. "It's pathetic to hold a grudge this long. Especially when it's clear you've got a good fuck buddy in Makar here."

Makar's face hardens, but Xena's expression brightens. Right there is my answer. "Jealous?" she asks.

"Hardly. I'd rather cut my dick off than let it anywhere near you."

Slowly, Xena's smile drains away. Her dark painted lips twist into a frown. "I think it's time to see if you're a man of your word, Nikolai."

I snort. "Are you gonna say I have to fuck you or cut my own dick off?"

"You're not so far off," she says. "I'll give you a choice: fuck me right here, right now, and I'll let you leave with your bride. Say no, and… well, I'll let you fill in the blanks."

Belle snaps her attention back to Xena, absolute murder in her eyes. If Makar wasn't holding her back, I think Xena would have her hands full fending off Belle.

But there's no need.

I bark out a laugh. "God, you're desperate."

"You're the one preoccupied with who I'm sleeping with."

"Only because you're paying for loyalty with your pussy. I'm trying to gauge how dedicated the man next to you is. Thus far, my read is 'not very.'"

"Come and find out, Nikky."

I roll my eyes. "None of this matters. I'm not touching you. Why would I put myself through that kind of hell when I could just kill you and leave with Belle instead?"

"Because you'll have to go through Makar," Xena says, pushing the man towards the middle of the floor.

Makar stumbles forward, taking Belle with him for a second before he lets her go and turns around to face Xena. "What is—I was here to deliver the girl. I thought—"

"I thought you were loyal to me," Xena interrupts flatly. Whatever kindness she's usually able to piece together is gone from her expression. She's cold as ice. "You came to me after you left the Zhukova Bratva. You told me you admired my ferocity."

"I did," Makar says quickly. "I do. But I didn't think I was coming here to fight."

He didn't think he was coming here to fight *me*, more precisely. And he's right to be hesitant. I'll fucking kill him.

"Life is war, baby. You have to be ready all the time. If you want to work for me, you have to fight for me." Xena steps forward and drags a seductive finger down Makar's chest. "Can you do that?"

The man practically moans at the slightest bit of contact. It's pathetic. In one touch, his uncertainty falls away.

He turns to me, shoulders back, chin high. "I can do it."

"By 'it,' do you mean 'die'?" I ask. "Because if so, I agree. You can do it right up there with the best of them."

Xena lays her hand on his shoulder, drumming her long fingernails across his shirt. "Take him down, Makar. And make sure he lives up to his promise."

Makar looks back at her. "What promise?"

Xena looks past him to me, her mouth turned up in a smile. "Cut off his cock. I want it."

"Maybe the two of you aren't fucking after all," I muse thoughtfully. "I mean, if you're that desperate for my dick, Makar is either severely lacking in that department or—"

In the end, it's the small penis joke that pushes the last of Makar's hesitations to the side. He charges at me with a battle roar, spit flying. I jump out of the way just as Belle screams my name.

"Who said you could take off your gag, bitch?" Xena shoves Belle back. If I wasn't busy with Makar, I'd kill her for that alone.

"Don't worry, Belle," I tell her, squaring off with an already-sweating Makar. "I'll be with you in a moment."

"Say your goodbyes. You'll never see each other again," Makar growls as he charges again.

I dodge him, letting him tire himself out a bit before we get into this. "I'm almost embarrassed to admit you ever worked for me," I say as I watch him pant and heave.

"Because I'm not a brainless sheep, following you into ruin?"

"No. Because you're a shitty fighter. Either Xena has never seen you fight or she is knowingly sending you to your death. You don't stand a fucking chance."

Makar's face turns red, anger coloring his neck and chest. "I've trained enough."

"There is a big difference between punching a defenseless bag in the gym and the task in front of you here, brother. This target hits back."

To prove my point, I fake to the right, sending Makar leaning wonkily in the other direction. I meet him there with a hard left hook. His rib crunches under my knuckles.

He groans and tries to fade back out of reach, but he stumbles.

"It's almost too easy," I sigh over his shoulder to Xena. I'm guessing this is her first time seeing him at work, too, because she looks pissed.

Makar doubles down, growling as he lunges. This time, he manages to get his arms around my midsection. My gun slips out of my pants and clatters across the cement. Makar actually forces me back a couple steps, but as soon as I plant my feet, I drive my knee straight up into his chest.

He wheezes, gasping for the breath I've just knocked out of him.

Panicking now, he tries to move towards my gun, no doubt hoping to grab it and end this before I kill him.

But no such luck. I spin around behind him and hook one arm around his neck, the other around his rib cage. I squeeze tightly, pinning one of his arms against his already-broken ribs. He cries out and tries to pry my arm away from his neck, but I squeeze tighter. More things break.

"You should have shut your mouth and fallen into line," I growl in his ear. "And you definitely shouldn't have put your hands on my wife. Because now, I have no choice. You made the choice for me."

He tries to say something, but he doesn't have the air. It comes out like a death rattle, rasping through his blue lips.

Meanwhile, Xena doesn't do a damn thing. I choke the life out of Makar's body, constricting around him like an anaconda while he spasms and dies, and Xena just watches with pure disgust on her face.

After a couple minutes, I lower Makar's lifeless body to the floor and then stand up and face Xena.

"I went through Makar," I sigh, brushing off my hands on my pants. "Now, give me my wife."

Her eyes narrow to slits. "Do you really think I'm done?"

I sigh. "No, I suppose not. Nothing with you could ever be that easy."

"You know me so well." She throws a sharp-edged smirk at me and then grabs Belle by the roots of her hair. "Come on. Help me reveal my secret guests."

"I'm not going anywhere with you," Belle snaps. She tries to pull away, but Xena pulls out a gun, and Belle goes perfectly still.

"I'll kill you in front of him," Xena says. "I'd enjoy that, actually. So give me a reason."

"This wasn't part of your deal," I growl.

Xena presses the muzzle under Belle's chin and smiles back at me. "I wanted to keep things interesting for you."

Belle walks stiffly with Xena to a wooden door on the opposite wall. Without taking her eyes or the gun off of Belle, Xena reaches over and opens the door. Then she backs away, keeping Belle at bay with the pistol.

I want to charge her, but she's too far away. She'd sense me coming, and I don't doubt for a second that she'll actually kill Belle. So for the moment, I'm stuck watching from the sidelines as her little plan plays out. Just like she wanted.

"Come out," Xena barks to whatever is waiting. "And don't forget that I'll kill you all without blinking."

I have no clue who she is talking to…

Until a familiar strawberry blonde head comes shuffling out of the closet.

"Elise," whimpers Belle, nearly folding in half at the sight of her sister. "No. No."

"I'm okay, B," Elise says quietly.

Howard follows Elise out. Unlike Elise, his face is up and he's alert. There's a deep purple bruise around his eye and a bloody cut on his lip. Whatever happened to them, he clearly fought hard. My admiration for the man grows yet again.

"You thought they were safe?" Xena looks back at me, her eyes raking over me so she can eat up every flicker of emotion. She wants me to be shocked, horrified. She wants me to be angry.

I don't give her anything more than a shrug. "I hoped you'd be lazy and leave them alone."

"Hm. Maybe you don't know me well after all." She grabs Belle and drags her away from Elise and Howard. "Because when it comes to revenge, there's no such thing as too much effort. I want all of you to die knowing how foolish it was to keep me from what I want."

I take a step sideways towards my gun. It's fifteen feet away, at least. But Xena catches the shift.

"I'll shoot her," she warns. "Move again, Nikolai, and I'll shoot her."

I believe Xena *would* kill Belle—but the more I think about it, I don't think she *will*.

"No, you won't. Because Belle is the only reason you have any control over me. Without her, you know I'll have nothing to lose." I wait for her to argue, but Xena just stares at me. "I fucking knew it."

I smirk and take a step.

Xena raises the gun.

"I wasn't talking about Belle," she says.

Then she turns the gun on Elise and pulls the trigger.

41

BELLE

Since the moment Elise and Howard stepped out of the closet, I've been frozen with horror. I thought Iceland was far enough away from Xena to be safe. I thought I'd sent my baby sister to a place where she couldn't be touched by the chaos I brought into her life.

But I was wrong.

Everything happens so fast and so slow at the same time. Xena raises her arm and that only takes a blurred fraction of a second. Then I hear the bang, and that sound echoes for an eternity. I'm fairly certain I can see the bullet spinning through the air. The striations on it, the way the air slices open to let it through.

Toward my sister.

"Elise!" I scream, reaching for her helplessly. I'm too far away to do anything. It won't make any difference.

Something else happens, too fast to comprehend. A body moves. The bullet meets flesh.

And when that body hits the floor, Elise is left standing there, completely unharmed.

I only realize I've closed my eyes when Elise's voice breaks through the devastating silence. "Dad?"

Then I wrench them open and see Howard crumbled on the ground.

Elise is kneeling at his side. "Dad?" she says again in a tremulous voice that makes my heart break.

A crimson stain spreads across his chest. Elise presses her palms against the wound to staunch the flow, but it seems to just bubble out of him even faster.

"Help him!" Elise cries out. "Please. Help!"

I want to run to her, but there's nothing I can do. Nothing anyone can do while Xena is still alive.

"There are other ways to hurt Belle," Xena says, looking past me to Nikolai. "And when I hurt her, I hurt you."

She's talking past me like I'm not even here. Xena just shot at my sister, hitting Howard instead, but it was all to hurt me. And she only wants to hurt me so she can hurt Nikolai. It's convoluted and it's messy and, ultimately, it's all for nothing.

"He doesn't care about me!" All of the emotions I've tried to bottle up are finally bursting out. "Nikolai doesn't even love me. You're punishing everyone for a lie you made up in your head. He didn't love me. He didn't love you. All of this is for nothing. Don't you understand that?"

Xena's lips are pulled back from her teeth, making her look like some kind of feral animal.

"You wanted Nikolai to marry you," I continue in a ragged pant. "You are hurt that he chose me instead."

"I wanted Nikolai to give me control of his Bratva," she corrects, tipping her head to the side like she can't understand how I could have ever been confused. "And I'm not hurt that he chose you—I'm merely puzzled. Who would want you when they could have me?"

"Anyone with eyes," Nikolai snarls.

Xena can say what she wants about not caring that Nikolai doesn't want her, but I am close enough to see the anger flash through her. Her nostrils flare. She doesn't even look human anymore.

She is vengeance incarnate.

I can hear Elise weeping over Howard behind me, but I can't focus on that because Xena is zeroed in on Nikolai. I know this isn't going to end well.

All of the pain and suffering—it will continue. This feud between them won't end until we're all dead or until Xena feels she's gotten what she's owed… whichever comes first.

As for me? I'd like to end this death train before it reaches my sister.

That's all that's left to care about.

"Kill me," I say suddenly.

Xena blinks and looks back to me. "What?"

"Kill me," I say again. "If revenge is what you want, then kill me. I'll be punished for ruining your plans. And if Nikolai loves me the way you think he does, he'll be tortured. Win-win."

But I know better. I know Nikolai won't be bothered. He can find another woman to fuck, and one day, maybe he'll even find a woman to marry. Someone he actually loves.

The thought of that alone makes me wish Xena would press her gun to my temple and get it over with already.

"Let everyone else go," I beg. "Take me instead. Kill me."

Nikolai roars, "Don't touch her!"

"Kill me," I say softly, repeating the words like a mantra. "Kill me. Kill me."

Xena looks from me to Nikolai and back again. Her finger shifts over the trigger. all the noise around me fades. Elise's crying, Nikolai's shouting, then it's all gone, like someone turned the volume of the world down.

Everything goes quiet.

I close my eyes.

I wait.

The bang that ends my world is deafening. I feel the heat of the shot, the singe of gunpowder against my skin. And I wait for darkness to take me. For pain or a blinding light or the warm numbing sensation of death.

But there's… nothing.

There's nothing?

When I open my eyes, Xena isn't in front of me anymore. She has turned away and is pointing her gun at—

"Nikolai!" His name tears out of my throat. I'm up and running towards his slumped figure before I can even worry whether Xena will shoot me, too.

What does it matter now anyway? By shooting Nikolai, she got me right in the heart.

I drop to my knees on the concrete next to him, barely feeling the pain of the stone biting into my skin because I'm too preoccupied by the puddle of sticky blood under me. It's warm and pulsing out of him too fast.

"Soak it in, lovebirds," Xena calls. "These are your last moments together."

"Nikolai," I gasp. My hands hover over his stomach, shaky and uncertain.

He's flat on his back with his head turned towards me. His gray eyes are laser-focused on me. He grabs my hands and presses them against his wound, but I'm not sure if either of us believe it will do anything. Maybe it's just to feel his heat one last time.

"You... you didn't... lose..." he murmurs through lips that barely work.

I've never seen him like this, wounded. Incapacitated. I hate it. I can't stand it, and it's so overwhelming that I can't focus on what he's saying. "Nikolai, you—"

"Belle," he rasps, grabbing my wrists. "Listen... listen to me. You didn't lose the baby."

I look up to his face. To his full lips and strong jaw. His skin is paler than I've ever seen it. "What did you—What? I didn't?"

"I thought you did," he explains haltingly. "The doctors messed—I told you that because I thought it was true. And because you said I only cared about the baby. But... I thought the baby was gone."

That means something, but there's too much information flying for me to cling to it. Nikolai is still talking, the words pouring out of him as fast as the blood.

"But the hospital called me right before you were taken. It was a mix-up. A clerical error. Do... do you understand?"

"Nikolai, you're bleeding." Tears are streaming down my face and it's all I can think to say. What else can matter in the face of this?

He squeezes my wrists until they hurt. Until my fingers start to tingle. "You might still be pregnant. But it doesn't matter, either way. I lied, Belle."

I frown. "You lied about the baby? I don't understand."

"I lied back at the house. Before you fell down those stairs." He lifts his head with visible effort and looks into my very soul. "I love you, Belle. I love you so much that, for the first time in my life, I was scared."

My heart is being pulled in two different directions. It wants to crack in half at the sight of Nikolai bleeding out on the floor, but his words make it feel close to bursting.

This could be his last moment. Our last moment together. And as much as I want to hear these words from him, I don't want it to be a lie.

I shake my head. "Don't say it if you don't mean it."

"I mean it." He pulls my bloody hand to his mouth and presses a kiss to my knuckles. "I love you, beautiful Belle. 'Til death do us part."

My face is wet with tears as I bend down and kiss his lips. "I love you, too, Nikolai. You can't go. You can't die. I just got you."

He shakes his head. "You've always had me, Belle. From the start."

I hear Xena moving closer. Her heels click across the floor. We have a minute left together. Maybe less.

I sob, relief and heartbreak rattling through me. "This can't be over, Nikolai. It can't. What can I do? Tell me what to do and I'll do it, I swear I will."

Slowly, Nikolai drags my hand closer to his hip. His eyes are burning into mine, trying to relay something I don't understand.

"I love you," he says again.

Another sob starts to bubble up in me.

But then I feel it. The hard length in Nikolai's pocket. The intricate handle poking out of his pocket.

It's the knife Makar gave me on my wedding day.

Nikolai's chin dips slightly, and I understand all at once what he wants me to do. What I have to do.

"I'm sorry." His voice sounds weak, and I know all at once what he means. What he wants to say but can't because Xena's shoes are clicking closer every second.

I'm sorry I lied. I'm sorry I got you tangled up in this mess. I'm sorry you have to be the one to kill the person who did this to us.

I lay my body over his, carefully pulling the knife from his pocket and tucking it against my forearm and palm. "You have nothing to be sorry for, Nikolai. I don't have a single regret."

"Come on!" Xena screeches. "Get up. Goodbyes are over."

I look at Nikolai again, hoping and praying it won't be for the last time. He tips his head slowly, a silent encouragement, and then falls back against the floor. His lids flutter closed, and that's all the encouragement I need. He doesn't have much time.

"Up!" Xena yells again.

Slowly, I stand up with an exaggerated sob and back away from Nikolai. Xena is somewhere behind me, so I want to get as close to her as I can before I turn around. Before she sees my face and realizes I'm lying.

"Turn around," she snaps. "I want to see you when I kill you."

I bow my head, my shoulders shaking. It's not so hard to fake. Seeing Nikolai quiet and still on the ground is terrifying. I'm worried he'll never get up.

"No!" Elise moans from a few yards away. "Please. No."

I don't know if she's talking about me or Howard, but it doesn't matter. Not in this second.

Right now, the only thing that matters is not missing.

Xena groans in frustration. "Would you fucking turn around, you—"

She grabs my shoulder and spins me around. As I turn, I slide the knife down into my fingers, hook my right arm around, and slash out at her neck with all my strength.

Xena reacts quickly, raising her right arm to try and block the attack. Instead of cutting her throat open like I intended, I catch her on the forearm. The blade bites into her palm and the soft underside of her wrist. Blood sprays out like a mist.

She tries to get a hold of my arm, but my skin is slippery with blood—both hers and Nikolai's—and she can't keep hold of me.

"Let go!" Her shrieks sound like a trapped animal now.

I can do this. I can fucking do this.

I'm going to kill her.

Suddenly, I see someone approaching. For a second, I think it must be backup. Must be someone else Xena had hidden away in the room, here to finish the job in case something went awry.

But it's Elise.

She grabs Xena's uninjured hand and starts prying her fingers away from me.

"Elise!" I shout. The single word is enough for her to know what I mean.

Be careful. Stay safe. Get out of here.

Xena stumbles, falls, and lands back on her ass. Her eyes are wide as she tries to scramble away like a crab.

"You can go," she gasps, clutching her shredded arm to her chest. Her fine clothes are bloodstained and dusty from the warehouse floors. I've never seen her so out of sorts, so uncomposed. "I'll let you go."

I move towards her, brandishing the knife. "You're not going to *let* me do anything. I'm calling the shots now, you fucking psycho."

"Please," Xena begs. "Please, Belle. I wasn't going to kill you. I just wanted to scare you. I didn't want anyone to die. I can get a doctor here in a minute to save Nikolai. Let me live, and I'll save him."

A dark part of me wants to let Xena beg. I want to make her plead for her life the way she wanted me to. I want to give her hope that I'll be merciful and then snatch it away. I want this powerful woman to be brought to her knees and know what it means to be afraid.

But that would make me just like her.

Instead, I don't say a word. I just raise the knife high over my head.

"No, Belle!" she gasps. "Please. Don't do—"

And I bring it plunging down into her chest.

I let it go and stumble backwards, wheezing from the effort. I watch her the whole time. I'm expecting her to rise up again. To, against all odds, stand up and lunge at me.

But she doesn't move. Doesn't breathe.

Xena Simatou is dead.

I'm still watching her when Elise runs to me and throws her arms around my middle. "Belle," she sobs. "What do we do? What do we do now?"

Numbly, I hug her back. I can still feel the vibrations of the blade striking bone as they careen up and down my arm. I have a feeling this sensation will be seared into my body's memory for the rest of my life.

Over Elise's shoulder, Howard is lying in a heap on the floor. Then I turn around and see Nikolai. He looks peaceful, almost like he's napping. Like this could all be a bad dream.

I wish it was a dream.

I shake my head. "I don't—We get help. We need help."

As the words come out of my mouth, I hear a commotion at the front of the building. Instantly, I pull Elise behind me.

If it's the Greeks or the Battiatos, I can't take them with one knife. But maybe I can buy time for Elise to escape.

Then Christo bursts through the door.

His eyes land on mine. For a second, neither of us know if we can trust the other. Is he working for the Greeks? Am I?

I do the only thing I can think to do—I point to Nikolai's body. "Help him. Please."

Christo sees Nikolai and curses under his breath. He sprints across the warehouse floor, a string of men flocking behind him. A rail-thin older man surges past Christo in a surprising burst of speed and drops down next to Nikolai.

"My son."

Nikolai's father. I can see the family resemblance. The strong jaw and broad shoulders. They have the same build, though his bulk looks to have been eaten away by hard years.

He presses his fingers to Nikolai's wrist, and I hold my breath. I prepare myself for the news I will never be prepared for. For the heartbreak I know I won't survive.

"Well?" Christo snaps.

Nikolai's father sighs. "He's still alive. There's a pulse."

I want to collapse with relief. But this isn't over yet.

The small faction of men moves quickly. They carry Nikolai out and then Howard. Elise and I trail behind in a daze, arms wrapped around each other, too shocked to speak or act.

We're caught in the wild current of the night—of this life—and the only thing to do is hold on.

Hold onto hope.

Hold onto faith.

Hold onto each other.

EPILOGUE: NIKOLAI
ONE YEAR LATER

I drop down onto the bench I donated to the cemetery and look over the headstone. It's white marble, tall and narrow, shining in the early evening light. Very phallic.

Arslan would love it.

"Happy birthday, you miserable bastard," I say, hanging the wreath of white roses off the side of the headstone. "I never would have gotten you flowers if you were still alive, just so we're clear. But I can't get you anything else, can I?"

I pause, waiting for a response I know will never come.

It's strange—even after over a year without my best friend, I expect to hear his voice all the time. But I cover over the sadness with the sound of my own.

"Actually, that's not true. I lobbied for my son to be named after you, but Belle and I had a girl. And we both know it's the thought that counts." I sigh and lean back on the bench. "Maybe next time. Fuck, do you hear me?" I snort. "'Maybe next time'? Apparently I'm a man who is casual about having a family now. If you weren't already dead, you'd die hearing that. I can't believe it, either. But Belle makes it easy."

Belle makes everything easy.

She killed Xena and put to end one of the most dramatic chapters of my life. While I was recovering from my gunshot wound, Belle took care of me even as she was growing our daughter. And now, Inessa is five months old and, despite not ever having a parent as an example of how to raise a child, Belle has been a wonderful mother. She's completely devoted to our daughter.

My phone rings and I pull it out of my pocket. "Speaking of the devil." I answer. "Hello, honey."

"Don't 'honey' me," Belle laughs. "You were supposed to be here by now."

She and I have been invited to a ceremony, but there wasn't time to drop off Inessa at the babysitter's and stop by the cemetery, so we split up. My chore is taking a little longer than expected, though.

"Everyone is looking at me like I'm a leper," she whispers into the phone. "I can't decide if it's because I'm a Zhukova or because this dress is fitting my postpartum body weird."

I'm a Zhukova. Hearing her claim her new identity still sends my blood pumping in a distinctly downward direction.

Plus, the thought of her body is verbal Viagra. Postpartum or not, she still does it for me.

"The Greeks look at everyone like that," I tell her. "And I'm positive you look incredible. Go find Christo. He'll take care of you until I get there."

"Which will be when, precisely?"

I check my watch. "Fifteen minutes."

She sighs. "Fine. Did you give Arslan my gift?"

Epilogue: Nikolai

I pat the inner pocket of my jacket. "Oh, shit. No. But I will."

"You're a good friend," she says, a smile in her voice. "I'll see you soon."

I hang up and pull out Belle's gift. The liquor bottle is so small I almost forgot about it. I pop the lid and dump the shot out on the velvety grass. "God, you would have really liked Belle, man. She got you a better gift than I did and she barely knew you."

The alcohol soaks into the ground. There will probably be a brown spot in the grass, but I know Arslan wouldn't care.

I push up to standing, slap the headstone lightly, and then head back to the car idling along the curb. I'm a few feet away when the driver door swings open and my dad runs around the back of the car.

"I told you," I sigh, "you don't have to keep opening the door for me."

He pulls the door open and stands tall. "It's what drivers do, isn't it? And I'm your driver."

"Yes, I'm aware. It's been almost a year now. And none of my other drivers have ever bothered. It's really not necessary."

My dad shrugs. "Just wanna make sure I'm earning my keep, son. The Zhukova men are no freeloaders."

I roll my eyes and slide into the back seat. He closes the door behind me and heads around to the driver's side.

On the night Xena shot me, my dad ran into Christo and my outfit of men outside of the warehouse. The few contacts he still had in the underworld told him that Belle and I might be in trouble, so he showed up to help.

While I was recovering, Belle and I agreed to hire him to help drive me to doctor's appointments and help out after surgeries. Eventually, the job became permanent. Now, I give him a salary to help him stay off the streets and away from his vices, and he drives me where I need to go.

It's not a normal father-son relationship. But it's something.

When the car pulls along the curb in front of the hotel, I climb out before my dad can open the door. But he still meets me at the back of the car.

"Will you need me to drive you to the airport tonight?" he asks. "I don't mind. It would actually make me feel better to know you're getting there safely."

"Christo arranged for rides for all of the guests. There's an open bar, so…"

"And you trust him?" It's a blunt question. Most people would tiptoe around it, not daring to even look like they might be questioning my judgment. But my father doesn't like to mince words these days. It's one thing I admire about him.

"I wouldn't let my wife be inside by herself if I didn't," I say. "Plus, Christo saved my life. He helped me eradicate what was left of the Battiatos. And the last year, with the Simatou mafia under his leadership, has been peaceful. We are allies."

My dad bows his head. "Enough said. If you trust him, then so do I. Text me when you are on the plane, please. If you don't mind."

I nod and he ducks back into the car and pulls away.

When I turn towards the hotel, I'm stopped dead in my tracks by the most beautiful woman I've ever seen.

"Don't look at me like that," Belle snaps, waving her finger at my face. "Don't give me that sexy smolder and assume I'll forgive you for being late. I've been making small talk in there for half an hour, Mr. 'Fifteen Minutes.'"

She moves down the steps towards me. Her champagne-colored dress shimmers in the ambient lighting, flowing over her curves like water. Her hair is pinned behind one ear with luscious waves tumbling over her shoulders.

"You're a goddess," I murmur, grabbing her waist and pulling her against me.

She lets me kiss her lips and then presses a finger to my chest. "Then I smite you."

"Consider me smote."

She bends back and narrows her eyes. "You shouldn't look so happy when you're in bad standing with a goddess."

"You're right," I say with all seriousness. "Getting back in good standing is of the utmost importance. We should probably leave right now so I can do everything humanly possible to please you."

Belle's hazel eyes burn and her skin flushes. It's clear she wants this as much as I do. We've both been insatiable the last couple months. Belle was so uncomfortable in the third trimester of pregnancy, and then there was the recovery once Inessa was born, and then the sleepless nights with Inessa crying.

We're only just getting back into a rhythm with each other. We have a lot of making up to do.

Still, Belle tows me towards the hotel's front steps. "It'll have to wait," she decides. "It would look bad if you didn't show your support for Christo."

"He's been leading the Greeks for a year," I retort, nuzzling her neck from behind. She smells like lavender as I press a kiss against her quickening pulse. "This is just the bullshit formal ceremony to make it official. He won't miss us."

Belle pushes me away gently. "Would you really want to risk the peace you've created for a quickie in the backseat of a car on the way to the airport?"

"That is exactly what I want, yes."

She laughs, unable to hold it back. Then she loops her arm through mine. "You're ridiculous."

"You're gorgeous," I say, draping her hand over my forearm.

"You're incorrigible," she whispers back as we near the front doors.

The doorman stands to attention, but his eyes drag over Belle in her gown for a moment too long. I drop her arm and slide my hand around her waist instead, pulling her tightly against my side. "And you're mine."

Her lips press into a tight knot, fighting against her smile. "Am I? I think I've forgotten. As soon as the ceremony is over, maybe you can remind me. From behind."

I bite down on my knuckle. "Do you want peace between us and the Greeks or not? Because I am dangerously close to carrying you out of here and making you make all my favorite noises."

Belle just laughs and pulls me into the crowd.

∼

The babysitter is already on the plane when Belle and I arrive.

"Inessa went down like a dream," she informs us. "She'll sleep for a few hours, I'm sure. So now that you're here, I'm going to go sleep, too, if that's okay?"

Belle waves her on. "Of course. That's the benefit of getting the jet with the private rooms. We can actually relax."

"Because we won't relax enough in Iceland," I chuckle.

In all the chaos after Xena died and Christo took over, Belle and I never had a formal honeymoon. So now that Inessa is old enough to travel and allow Belle a bit of free time, we're heading to the same resort we went to what feels like a lifetime ago.

Epilogue: Nikolai

Belle thanks Brienne for her help and then starts to settle in for the long flight.

While the plane takes off, she brushes her hair out and washes her face. And as soon as we're cruising, she slips into the bathroom to trade her formal gown for a lounge set. A few minutes later, she reemerges. The shorts flounce around her toned thighs and the V-neck dips dangerously low across her chest. She told me she bought it because it was "nursing-friendly," but right now, it looks made for me.

"Aren't you going to change?" she asks me. The seats across the aisle have been laid back to create a full-size bed. Belle drops down onto it with a satisfied sigh.

I eye her over the top of my drink. "I didn't see much point."

She swallows, but plays dumb. "Sleep in a suit if you want, I guess. I prefer to get comfortable." She makes a big show of pulling a blanket over her and rolling away from me onto her side.

She's playing hard to get. My favorite.

Silently, I set my drink aside and loosen the knot of my tie. I toss my jacket over the back of the seat in front of me. I can practically see Belle shivering with anticipation. As I crawl into the space behind her, she instinctively arches back against me. She gasps when she feels my erection against her ass.

"I'm trying to sleep, Nikolai."

I press a kiss to the back of her neck. "Too bad. You're mine, remember?"

"Well, this wife of yours is going to sleep."

I slide my hand down her leg and then pull her towards me, twisting her hips and opening her legs to me. My fingers slip between her thighs and cup the warm curve of her sex. She presses gently into my palm, and immediately, I pull my hand away.

"Unzip my pants," I whisper in her ear.

She rolls over so she's facing me, an eyebrow arched. "I thought you were the one who was supposed to please me."

"Give a little to get a little, *kiska*."

Belle stares at me for a moment before she reaches for my pants and does as I ask. She makes quick work of it, shoving the material down my legs and pulling me free. Her hands are small and warm, and I pump softly against her silky skin as I growl deep in my chest.

"Touch yourself," I tell her.

Instantly, Belle slides her other hand between her legs and inside her shorts. She strokes herself, matching the rhythm to the slide of her palm over my cock. In no time at all, we're both thrusting to the pleasure.

"Do you want me to touch you?"

Her eyes are glassy and unfocused, but she nods frantically.

"Tell me, Belle. Say it."

"Yes," she breathes. "I want you to touch me."

"Aren't you worried someone will see?" I whisper, taunting.

The flight attendant knows better than to bother us without first being summoned. And I don't plan to summon her anytime soon.

"I don't care. Let them see." She gives me a rough stroke, drawing a groan from between my lips. "I need you."

I slide my fingers down her stomach and lower, replacing her hand with my own. "You're so wet."

"I'm ready for you." She lifts her hips up, taking my fingertip inside.

I push into her, stroking and curling into her warmth. She arches her back and lets her eyes flutter closed. I add a second finger and she starts to match my movements, riding my hand at the same pace I'm finger-fucking her until she's breathless.

All the while, Belle strokes me. It's constant and firm, driving my desire higher and higher until I'm physically aching to push inside of her.

Reading my mind, Belle opens her eyes. "I want to come with you inside of me, Nikolai."

Maybe at one point, I would have resisted the pleasure. I would have held off and forced her to come on my hand before we moved on. But as much as this woman is mine, I am hers, too. And I want nothing more than to give her exactly what she wants.

I slide out of her and we shed our remaining clothes quickly before falling back on the bed together. Belle wraps her hand around my neck and draws my mouth to her plump lips, opening her legs for me. I situate myself between her soft thighs and, inch by inch, press into her.

When I'm fully immersed, Belle rocks against me and moans. "God, you're so deep inside of me. I want to stay like this forever."

Slowly, I draw myself all the way out of her before I plunge back in with one thrust.

Belle cries out. "God, yes. That. Do that forever. Forever and ever. Never stop."

I thrust into her again and again. Each time, Belle falls apart a little bit more.

She claws at my shoulder blades and presses her heels into my lower back. She moans and cries out and whimpers and it's all fucking perfect.

Finally, I feel her clench around me with a low groan.

"I'm coming," she gasps, rolling her hips against mine and arching her back off the bed.

I thrust into her until she sinks back into the mattress, her arms thrown lazily over her head. When she opens her eyes, she looks drunk. "My God."

"Good?" I ask, even though I already know the answer.

"Incredible." She leans up and kisses me, her tongue swirling into my mouth, her teeth nipping at my lower lip. "I wonder if I'll ever get tired of that."

I pull away quickly. "You have to wonder?"

She laughs. "I didn't mean it like that. I just meant—"

I don't let her finish. In one swift move, I roll her onto her stomach and grip her hips. I move onto my knees behind her and stroke my tip against her opening.

"You don't have anything to prove," she moans, wiggling her hips in front of me.

"Apparently, I do. I need to remind you who you belong to. Who you'll always belong to."

In one movement, I slide home in her. Her back arches, and she tips her head back in a cry. "Nikolai."

I smile and drag my hand down her back. "Exactly."

EXTENDED EPILOGUE: BELLE
FOUR YEARS LATER

Want to see Belle and Nikolai moving Elise into her college dorm, the reappearance of Belle's mother, and the birth of the Zhukova twins? Check out the exclusive Extended Epilogue!

CLICK HERE TO DOWNLOAD